Praise for Alisa Valdes-Rodriguez and her Vibrant Novels

Playing with Boys

"A funny, guilty pleasure of a novel."

—*Publishers Weekly*

"As Marcella, Alexis, and Olivia grapple with men and their careers, they really don't seem all that different from Bridget Jones herself."

—*Miami Herald*

"Valdes-Rodriguez brings savvy, and sometimes savage humor, to chick-lit."

—*New York Daily News*

"Once again, without resorting to didacticism, her novel becomes a subtle vehicle for demonstrating the rich diversity of Latina culture."

—*Library Journal*

"The three amigas—a television actress, a single mother, and a manager of musicians—each has her own distinct lifestyle, quirks, and notions of romance, yet each manages to help her friends find balance, along with loads of good times."

—*Sacramento Bee*

"Entertaining. . . ."

—*Entertainment Weekly*

"Humor abounds in Valdes-Rodriguez's new novel . . . women of all ethnicities will identify with the real-life trials of this novel's three friends."

—*Romantic Times*

. . . and The Dirty Girls Social Club

"The feel of a night out with the girls . . . charming . . . undeniably fun."

—*Miami Herald*

"A compulsive beach read . . . smart, brassy, and messy enough to make you pause mid-sunscreen slathering."

—*Entertainment Weekly*

"Delivers on the promise of its title . . . a fun, irresistible debut."

—*Publishers Weekly*

"Laugh-out-loud read . . . with no-holds-barred humor."

—*Dallas Morning News*

"Wonderful writing, delicious humor, biting sarcasm, and impressive intelligence."

—*Detroit Free Press*

"Alisa Valdes-Rodriguez's writing style is raund
it's the complex, finely drawn characters who m

also by alisa valdes-rodriguez

The Dirty Girls Social Club

PLAYING
with BOYS

alisa valdes-rodriguez

St. Martin's Griffin ☙ New York

This book is dedicated to the wonderful actress Mara Holguin, who taught me you're never too old to make a new friend; and the brilliant Elsa Menendez, who made me realize a friend had been there all along. (Gracias, Faustino, wherever you are, for bringing the 'burque girls together again.)

www.stmartins.com

Library of Congress Cataloging-in-Publication Data

Valdes-Rodriguez, Alisa.
    Playing with boys / Alisa Valdes-Rodriguez
        p. cm.
    ISBN 0-312-33234-3 (hc)
    ISBN 0-312-33235-1 (pbk)
    EAN 978-0-312-33235-8
    1. Hispanic American women—Fiction. 2. Los Angeles (Calif.)—Fiction.
3. Female friendship—Fiction. I. Title.

PS3622.A425P55 2004
813'.6—dc22   2004046859

10 9 8 7 6 5 4

Acknowledgments

Thanks again to my husband, Patrick, for putting his own writing on hold so I could flutter mine all over the world. And thanks to our son, Alexander, for being smarter than both his parents combined. Thanks to my dad, for everything. And to Leslie, for believing in me and fighting for me. Thanks to Stephanie for selling me all over the world, and to Ron for hawking me in Hollywood. Finally, thanks to Elizabeth Beier and everyone at St. Martin's Press for unwavering support, patience, and good humor.

Autumn

Charm is a product of the unexpected.
—José Martí

ALEXIS

There were times that made me s'dang proud to be a Mexican I wept 'til my mascara melted—say, when Vincente Fernandez sang "Cielito Lindo" for the Republican National Convention in 2000. But darlin', *this* wasn't one of those times.

I stood alone in a black-tie crowd, at a private outdoor cocktail party, on a terrace of L.A.'s Getty Museum, faking interest in a cube of raw tuna on a silver tray. It was like a wobbly, wet, red dice—or was it die? Correction: Was it *dead*? I jabbed it with my designer toothpick, just to be sure.

"It's only Jell-O, sugar," I whispered as I closed my eyes and shoved it into my mouth. But it was nothing like Jell-O, unless they'd come out with a "slippery acrid" flavor I hadn't seen yet. What I needed was a steak, well-done. Fat chance.

Suddenly, the chatting dimmed and all eyes turned toward a doorway as I held my breath and prayed for patience.

One by one, the members of Los Chimpances del Norte—the *norteño* band I had stumbled, dear God please tell me how, into managing—strutted single-file onto the terrace in perfectly matching toucan-vomit-meets-cowboy outfits.

I'd asked them to wear Armani. Black Armani. As usual, they'd ignored me. I instinctively fingered the little pink pearls around my neck, and smoothed my hands along the sides of the size 14 Ann Taylor cocktail dress I liked to think of as my "little black," but which was, by L.A. standards, more like a massive, flapping black.

A woman behind me gasped. "What are they wearing?" A man comforted her by saying, "I believe they're going for post-modern kitsch." No, I wanted to say. They think they look good, and there is a large percentage of an entire nation— my ancestral nation of origin—that agrees. I was not among that percentage, but then, I was raised in Texas, not Mexico.

Lime-green fringed blazers aren't for everyone. Neither are banana-yellow Wrangler pants worn tight as skin on a sausage. White ten-gallon Stetsons look good enough on Toby Keith. But twelve of 'em, all in a row, stuffed over waxy Mexican mullets in the middle of a modern museum? Lordy. And who knew twenty-four maroon snakeskin boots could look quite that bad, all lined up together like the keys of Satan's own little player piano?

We were here this evening, enjoying the gardens of this curvy modernist masterpiece of a museum perched in the gently smoggy hills of Los Angeles, for an exclusive private party. A celebration. What were we celebrating? This: the fact that Los Chimpances del Norte (the Chimpanzees of the North) had just donated $5 million to UCLA's Center for Chicano Studies, for the study of previously neglected U.S.-Mexico border music of the oom-pah type they themselves had inflicted upon the public for the past twenty years.

I was a Dallas girl, born and raised, armed with an arsenal of acronyms—BA and MBA from SMU, darlin'—but I was trying to become a California girl, with mixed results. I came to Hell-eh because I thought it was shameful that in a city where the top three FM radio stations now played Mexican music, the big PR companies were oblivious to the talent and riches in Spanish-speaking America. I was the first to offer artists like the Chimps *American*-style publicity, complete with professional press releases, follow-up calls, lunches—as opposed to Mexican-style publicity, which usually meant buying reporters off with things like cocaine, or island vacations.

My clients at Tower Entertainment, the Whittier-based firm I worked for, had been on *The Tonight Show, 60 Minutes,* and in the *New York Times,* which impressed *me* but rarely impressed my clients. As I often had to tell reporters, America was changing, fast. Tortillas now outsold bagels. Famously, Americans now ate more salsa than ketchup. Wal-Mart carried plantains, yuca, and Goya products. Kraft in the U.S. had come out with something they called "mayonesa," a Mexican mayonnaise with lime. Why? Not because they were nice. Because they *had to.* The top FM stations in New York, Los Angeles, and Chicago now broadcast in Spanish, and the U.S. had become the world's fourth-largest Spanish-speaking country. I was one of those lucky people who had long existed in a United States that spoke Spanish and English with matching facility. I swung with ease between the cheesy comedy of *Sábado Gigante* and the cheesy comedy of WB sitcoms. Some academic types, like my professors at Southern Methodist University, called people like me bicultural. But with Latinos poised to make up one in four Americans in the blink of a big brown eye, I preferred to call it *American*.

Of course, most people at this party didn't care about any of that. They cared that there was a "Latin" band that lived in Los Angeles with this kind of money—a band they'd never heard of until the *L.A. Times* ran a story on the donation. Everyone knew the statistics about the growing Hispanic population, and for money reasons wanted to connect with us. So they came. But they had no idea what they were getting into with my boys. Mine? Well. I called the Chimps mine, but really I was theirs: their *manager*, their *agent*, their *publicist*, their whipping girl.

Five million bucks was the sort of gift American schools traditionally got from benefactors whose non-Spanish last names were read in soothing monotones at the end of programming on NPR and PBS. And a private Getty shindig was the sort of shiny event people attended in cocktail dresses and bow ties.

In other words, there was something horrifying to my sorority-girl brain (Sigma Lambda Gamma, y'all) about the Chimps showing up in neon cowboy gear like rowdy goat-humping bumpkins from Chihuahua. I knew, of course, that the Chimps had made their millions (yes, millions) playing "workingman's" music in rodeo arenas from Zacatecas to Whittier, and that they, bless their hearts, did not forget this, though they had amassed enough of a fortune to forget whatever they pleased. Maybe the goofy getups were a statement to the effect. Either that, or they just had no clue.

So, while I was proud of my guys for being able to give away enough money to attract the movers and shakers of this achy-quakey town—and, I should add, support me and my potentially unhealthy handbag habit—I was also a well-bred woman of twenty-nine, whose lovely, Avon-selling momma had worked herself near to death to give me the kind of life she'd never had. The kind of life where I made good money, where I was never assumed to be stupid for lack of credentials, where I knew what side of the table-setting the bread plate went on; like Momma woulda been if *her* parents, my dear but insanely backward Granny and Grampy Lopez, hadn't been the kind of old-world first-generation Mexicanos who said things like "Only easy women go to college," and "Don't talk so much or act too smart cuz no man's never gonna go fer no woman like that." Sigh.

It had been *my* idea to give "chimp change," as I called the hefty donation, to UCLA. I suggested the academic gift as a way to raise the group's visibility among mainstream Americans, and in the process raise the profile of all successful Mexicans and Meximericans here, which, in the end, might improve my life, too. And, who knew, maybe if L.A. powerbrokers started to see that we Messicans had money—*real* money—and not just, I dunno, pruning shears and toilet brushes, they might start to produce movies where *The Mexican* was a person and not a *gun*, and *Hidalgo* was a human instead of a stinkin' (but determined) *horse*. It was a long shot, but so was everything worth doing, in my humble opinion, and in Hollywood, there was plenty that needed doin', Amen.

"*Orale*, Alexis!" shouted Filoberto, the bandleader, spying me. His lips pulled back to reveal a checkerboard of yellow and gold teeth, one or two outlined with what looked like brown eyeliner. He slowly lifted one hand, then flicked it toward the floor, in one fast snap, as if a roach had landed there and he wanted it off. This was Filoberto's *"mero mero"* mime-speak for "I'm here and I'm manly, *ahua*, Amen."

I hurried to greet my band.

"Filoberto," I said, kissing him on the cheek as was our custom. He smelled unwashed. "Hi, honey."

I leaned close to his ear and whispered, "Didn't you want to wear the Armani suits?"

"*Pues, no,*" Filoberto replied. Both his hands dove to his crotch area, and I cringed. I didn't want to look, but I did. He gripped and shook his enormous belt buckle up and down, and a few of the Chimps followed suit, in a strange approximation of a circle jerk. I was relieved. I'd feared Filoberto was going to whip "it" out, as he'd done backstage last month when I suggested he be nicer to a reporter. "Who's the man here?" he'd asked as "it" peered out like a deflated one-eyed slug.

In general, belt buckles are a good idea. They keep your pants up, hold the belt on. They're useful. But when they are the size of a salad plate and encrusted with red, green, and white gemstones sparkling in the shape of a Mexican flag, there's something unforgivably, I dunno, Liberace about them. Particularly when they cut deep into the flesh of a beer belly. I looked down the lineup of Chimps. They all had them.

"Why?" I whispered to Filoberto.

Filoberto stared hard into my eyes. "Look," he said, in the perfect English he often pretended he didn't speak. The Chimps were from Sacramento, California, but pretended to be from Sinaloa. "*Mexicans* gave us the money that we gave to the school. We owe our careers to *Mexicans*. We are *Mexicans*. And we're not going to dress like gringos just to make your little ooh-ooh friends here comfortable."

Ooh-ooh? Nice to see Filoberto not only speaking English, but enhancing it as well.

"I didn't ask you to dress like a 'gringo,'" I said, cringing at the racial slur. My stepdaddy was a "gringo" and the nicest man in the world. "I asked you to wear *Armani*."

"And I should ask you to suck it," he whispered in my ear. "Because this is my band and we do what I want. Got it?"

"Okay," I said, forcing a smile once more. "I understand. It's your choice and I respect that. I hope I didn't offend you. Good luck tonight." I started to walk away. Whenever anger bubbled up, that was the best policy. Back away, calm down, then talk.

"It's not us that need to change," called Filoberto, pointing to the crowd. "It's them."

Blah, blah, blah. Filoberto still thought we were fighting the Alamo.

"You're right," I lied. "I'm proud of you. Knock 'em dead, sweetie."

Many of the elites assembled here did not seem to know quite how to regard the Chimps, and seemed to be searching for the right facial expression. Condescending benevolence did not work. But neither did obsequious curiosity. Mostly, those unfamiliar with the border gangsta-polka world—folks who had, I think, come expecting a salsa band—stared at the Chimps in disbelief. Heck, I stared at them in disbelief. But why *not* have the Chimps at the Getty? After all, the Chimps *lived* in the U.S., paid *taxes* in the U.S., and made as much money off their music as many major U.S. pop stars, even if *Rolling Stone*, *Spin*, and every pop music writer in the land ignored them with almost vicious regularity.

With relief I saw three representatives from UCLA emerge from inside the museum and walk toward us in three-piece suits. At least they got it. The cute one, Samuel Reyes, managed to be cute even though he was balding. He smiled at me and my pulse quickened.

As the university people got closer, I stepped forward, past Filoberto, to be the first one to greet them. I heard Filoberto sigh behind me, dismayed yet again that I believed I could, you know, wear pants.

"Samuel," I said with a huge smile. I gripped his hand and shook it with authority. He held it longer than he needed to and searched my eyes.

"They look great," he said. "They're courageous."

"Yes, they are. This is a wonderful event. You've done such a good job."

Samuel nodded. He agreed he was great. A proper Texan man would have returned the compliment. But, Toto, we weren't in Texas anymore.

As the university people mingled with the Chimps and prepared to present the award, I strolled off to schmooze. After harvesting a few business cards for later use—yes, I hoped to one day escape the Chimp world—I stood back to observe the Chimps. I soon wished I hadn't.

First, a well-known Pacific Palisades socialite and her husband timidly approached Filoberto to introduce themselves. Filoberto made eye contact only with the man, though the woman was the one speaking to him.

"So nice to meet you," she said. "Congratulations."

Filoberto addressed her large, buoyant breasts, a perfect pair of surgically constructed half-grapefruits like so many in Southern California. "So nice to meet *you*," he leered. Then, to her husband, he added, "Congratulations," with a suggestive chortle.

The couple quickly hurried off to inspect a sculpture.

As I headed back toward Filoberto to give him a quickie etiquette lesson, a tall, gorgeous waitress sashayed past the line of Chimps with her tray of shrimp. Filoberto slapped her ass. He needed a lot more than etiquette. And I needed a new job.

The tuna cubes floated past once more, and though I was hungry, I couldn't do it. I couldn't. Once was enough. See, at the center of my fat-saturated heart, I was a steak-and-potatoes girl who didn't like exercise unless it involved a man in my bed. I was Christian, and unapologetically Republican, as my momma and daddy raised me. You can *imagine* how far this got me in Hell-eh, where it seemed to me everyone wanted to spend their free time doing yoga, volunteering for liberal causes, or lecturing the rest of us to join them. Oh, and I had a flat chest—a crime in Southern California.

Anyhoo. Schmoozing. I walked with confidence to a small cluster of beautiful people and planted myself among them.

"Hello," I said, sticking out my hand to the friendliest-looking person. "I'm Alexis Lopez, manager for the group we're honoring tonight. Thanks for coming!"

The assembled screenwriters, actors, and lone MTV animator shook hands with me. I stood with my toes turned out ninety degrees, in ballet's third position, because to point them directly toward the subject of your current conversation meant you had committed to them, and nothing was more fatal in room-working than committing to a single person or group.

I *had* friends. Granted, they were mostly in Dallas, but still. I didn't come to cocktail receptions to make friends. I came to make contacts. I took everyone's card, even the animator.

After listening to them complain and gossip for three minutes, I pretended to see someone I knew. Time to move on.

"Guys, really great to meet you." I opened my business card holder and dealt like I worked a Vegas craps table. "Thanks again."

I strolled away with the uneasy sense I was being followed.

"Those idiots yours?"

The female voice was dusky, and close to my ear, and I felt the red tones of her wine breath, laced with dark, musky perfume, on the back of my neck. I knew that voice. I had perfect voice recognition.

I turned toward the voice and saw the tall, slender cocktail waitress Filoberto had smacked. Dressed in a well-fitting white blouse (okay, truth be told, it *strained* at the bosom as if she carried water balloons in her bra) and black slacks, she had lustrous long hair, brown with gold and honey highlights, wavy and down to the middle of her back. Beautiful gold earrings I recognized as $550 Paloma Picasso designs (I also had perfect price recognition) flashed on her lobes, and I felt ashamed for wondering how a cocktail waitress might afford something like that. She was almost six feet tall, but must have weighed about 130 pounds. I had perfect weight recognition, too. Her electric blue eyes danced with amusement and what appeared to be controlled rage. The golden brown skin reddened on the cheeks as she prepared to speak. I recognized her from somewhere. She was the kind of woman you couldn't take your eyes off of, even if you wanted to because she reminded you of how you'd never be that thin or gorgeous without surgical and divine intervention.

"You mean the boys in the band?" I asked her.

She nodded.

I glanced at Filoberto. He had hoisted his barrel-body onto the small stage and planted his feet apart, like an easel. It was the stance he took when he was about to sing. It wasn't time to sing, but Filoberto did not care. Without a microphone, he began to belt out a few bars of his favorite ditty, "El Rey," by José Alfredo Jimenez.

"*Yo se bien que estoy afuera,*" he began. I did a quick check of the faces in the room and realized that, to them, Filoberto was quaint, a glorified restaurant mariachi, while, to him, he was the King of Mexico.

"They're mine," I sighed, thinking, *For better or worse and mostly worse.*

"Okay, then." Her woodsy voice was as familiar as her face. She scowled and placed a firm hand on my shoulder. "Tell the fat one to keep his fucking hands to himself unless he wants to swallow his tiny balls. *Whole*."

Filoberto sang on: "*Con dinero y sin dinero, hago siempre lo que yo quiero . . .*"

"I'm sorry," I said to the cocktail waitress. "He's a bit . . ." I searched for the right word and smiled so strenuously, and with such artifice, that my face cramped. It was just like Momma used to say, you did things for work that you'd never do in real life. "He's a bit old-fashioned."

The waitress laughed at me as if I had told her a transparent lie, tossed her glorious mane, and it struck me that in this party full of beautiful people, she, with her large chest and flat belly (I, for the record, was the precise, schlumpy *reverse* of that) was probably the *most* beautiful.

"He's a *bit* of an *asshole*," she corrected me. "And if you don't take care of the problem, I'll take care of it myself." She held up a fist before smacking it into the palm of her other hand. "Black belt in karate, girl."

Something about the way she grinned was incredibly familiar.

"Have we met before?" I asked her.

Her large eyes narrowed as she inspected me, a manicured finger to her full, pouty lips, and finally she shook her head. "Did you go to Cate?" she asked.

"Where?"

"The Cate School, in Santa Barbara. But if you have to ask, the answer's no." She looked me up and down. "Nope," she said. "We've never met."

"Then I apologize," I said, aware of my thin lips and double chin. It looked like the waitress had porcelain caps on her teeth; at a thousand bucks a tooth, I wondered, again, how it was possible. I remembered the first time I went to get a manicure in Los Angeles, when the Vietnamese nail lady told me in shock that I was "pretty, but natural pretty, chubby pretty," as if this were rare. In L.A., even the help had invested in cosmetic surgery. "I just really thought I knew you from somewhere."

Her posture softened and she lowered her voice the way a friend might, if she were going to say something not exactly appropriate for the setting, something conspiratorial and delicious the way my girlfriends back in Dallas used to do. How I missed my girls! "Do you ever watch *novelas*?" she asked.

I nodded.

A *novela* was a Spanish-language soap opera, a dramatic miniseries that played every night of the week on Univision or Telemundo for a season, and if your family was from West Dallas, like mine was, there was little chance you'd escaped them growing up, especially if you had a grandmother like Granny Lopez, who lived for the melodrama and happy endings.

"That's it!" I exclaimed. "You played that illiterate peasant girl who fell in love with Fernando Colunga on *Sus Raices*!"

Sus Raices, or "Her Roots," had been the only *novela* I'd watched as an addiction—with my sorority sisters, religiously—and this comely cocktail waitress had been not only beautiful, but a very competent actress we'd envied and admired. I'd even bought a copy of that Spanish-language gossip rag, *TV y Novelas,* when she was on the cover, and remembered having been surprised to learn the actress with the perfect Spanish was actually half-Dominican and half-French, born and raised in Santa Barbara, California. From a rich family. That explained the teeth, earrings, and, quite possibly, the boobs. But why was she working *here*?

I grabbed her arm and heard my voice rise up in excitement. "Oh my gosh! You're Marcella Gauthier Bosch!" I remembered her name, even though it had been almost ten years since the show aired. That probably made her somewhere around thirty now. I remembered reading something, too, about how she had hoped to give up Spanish-language TV for mainstream Hollywood. She'd quit *novelas* around the same time as Salma Hayek, but apparently had not fared as well.

"Weren't you going to do some English work?" I felt awkwardly starstruck, and a little embarrassed and confused that this woman was serving cocktails. It wasn't right. She nodded, confirming the fact that she was the actress I had in mind.

She said, "Uh-huh. But I refuse to play a maid with an accent, or a crack whore, so I guess you could say I'm taking my time finding the perfect role."

She glanced worriedly over her shoulder at a tall, stern man in black pants and a white shirt who stood behind the bar tapping his watch in her direction. He looked like Moby.

"Yeah, okay, you relentless, meaningless sphincter," she said under her breath. Then, to me she added, "Please ask that fat piece of *corrido* chimpanzee shit to leave me alone, okay? Or I'll get him. Wax on, wax off." Her hands spun in front of her face and she let out a low crazy karate wail that made me think of Angelina Jolie. She actually rather resembled Angelina. Her, and Carmen Electra.

"Wait!" I cried as she kickboxed away, far too graceful and angry for her job. I didn't say it, but I thought, *What on earth are you doing serving cocktails?*

I wondered, with no small amount of self-interest, if she had good representation. I noticed that more than one of the elites, the men in particular, stared at her. It was a huge accomplishment to turn heads in Los Angeles, a city with perhaps more good-looking people per capita than any other in the world. I knew L.A. was brutal, but the apparent fall of Marcella Gauthier Bosch made me want to cry.

At the stage end of the terrace, a microphone screeched feedback as the top brass from UCLA prepared to hand the Chimps some sort of plaque and answer questions from the press. The band was supposed to be up there, next to the university people in a photo-friendly chorus line, but they were scattered around the terrace, doing other things, like throwing pennies into a fountain that was actually a sculpture you weren't supposed to touch. I intercepted Filoberto as he began to move toward Marcella Gauthier Bosch again, licking his lips.

"Don't touch the help, and don't talk to them," I told him. "You need to get over to the podium and talk about how exciting all this is for you. How *honored* you are. The importance of education for your people, etcetera. Remember what we talked about?"

"Don't tell me what to do," he countered with beer breath. "You do your job, I do mine." His eyes did not move from Marcella's lovely body as she waltzed here and there with the tray, a mixture of hope and fury in her eyes. I truly hated women with flat bellies and big chichis. I *did*. I hoped Jesus would forgive me. Envy was such an ugly thing.

"Please," I said. "It's not a strip club. It's a museum. Act like a gentleman for Pete's sake. Everyone's here. The *Times*, *The New Yorker*. Everyone."

Filoberto, high on the fact that he was being celebrated as rich and powerful by a bunch of "gringos," seemed to feel invincible and shrugged out of my grip, moving forward on his mission to find and fondle Marcella.

"Trust me," I said, pulling on his lime-green fringe, "there will be plenty of other women in your life."

"*Me vale madre*," he said, steamrolling on. "*Quiero esa buenota.*" Polite translation: I could give a rat's behind.

I thought, frantic.

"She's *pregnant*," I lied, in loudly whispered Spanish. His expression changed instantly, to fear. I put a kind hand on his forearm, like an older sister offering a kind-hearted suggestion. "I know her, and . . ." I thought hard. "And I think she's sick, *amorcito*, that's why she's so skinny. You deserve better. I'm just looking out for you."

Filoberto made a disgusted face that I thought went nicely with the ensuing crotch-scratch and loud exclamation of "*nimodo*," and stopped following Marcella.

Yes, ma'am, there were times that I was proud to represent this band—but this was not one of them. I didn't know whether to be proud of myself for smoothing the situation, or ashamed to my bones for lying. But Los Angeles was nothing if not a lie factory, and the longer I lived here, the more lying—like asthma and Starbucks—became essential.

I dragged Filoberto by the hand to the podium, and released him to the care of sexy Samuel. The professor stood with a tiny, pretty woman, no more than five feet tall, with fierce black eyes and shiny dark shoulder-length hair streaked with a few strands of white and cut carelessly and stylelessly, as if she might have done it herself with sewing scissors while absently listening to NPR.

"Alexis," said Samuel, "I'd like you to meet my wife, Olivia."

Dangit. He was married? I'd been hoping he wasn't, and was a little surprised, given the shameless way the boy had flirted with me, that he *was* married. Or at least I thought he'd been flirting. But that was the problem with me. I misread men all the time. I thought they wanted me when all they wanted was a sandwich. And I had, more than once, ignored a wonderful guy who loved me because I did not believe in my ample gut that a guy like that could in fact love a woman with an ample gut. All the good men in this town were either married, or gay, which is why I was stuck dating a loser of a newspaper writer named Daniel, who was supposed to be here with me but who'd had a last-minute assignment covering a rap-world shooting. I shouldn't have been relieved Daniel was elsewhere, not to mention an elsewhere involving violence, but I was. He was almost forty, and wore his baggy jeans so low you could see his Fubu underwear; worse, he thought that was cool. I used to think he'd improve with time, but recently it was looking like that wasn't going to happen.

Olivia held her hand out to shake mine and I was impressed by her strength. For a petite, slouching wisp of a woman, she was powerful. Even the tendons in her forearms looked toned, as if she never ate fat and ran marathons for fun, like Gandhi. Samuel took Filoberto to one side and began prepping him for the press conference, and I was left with his wife.

She hunched and cowered as if she were afraid of something. Me? Was she actually afraid of me? How silly. She clutched her sweating wineglass with two hands, and sipped cautiously, her eyes closed to slits, observing everything around us with what I took to be judgmental amusement sprinkled with paranoia.

She wore a simple, linty black jersey dress with a too-long skirt; it would have been just right for a Mormon schoolteacher, and looked like it might have seen better years. Her jewelry was a stained-looking sterling silver in need of a polish.

Her navy blue pumps were worn out and dusty, and did not match her dress; she stood awkwardly in them, as if she were more accustomed to boots, or running shoes. Or no shoes at all. She wore no hose, and the tops of her feet had a couple of ugly black hairs sprouting on them. What, she hadn't heard of hot wax? Nair? A razor? Something. Her purse was the kind my granny used, from a Wal-Mart or a Target, sort of a mesh material with nylon underneath it. Pinned to the strap were about a dozen buttons with left-leaning political slogans in Spanish and English, the usual sort of United Farm Workers/Frida Kahlo kind of nonsense I'd seen so much of since moving here, and a particularly disturbing pin that looked like a Bush/Cheney bumper sticker but in the place of "Cheney" was the word "*Chupa*," Spanish for "sucks." The *nerve*.

Still, Olivia radiated intelligence and the intangible quality of *grace*, almost as a defense mechanism, in inverse proportion, it seemed, to her shabby wardrobe. She had to have been aware of the many gorgeous gowns in the room, and the fact that she wasn't in one. In spite of her politics, and likely because of my generous reserves of pity, I liked something about her. My momma always accused me of "collecting strays," meaning that of all my Latina sorority sisters I was the most likely to befriend the homeless and drug-addicted people we met during service projects, the one most likely to hang out with needy folks, the one most likely to want to adopt a foster child in the event that I failed to produce a child of my own—which, considering the odds lately, was more than likely. This little Olivia person seemed a little needy, and I wanted to ease her suffering somehow.

"So, you're married to Samuel?" I asked. It was an idiotic question, but I didn't know what else to say to her. We certainly couldn't talk about *fashion*. I stopped myself from the thought because it was *so* not nice and I had been raised to be nice.

Leave judgments to God, I said, but it wasn't always easy.

"He's really nice," I said of Samuel. "He's been a great help to me." I also imagined he'd be good in bed, but didn't raise the subject.

"For ten years now," she said with a smile sadder than I thought should accompany such wonderful news. Her English was tinged with a slight Spanish accent. She sighed. "We've been together a long time."

"Are you in academia, too?" I asked, assuming, given the collection of horrible pins and the shoes, that the answer would be yes.

She shook her head and sucked at the wine with a loud slurp, shrinking even further into the thin shell of her shoulders.

"I used to be a technical writer for a medical journal, but I quit my job when we had our son. Jack. He's two." She finally looked me in the eye and smiled at the thought of her child. *That's* why I liked her, I thought. She was a good mother. "I don't believe in nannies or day care."

I liked that, too. I would never hire a nanny. Never. Well, maybe if I had to.

She sneaked a look at my left hand, and asked the question the very bareness of my ring finger made glaringly clear.

"Are you married?"

"No," I said, and saved her the thoughts that followed. *I'm heading on thirty and still can't find a man who can stand me. I'll never have children unless it is through surgical intervention. I am thinking the best remedy for all of this is to adopt three hundred cats, one for each pound I plan to weigh soon because I can't seem to stop spooning cookie ice cream into my gaping maw thanks to my increasingly realistic fear of being single forever, Amen.*

"Lucky you," she joked. I did not see the humor of it. What was wrong with being married?

"Do you like staying home?" I asked her.

"It's great," she said with a tinge of counterfeit happiness. "Really. I love it. I love my son." It sounded like she was trying to convince herself, and me.

"Good."

"So, you manage the band?"

"Uh-huh."

"They're great. They really connect with the people." She looked like she actually *liked* the Chimps, or admired them, or felt pride in them. "How do you like your job?"

It was the first time I could remember in Los Angeles that a person had asked me a question this direct, simple, and personal. I answered honestly, telling her of my dream to have my own talent agency someday and be done with the Chimps.

"Wow." Her eyes lit up with surprise. "I guess we all have dreams."

"What's yours?"

The men were taking their places at the microphone, and we had begun to hold our conversation in whispers.

"I want to write a movie." Her eyes focused on her hairy feet and she blushed.

"That's great." I tried to be enthusiastic.

Everyone I met in L.A., from bartenders to cosmetics salesgirls, said they were screenwriters or actors, it seemed, but this Olivia person didn't seem to have any ego involved in the statement at all. In fact, she seemed oddly humiliated by it. I took this to mean she had something to say, and guessed that with her tendency to shrink away and watch everything around her (which also, frankly, could be considered antisocial) and her prior employment as a technical writer (whatever that meant) she might make a halfway decent screenwriter. Or at least as good as half of the wannabes in this town.

"Well, actually, I wrote it already," she apologized. "I just don't know what to do with it."

Samuel, her husband, was tall and cocky. He took his place at the microphone on the stage, tapped it once or twice, cleared his throat with deliberation, and began his very flattering and informative introduction of the band.

"I'd love to read your movie," I blurted to Olivia, wondering, as I said it, if I had made a mistake. Sometimes the charitable impulse was too great in me.

Olivia stared hard into my eyes. I didn't know why I'd said that I wanted to read something I didn't know anything about, other than the fact that it made me feel like I might actually be capable of starting my own firm someday if I were able to say things like that and make someone flinchy feel like I was that important.

Olivia whispered, "Would you? It might suck. I need an honest opinion. Samuel says it's good, but he's my husband." She glared at him. "And men *lie*."

I smiled as politely as I could, to try to let her know I thought it was time for us to keep quiet and listen to the speakers. I also didn't know her well enough to start talking about how she mistrusted her husband and men in general, and was not comfortable with her apparent and unearned comfort with me. She got the message instantly—she was nothing if not a sensitive woman—and moved a few feet away from me with some sort of mumbled apology. I hoped I hadn't offended her, and fished a business card out of my bag.

"Call me," I mouthed. "Send me a copy of your movie. We'll talk."

She nodded, sullen, and slouched away.

Once the press conference ended, with rousing applause and polite smiles all around, Filoberto swaggered off to the drink table once more, one hand inexplicably stashed in the waistband of his pants as if he were posing as a body double for Napoleon. Olivia slinked off on her husband's arm, with a wincing sort of half-smile in my direction, and I stood, alone, surrounded by a murmuring crowd of elite Anglo-linos.

I assessed the room, wondering who to introduce myself to next. There was so much power here, I could hardly stand it. Finally, I spotted a couple whose pictures were familiar to me from gossip magazines. The man, Darren Wells, was a big-time TV drama producer who had made his fortune with a show about anxiety-ridden non-Hispanic white kids in Beverly Hills, starring his very own son. Short, with a dyed brown comb-over and trendy, artsy eyeglasses, he wore a fake tan under his black sweater and sipped wine with studied indifference. His equally bronzed wife was a walking tribute to Botox, Chanel, and starvation, dripping with waist chains.

"Hi there," I said with a big cheesy smile. I stuck my hand into the space between me and Mr. Wells. "My name is Alexis Lopez, and I'm the manager and publicist for the band being honored here tonight. Thanks s'much for coming out."

Mr. Wells took my hand in his and I was impressed by its softness and heat. My own hands were like ice. His face opened in a warm smile, which I didn't expect, and both he and his wife acted more than pleased to meet me.

"This is such a treat," said Darren Wells. "I've been looking to get something with a Latin flavor going, and some people I know thought I might make some contacts here."

My smile went from forced to fabulous. "What sort of Latin thing?" I asked.

"Oh, a show. I do TV shows. Name's Darren Wells."

"I *know* your name, Mr. Wells," I said, with a wink. "And I *know* you make TV shows. Everyone in the world knows that! And no one does them better. I think you are a genius and when I saw you here, I just thought, omigosh, I can't *not* meet that man. We're honored you came. Truly."

He smiled modestly and brushed off my shameless gushing, but seemed to like the compliments. I continued: "No, really, sir. You are. I mean, I just love everything you've ever done." I listed the shows I knew of his, and the names of the actors and writers that I could remember. First rule of good public relations: Flatter. Second rule: Know who you're talking to and what they've done. He and his wife seemed impressed, and she put a hand on my arm.

"Are you from the South?" she asked. "You speak beautifully. So articulate. Isn't she articulate, honey?" He nodded.

"I'm Texan," I bragged.

"How charming," smiled Mr. Wells. They both looked surprised that someone who looked like me—that is, someone with dark skin and hair—might be Texan. It happened all the time out here. Hollywood thought Latinos only existed in East

L.A. I let it slip because, honestly, it didn't bother me. Well, maybe it bothered me a little that people might be surprised I was "articulate" or Texan. But I loved being an ambassador for my state.

After a bit more small talk, he told me that he was putting together a *Baywatch* clone beach-bunny lifeguard show, and that he was hoping to cast a Latina in the lead female role to reflect, as he called it, "the real L.A." Loved that.

"The only problem with this damn town is that everywhere I go they say, 'Darren, there aren't any gorgeous Hispanics. Look at that George Lopez.' That's what they say. They always talk about George."

I gasped. "They don't honestly say that, do they?" Privately, I had to admit, I had thought once or twice that there were better-looking men in the world than sweet, funny George Lopez, but I didn't see how Hollywood could assume that he was the physical prototype for all of us. That was like saying all non-Hispanic whites looked like Rodney Dangerfield or David Spade.

"They do say it. All the time."

"What about J.Lo?" I asked.

"Well, that's just it. They think it stops and ends with her, and, you know, she isn't the cuddliest woman to work with and nobody's breaking down doors to ink a deal with her since *Gigli*."

"I hear she's vulgar," said the wife.

"Anyway, I can't get an agency in town to send me anyone worth looking at. I'm close to giving up and casting another Barbie doll, but I don't want to. That's what the networks want, but I think it's rotten and stupid. Unimaginative sons of bitches."

"We go to Los Cabos all the time," said the wife. "And there are so many lovely women down in Mexico."

I listed the names of some well-known Latina actresses who happened to be gorgeous, and Mr. Wells shook his head. "Too famous, all of 'em," he said. "I want hungry. Someone new to put out there the way we did for the kids on *Beverly Hills High Life*. I don't want the show to be about the star. I want people to believe these actors are the characters because it's the first time they're seeing them."

It was a genuine Alexis lightbulb-moment after that, and if I'd been a cartoon character—which sometimes I rather thought I was in this town—I might have sprouted a bubble with a sixty-watter going "Bing!" above my head.

"Are you a religious man, sir?" I asked. The couple stared at me in horror. I had forgotten you didn't ask that sort of question in Los Angeles. You got the same reaction you might if you asked someone if they liked porn. "I mean, spiritual," I said, using the word that, to me, meant the Bible, and which, in L.A., meant hemp T-shirts and vegetarianism.

"Well, sure." He looked worried about where this might be heading.

"So am I," I said. "That's why I think we met tonight. There's someone here I think you need to meet. The perfect actress for your show."

I looked around the room for Marcella, the cocktail waitress, but didn't see her. I asked Mr. Wells if he would mind waiting right where he was for a few moments while I found someone, and he agreed. I raced around the gallery, but could not find her.

"Excuse me," I said to the Moby man, who I assumed was her boss. "Could you tell me where I might find Marcella, the real pretty waitress?"

He snorted. "Hell if I know."

"Pardon?"

"Bitch quit ten minutes ago."

"Quit? Where'd she go?"

"I don't know and I don't care."

"Do you know how I can reach her?"

"Why would you want to?" he asked. "She's a psycho."

"I'm an old friend and I want to catch up," I lied. Again with the lying. It was getting too easy.

The man fished beneath a box of cash for a tattered piece of paper with a list of phone numbers on it. He pointed hers out to me. I took my Palm Pilot out of my white-fringed Tod's handbag and tapped the number in.

I returned to Mr. Wells and explained the situation to him, embellishing it a little by saying I had just signed her as a client. He said he remembered having seen her, and was not surprised she'd been a star before.

"A hot girl," he said.

"She's fabulous," I said as I handed him a business card. "The new Salma. And as you can see, she needs the work. I can send you tapes of her work, if you'd like, and I can arrange a meeting."

He looked doubtful, but his wife seemed confident. It reminded me of the saying that behind every great man is a great woman. *So* totally true. "Why not, honey?" she asked. "It might not work out, but it might be the smartest move you ever made. It's why you came here, right?"

"Yes, but a waitress?"

"She's a star in Spanish," I assured him.

"Jennifer Aniston was a waitress, honey," said the wife. "And Brad used to deliver refrigerators."

"But we need her in English," he objected.

"She's from Santa Barbara, sir, fully bilingual, no accent either way. She went to Cate."

"Really?" he asked. "We have a niece at Cate."

I had never heard of Cate before tonight, but I did know the power of prep school name-dropping.

Mr. Wells took my card and put it in his pocket with a shrug that made me think of Woody Allen. "We'll see," he said. "Thanks for the lead. I'll call you, Alexis."

I wandered through the room, gathering business cards for a few more minutes, and finally checked in with Filoberto, still holding court by the drink table. I asked if he was okay, and when he said he was fine, I asked to be excused.

It had been a long day, and I had a longhaired Chihuahua named Juanga, after Juan Gabriel, my favorite singer of all time, and a pint of Chunky Monkey waiting for me at home in my Newport Beach condo. Juanga the dog was a girl, but so might as well have been Juanga the man, in his shiny patent leathers and capes.

The drive to Orange County was not short—but worth it because O.C. was the only place in Southern California where I didn't feel like I had to apologize for being a card-carrying member of the G.O.P.; I *almost* fit in there. Even though I loved speeding around in my pretty little cream-colored Cadillac, I dreaded the hour-plus I had yet to spend on the freeways of Southern California tonight. Thank goodness for CDs; a rockin' eighties compilation would be my company tonight.

"Go," huffed Filoberto, as if he not only did not *need* me anymore, but had *never* needed me and would never need me again. I smiled in spite of him.

"You did a wonderful job tonight, darlin'," I said. "I'm s'proud of you! Everyone is. Thanks for all your hard work and generosity."

Filoberto chugged his beer and observed me from the corner of his eye. Then, to my surprise, he belched softly and pulled me into a fatherly hug.

"Come here," he said. "I know I'm hard on you. Maybe, you know, maybe you were right. About the suit. But I think I look good."

Then, as quickly as he had gotten mushy, he hardened up again, pushing me off as if I'd been the one who embraced him. I stood, staring, a sap, with tears bubbling up in my eyes.

It was the girly girl in me; I cried for near 'bout everything. Babies born, planes that landed on time, douche commercials, the satisfying ding of the bell on my clothes dryer. Everything.

But if it was something that reminded me I hadn't known my (Mexican) biological father until I was eighteen, forget it. I wept like Tammy Faye in a Barbara Walters interview.

I had been eighteen when Momma and Daddy finally told me the truth: The male provider of my spectacular DNA had been none other than Pedro Negrete, the famous Mexican film and mariachi star. He was, and continued to be, Mexico's most beloved and heavily mustachioed middle-aged romantic singer, as popular in grainy movies aired late at night on the Telemundo network as he was in recordings; a long, roguish slash of a man with exceptionally tight pants sewn down the side with shiny things resembling quarters, and short embroidered jackets that just brushed the top of his widening, pork-loving arse. He kept ranches in Mexico, and in McAllen, Texas, filled with fancy white horses that pranced like big show-poodles during his concerts, which were generally held in rodeo arenas. Pedro sang on horseback whenever possible, and women of advancing years and descending breasts threw increasingly wide, pork-loving panties into the hoof-beaten dust. At first I thought they were joking when Momma and Daddy told me, but I soon realized it was the truth.

I think Momma was temporarily insane when she had her one-night stand with Pedro in 1974. But in West Dallas, Pedro Negrete was like Elvis or the Beatles. So when my Aunt Dolores took Momma to one of Pedro's concerts to celebrate her graduating from SMU (she was the first in the family to go to college, against her parents' wishes), Pedro picked Momma out of the audience because he thought she was so pretty with that reddened bouffant hair helmet and the turquoise minidress with white *Laugh In* boots. I've seen pictures; she was twinkly, and cute as pie. People think only rock stars cull chicks from the audience, but ranchera stars do it, too, apparently.

Even though Momma's Methodist now, like Daddy, she was *raised* Catholic. Terminating me was never an option—thank you, Jesus, Joseph, and Mary, Mel Gibson, et al. She lived with my grandparents when I was born; they insisted the "situation" (aka *me*) was *exactly* what you could expect when you sent a *female* to college. Dolores defiantly went on to graduate from SMU, too, and *her* decision to kiss the (upper and lower) lips of women *only* entirely solidified my grandparents' view of college as Satan's Sinful School for Girls. Momma waited until I was two years old to get a job with an oil company as a secretary; that's where she met Daddy, then a member of the junior sales force. Daddy, as in the man who *raised* me.

"Filoberto," I stopped, words stuck and wrong in my mouth. I wanted to say something, but I realized it wasn't Filoberto I wanted to say it to. It was all scrambled up in my head sometimes—men, who they were and what they meant to me, what I wanted from them and why.

"You still here, woman?" He wiped a tear from my cheek with his calloused thumb and smiled. "Go on home, *gueda*."

MARCELLA

t was supposed to be the hottest thing in fitness classes, but I was unprepared for the big black drag queen. Let me rephrase that. I *was* prepared for the big black drag queen. Of course I was. This was SMASH Fitness in West Hollywood, after all. One in every three people there tended to be a big black drag queen. But I did not expect him to strip down to his hairless, shaved birthday suit in a room full of people, however cutting-edge and open-minded we were.

The class was called Pole Hopping, and, as you might imagine, involved a pole, disco music, and stripper moves taught by a real-life exotic dancer with CPR certification. I'd been reading about it for a couple of weeks in all the fashion magazines, about how it toned the abs and inner thighs, and I'd stood outside the class gawking the week before like everyone else at my gym. It seemed harmless enough, and I'd been looking forward to participating. I might have liked to be a stripper, in real life, for reasons too complicated and unpleasant to consider most of the time. I had the tits, but I didn't have the guts. This was close enough.

I'd come here under the assumption that nothing took your mind off the fact that you'd just quit your fifth job in a month faster than hard-core exercise. I also needed to take my mind away from the fact that Ryan Fuckwad, the only nice guy I had met in the past year, had turned out to be another loser in an Abercrombie sweatshirt.

Just yesterday, *Cristina* magazine had printed photos he'd sold of me running topless on that beach in Tulum, Mexico. The magazine feigned titillated horror, and failed to mention the fact that it had been a *nude beach* and that in my bikini bottoms I had been the only woman not showing *bush*. I'd been positively conservative in context. But *Cristina* whooped it up about how I'd hit complete rock bottom. The magazine had even mentioned that I was more than a hundred grand in credit-card debt, which was unfortunately true. Ryan must have told them about that, too; I'd trusted him, and this was what it got me.

The Latin media had been covering the scandal of me for years, starting with my fake boobs when I got them at eighteen, halfway through shooting *Sus Raices*. They'd moved on to how I told off a bunch of Mexican and Brazilian producers and "lied" about them demanding I suck them off for parts on their idiotic *novelas*. (Not a lie, obviously. No *chupa*, no job, *asi fue*.)

The media giggled about how I'd bragged about quitting Latin TV because I thought I was smarter than everyone else and could actually make it in Hollywood. I'd once said in an interview, quite honestly, that I thought Latin television in the United States and Mexico was just about the biggest piece of sexist and racist shit you might hope to find on the planet, and I'd hinted that if any major mainstream English-language network in the nation had tried to do some of the things they did on Univision they would lose their FCC license for indecency or stupidity or both. I'd also said that Don Francisco looked like a muppet of Doctor Ruth, in drag. The mediocre media mafia in Miami never let me forget I'd said any of this, of course, and soon I was about as blacklisted as you could get in Latin TV.

You'd think my own people might support me a little in my attempts to do something somewhat more meaningful with my life than jiggle on *Sabado Gigante* or wrestle with G-string midgets on *Cristina*, or get dragged around the set by the arm by a man with a moustache in the obligatory *novela* "macho man, timid woman" scene; but it was crabs in a barrel. I'd been a *novela* star and *that* crowd would not let me go without doing their best to destroy me. Lately, they'd been salivating over the fact that I had gone from being a pampered prep-school kid from California to being a *novela* star to being one of the least-busy actresses in L.A., waiting tables and running naked on the beach with my mouth open because, they guessed, I could not pay my debt, all of which was essentially true.

They peed with joy that my rich parents had cut me off because they were ashamed of me. This was only half true. They'd cut me off, yes, but it was meant to inspire me to work harder at what my parents thought was "real" acting—not TV. I waited tables and used credit cards because I didn't *want* to be dependent on my parents for the rest of my life. Now, this. Me and my boobs all over the cover of the magazine, with little red stars to cover the nipples, as if nipples themselves were not little red stars, and a superimposed photo of my once-famous French cinema star mother, Brigitte Gauthier, from one of her lame-ass art-house movies, with her hands raised in horror to her face and her own mouth open in a Hitchcockian shriek.

Ryan had taken the photo of me with my mouth open as a joke, but on the cover of the magazine it made me look like I was insane. "Sexaholic," they cried, "nymphomaniac." A rebuke to her elegant mother and powerful father, the famous Dominican business lawyer and writer. A lunatic, the ultimate shallow, sex-crazed, Americanized nightmare of every Latin or European parent. And all this because Ryan had apparently sold the photos as a big, fat, parting "fuck you" to *me*, for dumping his ass after he nearly bored me to death. I had never come with any man, ever. (Long story, sad ending.) But it was only during the snoozy, garlicky act of sex with Ryan Fuckwad that I had actually fallen fast-snoring *asleep*.

So, attention. I needed it, wanted it; I allowed the envious, miserable stares of strangers to soothe me into the illusion that I might in fact be something special and therefore did not need to get depressed about the way the world seemed to be out to get me. I was the kind of woman who couldn't keep friends, who somehow always ended up offending them even though I didn't mean to. So I got attention where I could. Therapy, years of it, forced upon me by my concerned/embarrassed parents, had done nothing to help, so I indulged myself. I was an actress. What else was there to know about me? I needed attention. That was all there was to it. And the gym, if you had a body like mine, was one of the world's greatest places to seek attention.

But the drag queen, alas, was getting more than I was. I should have gone to Step. There were no needy people in Step.

See, I wasn't mellow enough to appreciate or benefit from Pilates; I wasn't angry and judgmental enough to believe yoga or kabala would calm my ass down; and I wasn't corny enough to go to Step anymore (even though I still loved it, I'd never admit that to anyone important) and I hated the numb vulva I got in Spinning. Pole Hopping seemed just right. Or it had. Until the naked, shaved thing. It reminded me of something Julia Roberts once said: *"For me, to act with my clothes on is a performance; to act with my clothes off is a documentary."* This class was a documentary for the big black drag queen.

No one got naked in Pole Hopping the week before, when I had watched; they just got sexy. I was used to sexy. The three *novelas* I'd done were all about sexy, even when I was supposed to be in mourning for my evil twin, or beaten down by the boss man on his horse; in Mexican drama, it was all about sexy for women, all the time.

It wasn't so different in Hollywood, actually. I had, in my own mind, transmogrified the entire notion of female sexiness into a personal philosophical doctrine involving post-feminist social illusions, all of which made it easier to justify my choice of roles to myself, Mère Brigitte, my sister, and Collis, my best friend from high school and the only real friend I had anymore. But even Collis was disgusted by my tight ass-cleavage pants and low-cut shirts. She, like the rest of the world, didn't get it. Or me. Nobody got me. It wasn't women's sexuality that was wrong; it was the way society thought you had to deny it in order to get ahead. I didn't want to have to make men feel comfortable and unthreatened to get ahead. I wanted to terrify them every step of the fucking way.

Forty years after Betty Friedan and twenty-five since Madonna first writhed on the floor in a wedding dress, and our screwed society *still* balked at women owning their sexuality. *Que estupidez.* I was single, independent, successful, attractive, and yet people like my mother, sister, and Collis squirmed at the fact that I had worn a bikini on international television, as if this were somehow *oppressive* to me. What, they never heard of the Taliban? What I did was so anti-Taliban. This was why I was drawn to Pole Hopping. I thought people here might be like-minded and open to a new world order. The naked man was about to be the reason I fled.

At a more banal level, however, I thought the class might be fun. I also hoped I might meet someone who would ask me on a date. There were lots of good-looking men at SMASH. I even dressed sexier than I usually do to work out. I wore low-riding Pezzi jersey short-shorts and a barely there Marimbondo sports bikini top, all in the name of fun. I wore those long athletic socks with the stripes on top, like basketball players from the seventies used to wear, so they were like elastic go-go boots, with my gold and gray Nikes. I usually kept my long hair back in a pony-tail when I exercised, but I thought it would be fun for this class to leave it loose, hanging down my back just past the bikini strap. I stuck the platinum belly ring through the hole in the skin at the top of my belly button.

It might not have been so shocking if he hadn't been standing right in front of me, and if he hadn't smelled so horribly *nude*. There's a certain naked-guy smell, a cross between farm animal, yeasted dough, and old lime juice that I had not hoped to experience in an exercise class, and there it was. Jesus, but it was rank. People said women smelled bad "down there," but I'd take puntang and beefy menstrual blood over crusted semen and ass hair any day. I had Huxley on the brain, and the words rose from my mouth into the disco din: "*Maybe this world is another planet's hell.*" Fer sure.

We were about half an hour into the one-hour class and each of the attendees were taking turns at the pole in front of the class, trying to imitate the instructor's slithering. I'd just gone, and was still a little dizzy from the part of the routine where you turn yourself upside down on the pole, hold your body aloft with your arms, and spread your legs, like a big Y. It's significantly harder than it looks. I thought my face had looked funny and sort of old in the mirror upside down. I'm only twenty-eight, but I've already scheduled my first face-lift, a trick of the trade. Collis had a coughing fit when I told her about the face-lift, and didn't talk to me for a couple of weeks. You dreamed of keeping the same friends all your life, but it rarely happened. More often than not, you traded friends as you grew up, fitting them into your life as made sense. Or at least I did.

I'd walked back to my place in the exercise studio, high-fived Krista Brooks, a pretty actress I recognized from a USA Network show that would soon be yanked off the air, turned around, and there he was, doing his own thing that had very little to do with the routine. To be precise, he pulled his clothes off as if they were on fire, bumping and grinding away while other people squealed, cheered, and egged him on. *You see?* I thought. A smart, capable, independent woman like me or Krista Brooks wears a bikini on television and the world pities us our tragic loss of humanity and morality, but a lunatic drag queen wants to shake his shrunken weenie for the world to see and everyone applauds him. That, in my opinion, was not progress, thank you. That was patriarchy adjusting to the new modality.

SMASH was known for bending the rules of fitness instruction and for attracting cutting-edge fashionistas. I'd been to Step classes with women who taught in sparkly platform boots—that was during the Spice Girls craze. SMASH was also where I'd been happily attending fire-fighting fitness classes, where the props included real fire hoses and axes, and two real-life hunks who taught the class in G-strings and bow ties. SMASH was very West L.A. and so, I thought, was I. But the naked, self-fondling drag queen, with his hormone-shriveled wiener, shaved pubic hair, and hormone-prompted breast mounds just about made me hurl.

At the Cate School I had been required to volunteer at an AIDS hospice for one summer, so I knew it was important to be open about sexual orientation. And, if I were completely honest with myself, I had to admit that I sometimes got *more* turned on by the thought of a beautiful woman's body than a man's, though I didn't believe this made me anything *close* to gay. I had a simple appreciation for the female form, in part because I worked so hard on *mine* and could appreciate greatly when another woman worked as hard as I did; and because as an actress it was much easier to imagine myself in the body of the *female* porn star than the *male* and so *she* was the one I focused on. Not to mention the fact that most male porn stars still resembled British sitcom actors or Luis Guzmán. But *still*. I did *not* want to see *this*. I really didn't.

☆ 27 ☆

I bolted from the room, grabbed my keys and purse from the locker room on the way out, and fled the gym into the outdoor mall. I slowed to a walk and found myself sitting on a bench in front of the downstairs fountain, trying to ignore the luscious butter breeze coming from Wolfgang Puck's restaurant. I fished for my cell phone with an urgency that almost snapped one of my acrylics.

I flipped open the phone and dialed Nicolás, my lawyer brother. He was back in L.A. preparing a case and visiting some old friends. Nico was one of those people who kept his. He answered on the first ring.

"Nico," I said. "I wanted you to be the first to know I just saw a big, black, naked drag queen shaking his dicklette like a Chiclet."

It sounded like he sucked his teeth before answering. "Where are you, Venice Beach?" Unimpressed.

"No. He was in my fucking *exercise* class."

"Chiclet dicklette. That's good. You should rap, *princesa*. Do a record like J.Lo. Maybe that's your ticket out of this waitressing shit."

"Shut up."

He sighed. "I keep telling you Miss Kitty's Chatsworth Skin Palace ain't a gym, but do you listen?"

"Nico! Listen to me."

"What?"

"I lost another job."

"Lost? Or quit?"

"Quit."

"Congratulations. I'll call you later. I'm busy."

He hung up on me. My nerves were shot. I needed to talk to someone. Who could I call? *Mère*? She would lecture me on being open to gender-bending as an art form, or find some way to link cross-dressing to Jean-Paul Sartre or Samuel Beckett.

Who to call, then? My agent, Wendy? I hated Wendy. I needed to fire her ass, but after firing three agents in one year, I was trying to cut back.

Papá. He'd understand. We were more alike than not, I thought. He took no crap, I took no crap. He might have even found the drag queen thing amusing.

So I called my father, the big-shot international business lawyer, but soon wished I had not. He was in Halifax, negotiating a contract, and even through the crackling of his cell phone I could hear the disgust in his voice. He "uh-huh"ed his way through the drag queen story, and promptly asked about my job, his favorite topic; being Marcella, I told him the truth: That I'd quit because I was smarter than my boss.

"What do you mean, you *quit* another job?" he shouted in Spanish, his language of stern reprimand.

"What?" I asked. "You want me to put up with the insults, Papi? Sometimes you have to defend yourself. I couldn't take it. I'll get another job."

He sighed. "Marcella."

"What?"

"Why must you always think everyone is out to get you?"

"Because they are. Have you seen *Cristina* magazine? They're out to get me. People *are* out to get me."

He laughed dismissively. "I'm sure the magazine made you take your shirt off at that beach, right? Marcella, it was you. You did that. When are you going to accept some responsibility for the things that happen in your life? It's called growing up."

"It was a nude beach!"

He sighed. "Why can't you be more like your sister?"

"Mathilde's stupid, and I'm smart. That's why. Thought you knew that."

"She'll have her PhD before the year is out."

"In Women's Studies? It's a completely false area of research."

"Or your brother? Why can't you be like Nico?"

"Isn't one clone enough for you?"

"My point, Marcella, is that they went to *college*. They have *careers*."

"I have a career. I'm an actress, like *Mére*. She never went to college and I don't hear you ripping her about it. Jesus. Oh, but that's because you support her. Oops."

"Your mother was a *real* actress, Marcella. When's the last time you had an acting job?" he asked, in interrogation lawyer mode.

"Last year."

"That tortilla commercial where you were nearly naked?" He laughed again.

"It was a job. I had a sombrero."

"Marcy, you're pretty and young, but you won't be that way forever, and you can't keep burning bridges everywhere you go. You are almost thirty. There's a limit to how much childishness people will tolerate. You need to focus on something realistic. And respectable."

"There's a *limit* to how much shit you can take on the job, too, Papi." Or, I added silently, from your family.

"Watch your language."

"Okay. I'll fucking watch it, it's a goddamned promise." I was seconds away from hanging up, and he knew it.

"Marcy. Please."

"Sorry."

His voice turned tender. "Do you need money?"

"Not yet." My father was the king of secretly depositing money into my account, whether I asked him to or not, and I was accustomed to a couple thousand a month just sort of popping up. I knew I was supposed to be "cut off," but I really wasn't. "The last deposit has a little left."

Again, the sigh. "I just hate to see you wasting your youth with bad decisions. You could have done *novelas* again, but no one in the industry wants to work with you. You have a reputation for being difficult. Everywhere I go, I hear about it. Can you imagine what it's like to be your father for a minute, Marcella? All I hear about is how troubled and crazy you are."

"It's accurate." I watched as a group of female friends walked, gossipy and laughing, out of a boutique; I wondered what it would be like to be the kind of woman who had friends like that, as opposed to troubled and crazy.

"You should take the jobs Uncle Hubert offers you."

"I'd rather eat rat poison."

"You see? You're crazy. You set yourself up for failure."

"Crazy because I won't work with an asshole?"

"It's Broadway, *princesa*, Hubert is a *Broadway producer*. Where else will you get a shot like that?"

"I don't know. I'm not interested in Broadway. I'm interested in TV and movies."

"What have you got against your uncle? He comes to see us, you stay in the other room. He calls to talk to you, you won't talk to him. He's a fan of your acting. He says so all the time. He's one of the *only* people I ever hear say that, actually."

"Now wait a minute," I roared, my adrenaline levels shooting up at the insult. "That's not true. You know that's not true. People might call me crazy or difficult, but no one ever says I can't act. I *can*. You *know* I can."

"Perhaps. But you don't have to prove to everyone that you can do it alone. None of us can do it alone. Let your uncle help you."

I said nothing, because there was too much to say and I didn't know how. Uncle Hubert, the husband of my mother's oldest sister, was a dashing and celebrated theater producer and actor who hung out with people like Joan Didion in New York. He had decided when I was fifteen that it was time to set up a secret camera in my bedroom, to tape me dressing—and more importantly, *un*dressing. I found the camera, and after feeling sick and scared, set one up in his house, to tape him beating off to videos of me, his niece, changing clothes. He had no idea I knew and I'd never told a soul. He'd been in his late thirties then, already famous, and handsome, and I had not known at first whether to be terrified or flattered. He'd find any excuse to visit my parents, a few times a year, for business, and he always pretended to enjoy talking with them late into the night over cognac and cigars. And then, I could count on it. Hubert sneaking into the hall closet by my room, to check on his weird little video production setup, behind boxes of old family photos.

I was seventeen when it stopped, and it stopped because I had moved out to be a *novela* star and never invited him to my shack in L.A. I still had the videos of him masturbating to videos of me, and I had videos of his creepy surveillance system, and of him sneaking in to fiddle with it. You never knew when something like that would come in handy.

He continued to tell my parents he wanted to work with me. He also made a big show out of telling my parents that I was his favorite niece on those rare occasions that we all ended up in a room together.

I'd tried, in a way, to tell my parents I'd been hurt, by cutting my arms to shreds with razor blades, ditching school enough to nearly get thrown out, sleeping my way through all four of my high school years with little regard for the gender or appearance of those I bedded, reading morose poets, and nearly starving myself to death. My parents decided I was a loser and a slut—or, as they put it, pathologically underachieving and promiscuous—and to remedy this they'd shipped me off to a doctor who pumped me full of meds, and never found out what was wrong because I didn't tell them, and I didn't tell them because I knew how evil people were and I pretty much knew by then that everyone would blame *me*. They wouldn't have believed me, because the entire family, from the grandparents in Santo Domingo and Paris to my own siblings, figured I was some kind of psycho who would say anything to get attention. The drama queen. The wayward beauty. The whore. The wild child, spoiled rotten, they thought. Didn't know the value of money or hard work, hopeless. But they didn't know me. No one did. And I liked it that way. This was where acting came in very handy; if I could pretend everything was fine, then it was fine. That was the actor's gift, and it was how I had decided to live my life. Pretending I was happy.

Blissfully, my call-waiting bleeped. "Dad, I have to go. I'll talk to you later."

"Call your mother but don't tell her I gave you money. Get a job. Call Hubert."

"Bye."

I flashed over to the other call.

"Marcy, you there?" Wendy, my miserable agent, was the only person other than my father who called me that dreaded name, and no matter how many times I'd asked her not to, she still did. She'd heard my dad do it once, and was relentlessly insensitive.

"Hi, Wendy. How are you?"

"Tuesday at ten. You free?"

Like many people in the entertainment business, Wendy could never be bothered with small talk. In this town, it seemed to me, people tried to sound as rushed, busy, and important as possible, often in inverse proportion to their actual importance. They had male assistants call you—and the gayer they sounded, the better—to seem more important than the task usually required, probably because they liked to hear their own voices saying, "Get me so-and-so, on the double!" They did conference calls for no real reason, other than mass confusion as you tried to figure out who the last person to talk was. It was all part of the Hollywood game, a game that required many useless meetings where people had the chance to seem important for the sake of seeming important. I paused for a moment too long, trying to remember my schedule.

"Marcy?" Wendy barked. "You hear me?"

"Yeah. Hi."

"Ten Tuesday."

"I heard you. I was thinking."

"Truman wants you to read for *Light House,* that new project he's doing with Morgan Freeman."

"I hadn't heard about that one," I said, digging once more through the bag for my Pocket PC.

"Where've you been? *Light House,* Marcy. The part is perfect for you."

"Ohhhh," I said. "Isn't that the one with Jennifer Jason Leigh? Morgan plays a sharecropper's illiterate son and she plays a rich Southern lady who befriends him and teaches him to read even though he has Alzheimer's because she feels so guilty for letting her black nanny drown when she was six?"

"Yeah."

I'd almost gotten used to the typical Hollywood take on race. All blacks were portrayed as violent, poor, downtrodden or stupid, or they were rappers, or psychic or otherwise endowed with supernatural qualities they used only to better the lives of white folks, with the "best" movies featuring blacks who were all of the above, all at once. All white ladies were shown as rich, benevolent, and sexually frustrated. All Latinas were shown as "spicy," which I was sure was an overused cliché only because it so closely resembled "spic." And there was no physical variety of Latina; we were all supposed to be brown. We were supposed to be "hot," too, longing to be stripped naked in a tub of red chili before heading off to turn tricks and clean commodes. Rarely were we allowed to speak English well. I used to think there'd be lots of roles for people like me out there, but I had sort of given up finding them. I turned on my Pocket PC, only to find it had once again deleted everything I entered. "Shit," I said, before I could stop myself.

"What? Don't fucking tell me you got a problem with it, Marcy. I told you, you can't expect to go right to leading roles from television." It didn't occur to her, I guessed, that Jennifer Aniston had done just that. But, then again, Jennifer was a "Friend," and Greek, which they considered white, and not me.

"No," I said, and fought the urge to dash the electronic calendar against the bench. "I lost everything on my PDA. Sorry. Go ahead."

"So you can't do it?"

"No, I don't *know*. That's what I'm trying to say. I don't *know* because I lost everything on my Pocket PC."

"Fine," said Wendy with an exasperated sigh. "Look, write this down. You got a pen?"

I dug again, this time for a writing implement. I found one in a bloodred lip liner, and pulled out a receipt from Fogol, my favorite Rodeo Drive lingerie boutique. I spent entirely too much money there. "Okay," I said.

"Universal Studios, ten. Meet me at the agency and we'll go together," she said.

"What's the role?"

"It's for a working girl. But she's recurring. You'd get about six minutes of talking time, lots more silent. She's pivotal."

"*Working* girl? What's her name? Does she have an accent? Please tell me they don't want a Spanish accent."

"Call coming in," Wendy said, importantly. She clicked over to another call, clicked back to me a minute later.

"Okay," she said when she got back on the line. "So I'll see you here at nine? Let's say eight-thirty, that way we can grab a coffee and head over with plenty of time for traffic."

"What's the character's *name?*" I asked again.

"Oh, *that.*" Wendy pretended she didn't know what I was talking about.

"Yes, please," I said.

"Well, that's just the thing. She doesn't exactly *have* a name."

"What do they call her, Wendy?"

"Okay, Marcy. But don't get all pissed off on a crusade. It's a good opportunity to get out there and be seen."

"Okay."

"Uhm, I've got the script here somewhere. Okay. Ah. Here it is."

"And?"

"The character is called 'Hispanic Stripper Number One,'" she said.

I said nothing.

"Trust me, Marcy. It isn't as bad as it sounds. You could bring a lot to the character. She doesn't want to do this for a living, she has to, you know? Like she has a family to support. You could give her a lot of dignity. She gets six minutes. That's a shitload."

"Okay, Wendy."

"See you then?"

"Yeah. Thanks for calling."

I snapped the phone shut and stared for another minute at the water spraying from the top of the fountain, one never-ending festival of imperialist jism. I took my new book out of my handbag and tried to read. It was *Who Stole Feminism?* by Christina Hoff-Sommers. I needed ammunition against my sister Mathilde and her ilk, and this was just the book. I read through something about feminist epistemologies and science, but I couldn't concentrate. The spewing water was too penis-like, too Ryan, too loud an ass-pain roaring in my ears.

Just then, a couple of men from the Pole Hopping class, which was now either over or in full-blown health code violation, walked by me, and one said to the other, "Look, darling, there's that silly homophobe." Darling clicked his tongue, *tsk tsk*, and said, in Spanish, "Well what do you expect, sweetums, she's the one who's always flashing her implants for the camera." They grabbed each other in a shared peal of laughter and both said, "Tulum," as if it were the funniest word in the world. One of them, the little bitch, lifted his shirt as if he were flashing *me*. Okay, too fucking many naked gay men in one day. Jesus.

I thought of calling Ryan and telling him how much he'd hurt me when he sold those photos, but he'd probably record the call and sell it to *Al Rojo Vivo*, where it could be sandwiched between a sobbing noseless Michael Jackson and a drunken Britney Spears. Nico thought I should "just ride it out," and wait for the next Latin tabloid scandal to push mine off the radar. But how did you just ride out two men snickering at you, right in front of your face?

What were they talking about, *homophobe?* I was okay with gay people. I really was. I just didn't like them taking their *clothes* off in class, especially if they were male and shaved off their pubic hair. All their pubic hair. Even I left a landing strip down the middle, so guests could find their way.

I fished in my handbag for my car keys. As I pulled them out, a handsome older man walked out of the nearby bookstore, looked at me, looked away, then looked at me again. He smiled shyly, and walked up to me. Maybe he didn't know who I was and just wanted to say hi or ask me on a date. That would be nice.

"Marcella?" he asked, nervous.

Or maybe not.

He wiped his sweaty palms on his jeans and spoke to me in Spanish. "You're Marcella Gauthier Bosch. I know that because, look." He opened the shopping bag in his hand, blushing. "I just bought your calendar."

My calendar. I'd forgotten about it. It was Wendy's idea to package some of the racier photos of me from the *novela* days for a calendar with limited distribution in the major Latino markets in the U.S. I didn't think anyone sold it, much less bought it.

He stammered, nervous. "I could have bought the Pam Anderson. But I bought this because you're in it. I don't like blondes."

"That's fascist talk," I said. He blinked at me as if I'd spoken another language. "Never mind," I said.

He held the calendar out for me to see and stared at my breasts. "Can you sign it for me?" he asked.

"Sure," I said. He wasn't bad looking. Actually, he was really, really attractive. I wanted to ask him if he was straight, or if he'd like to go out sometime. Regular men were too intimidated to ask me out anymore, just like regular women were too intimidated to be friends with me. But he might turn out to be a serial killer. Oh, and he wore a wedding ring. Not that this particular bit of jewelry often stopped men from dating and fornicating, I had learned. Often, it seemed to promote such behavior.

"So," he asked, in English, before walking away. "When can we see you on the silver screen, Marcella? I remember a few years back everybody talked about how you were going Hollywood." Only non-actors called it the silver screen.

"Soon, I hope."

"It's great to see strong Latina role models for our girls," he said. "My daughter loves you almost as much as I do. I mean, I don't let her see the naked stuff from *Cristina* and all that. We watch reruns on the Spanish stations. You're the only Latina my daughter looks up to on television. She's a California girl, like you."

My heart sank as I handed back the calendar and thought of that poor child with nothing but me for a model. "Thanks," I said. "I appreciate your support."

"I'll look forward to your movie debut," he said. "I'll be sure to take my daughter."

"Great," I said, thinking of Hispanic Stripper Number One. "But, listen, please don't do that to her. Seriously. Bad idea. Try to get her to dig Reese Witherspoon or Catherine Zeta-Jones. It's called good parenting."

He stared at me in confusion as I walked away.

As I walked through the front door of my little Spanish-style cottage in Laurel Canyon, two emotionally troubled orange tabby cats swirling around my ankles, my phone was ringing. I ran to answer it, but wished I hadn't. It was my mother, purring.

When furious and prescription-drugged, which was her normal state, my mother, a heavy smoker, tended to sound like a Bobcat with a bloody little rabbit in her mouth. It was more of the same: How could I quit, how could I disgrace her, how could I be such a loser, why didn't I call Uncle Sick-Fuck, when was I going to do real acting like she had done? Unlike my father, however, my mother began to threaten to kill herself if I didn't get my life together. I was the most like her, she said, and as such I was the biggest disappointment. I wondered what she'd been popping.

I hung up and wandered around my little house, looking for a good book. I ran through about five a week. As I settled into my patio chair with a copy of *Wild Grass: Three Stories of Change in Modern China,* by Ian Johnson, the phone rang again. Sure it would be one or another member of my miserable family, I answered with, "Leave me the fuck alone. Good-bye."

"Uh, hi there?" a sweet Texan voice said. "I must have the wrong number. Sorry to have been a bother for you."

"Who are you trying to reach?"

"Marcella Gauthier Bosch."

"That's me. I'm an ass. My bad."

"Oh." There was a pause. "I guess you were expecting someone else."

"Dreading, actually."

The woman explained that she was Alexis Lopez, the manager I'd met at the Getty last night. She told me that after I had left the museum, none other than Darren Wells had voiced interest in meeting me and having me audition for a new TV show he was putting together for an important network.

I told her she'd have to go through my agent, Wendy, and she quickly told me that she had lied and told Darren Wells that she herself was representing me. "He's getting on in years," she said of Wells in a kindly whisper. "I don't want to confuse him. Might I go with you on this one?"

"You told him *what?*"

"Darlin', it was a great opportunity for you," said Alexis in a voice as sweet and Southern as anything I'd ever heard. "I'm sorry for having been dishonest.

Seriously. I am. You have no idea. But sometimes in this business you have to be. We'll tell Wendy later. How's that?"

"Oh, we will? Says *who?*"

"Oh, I'm sorry. Did I offend you?"

No, I thought. *You impressed me.*

She continued, "I just thought it would be best to tell her later. I'll call her now if you want. But here's the thing. Mr. Wells said he'd had feelers out at all the agencies, including yours, and that no one had sent him anyone. With all due respect."

I thought of the jobs Wendy had been lining up for me, and without exception they had all been for hackneyed Latino stereotypes. Crack whores, maids, gang members, dying yet sexy heroin-addicted abusive moms giving sweaty birth in the ER. I'd been close to firing her, except that my father talked me out of it because, as he reminded me, I was slowly burning every bridge in town before I crossed it.

"I don't care if you leave her out of the loop," I said. "But know that if I get the job you'll have to share your money with her. It's in the contract that she gets fifteen percent of everything I do, even if she doesn't arrange it. You can duke it out with her."

"Oh, darlin', I don't want none y'all's money," said Alexis, in a playful way that assured me she did not regularly practice such miserable folksy grammar. "You didn't ask me to do this for you, so I'll do it pro bono. But if it works out, I'll ask you to consider me as your manager. That's all. You can have Wendy for an agent and me for a manager. Plenty of girls do it like that. With all the extra work I getcha, you won't even feel my piece of the pie missing."

Alexis then proceeded to give me the address and date of my appointment for an audition, two weeks down the road, and the address of the restaurant where she and I would be having coffee beforehand, to talk it over. She apologized for not arranging for an earlier audition, but said she had to go to "yoga hell" for a week with "another client."

"I'm not your client," I said.

She rattled on as if I hadn't spoken. "So, is that date free? Are you game? We'll head over there together, if you're not busty."

She gasped and I heard a slap I figured was her hand over her mouth, followed by a giggle.

"Oh gosh! I mean *busy.* How's that for a Freudian slip? Jeez Louise! You might have noticed I'm flat-chested. That's where that came from. Oops. So, you game? You busy, busty girl?"

Yeah, I was busy. Busy sitting around my house, feeling sorry for myself. Busy going to the gym only to be assaulted by naked drag queens. "Fine," I said. "I'll go. But with one condition."

"What's that?" she asked.

"That we shop instead of eat. I think better that way."

"Whatever you want, sugar. Shoulda guessed you weren't the eating type."

OLIVIA

Don't scream, she says to me, and her eyes look like an animal's. Her hand clamps to my mouth—it tastes like masa and onions—and her other hand over my baby brother's puckered lips, and the other brother is so little, almost newborn, so he's still asleep and I hope to God he doesn't wake up laughing like he does, the most cheerful baby in all of Perquín. She tells us to be quiet, she says this all the time of course because we are kids but this time she says it and we know she means it. Her breath is bad the way breath is bad in the middle of the night, thick and pasty, and I have to pee and she's in close and it's late and I can't remember how we got here under the bed at the doorway, the little door my father put in the floor, the one she made fun of and said we'd never need, a door smaller than any door I have ever seen, with spiders and darkness on the other side. We practiced once, the whole family, squeezing through that hole, to the open underside of the house, shimmying on our bellies toward the light of the yard.

We huddle together, a woman and three children under the bed in the dark room, and we don't move, barely breathe. She is twenty-seven years old, her name is Soledad, and she is my mother. And I hear them kick the front door down, the cracking of wood, the sharpest, most horrible sound I have ever heard in my ten years of life. And I hear them speaking in their loud man voices and I'm young but I know how men sound when they are drunk; if asked I'd say no, I don't know, but I do. I hear them say they are looking for my father, they call him communist, Marxist, Fidel's whore, worse names, awful names, words my mother won't let me say. And I can see him, my Tata, on the other side of the room curled up in the chair, then he's up standing behind the door with a gun in his trembling hand and his other trembling hand slices the air to tell us to stay down. He wears just his underwear like he does to sleep and a plaid shirt, bitten through with moth holes. All of this makes him look like a little boy. His hair is messy with sleep and he is so skinny, so young, I see that now. I see his bony knees and his too-long second toe. I see how small he is and this frightens me because my father has always been so tall and brave to me, the world to me. He looks at me and smiles to let me know things will be okay but his eyes tell the truth. His teeth are stained brown in the front from the minerals in the well water in the small town in the hills where he was raised to be honest and kind. I know enough to know he's lying, in the same way I already know how drunk men sound, I also know what lying men do with their eyes. My father was never good at lying. That was his best quality and his worst. Tata always told the truth and it was not allowed. He was a loving man and kind to animals, so kind he didn't even eat them, he was a Buddhist and everyone in our neighborhood and town thought that was crazy and did their fingers in circles like guns pointed toward their own heads, que loco, que loco.

I know the gun has no bullets, that my mother removed them one day when my dad was at school studying to be an archaeologist with the dream of documenting the mass murders, the anonymous burials of his people, my people, our people. I know this because I saw her take them out and she told me why she did it as she did it, said she didn't think we needed a gun. "No house with three children should have a loaded gun, that's a sure sign of a society's downfall," she said, and she kissed me on the head and threw the bullets in the trash. "But Tata said he might need it," I said. "They're out to get him, Roland Reagan." "Ronald," she corrected me, and laughed and tousled my hair. She clucked like a chicken at me and said she didn't think the problems would reach us, didn't think things would get this bad, and she was afraid to have a gun in the house, more afraid of the gun than the death squads.

I always trusted my father because he told me stories at bedtime and brushed my hair with the silver hairbrush and I didn't know any other Tatas who did that, most other Tatas I knew sounded drunk and had lying eyes. I didn't know what these things meant but I knew my mother took the bullets and my dad wanted them in the gun. And our heads peek out from under the bed, I watch it all and I started then to hate my mother.

And they exchange a look my mother and father and he says with his eyes he knows there are no bullets so he is scared and she says she's sorry and he says it's okay and she cries without noise and grips my hand until the fingers are numb. And my father the Mayan Buddhist begins to pray a Catholic rosary he learned as a kid and thought he forgot and I hear the words tumble out, a waterfall of words, and my mother's head hits the floor and she bangs it there three times and says she is a fool and I don't disagree with her.

We listen and listen and they dump and rip things in the other room, our only other room, it's a small apartment, we don't have much money, we share space and food and do the best we can and only later do I understand that we were poor. And they don't knock on the bedroom door. They kick it in. It is not locked and they could have turned the knob and walked right in, that's what I think as I watch the dark green canvas and rubber boot come through the wood. My mother's grip tightens and now my whole arm is numb. It's not even a nice boot because these men are illiterates, they are boys who are drunk and don't know why they kill, who kill because they think the money they earn from it is a lot. I see the boot and the rifle and then the men, and there are five I can see and more I can hear talking in the other room, laughing. That isn't fair, I think in my child's mind, five against one, even if the one is my father and he is big and strong or used to be before my mother stole his bullets and he went to sleep without his pants on.

I will never forget how small my Tata seemed with his empty gun at his side, his legs so thin like a flamingo's legs, him trying to smile and shrug, trying to seem harmless. He tried to reason with them in his soft voice and I hated my mother for taking his bullets and she pulls us against her like a stack of tortillas and puts her body over ours, her arms, her legs, we are wrapped in her and I feel her sobs heaving, shaking us, and now my feet are numb.

"Don't watch," she says, and I don't know what she's talking about and then I look up and my Tata's head explodes red and gray and a piece of his scalp with the shiny black curly hair goes flying across the room and sticks to the wall. There was hardly time to understand it and it had already happened. And I hear the shots come later like delayed and the men laugh as my father's body thuds to the floor like a basket of potatoes, something heavy and inert and they shoot him again and again and I want to scream and I can't, my mother won't let me and this is her fault and I hate her. I smell the gunpowder and the blood. Blood smells like metal. I didn't know until that day that blood had a smell at all. My legs are numb.

It doesn't hit you right away that your father is dead, that in a tiny piece of time, a shred of time, that men could take him from you so easily, that people are so fragile, disposable, that we hang on by the thinnest of threads, that at any moment someone could decide to explode your head. That comes later in your dreams, for the rest of your life, in the way you cling to people and situations you shouldn't, in the way you turn a blind eye to bad things, bad people, in the way you don't want to let anyone go no matter how poorly they treat you especially men and in my dream one of the men in the death squad is my husband, Samuel, drunk and laughing at me.

And my mother, trembling, cursing, whispering, pulls a knob under the bed and it's a hole under the house and she rolls us one at a time through it and I can't feel my back when I land on the ground and we feel our way along the tunnel and come out in the backyard and she pulls us to her and lifts us because we are too scared to move, me and my little brother who is five and he is quiet, so quiet, I can't believe it's the same child who makes so much noise during the day you want to slug him and the other one is still asleep,

I can't believe it even after my mother rolled him like corn paste along the ground. It's good the soldiers are so drunk, they sing and shout to celebrate the kill that will bring them gold, because they don't hear us until we are already out of the house in the yard and running toward the only place that is still safe: the Catholic Church.

And I want to go back to the house to kill the men and my mother says no and my mother tells us this is how he wanted it, that we would wait until they were in the house until they had him and then we would leave, that this was the best way and the only way. She says, "This isn't happening," again and again and I hate her resolve, her fatalism, the way she just let it happen and she lifts us, throws me over one shoulder, the boys over the other, and she is small and skinny but she runs and I feel the salt heat of her tears and they aren't mine, they are hers, they taste bitter like metal and sick in my mouth. My mother's tears drench my shoulder and she runs barefoot through the middle of the night and the bullets fly and they try to stop us.

And now my mother the Mayan atheist socialist prays too that God will deliver her and her children to the church, that we'll get to the church where we'll be safe and the night is so dark I can't imagine there will ever be light again and the bullet hits my brother, the tiny one, the newborn, in the foot and he howls, he will lose the foot and never walk right but he will live and he will be a doctor and he will help children refugees from wars everywhere and now I am so numb I can't feel anything at all. . . .

"Noooo!" I woke up drenched in sweat, screaming.

"Olivia. *Tranquilízate, calmate.*" It was Samuel's voice, his hand soft and warm on the goose bumps on my arm, his Spanish forced and clumsy but loving.

He still smelled unfamiliar, and I couldn't place it.

"It's just a dream," he said. He rocked me like a baby. I blinked through the darkness, at the small bedroom walls, too close, at the cheap Ikea dresser with the warped mirror, at the chair across the room, at the "Boycott Grapes" United Farm Workers poster my mother had given us for our anniversary, at the woven wall hangings from Peru, with the hills and llamas walking. I glanced behind me at the Ikea headboard. Then I looked at the face of my husband, strong, kind, with dark, mournful eyes.

I rolled into his embrace, shivering. "No," I said. "It's not just a dream. It's *the* dream. My Tata."

"You need to see someone about this," he said. "It's getting worse. It's killing you."

"Don't say kill," I said. Dream talk. What was that smell? He was so warm. Gunpowder. No, metal. Dream smell. Not real. Samuel, smelling of blood. I heard my mother's voice, so close, and saw a mouth moving in the air. *This isn't happening, this isn't happening.*

"You were there," I snapped. "You shot him this time, it was you." I slugged him, slapped him, opened my mouth to bite him but he dodged me.

"Shhh," he said. He wrapped his arms around me like a straightjacket. "Olivia, listen to me. I know you want to write your mom's life story. I know that's important to you. But the longer you work on the screenplay the sicker you get. You should let it go for a while."

A bullet sound cracked through the night, and I jumped and screamed.

"Shhh," he said again. "It's nothing. That was the heater going on. You're in L.A., it's October, it's a cool night. Did you hear me? About the script? I don't want you working on it anymore."

"They're going to kill me," I said.

"No one is going to kill you. You're safe. Can I get you some water?"

"*Noombre!*" I said, frantic. "Go see if Jack is okay. *Fue la pelona.*" Death was here, in the room, snorting in the corners like a pig. I could feel it.

"I'm sure Jack's fine, Olivia. Listen." He held the baby monitor up for me to see. Steady hum. It made no unusual sounds. Samuel smiled assuringly. "Don't worry," he said.

He tried to hold me again, but I kicked him away. "Go," I said.

"He's fine," he repeated.

"But his foot," I cried. "The baby lost his foot." I wrestled from his grip. He grabbed for me again, but I kicked him away, hard. "No," I hissed. "Go check the baby."

Samuel recoiled. "Okay, okay. I will. But are you going to be all right if I leave you here?" he asked.

"Make sure Jack is fine." I shivered. "They shoot babies. They don't discriminate."

Samuel crept up in the half-light of the nighttime bedroom, careful not to expose his back to me. I saw his strong legs, powerful from cycling, and the muscles of his abdomen. He had no right to be so much stronger than my Tata. Why had he been there, I wondered, shooting my father? "I'll be right back," he said.

As soon as Samuel left the room, the voices swirled in on me. I stared at the ghosts flitting along the walls and waited, numb and cold. I pulled the sheet over me and tried to get warm again. "Go away," I said to the ghosts. They laughed. I tried to forget the dream and the way that smell stayed, even after Samuel left the room. It hung in the air, phantoms everywhere I looked, most menacing skulls, but one full face, with a beard and kind eyes.

"Tata," I said. He smiled sadly and sliced his hand through the air, telling us to stay down, stay down. I wanted to warn him, to tell him what was going to happen, to get him to run for his life, to come with us, why didn't we all just leave, why did he stay and fight, but my tongue would not move.

I jumped out of bed and went to the mirror. I wasn't a little girl anymore. Looking back at me was a woman of thirty-four, who looked young for her age, with cinnamon skin and chin-length dark brown hair laced with white. I didn't do anything to my hair anymore, though I'd put some effort into it and the rest of my appearance in college and high school. There was no time anymore, and no one cared how I looked anyway, not even my own husband.

Olivia, the ghosts called out. *Where are you?*

"Right here," I said to my reflection.

We can't see you.

I was a woman people always thought they recognized from somewhere, though I didn't know many people. I had an oval, open face people trusted and believed they'd seen before. I wore makeup so rarely that I'd forgotten to take it off the night before, but somehow the mascara had smeared in a way that looked intentional, as if I were wearing eyeliner and trying to look pretty. Blush still pinkened my high cheekbones. I ran my fingers across my narrow neck, down my collarbone. I shivered.

Olivia, we're coming for you.

I was a little more than five feet tall, strong and lean from many years of daily runs, and the swirling of the ghosts against the ceiling made me feel even smaller. I was not big enough. I heard footsteps, and sprinted back to the bed, diving beneath the covers, trembling.

Samuel returned, padding along the Berber carpet. The ghosts scattered like cockroaches when he entered the bedroom.

"Is he alive?" I asked.

"Jack's fine," he said. He crawled back into the bed. "Come here."

He held me and rocked me in his arms. "*Ya, ya, mi amorcito,*" he said. "It's over now. You're safe."

I trembled and allowed myself to melt into the heat of his powerful arms. I looked at the red digital numbers on the alarm clock on the bedside table: 4:47. Samuel would be getting up in an hour to go to his office at UCLA to prepare for class. Still, the thuds came, one after another, feet scuffling, walking, drunk men out hunting, in the other room, in the green hills of Pequín. I closed my eyes against the sounds of the men's boots on the hardwood floor. I told myself there was no wooden floor here, it was carpet, new apartment carpet, I was in Calabasas,

California, not El Salvador, I was thirty-four, not ten, there was nothing to fear. The vinyl shade of the lone bedroom window glowed gray with the approaching dawn.

"Help me," I whimpered.

"Call that doctor," said Samuel. His cheek bled in a gash from my fingernails.

"I will," I said.

"Don't just say it this time, Olivia. Do it."

"I will." I burrowed into him and began to thaw myself free of the dreams. He held me and began to kiss my neck and shoulders, and then there it was. An erection. Against my thigh.

"Don't," I said as I pushed away from him.

"I can't help it," he said with an embarrassed shrug.

"I don't need that right now."

He rolled away from me. "I know. I'm sorry."

"Yeah," I said.

"How about pancakes for breakfast? Would that help?" he asked.

"Yeah," I said. "But it's barely five in the morning."

"You sleep," he said. "I'll do some cleaning. I'll get you up in a while."

"I'll try," I said.

"Hey," he said. He moved his head so that we could see each other's eyes. "Did you know I love you?"

I smiled as the last filaments of the dream dissipated in the air. "I love you, too," I said. Then, suddenly, my father's face appeared to me up close, on the bed with us, and then it zipped off across the room, clear as if he were alive, there, on the windowsill, smiling.

"Tata?" I called.

Samuel looked to where my eyes stared. "Do you see him?" he asked. Among other topics, Samuel taught the Salvadoran civil war at UCLA. He was American, of Mexican descent, from Oxnard, but he understood me.

"Yes," I said. But as I said it, the face disappeared and I was left cold, colder than I had felt in days.

Samuel kissed my hand. "He loves you, too," he said. "You have to remember that. And he doesn't want you to keep having these dreams, either. He wants you to let yourself be happy."

"I'll be happy as soon as I finish writing this story," I said.

"Forget about the story," said Samuel. "Focus on getting well, Olivia. That's the most important thing right now."

"Ay, Samuel," I said, and I snuggled against his chest. The scent of blood was gone. He smelled of musky men's deodorant. "Am I going crazy?"

"No," he said. "You're fine."

I felt nothing, just a spreading Novocain numbness that wouldn't stop. Samuel clicked his tongue soft and low, and he held me until the morning came and with it, light.

ALEXIS

I stood in the bright light of my upstairs bedroom, opened my dresser, and started to lob pastel yoga suits and bundles of white athletic socks into the yawning mouth of the duffle bag, a Vuitton, in the fabric and pattern of the season.

I'd saved for three months to buy this bag, and had mixed feelings about dragging it with me to the Ashram. And I was a rotten shot, in part because I lacked enthusiasm and in part because I was not athletic in the least, which only added to the pressure I felt of actually ending up for two whole weeks at the stinking Ashram. According to the Ashram Web site, I would be back in Orange County in fourteen days, "trim, toned, and tan"—everything that counted in Southern California. But my arms flopped at my sides, heavy and unmoving, staging their own little rebellion—against ashrams, against Lydia, my eighteen-year-old mariachi-star client and the person who was dragging me against my will to two weeks in yoga hell, and against So Cal, this massive, hazy spill of freeways that fancied itself a city or two or three. I'd lost count.

I looked out the second-floor window at the perky green fronds of the palm tree in the little backyard of my condo. The sky was a washed-out aqua, the color of hard-chewed wintergreen gum, the closest you got to a clear sky in Orange County, which, like the rest of Southern California, suffocated beneath a permanent gray smear of ozone, sulfur oxides, particulates, nitrous oxide, and carbon dioxide, a smog soup the locals cheerily and knowingly mislabeled "marine layer." Denial was darn close to an art form in these parts. Heartier forms of plant life, my happy palm tree included, thrived on the noxious haze. Asthmatic me and my pinched bronchial tubes? Not so much.

They said you got used to it, the pollution here. But all I'd gotten used to was grasping desperately for my inhaler, which was still exactly what it was even if it came in a cute round purple plastic container called a "diskus." I didn't care how hard the drug companies tried to make them look trendy, *inhalers*—like back braces and orthopedic shoes—would never be fashionable, in my opinion. But with megalopolises all over the world longing to be like this one, you just never knew. I supposed in twenty years or so inhalers might be the must-have accessory for all wannabe actresses and models, worn around the neck like big plastic jewels.

Wheezing, I grabbed mine off the nightstand, pressed the button, and sucked down the sickly sweet white powder. I held my breath like Cheech and Chong at a block party. Then I convulsed, coughed, wheezed with a strained pitch like a cat strangling, and stared again at the duffle. I knew the American TV-viewing public had ripped tuna-challenged Jessica Simpson for camping outdoors with *her* Vuitton bag, but I doubted anyone in L.A.—particularly at something as trendy as the Ashram—would object. In fact, they might not even let me *into* the Ashram without a Vuitton. One thing you learned quickly in Los Angeles: The people who *made* TV were nothing like the people who *watched* TV. I was more of the ilk who watched, but by virtue of my occupation was forced to fit in with those who made. It wasn't easy.

I was the first full-time mainstream media publicist for Tower Entertainment, my biological father's management firm in Whittier, and had a growing roster of artists to manage. Lydia, the golden-piped eighteen-year-old mariachi queen who was dragging me to the Ashram, was now the leading female Mexican music artist in the world, in spite of the fact that she was born and raised in Orange County and did not understand a word of the songs she sang phonetically. Just like Abba. She sold millions, the Chimps sold millions. I was doing fine. I wasn't rich yet, but there was a glimmer on my horizon and it looked like gold. I'd get there. No doubt about it. But to get there, unfortunately, I had to live in Southern California.

Even with success and the things that came with it, I never felt quite at home in Los Angeles. For better or worse, I was still a Texan. I preferred a rib-eye steak to tofu, and the NFL to yoga. Most women my age (twenty-nine) in my industry (show biz) would have loved for their prized female client (Lydia) to take them to the expensive (four grand a week) Ashram (yoga hell) for two weeks (eternity). It was the sort of thing people in the shallow end of the human gene pool flocked to Southern California to *do*. I should have been *happy*. But I wanted to go to the

Ashram about as much as I wanted a Tabasco enema. (I expected such a thing would soon be offered at Ashrams across the land, but what did I know.)

Yoga? For two weeks?

I pressed play on the CD player on my laptop, and Juan Gabriel's melodious voice filled the room. I wanted to lie on my bed and listen to him sing, eat ice cream, have sex with Daniel, watch *George Lopez* and sleep. Nirvana.

I didn't care how hard certain of my sorority sisters had tried to convince me Juan Gabriel was just Spanish for Barry Manilow, I still loved the man. Juanga rocked. I wasn't alone, either. Thirty million albums sold, and a star on Hollywood Boulevard, mansions in Malibu and Miami—Mr. Gabriel was dang impressive for a gay Mexican orphan from Juarez. I'd have just about killed to get him as a client. It was a goal. Down the road a ways. Then again, Juanga might also be a fan of ashrams. I needed clients who did *not* do yoga. That's what I needed. Was there such a thing in L.A. anymore?

I sat on the edge of the bed and tried to think of a way to get out of this Ashram business. I couldn't. I was an entertainment manager and publicist, and the Ashram was a *business* trip. In Los Angeles, yoga had become something of a job hazard. I turned off the CD and kept packing.

"Her name was Lola," I sang, sorrowfully. Juanga's ears and their assorted sprouts perked up, quivering at the sound of my voice. "She was a showgirl. With yellow feathers in her hair, and a dress cut down to there . . ."

I didn't honestly think Barry Manilow was half bad. He was prolific, and a skilled composer. If you looked at it objectively, it was obvious, in fact, that he was very talented. Barry just got a bum rap, like Fabio, Vanilla Ice, Pauly Shore, Debbie Gibson, Todd Bridges, or Siegfried and Roy. They were all talented people who'd come under attack for one reason or another by the media, usually because they looked funny, or were too attractive, or had been too popular.

I smiled at Juanga, even though I didn't feel like it, because smiling when you didn't feel like it was a mood booster. Singing was too. Back home, the solution would have been easy: I would not have gone to an ashram. Back in Dallas, publicists did ladylike things, like *coffee* and French *toast*, with clients. That would have been unthinkable in L.A., where, even though people inhaled more toxins in four average days than was recommended for a lifetime, the sunny yellow of cholesterol was still seen as public enemy number one, followed closely by the various other things I loved: sugar, caffeine, lard, and the Bible.

If I still lived in Dallas, I very likely wouldn't even know what an ashram *was*. If I'd so much as *heard* the word "ashram"—and I have no idea where I *might* have heard that word in Dallas, except on a TV show made in *Los Angeles*—I might have imagined it was a wraparound skirt you wore over a bathing suit, or an ancient language pressed into clay tablets with dried reeds, or a scary sex toy I discovered when I clicked on an e-mail I thought was personal but which was actually spam, you know, where they accidentally replaced the "h" with an "s." Come git yer hot diggity Ass-ram. And I would have been fine with that. Truly.

"I hate this place," I sighed as I began rolling the yoga suits into tubes, the recommended wrinkle-free route for traveling with such items. Then, realizing I'd slipped into a moment of unacceptable negativity—cynicism being another byproduct of living in L.A.—I corrected myself, with a smile. "This place has some good qualities. I'm just not feeling in tune with them right now." Smiling, even when you didn't feel like it, made you feel better instantly. So said Dr. Phil and I believed in that sexy, bald, Texan sage almost as much as I believed in Jesus. Why weren't there men like Dr. Phil out there? No-nonsense men, preferably one built like Alex Rodriguez, the baseball player? There had to be. But one thing was sure: He would *not* be at the Ass-ram.

With Juanga whining in her hot pink purselike carrier, I sat on the stairs and watched out the entry window for a sign of the pink limo. Lydia, a control freak, did not trust me to drive all the way to the Ashram on my own, and had decided it would be best to pick me up. I took out the cell and dialed Heather Simpson to catch up and apologize for not having been able to see her and the new baby when I was last in Dallas. Next, I called Jessica Maldonado to chat about all the boards she sat on in Fort Worth.

Lydia was late, so I had time to call my other best buds, high school pals and sorority sisters mostly—Heather Martinez, Madison Richards, Chloe Quinones, Charlotte Walker, Briana Perez. We'd volunteered together, worshiped together, drank beer together, watched football with our assorted boyfriends du jour together. They knew where I liked to shop, they knew what I liked to eat. (Rudy's Barbecue, girl!) We had sung Christmas carols door-to-door and no one laughed at us. I couldn't imagine doing anything like that in L.A. without getting a gun pulled on me for trespassing.

I hung up when the limo slid into view, and considered my life. Lydia emerged from the limo wearing short-shorts and a baby-doll T-shirt with the word DEEP across her chest. I opened the door and hugged my client. I even pretended to listen to her as she prattled on about a soccer star at her high school that she had a crush on, but I found I was thinking about Olivia Flores, the flinching little screenwriter I'd met at UCLA.

Her script had finally come in the mail today, and I planned to use any free time I had at the Ass-ram to look it over. I had read the first three pages, and thought it was excellent, even if I didn't agree with the anti-Reagan politics of a screenplay about supposedly U.S.-sponsored death squads in Central America. But I knew the public, and they'd believe anything. I wasn't above supporting a smart Latina whose views I didn't agree with; that would have been bad business sense. And now that I had all but scored the voluptuous and volatile Marcella Gauthier Bosch as a client, I couldn't wait to see the rest. Plus, Lydia had callbacks for a Will Smith movie about rapping cowboys on Mars.

Olivia's cover letter had said the screenplay, *Soledad,* was about her mother's life—a woman flees death squads in El Salvador and becomes a legendary labor organizer in Los Angeles. And even though my mind usually shut down when politics and history (and, Lordy, *labor unions*) were mentioned, my desire to be free of Tower Entertainment and gangsta polka bands outweighed politics. Plus, it was interesting that so many labor leaders were Salvadoran. Who knew? The Sundance crowd would eat the stuff up, with a side of seaweed.

"You okay?" Lydia asked, as the doors to the limo closed. "You look appre-heesive."

"Appre*hen*sive?"

"Totally." She smacked grape-smelling gum and twirled a long strand of shiny dark hair.

"I'm fine," I said. "Just thinking about a movie script I'm reading."

"Is it silence fiction like my movie with Will?" asked Lydia.

"*Science.* More reality-based," I said. "About a labor organizer."

"Oh!" cried Lydia as her mouth dropped open in glee. "I saw a show like that on TLC, where the women, like, give labor and *birth*. It was *way* raunchy. Reality TV *rocks*. I like that one show where people eat worms and drink vomit. Fo shizzle."

Juanga whined in her carrier and looked at me with sympathy.

"So," I tried to change the subject, "are you still psyched about the Ashram?"

"Totally! I'll finally lose this ghetto booty. But maybe I should keep it? It gives me street cred."

Lydia, a perfect size nothing, tried to pinch flesh from her midsection, but there wasn't any to grab. She also had no booty whatsoever, much less the "ghetto" one she so often lied about wanting to lose. Lydia was a beanpole with a good nose job her parents bought her for her fifteenth-birthday Quinceañera gift. But she was a beanpole who agonized over the mythical five extra pounds every dangerously underweight woman I'd met in L.A. agonized over. It was a way of bonding in Los Angeles, being thin enough to slip under a closed door, but never feeling quite invisible enough.

"I'm so glad my best friend is coming with me!" Lydia cried, hugging me. "Way ill!"

Juanga growled and snapped toward Lydia. I stifled a sigh as the limo pulled onto the northbound 405. I was on my way to the Ass-ram. With Lydia, a mariachi slangstress bright as a moonless night. But what was this feeling in my chest, heaviness and loathing? I believe it was known as misery. I'd never felt it so acutely in Texas as I did in California. I had decided that Los Angeles required unhappiness of native Texans, that this was part of her punishment against us for being sensible. I wondered if Dr. Phil, trapped forever in his Beverly Hills mansion, surrounded by makeup artists and all manner of shallow fools, would agree with me.

Honestly, I really, truly *did*. I *tried*. I sat cross-legged, staring at the Buddha statue in the meditation garden of the Ashram, listening to the buzzing drone of other people chanting. And I tried. To fit in, I mean. Hard. But my mind would *not* go blank. The yoga guide dug her icy California claw into my shoulder and commanded my mind to be blank.

"Otherwise," she whispered, "the chanting won't work. You won't get that which you most desire in life."

So, adios new Isabella Fiore tote (so *cute*!), and ta-ta husband and kids. So long, Rolex Oyster. Who knew chanting was useless unless the mind went, you know, zip, zilcho, nada. Not little Methodist me.

It was the *way* she said it that messed me up. She whispered in a weak and wispy falsetto that my mind had to go blank as a *crispy* white sheet. *Crispy?* Hello? To be fair, I'm pretty sure she meant *crisp*. But she *said* crispy, which made me think of *Krispy*, as in Krispy *Kremes*. Mmmm, Krispy Kremes. All I'd eaten in the five days leading up to that moment were fruits, vegetables, and brown rice—per Ashram regulations. How was a girl of 170 pounds, five foot five, with steak and potatoes written on her soul, supposed to maintain her glorious self on gerbil food? On Granny Lopez's grave, I swore I would just about have *killed* for a Krispy Kreme.

I mean, I let poor spelling and grammar go, for a good cause, like donuts; but I could not tolerate it when it was plain old silly, like *crispy* sheets. Suddenly, the Ashram, which had simply been *annoying*, became *hee-larious*. Under the gaze of a ninety-five-pound yoga maven, gasping for clean air and dreaming of glazed

donuts, I resolved: Someday I'd be gone, maybe back to Texas, but probably somewhere half-Texas, half-California, like Florida.

I sat under the palm tree, examining the Buddha statue with *his* big chi-chis
and smooth skin, but couldn't find meaning *there*. I wasn't raised to find salvation
in a grinning bald guy whose spiritual philosophy might be summarized on the
backside of a Snapple cap. Sorry.

Besides, I just didn't much think Buddha should have bigger boobs than me,
that's all. Miss Marcella the silicone wonder woman I could handle, especially because her implants would likely one day earn me a very nice salary, but I figured I
deserved a *prize* or something for being the only woman I knew in the entertainment industry who had never even *considered* implants. Could a woman go
nowhere in this dang town without being reminded of her measly A-cups? Jeez
Louise.

I glanced at Lydia. Blissed out, with C-cups. In yoga heaven. Good for her.
There was something so sweet and innocent about her, something so gullible and
trusting. I wanted to protect her, or run from her. I hadn't decided which.

Lydia and I had publicity powwows in her Laura Ashley bedroom, in her parents' beachfront house, where the multiplatinum singer still signed checks with a
pink Hello Kitty pen. Now, I'm all for stayin' a kid and holding on to your innocence, but there was a time when you were supposed to git gone. Lydia had a few
friends, but most of the girls she'd gone to school with found her early success in-
timidating (she got her first record contract when she was ten years old) and made
themselves feel better in the early years by sticking gum in her hair, and in the
later years by creating "I Hate Lydia Blanco" Web pages. Lydia cried about this sort
of thing all the time, and I guessed this was why she had decided that an overweight Texan going on thirty was her best friend. There were no other women in
her life.

I could not imagine what that was like, honestly, because I had so *many* friends,
or at least I did back home. I was the only woman in Lydia's entourage, and the
closest in age, even if I *was* eleven years older, so I sort of adopted the poor creature in out of the cold as my little golden-piped (Hello Kitty) pen pal. Lydia con-
founded me because she sang, in Spanish, with this great big deep voice full of
world-weariness and soul, and when she was done, she stuck "like" in between all
her words and seemed confused about almost everything.

Last year, Lydia and I had spent a month in Europe, on tour together. Her
parents had been too busy to go, so I was as much chaperone as publicist. I'd
forced myself to laugh at her jokes in Spain, France, Italy, and Portugal, so I suppose it was natural for her to think we were great friends. I wanted her to keep

thinking so, too, because now that she had several Latin Grammys under her tiny little mariachi belt, and now that Hollywood was showing interest in her as an actress, she was a hot commodity. I didn't used to think of people in commercial terms, but Southern California, and dating Daniel the Self-Important Entertainment Reporter, ruined me. People were now products to me. Wasn't that sad?

I was amazed by Lydia in Europe, incidentally. I'd worried about her lack of skill in Spanish, about the way sarcasm and sophistication never quite penetrated her brain. But she'd wowed crowds of multilingual, chic people from stages great and small in her huge (yet still feminine) pink-and-ivory velvet sombrero and tight white *charro* pants, belting out stereotypical and powerful, nearly operatic Mexican songs of love, booze, and loss. No one cared that Lydia had never taken even a sip of alcohol and scarcely understood the language whose lyrics she sang, because she was a fit, striking singer of uncommon conviction and operatic competence, and, you know, she was *nice*. Really nice, from the heart. Europeans, particularly the French, have no patience for niceness, of course; but even *they* liked Lydia. They couldn't help it.

"That one is a supernova," said my biological father, Papi Pedro, the last time he was in town and saw Lydia perform. As with most things he proclaimed with great feeling, he frowned deeply as he said it. "She is a giant, like Rocio or Ana."

I hunkered down, clamped my eyes shut, and added my voice to the drone of *nam-myo-ho-renge-kyo*. But when I came up for air, I was still Alexis, still dreaming of handbags and shoes, still missing Juanga. How was the bitty woof-woof holding up at the doggy ranch? I'd taken her with me to Europe, and I wanted to bring her here, but it was forbidden to have dogs at the Ashram. *Everything* I loved was forbidden at the Ashram. I was still furious I couldn't use a cell phone, read Danielle Steele novels, eat sugar, or watch the *George Lopez*, the four things that, to me, made life worthwhile. I was still hopping mad I couldn't have conjugal visits with Daniel during my sentence at the Ashram. I'd really looked forward to several days of essentially uninterrupted sex with Daniel. Now, Daniel wasn't my (or anyone's) dream man, and while he'd never sire my offspring, he was moderately better than a blank crispy sheet, tofu, and no romance novels.

Rather than being blank, my mind conjured up images of me standing side by side with Emeril Lagasse, the sexiest fat guy alive, with a long pole, fishing three-hundred-count Egyptian cotton sheets out of a deep fryer. A really *big*, silver deep fryer. Mmmm. Deep fryer. Grease, the foundation of my personal food pyramid. I made a mental note to hit Williams-Sonoma and buy a fryer when I got out of this place, and to fry everything in my kitchen just because I *could*—cheese, soup, celery, cereal, you name it.

Shoot, I could even fry up Juanga's doggie biscotti; my beloved longhaired Chihuahua also ate Iams wet food, twice a day. But the thought of *that* noxious slop frying and filling the house with the smell of horse shins or newt lips or whatever they poured into those cans was too much. Juanga might *like* fried *kibble*, though; God knew she loved pizza, cappuccino, and Cheez-Its almost as much as I did. Yes sir, I'd fry *dog* food, just because this was *America* and I was a free *woman* and I did not have to adhere to the Ashram view of life, nutrition, and fun. Heck no, and power to the people (and longhaired Chihuahuas) who loved Pringles, Amen.

Okay, so maybe there was a *little* envy in my Ashram rantings. I didn't *look* like Malibu Barbie's all-natural sister the way the *yoga* guide did. Though I'd been the kind of shiny-haired college girl people called "perky" (think a younger Sally Fields at SMU), somewhere along the way I had turned into the slightly chubby, rapidly aging woman who never looked quite right in jeans, who cute guys talk to in order to meet her *much* hotter friends.

I'd always loved junk food, but growing up in North Dallas, I seemed to exercise more; I'd played tennis, I was a cheerleader, things like that. But here in Los Angeles, I had almost become surgically attached by the pants to my car. I did not *willingly* make time for exercise, which was like torture to me. I was now the nice, jiggling woman with the hot friends *and* an inhaler. I ate too much, moved too little, wheezed—and when you're nearly thirty and *still* looking for a husband, that's a deadly combination.

I had not meant to look at the Russian; it just happened. My knuckles went white when my eyes locked with his, as I had mentally instructed myself *not* to look at him, ever. I'd been staring at Buddha's joyous belly button, and then—hello— there they were, the small gray stones of Boris's eyes, one fleshy red lid fluttering open and closed beneath the twitching unibrow.

Boris's mind must not have been blank as a crisp white sheet. I snapped my eyes shut, trapped, and then, without meaning to, I looked at him again, to see if he could possibly still be staring after I very clearly made the disgusted-with-life face intended to ward off lecherous older men in possession of massive quantities of back hair. He was. Still staring. And he seemed to believe my pained second glance was a come-on. *Eeew, eeew,* I thought, *get it off me.* The winking escalated, and he circled his hands as if trying to reel me in. He mouthed words: You, me, you and me. The stubby hands, whose fingers seemed all of a uniform size, quivered. I had instructions from Malibu Yogi to stay put, chanting and "self-discovering" for the next twenty minutes, but I jumped up and fled the stink-garden for the quiet wooden dampness of the circular temple up the hill. The guides didn't see me defect because they were busy preparing another tasteless feast of brown rice and soggy vegetables, seasoning it all, I imagined, with essence of Buddha butt crack.

I stared at the golden Krishna at the front of the clammy room for two full minutes before Boris came tripping with tiny, swollen feet over the well-worn wooden steps of the temple. He probably thought I came here hoping for "you, me" time. Oh, boy.

"Five feet, Boris," I announced. He staggered through the door and waved and smiled, misunderstanding my "stop, you creep" hand for a friendly wave.

"Oh, hello!" he roared. "I fall because I am not in so good shape. Every muscle hurt. So sore. And I am Burian, not Boris, thank you very much pretty lady."

I scanned the room for a weapon. The wooden ladle for the golden pot of stagnant holy water would have to do. "Stay five feet away from me at all times, Gadzook, or I'll call the police."

He exposed his gold teeth and opened his palms to the ceiling. "They'll never let you use the phone here. Phone forbidden, this is what they say." He shrugged.

I thought of the mobile phone stashed in my suitcase, under the cot in my ashram room. If I ran, I could get it.

Boris, as if reading my mind, smiled. "Cell phones no use here. The antennae, she not so good on big mountain."

One quick step toward the holy water and I swiped the wooden spoon, slashed it through the air, trying to remember everything from the Self-Defense Weekend at Sigma Lambda Gamma's main house my sophomore year. I could only come up with vague images of two Heathers duking it out. My voice rose an octave. "I'm warning you. Boris, I'm not joking. Get back."

"But I don't understand." He settled his square buttocks on one of the pews, licking his large, fleshy lips. He mopped sweat from his forehead with the large green hand towel wrapped over his shoulders. He dripped sweat like Whitney Houston at the NAACP Awards. I backed away, prepared to fight.

"I have no romantic interest in you, Boris," I said.

"That's fine," Boris said. He looked surprised. "Because I have no romantic interesting for you, either. I married man two times your age. I'm not lunatic." He thumped his chest with a fist. "Such trashing talk from you." A laugh erupted from his gut.

I realized Boris what's-his-face had never flat-out said he *wanted* me. He'd just followed me and told me all about his life. He'd even offered me part of his orange, pre-seeded by his muddy thumbnail, two mornings in a row. At the Ashram, that was like a come-on, wasn't it?

"What do you want?" I asked.

Burian swatted his thigh. "I am meaning talk you about something," he said. "But I didn't want rush it. I want wait until we friends. I thought we friends now, after orange today morning, but I think now we are not friends."

"No, we're not friends, Boris."

"But why?" He looked hopeful. Childish.

Maybe it was the vegetarian diet, or the fact that I'd lost seven pounds already, most of it, I figured, in my head. But I said, "What is it? Tell me."

"I am wondering: Have you ever hear great musician called Vladimir?" He snapped his fingers and gyrated his head, as if listening to a catchy Bollywood tune in his mind. He tried to do a beat box with his mouth, spit flying.

"No, never heard of him."

Burian's jaw dropped, his eyes widened. "Ah, you miss out then."

"How so?" I tried not to roll my eyes.

"He is very popular in his country. I think you would be very interesting in him."

"I'm sorry, Boris." I strode toward the door. "Now, if you'll excuse me, I have meditating to do. I'm chanting for a Rolex."

Burian chased me with short, urgent steps. "No, please. Give me two more minutes of your time, pretty lady."

Sometimes being polite was a pain in the you-know-what. "Fine," I said. "Two minutes. Go."

Burian grinned. "So I have a friend, a very good musician. This is purpose for my talking to you here now. He is Vladimir. He is big star in his country."

I held up a hand. Too many Vladimirs in one week. My girlfriend Heather hoped to have a second child in the next few years, and told me she'd love to name it Vladimir, in honor of his Russian daddy. One of the yogis at the Ashram was named Vladimir. And now this. A person shouldn't be forced to hear the word "Vladimir" so many times in one month. It wasn't right. Besides, my world-music browsing taught me that any Russian singer worth his weight in pickled tongue and vodka would have a name other than *Vladimir*, which was reserved for incontinent old men. And, I realized, a real star wouldn't have a furry, trembly-eyed ashram-going letch for a friend.

I thanked Burian for his time, turned, and walked out of the temple. Burian came tumbling after, eyes crazed.

"I don't want to know," I said, increasing my pace. "And you shouldn't go around calling strange women 'pretty lady'—not unless you want them to think you're romantically interested in them."

Burian flapped his wings alongside me, like someone doing the chicken dance in an old folks' home, panting from the effort. "Do you wish I to be romantically interested in you, then? A little adventure with foreign man?" He winked. "Something to scandal the family?"

"No, thanks." I trotted down a path in hopes of losing him, but he stuck to my side. "Plenty of scandal in the family as it is."

"You are sure?" He smiled the gold teeth and laughed deeply.

"Quite sure." I sat on a bench near a rose bush. Burian plopped down next to me. "Boris," I said. "Please finish what you were saying and then leave me alone. You were talking about your friend, the singer. Vladimir."

"Burian."

"Sorry."

"He lives in Glendale." Burian beamed as if this were the most fantastic thing in the world, living in Glendale.

Ah, yes, I thought. *Vladimir of Glendale.* Glendale, that hotbed of pop powerhouses. Burian noted my doubtful expression.

"He is very poor for his fame because his music is outlaw in his country."

"Ah."

"All bootleggings. Four or five million bootleggings. If they pay for Vladimir records in his country, he be a very rich man. But no one pays. Is this how you say? Bootlegging?"

"For what? Illegal copies of a record?"

Burian smiled and nodded. "Exactly. All people love the music of Vladimir." His unibrow vibrated.

"Ah," I said, and searched for the quickest escape.

"And he has many fans here."

"Ah."

"Vladimir is big fan of Lydia, your artist. So pretty a girl, Lydia."

"And?"

"And he wants so much to do Spanish album with her. He say to me the other day, 'Burian, my friend, I want so much to do Spanish album with Lydia.' You see? I come here, see you and her, I say, incredible! I say, I will arrange it for Vladimir!"

"That's nice, Boris. But Lydia's a huge international star. You can't just come up to us and say your *friend* wants to make a record with her. That's not how things work. I'm sorry. Look, I've got to go."

I scurried away, but he pursued me, faster, turning to face me as he walked backward and gesticulated.

"Go? Where? You are two more days at Ashram. I want give you this two tickets for to go Vladimir concert next weekend in Anaheim, ask you and Lydia to please come."

Tears filled his eyes. I slowed down and put a hand on his shoulder. I'd been rude from lack of In 'N' Out burgers. "That's nice, Burian. But we're . . . busy."

"Take them anyway," Burian said. He shoved the tickets in my face. "Just in case you are un-busy."

"Are you his manager or something?"

"No, I am tax man. Vladimir have no manager."

"That's great." I took the tickets, damp from Burian's pocket, and stuffed them into the pocket of my pink Juicy Couture zip-up sweatshirt.

"Well," I smiled, "best of luck."

"I see you think me crazy," Burian growled, tapping his temple with a stout finger. "But I ask you, keep open mind. You are mean and tough. You are real, how do they say in America? You are real bitch!" He smiled as if this were a compliment. "Yes! That is good. Very good." He chuckled to himself.

I trotted back to the meditation circle just as the guides floated over to herd everyone into the fly-infested eating tent. Lydia grabbed my hand and kissed my cheek as we walked.

"Isn't this so cool?" Lydia asked. "I feel, like, way lightened already."

"You mean enlightened?"

Lydia looked confused. "That's what I said. *Duh.*"

"Ah," I said.

Brown rice, steamed vegetables, and tepid water in greasy-looking glasses bearing yogi fingerprints. That was dinner. That was what had taken the guides so long to prepare. My stomach cramped in a knot, begging for Burger King. You'd think if they forced you to hike five hours, twist through yoga two hours, exercise in various other ways another two hours, that they might at least drizzle a bit of olive oil on your food or something. But no. They might as well make us eat wood, I thought. I wanted to ask the guides if sprinkling soil on dinner for flavor was allowed, but held my tongue, for Lydia's sake.

"It's totally amazing how awesome you feel when you really take care of yourself," Lydia said as she sipped the water, pinky out. She inhaled deeply, nostrils flared, and smiled like Krishna as she blew the air out. "I'm like a new woman!"

"Yes," I said, dreaming of the hearty crackling of the Del Taco drive-through speakers. I remembered reading an interview with the wife of one of the men who died in one of the hijacked planes on September 11, how she said she looked forward to sleeping so she could be with her husband again. I could hardly wait for lights out so I could crawl into my cot and spend the eight-point-five hours allotted for sleep dancing with chicken quesadillas and Ding Dongs.

"Thanks for coming here with me," Lydia said, her eyes rolling back in ecstasy as she savored a hunk of lifeless bean curd.

"Just doin' m'job, darlin'," I said with a sigh, biting into what I hoped would be my last tofu meal for a long, long time.

CARIDAD

Forwarded mail from Chicabata@cubalinda.cu
To: Goyo528@rappermail.com
From: JulindaLinda@cuny.edu
Subject: Miss you—I messed up
Note: Forwarded message attached

Hey Goyo!
My name is Julinda and I got this note for you from a friend in Paris. It came in a language we didn't understand but we found someone here at CUNY who knew it was Angolan. Angolan?!?! You a spy or sumpin? Daaaag. We got someone to translate it for you and here it is!! Boy, this Caridad girl must really love you! Is it true you're opening for Cypress Hill? Wow! Done heard your music, boy, and you da bomb. I'm trying to make it as a chick DJ and I'd love to meet you if you're ever in New York. Peace out, Li'l Juli

Mi querido Goyo,
Havana is not the same without you.
The guys from Grupo Changó signed forms denouncing you. They started doing those pro-Fidel raps like everyone else. Everyone is so scared since the crackdowns. Did you hear about it? I got locked up for about a month. They

think I helped you build the raft. They took my Batá. They said a woman shouldn't be playing a sacred drum and had a babalao lecture me. They took my job away. My rations don't last long enough and we go hungry the last half of every month. They canceled my telephone and our neighbors won't let me use their phones because they're afraid of seeming nice to me. My mother says some government men came by the apartment asking questions. Eniguay. Okei. I'm still practicing my English, as you can see. I see on the Internet that you're opening for Cypress Hill and Orishas on their new tour! I'm real proud of you, Goyo. You've only been in Los Angeles for six months and you're already making your way. But we always knew you were da bomb. Felicidades y que Diós te bendiga. I'm sorry we fought. Please don't forget me, your Cuban girl and favorite percussionist. I love you. Un abrazote muy fuerte pa'ti mi compai.

—Caridad

MARCELLA

I dressed for the part of Hispanic Stripper Number One, as advised by Wendy, in a miniskirt and a tight, cropped, baby tee with two bras underneath, one to strip off and one to leave on per Screen Actors Guild (appropriately known as SAG) rules. I wore stilettos, God's gift to leg length. I applied lots of makeup, teased my hair out large. "It's the land of the literal," Wendy told me. "Don't make them have to imagine anything."

I'd been on enough auditions to know what to expect. Wendy, at the wheel of her dark green BMW sedan, Josh Groban warbling like an autistic kid on the stereo, guided me through the studio gates and guards, and I just sat there, the star, in my big-ass sunglasses, wondering why the hell I was auditioning to be a Hispanic Stripper Number One, for a movie that would probably be stupid and tank after one weekend at the box office. Was I really this desperate? In a word: yes.

"Hey, Marcella," said the security guard, a young chunk of a man with a trace of a Spanish accent and nice eyes. "My name's José, I'm a big fan! *Raíces*, man!" He gave me a thumbs-up.

"Thanks, José."

He asked for an autograph on a pink phone message pad, and I gave him one even though Wendy gave me a look that said we were late and José was scum of the earth. Wendy thought all people who made less than $300,000 a year were scum of the earth.

We found the sound stage where the three producers sat on three director's chairs. Yes, they actually sat in director's chairs. Other than that, it was nothing like it looks in the movies, where you have cattle calls with dozens of girls. I'd been on that kind of audition, so they existed. But this was another level. You only got to audition for this level of film if you had connections and a powerful agent.

"We've seen your shows," the casting director said by way of introduction. "Er, I mean we've seen the shows you were *on*. In. So we know you can . . . act. That's fine. What we're concerned with is your ability to strip. I mean, we know you look terrific with your clothes off, or in a bathing suit. That's obvious. What we need to see today is that you have the ability to remove the clothes in a sexy and seductive way."

"And a passionate, Hispanic way," chirped another producer.

"Right, totally hot," gushed the casting director.

Hot, passionate. Code words for *spic*.

"Marcy's hot, don't worry," said Wendy as she shot me a look that meant she wanted me to keep my mouth shut and not make a big deal out of this shit.

"Get out there," she said, pointing me toward the center of the room. I dropped my purse on a chair, and situated myself before the producers. The casting director instructed an assistant to "hit" the music. A stereo system blared the latest, surprise surprise, Ricky F-ing Martin hit, something sort of flamenco and hip-hop, very sexual in that I'm-gay-but-will-pretend-I'm-not-to-make-money way of his. Why did he sound so much like Robi Rosa?

"Go," said the casting director.

I smiled, winked, and started to shake and shimmy and do my thing as I'd practiced, real va-voom, sexy, the whole thing. But I kept hearing my mother's voice in my head: *vulgaire*. And I kept thinking about Alexis, the manager, and how smart she'd seemed. She got me an audition for a real leading role, in a TV show. I had that. I didn't need to do this, did I? I didn't need Wendy, did I? I thought of the man who'd asked me to sign his calendar, and of his daughter, and of how it might screw her up to go see a movie where a prep school girl from Santa Barbara is forced to play a stripper simply because of her ethnic origins.

"You look totally hot!" cried one of the producers.

"Thanks," I said.

But I felt cold, and I hated it. I didn't want to do this.

And then, just like that, I stopped moving. I almost stopped breathing. And, amazingly, it felt as if I'd taken flight. This was how it always was when I quit a job, or told someone off who desperately needed telling off. I was free.

"Keep going," a producer said, as if I'd misunderstood. "You were doing great."

"No," I said softly. I smiled and walked over to gather my purse. Then I turned down the volume on the stereo and stood grinning at them all.

"What's wrong?" asked Wendy.

"Nothing," I said. I meant it. Nothing was wrong. "I just don't feel it. Sorry."

I shook everyone's hand, and thanked them for giving me the chance. "I'm really sorry," I said. "But I just don't think I'm the right girl for the job."

The casting director disagreed, and said that I was all but assured the job if I wanted it.

"That's just the thing," I said. "I don't. I *don't* want it. I want to play a doctor, or a president. Anything like that in the script for a spic with big boobs?"

They all stared at me with open mouths. "You're crazy," said Wendy. "Everyone told me I was crazy to take you on, but I was like, no, she's fine. But they were right. You're crazy." To the producers, she said, "I'm so sorry. She's on the rag, something. I don't know. She's crazy."

I nodded and thought for a moment. I said, "*'You know, a long time ago being crazy meant something. Nowadays, everybody's crazy.'* That's Charles Manson."

Wendy and her pals shook their heads and tried to laugh, as if I might snap out of it. "Oh," I said. "And Wendy? You're fired."

"I'm what?"

"My new manager is twice the agent you are."

"What? What new manager?"

"Here's another one for you," I said, and began singing my favorite Ani DiFranco lyric: "*'They can call me crazy if I fail, all the chance that I need, is one-in-a-million and they can call me brilliant if I succeed.'* See ya."

I whistled the rest of the tune as I walked out of the studio, across the bright light of the parking lot, past the security gate. I waved to José on my way toward the chaos of Ventura Boulevard, and kept on whistling as I waited for the bus.

ALEXIS

Daniel picked me up from yoga hell early in the yellow morning on the glorious, deep-fried day I was released from the Ashramitentiary. Lydia opted to stick around for one last "bonus" butt-tightening yoga class and I really couldn't imagine waiting around through *that* for the pink limo. No siree. I was ready to leave, just as I'd been ready to leave as soon as I got there two *weeks* before.

Half an hour before Daniel arrived, I stood in the Ashram parking lot, surrounded by the dusty trees and jagged rocks of Malibu Canyon. The soft white-blue of my velour sweat suit matched the color of the sky. I imagined the rush of freedom filling my body was something like what it must have felt like the day after the emancipation. I listened to the dirt road crunching under the tires of my Cadillac and did a little dance of excitement, happy and hungry as a child finally adopted out of a Dickensian orphanage.

True to hard-boiled form, Daniel, a newspaper reporter his bosses called a "crackerjack," skidded through the gravel in *my* Cadillac, blasting an old Tupac CD. His 1990 Toyota Corolla was in the shop again, and he was too cheap to get a rental car. The *L.A. Times* provided a generic white company car during working hours, he reasoned, and after work he bummed rides with me. He always wanted to drive my car, and, against instinct, I let him. Even though he was thirty-seven years old, he reclined the seat as far as it would go, wore his baseball cap sideways, and steered with only one hand on the wheel, feeling, I was sure, very supa dupa fly and gangsta fresh as rap subwoofed from the speakers. Since he'd begun to leave clumps of light brown hair in whatever drain he'd recently bathed near, Daniel had begun wearing baseball caps, though this thing with the bandana tied up underneath was new, I noted. I didn't know how much more of Daniel I could take. I was thirty, yes. With a waning egg supply, sure. But no matter how hard I tried I couldn't see any of that happening with Daniel. I could not imagine him with an infant in a Baby Bjorn carrier, I truly could not. Maybe if Fubu started a Mack-Daddy line, or something, he'd go out for a walk with a baby. And a pit bull.

The car rolled to a stop in front of me and the tinted glass of the driver's-side window slid down silently. "Hey, boo," said Daniel. "Hop in." Just like that, like he owned the car, or at least like he deserved it, which I didn't think he did. I was just too dang nice, that was the problem. Too dang Texan, a girl with manners; Daniel took advantage of that. He smiled at me and took a swig from a coffee travel cup I recognized as my own, from my kitchen cabinet; Daniel had keys to my condo and I was pretty sure he'd stayed there the whole time I was gone, even though he'd said he wouldn't. I'd asked him to water my plants. He'd probably had a party.

Daniel hadn't stayed in his unfurnished, shared Echo Park rental for weeks. And, really, why bother sleeping on a black beanbag surrounded by empty Ramen noodle containers and dirty white plastic spoons when you could crash on my Thomasville king-sized bed with my silky Yves Delorme linens for free? Why stand in the cramped shower stall at home, fighting roaches for the slim brown trickle produced by the exposed pipes, when you had my two full bathrooms, each with jetted Jacuzzi tub and separate shower, to choose from? He loved to sit in my homeowner association's swimming pool, too, with his "homies" from the *Times*, a bunch of youngish, geeky reporters who'd collectively spent thousands on pocket protectors in their college years and who now thought that covering the entertainment industry for the nation's biggest daily newspaper made *them* entertaining and important, in spite of buck teeth and flaccid arms. They sipped the type of expensive champagne popular in the rap videos Daniel obsessed on, directly from the bottle, like has-been New Kids on the Block, and dropped names. *I was talkin' to J.Lo the other day, and she told me to call Bruce directly. Oh yeah? Well I had a meeting with Jimmy, and he made a deal with me—he told me who they're puttin' their money on next year. Jimmy who, dog? Iovine, you dumbshit. Oh, right—they keeping Whitney? No, man, she's so coked up and beat up I don't know why Bobby doesn't just leave her ass. That's what Christy Milian told me when we did lunch. You did Milian at lunch? Ha ha, I wish! Hey, you think Britney's boobs are fake? Probably, but that won't help her get past the Britney backlash. I wouldn't mind lashing Britney's back. Smack it up, flip it, rub it down—hey! I need a body bag. Dude, I'll give her your number. Yeah, right! No, I'm serious, she's told me she's lonely because guys are afraid to ask her out. I can't ask her out because I write about her all the time, but you cover TV and radio, man, you can do her. I have her assistant's mobile number right here. Or I did. No, really. I did too!*

Of course, Britney and Christina had no idea who these guys were. But after three years covering the segment of the music industry he had begun to call *thug life*, Daniel had begun dressing twenty years too young and using words popular with high school kids two or three years ago. His friends from the *Times*, a paper that prided itself on covering pop culture with the same depth and respect the *New York Times* reserved for the symphony and canned chipotle peppers, were just like him. If he wasn't so good below the belt and in the dark, I might have let him go by now. It was inevitable. It was about that time. He was starting to get tired, as he liked to say, a tired playahayta—or whatever.

"I thought you were through with Tupac," I said as though I really cared, as I threw my Vuitton duffle bag into the backseat and climbed into the passenger seat.

"Suge called with some new information," Daniel said, lowering his shades to reveal the devilish gleam in his nondescript hazel eyes. I didn't think he had eyelashes. I couldn't see any. I kept waiting for them to grow in or something, but they never did. His eyes were raw and exposed, like a newborn kangaroo's. Maybe he pulled the lashes out. Trichotillomania. "Wickety wack, step on back. I'm still the Mack. You know, you know."

"No," I sighed. I'd forgotten about the jive-talking. I wasn't in the mood. "I forbid you. No more Tupac, no more Biggie."

"You look good, sugar," Daniel said as he pulled me in for a kiss. Sugar was *my* word. I didn't like the unformed chameleon using it. "You lost weight."

He pulled the car off the dirt road onto Las Virgenes Road and headed toward the Ventura Freeway. I pressed my cell phone on and checked the messages.

Olivia, the odd little screenwriter with the linty dress, had called three times, wanting to know what I thought of her screenplay. I called her back, and as Daniel drove, told her the truth: Her movie script was very good, but a little long and unfocused.

"You hate it," she said.

"No, I like it. I just think you need to polish it up a little."

"God, I'm so stupid. I'm sorry you had to read it." She sounded crushed, like she wanted to die. I suggested we get together for lunch and talk about it some more. She agreed, without much convinction, and hung up.

"Did you hear me?" Daniel bleated. "I said you look good."

I dropped the cell phone into the holder on the dash. Poor Olivia. She was fragile. I had never known anyone that fragile. My eyes darted back and forth like those of an escaped convict. What was I looking for, exactly? Junk. Food.

"I *said* you look great," barked Daniel. "Can't believe you finally dropped the weight, sugar."

He said it again! My word. I scanned the horizon for a donut shop. I spied nothing but open space and green hills with sheep on them. Drat. "That's what happens when you starve a person. Grease. I need grease."

Daniel steered with great confidence, grinning beneath his oversized tough-guy sunglasses. Cop glasses. I disliked them almost as much as I disliked his vintage Adidas sweat suit with the gold chain around his neck.

"Didn't dig the Ashram, boo?" he asked. He put a hand on my thigh and squeezed.

"I don't want to talk about it." I put my hand on his, mostly out of habit. Almost thirty. Would I ever find another guy if I broke up with Daniel now? Could I get used to him? Was he beyond hope? Why wasn't there a rehab center for the hopeless loser?

"What was it like?"

Did I not just tell the man I didn't want to talk about it? Hello?

Daniel was a reporter all the time, not just when he was working. Daniel was nosy and couldn't stop asking questions.

"Let's talk about you," I trilled. I regretted the invitation for Daniel to talk about Daniel almost as soon as I uttered it. It was like sitting in those dunking booths at state fairs—you did it to be charitable and kind, but kicked yourself the entire time because you really did not want to go down in a tub of suds.

"What do you want to know, boo?"

He drove toward an intersection involving a Jack in the Box and a Starbucks, and my heart fluttered. Should I ask him to stop? Not here. I wanted to get as far from the Ashram as possible. The guides might be following.

I said, "Tupac? Daniel, are you crazy? Nobody cares about that story. Give it up. It's not worth it." It was what Daniel wanted to hear and talk about, his big story that he'd been fretting about for almost the entire year I'd been dating him.

Daniel laughed the investigative reporter's laugh, scary and crazy, high on his own misperceptions of power. Daniel, who smelled of coffee and ink, believed what he wrote mattered to millions of people when, in fact, it didn't. Most people didn't read the paper, and those who bought it probably made it two paragraphs into his stories before using the *Times* for other things—wrapping dishes for a move, lining the birdcage, protecting the crafts table from acrylic paint splatters, wiping their hobo bee-hinds. I knew Daniel's attitude well—the pounding of the steering wheel, the adrenaline-crazed flooring of the gas pedal; it meant he believed he had another scoop to end all scoops. It gave him a woody to think he would beat *Daily Variety* and the *New York Times*. I pitied him.

I met Daniel over a sculpted ice dolphin at the sushi table at a Grammy party little more than a year ago. He knew his sushi, and I thought he was cute; I mean, he was decent looking but not so cute he'd never date *me*. The issue of the lashes and all. And he'd seemed cocky in a charming sort of way, unlike anyone I'd ever dated before. When he smiled, it was sideways, a grin, which I loved. He was cynical, articulate, and, I thought at the time, important. I'd seen his byline and liked the way he wrote. We hit it off, at first.

Since then, however, Daniel had grown more and more out of touch with reality. He truly *believed* he was important, and not just important, but really *really* important. And that self-importance grew increasingly dangerous as he waded from the safety of faux-trend stories into the shark-churned depths of the music business involving drugs and guns.

Daniel constantly surprised me by getting excited when he stumbled upon an interview that informed him of (gasp!) corruption in the music industry. What planet did he live on that this was *news* to him, or that he thought it might be news to anyone else? I didn't tell him this, but I could have given him *so* many stories that would end up on page one, his holy grail, but of course those stories would lose me my job.

My own obese banda group, the Chimps, were likely involved with drug trafficking; they sang about it, snorted lines like wild pigs in truffles with those hollowed-out ballpoint pens they carried in their pockets. But like most people who made a living from this type of corruption, I chose to keep it to myself. That's the bit of the puzzle Daniel never seemed to discover; that most people who "opened up" to him were doing it for some other reason, to seek revenge on someone, to make a name for themselves. Real whistle-blowers did not, in my humble opinion, exist. There were few altruistic people working in any business, I figured, and even fewer working in entertainment. And even fewer than that, from what I could tell, working in the Latin music industry in the United States. Besides, at the end of the proverbial day, did it really, truly matter that a famous singer had bribed someone into playing his song on a radio station? Weren't there more important things reporters could focus on than rappers and record labels? Jeez Louise.

I truly did not want Daniel to have another scoop, especially not another scoop involving rap's two most notorious murders. He'd already won a Pulitzer—the committee said he wrote with a youthful exuberance appropriate to the subject matter, and had bulletproof reporting skills; he showed me the letter three different times. The "youthful exuberance" line is what made him start shopping in teen stores, I was darn near sure of it. I didn't adore Daniel, but I liked him well enough, and I didn't want to see him get killed over an article. He just didn't know when to stop, and it seemed to me he wrote mostly for the benefit of other reporters. He had his journalism groupies, squishy men with too-long arms that seemed to be stuck on backward, men who gimped around the newsroom in leather pants even though their lack of butt meat indicated they shouldn't, men who still thought the Rolling Stones and Bob "Bore-Me-to-Death" Dylan mattered; he spoke at conferences with his hat on sideways, and felt important. And here he was, driving my car too fast, talking to me like I was one of them, like I cared, which I didn't.

All I cared about just then was finding caffeine, a deep fryer, and a quiet corner to call Olivia back.

I watched Daniel next to me, and I could see that his mouth moved in speech. It almost looked like slow motion. The half grin indicated that he thought whatever he was saying was peachy. I didn't hear it. I listened instead to the obnoxious rap he adored and nearly blasted my speakers to Timbuktu with, something about bitches and capping niggas and a six-foot schlong in a doghouse. Charming.

If I weren't such a nice person I would have removed his CD and replaced it with one of mine, something upbeat and eighties. I was in the mood for some Bananarama. Eighties songs reminded me of happier times, back in Texas, when life wasn't as complicated and smoggy as it was now. When I was thin and believed I would have been married by thirty. When grown-ups kept their knickers on at nightclubs. I peeked at Daniel again, tried to visualize him behind a lawn mower or at a Little League game. Nope. It would never happen. He didn't notice me sizing him up, just kept on yapping with those snapping otter's teeth.

Man, I wished he'd just let it go. He'd already linked the Los Angeles Police Department and several L.A. gangs to the whole deal, and he'd had his tires slashed, his apartment ransacked, and his life threatened by two bad boys in ski masks. I had enough trouble with Los Chimpances del Norte, who sang about drugs, *did* drugs, and, I had been told once or twice, smuggled drugs in their accordion cases. I didn't need an English-language reason to hire a bodyguard. I needed a charming, debonair husband.

"No," I said, finally, hoping to shut him up. "Daniel, *please*. No. It won't change anything but your phone number."

"Oh, yes! Yes!" He bounced in the driver's seat with glee as he gunned my car onto the 101, only to come to a near complete stop at the end of the entrance ramp in stagnant traffic. "You have no idea how *yes*, shorty." Shorty?

"What is *this*?" I pointed to the cars. "It's not even seven in the morning yet! Who are all these people? What are they doing up? Go home! All of you!"

☆ 71 ☆

"It's going to be my biggest story yet and we're going to nail these sleazy fuckers," said Daniel, ignoring me as usual. He produced the travel cup from between his legs and gulped through an enormous, caffeine-stained grin. A brown coffee trickle snaked down his stubbly chin.

"Cup holder," I complained, pointing. "I told you, you drive my car, you use the cup holder. Hey, isn't that my cup?" He grinned like a little boy caught doing something bad. I continued, "This isn't your Corolla. You can't just throw trash around. Don't do the story, Daniel. It's not worth it."

"Sorry." He jammed the cup in the holder. "Habit." He shot me an accusing stare. "Of *course* it's worth it. You know how high up this thing goes? Oh, man. You have any idea how many fuckers in the LAPD are going to go *down* if this thing goes public?"

My lungs were closing in on themselves again. I reached back and dragged my Vuitton tote to the front seat. I pried my inhaler from a side pocket and sucked down the medicine. Daniel did not ask if I was okay, as might have been the polite thing to do. Rather, he kept talking about Daniel. That's when I gave up on Daniel for good.

"Gosh," I coughed. "This traffic is something else, isn't it?"

Daniel's eyes stayed on the road, crazed, as if he thought he alone, Mr. Special, might find a way out of this traffic jam, which took up five lanes. "I wish I could tell you what I found out. But I can't. It's mad confidential. But it's good. You'd cold flip, doll. Oh, man, is it good."

"Good like you're going to get *killed* good?" I heard the words come from my mouth, but the corresponding emotions—concern, alarm—were absent. I was being polite in a hollow sort of way, and he had no idea.

"Maybe." He grinned. He slurped more coffee and held the cup between his legs.

"That's not funny. These people wouldn't hesitate to take you out."

"They won't touch me."

"Why, because you're a reporter?" I snorted a laugh.

"Exactly. I'm impartial. They need me."

"Yeah, okay."

"It makes the boys at Rampart look like a bunch of little sissies."

"Daniel," I wheezed, my head pounding from caffeine withdrawal. "I don't need this right now. I need Krispy Kremes. Caffeine. Gosh, but I missed caffeine. Do you have any idea what it's like to live without caffeine for two weeks?"

I eyed Daniel's coffee cup. My coffee cup, but he didn't take the hint. He kept it tucked into his lap.

"Starbucks cool?" Daniel pulled the Cadillac into the illegal, pebbly, prickly shoulder lane and began speeding over bunny holes past the traffic. "This is Calabasas, right? Brandy bought a home here. Puffy hangs here sometimes. I don't think we'll find a Krispy Kreme here. More like, what are those things? . . . *Croissants* or something. This is mad high-class up in here, yo."

"Starby's is cool." I greatly disliked the way Daniel spoke of stars like they were his friends. At first, I really believed he knew these people and they cared about him. That's the impression he gave. But the truth was only that he'd met them, interviewed them, and that was it. He did not understand that they'd charmed him because that's what artists do to reporters. That's what publicists and managers like *me* trained our artists to *do* to reporters, anyway. Bring them to your house if you can, compliment them. Mention their last story if you can say you found it fascinating. Lie. Nobody got lied to more in the world than reporters . . . except maybe judges. But reporters, from what I could tell, didn't notice.

"I think Ja's even thinking of building a crib up in here," Daniel said. "That'd be dope."

"Jah?" I wrinkled my nose, wondering when, exactly, Daniel had met the Rastafarian God. I knew he thought he had some high-powered friends, but this was getting ridiculous.

"The Rule, bay-bay," he said, trying to sound like Ja-Rule, the has-been rapper, who sounded, to me, like Louis Armstrong on crack.

"Uh-huh," I said. I was hardly pretending to be interested anymore. I didn't have the energy to be nice to Daniel right now. He was too annoying. No man going on forty should imitate Ja Rule like that. *One last screw*, I thought, *and he's history*. A girl had her carnal needs, after all. Especially after two weeks at the Ashram.

Daniel swerved off at the next exit, and pulled into a minimall in downtown Calabasas. It was the first minimall I had ever seen with a giant Rolex in the clock tower. "Nice," I mused, wondering, for a moment, if this was the result of my chanting for a Rolex after all. But I felt like I should have a triple chin tuck before setting foot here.

"Livin' large up in Cali," Daniel "sang." "Woo-ha, woo-ha."

Okay, I thought. *Enough*. "Do you always have to talk like that?" I smiled weakly, trying to retain a civil tone. I rubbed my temples and closed my eyes against the sight of him.

"Like what?"

"Never mind, darlin'."

As we headed toward coffee, I decided to call Olivia. She answered and sounded as if she'd been crying. Bingo. I told her I liked her screenplay, and I hoped she wasn't hurt. She sniffled. Too dang sensitive for her own good. What was the deal with writers? Either they were arrogant all out of proportion to their talents, like Daniel, or believed they were nothing short of doggie doo, even when they were talented.

"It's just real competitive out there, sweetheart," I said to Olivia. "I want to make sure that when we send this thing out it's as darn near perfect as we can get it."

"So you liked it?" she asked.

"I did. It's a great first draft."

"Oh, no." She blew her nose.

"What's wrong, Olivia?"

"Well, I just destroyed the screenplay; I decided it sucked."

"What?"

"I just cut it up, with the help of my shredder and my little son, who likes to put papers into the shredder, and I smashed the disc with a hammer and flushed the pieces down the toilet."

It's funny, they never told you Norman Bates had a sister.

"Did you have it on a hard drive?" I asked, trying to sound as if this were normal.

"I did. But I deleted it."

"So you don't have a copy of it?"

"Just the one I gave you, but I assume you threw it away."

"Why would I do that? It was good."

"You said it was bad just now."

"I didn't say that! I said it needed work. But it was good. Everything needs work. Nobody gets it right the first time out! I can't believe you did all that, Olivia! Jeez Louise."

"Yeah, well. You don't know me very well."

The parking lot near the Starbucks was crammed with shiny new luxury cars. Daniel, being Daniel, parked my car illegally, at the curb in front, partly on the sidewalk, near the entrance ramp from Parkway Calabasas.

"You can't park here, Daniel," I said. "Park at the Ralph's and we'll walk."

"I'm in a hurry. I'm not parking all the way at Ralph's. And don't say 'the Ralph's.' It's like saying 'the AIDS.'"

I stared at him in disbelief. "There's tons of spaces over there, Daniel. It's a forty-second walk."

"We'll be fine here." Daniel cut the engine and put his ubiquitous, battered, poorly laminated green press pass with the metal chain on the dashboard.

"It's *my car*. I think I should have a say in where it gets parked!"

"Just get out, babydoll," he barked. "Don't front so much. The stress'll kill ya. Pigs don't front when they see the pass, boo. They know the score."

I acquiesced, but only because my body needed caffeine and the smell of brewing coffee overwhelmed me. I opened the door of the Cadillac, very narrowly missed getting clipped by a passing BMW, and dragged myself toward the café.

A line of stylish people shouting on small cell phones or cell phone wires snaked around the inside of the store and spilled onto the sidewalk outside. Daniel strode through the crowd with the limp he'd begun to affect lately. It wasn't a real limp, of course. He hadn't hurt himself or had surgery, nothing like that. Rather, it was a *gangsta* limp. He thought it was *cool*. Now that he was out of the car I could see that he had a pant leg rolled up the way LL Cool J used to do, decades earlier, meaning he looked like he was about to take a spin to the playground on his Huffy. A few people stared at him in confusion and alarm. I wanted nothing more than to stand far away from him. How did I end up with this guy? Why was he driving and illegally parking my car? Why was he staying at my house? Why couldn't I be more like Marcella, who told loser guys exactly what she thought of them? Here I'd been trying to fix her, but it was I who needed Marcella lessons, and quick, or I was going to end up with this jerk.

"Daniel!" A man with a large belly only partially hidden by a shiny blue suit, and with a hands-free cell phone strapped to his head, shouted from across the room. "Daniel Mehegan! You son of a bitch!" He sat at a table with a living, smiling Barbie doll in a tight pink T-shirt.

"Ross, my man!" Daniel called back, weaving through the generic beautiful bodies to shake the man's hand.

"How's things down Times-Mirror Square, Danny boy?" the man asked, standing.

"It's all good, you know," Daniel said. "But we aren't Times-Mirror no more. Got ate up by Tribune Company, wickety wack." He turned to look for me. I tried to hide at the back of the line, but all I had to hide behind were two Calabasas housewives, each as narrow as a bag of Starbucks coffee beans. It would take at least five of them to hide half of me. I had no interest in making nice, in mingling with garrulous fat assholes (pardon my French, but honestly, this man fit the description) right now. I had interest in maple scones and iced toffee-nut lattes with loads of fattening whipped cream.

"Alexis Lopez!" Daniel called. He pretended to be joking about the last name part, but I'd noticed he used my full name when he thought it might impress people who found such names exotic, as he himself apparently did. "Get over here. This is Ross Albertson, from Creative Artists Agency. I've been wanting you to meet him. Remember?"

I looked with longing at the pastry case, noted the three hollow-eyed zombies who trembled in caffeine withdrawal behind me in line. If I left now, I'd have to go to the back of the line again. I wanted to stay, to follow my own particular bliss. But, true to my upbringing, I did what I thought was the polite thing to do, which was make the man in my life comfortable even though I really didn't like him. At all. I left the line.

Daniel had this idea that I would be better off working for one of the big talent agencies in the city instead of at Tower. He'd been trying to hook me up, as he would say, with important people he knew. I could tell he thought this was one such person by the way Daniel opened his eyes wider as I approached, as if we shared a secret, which we didn't.

Ross jiggled my hand so hard my knuckles cracked. He wasn't only fat, he was strong.

"Damn good to meet you," he boomed as his jowls waggled. "I've heard a lot about you."

"You have?" I asked, smiling my nicest smile.

"Well, no, not really. But that's the shit you're supposed to say, right?" Ross cackled and smacked Daniel on the back hard enough to almost knock him over. Ross pointed to the smiling blonde at the table and said with what sounded like enormous boredom: "This is the wife. Betty."

The wife. His wife, I wondered? Or someone else's, out on loan?

"Betty! Good name." Daniel gave her the wink and the gun.

"Thanks." Her facial expression scarcely changed. I was familiar with the look. Botox paralysis. "I hate it, actually."

"No way, it's a cool name now, Betty, every thug boo wants to be called a Betty," Daniel gushed.

"Nice to meet you," Betty said to me with a roll of her big blue expressionless eyes. Lucky for her they still moved.

"Nice to meet you both," I said.

"Alexis manages Lydia Blanco, the mariachi star," Daniel said, trying too hard to pronounce the Spanish names in Spanish. Leeedeeeaaahhhh Blaaahhhhn-koh. Not even *Lydia* pronounced it *that* Spanish.

"Oh really?" Ross's face was blank, but he forced the old L.A. smile anyway.

"She's got a couple of Latin Grammy nods," Daniel added, speaking newspaper again. Only newspapers used "nod" to mean "nomination." "Hell of a singer, man, you ought to hear her. Pretty girl, too. Young and hot."

"*Latin* Grammys. Wow. Very impressive," said Ross, sincere as a car salesman. "I wish you all the best of luck."

"Ross manages rappers," Daniel explained to me with his eyes doing that wide-open secret thing again. "Lemon Joy, Booty Ransom, and what's that all-girl group you got now, Ross?"

"Heir Cunning-Lingus," Ross said.

Betty wrinkled her sculpted noselette, exposing white capped teeth very much like Lydia's, or Marcella's. Porcelain caps that looked great at first, but upon second glance seemed to be staining the wearer's gums blue-gray. I had started to think of it as Los Angeles mouth. They said you had to file the wearer's teeth down before putting the caps on, and that with time the expensive process would have to be repeated; I imagined that in forty years, Los Angeles would be full of has-been celebs who couldn't afford to have their teeth redone, and that the lot of them would have pointy brown witchy smiles.

"I hate that name," she said. It seemed she hated all names.

"Pretty disgusting," I agreed.

"It's a great name, man," Daniel laughed. "I'd buy their CD just to see the name."

"You know you never buy CDs, Danny boy," Ross bellowed. "You horde press freebies like all you news fuckers. Admit it." I cringed at this man's uncensored mouth. What a lout. And in the presence of ladies. But of course he was right.

"He knew Tupac back in the day," Daniel said with abject admiration.

"What agency you with?" Ross asked me. He made brief eye contact but soon found something more interesting to look at in the parking lot.

"Tower Entertainment." I smiled as politely as possible and tried not to look where I wanted to look, which was the pastry case. My daddy always said that if you exhibit good manners yourself, no matter how poorly someone treats you, you can always rest easy knowing that you were the better person.

Ross shrugged and stuffed a giant hunk of muffin in his maw. "Never heard of it," he mumbled through the crumbs.

"It's a Mexican company in Whittier," Daniel explained for me. "But don't let that fool you. They make a bundle. I'm talking hundreds of millions," he exaggerated. "They make serious benjamins on immigrants, man."

"I'm sure they do," said Ross, stuffing more muffin into his mouth. I wondered if Ross realized that "benjamins" was dated slang. "Sounds like horse shit, but Jesus God if Mexicans don't buy it like fucking tacos." The nerve! He swallowed, looked out the window for a few seconds, biting his lower lip, then continued excitedly, "I'd like to see some Mexican chick rappers, you know what I mean? Hard-core Mexican chicks with big knockers and hot pants and heels, and big lips."

"That's a fly idea," Daniel said to Ross as he scratched his private parts with great gringo gusto. "Hard-core Mexican chick rap."

"With big knockers," I said with a gentle sarcasm neither man caught. Betty made a face and shook her head, in spite of her own huge, tanned knockers.

"Yeah, like this, how about this: the Red Hot Chili Pussies," Ross said. "You know what I'm saying?"

"God, Ross, what's wrong with you?" Betty asked. "Did you take your medica-tion this morning?" Looking at me, she said, "I apologize for my husband's mental retardation. Usually, he's only mildly retarded. Today, I don't know."

I made a motion with my hand to indicate that I was fine with everything. As usual, easygoing li'l ole me.

Ross lapped the whipped cream off the end of his green straw, leaving smears across his upper lip. "I could do it, too. It'd be huge."

Daniel turned a chair backward, and straddled it, feet splayed in shiny Nike sneakers with zippers instead of laces. What was he, ten? He then removed his own unusually large, clumsy, and dated cell phone, for show, and pretended to check text messages. "Damn editors," he said. "They always want something, you know?"

"Red Hot Chili Pussies," Ross repeated, eyeing Daniel's cell phone as he might observe a shack in Calcutta. "Put a star where the second 's' should go, and you got it."

"Danny *boy*," I said at last. "I hope you don't *mind*, but I'm starving from two weeks at the Ashram, so I'm going to get in line. Okay?"

"Sure, not a problem."

"You were at the *Ashram?*" Betty Botox perked up.

"Yep," I replied.

Blank smile from Betty. "I like the Ashram."

"You would," Ross said. "She tried to get me to go there, but I told her I'd rather pull my fucking eye out with hot tweezers."

"You want anything?" I asked Daniel with a smile. "A cold shower, perhaps? Or, I don't know, *coffee?*"

"Nah, wired enough, boo."

Boo. I shuddered. Wired? Of course he was. No doubt the coffee in the travel cup came from my own pantry, too.

The line was longer than before, and I cursed Daniel under my breath. People stared at me, most having just overheard the nasty conversation my boyfriend seemed to enjoy. I absolutely hated that word: *pussy*. So ugly. What was I doing with a guy who used that word without a second thought?

When I finally reached the counter, I joyously ordered a frosted maple scone and a venti iced toffee-nut latte. I waited at the counter for my drink, even though the shop was crowded. When the drink finally came, I decided that rather than return to the table to hear more of Ross's brilliant cross-cultural marketing ideas, I would take a table for myself in the sunshine outside. I downed crumbly, sweet bits of scone, munching nonstop as the scornful, LASIK-corrected eyes of a few anorexic nonfat soy latte women inspected me. I was tired of being the biggest woman around. I wasn't that big, even. It was just Los Angeles. It made you feel inadequate. But it was nothing a little bit of shopping later on wouldn't cure, once I'd ditched Daniel. I still wanted to get the deep fryer. But I also needed some new sunglasses and a handbag. A girl could never have too many handbags. That was one of my mottos. "Daniel sucks" would be my new motto.

"I wish I'd ordered two," I mumbled, wishing I had the courage to say it out loud to them. "So *there*. Mmm. Yummy."

I downed the cold, sweet coffee, sat with my eyes half closed, concentrating on the drug as it entered my bloodstream, seeing if I could pinpoint the moment when it killed the vitamins and jolted me back to the shallow, buzzing reality I most preferred. Boom, there it was. Ahhhh. Energy, light, happiness. I closed my eyes, focused on—why, on *nothing* at *all*. Amazing, I thought—my mind is blank as a crispy white sheet at last. All it took was sugar and caffeine.

As I basked in the buzz of sunshine, thinking of all the delicious ways I could kiss Daniel good-bye and the fabulous greasy meals I would have afterward to celebrate, I heard the unmistakable trumpet line from one of my dad's mariachi songs wailing forlorn and Mexican from a rusty blue Jeep Wrangler. The driver was a gorgeous young black man who I thought at first was Alex Rodriguez, the light-skinned Dominican baseball player. A closer look showed me it wasn't A-Rod, of course; the highest-paid man in baseball would never drive such a junky car. The man behind the Jeep's steering wheel had clear light-brown skin and dark hair that appeared to be teased into short, thin little dreadlocks. He wore a black tank top that showed off a tattoo of some sort on his shoulder. He wore a narrow straw cowboy hat a little too far back on his head, but it didn't look hokey on him; it looked very Santa Fe chic. He had the sort of powerful arms with big deltoids I wished I had the sort of body to attract. He wore sunglasses, too, but nothing like the Poncherella sunglasses Daniel wore. This guy was *hot*, and not in the way Ross and men like him thought things were hot. He was sexy hot, a stud, with just the right amount of black razor stubble dotting his strong jaw. A closer look, and he now resembled Will Smith, a handsome, luscious guy—listening to my biological father on his car stereo.

Los Angeles, for all its problems, was always full of surprises.

I looked around and realized the two of us were the only darker-skinned people here. What on earth was a hot young black dude doing driving around blasting Pedro Negrete in a messed-up Jeep in Calabasas? I mean, there was a minuscule *chance* he was Mexican; I didn't like to generalize. I mean, there were lots of blacks in Mexico, especially on the east coast, and who else but a Mexican would listen to my dad at top volume like that?

But he looked American to me, the tilt of his head, the half grin on his face. The young man's gorgeous lips sang along to Papi Pedro's emotional, violin-drenched music. He didn't even have the decency to look embarrassed, which I somewhat admired; in fact, he looked a bit full of himself, confident out of proportion to his lame ride in a neighborhood where having a good ride mattered almost as much as having a dishonest accountant.

Good for him.

I slurped up the last drops of coffee and watery whipped cream and wondered what it would be like to have a handsome, sexy guy in my life, just once, a guy like *this* one. As he got closer I saw the tattoo was a heart. I also saw that he held a toothpick between his full, soft red lips. As he sang, it wagged up and down. Dang. He was the sweetest thing I'd seen in a very long time. And dangit all to you-know-where, I wanted him.

Since college, as I had gained weight, most of my men had been variations on the Daniel theme, men who had something charming about them but who were odd or ugly enough not to scare me away from approaching them. My best hometown friends tried to give me pep talks about it. They said a good man wouldn't care how much I weighed and showed me studies about men valuing friendship and sense of humor most in their wives, not sex appeal. But I knew it was true that most men cared, and Marcella, the queen of sex appeal, backed me up on it. Marcella got guys like this, not me. A guy like *that*. What would that be like? I could almost see him on the cover of a romance novel.

Finally, the brother in the Jeep noticed me staring at him, and did the same kind of uncomfortable double-take with me that I had done with Boris days before, as if he feared me and hoped I didn't catch him looking at me. Of course. He was hot, I was not. We could be our own sitcom or something. *The Hot Guy and the*

Chunky Girl, a real hoot. I looked away, but looked back immediately as I heard an awful metallic crunching.

The hottie in the Jeep, distracted by my shameless and possibly terrifying stare, had just crashed into the back of a car. My car. He turned his music off. All the eyes of Calabasas were on him.

He turned the Jeep engine off, and stepped out. He wore fashionable jeans, not too baggy—the way Daniel had begun to wear his—and not too tight—the way Papi Pedro wore his. Perfect pants over a perfect li'l butt. When he turned, I could see that the jeans had faded slightly in the outline of his, well, you know. A good-sized you know, too. Yikes. He was more than *six feet tall,* I figured, and walked with authority.

I walked over, hand on my head. I should have been more concerned about my car, of course. But I was more concerned about the electric nest that was my hair. Conditioner was banned at the Ashram, of course, so here I was, lookin' like Roger Daltry again.

"This your car?" the young man asked. He had a thick Spanish accent. Needless to say, his *Español* increased his fantasy potential for me. Absent biological father and all that. Didn't want to think too hard about it. I patted down my hair and smiled, coy as possible.

"Yes." I answered in English. I spoke Spanish but not as well as English. And I blushed, for him having wrecked my car, and for the moistness he caused in my panties. I know, it isn't polite to talk about things like that, but, dangit, they happened. Particularly in the presence of a man this fine. My last six eggs rushed to the precipice, ready to duke it out for a shot with this package of genetic material.

"*Ay, Dios,*" he said. His hands moved through the air as he talked. His accent sounded unusual, one I couldn't pinpoint. The Mexicans I dealt with most of the time came from Mexico City, or, for some reason, San José, California, and they didn't talk like this. In English, he said, "Look, miss, I'm really sorry."

"It's okay." I was still blushing.

Out of duty to my car, I walked in a slow circle around the Cadillac. The man circled right behind me. He smelled of coconuts and grapefruit. "I'm so sorry," he repeated.

"It's a little dent, not a big deal," I said. "I shouldn't have been parked on the sidewalk."

"Let me give you my insurance information and my number," he said. "Come."

I liked the way that sounded coming from his mouth. Too much. I imagined him saying it in more savory and private conditions, and obeyed. He led me to the glove-box side of the Jeep, reached in, and opened it. A plastic file of photos fell onto the seat, the kind a man might keep in a wallet, filled with pictures of the same sorrowful but pretty, serious-looking young woman and her large, pretty, bright green eyes. I felt a shock go through my body as I realized her eyes looked like mine. Almost too much like mine. It was weird.

He lifted a stack of what looked like e-mail printouts from the glove box, and fished until he found his insurance card. "Here," he said, removing a pen and a piece of paper from the box. "Let me write it for you." He scribbled on the back of the paper, handed it to me. I folded it without looking, and tucked it into the outer pocket of my newest striped Kate Spade bag.

"Do we have to call the police?" I asked. Still blushing.

"We should, if you want the insurance to cover it." His face was kind and focused on me, as though he were listening closely, as though he were not being stared at by dozens of concerned Valley residents.

I realized I'd been speaking only in English to him, even though I could speak Spanish perfectly well—or reasonably well. I switched languages, hoping it wouldn't offend him. "That's so honest of you," I said. "You from L.A.?"

He laughed and continued in Spanish. "Yeah, I am."

Then it hit me. Cuban. He sounded like a Cuban. Now that I heard him in Spanish I could tell.

I asked, "You sure? There are no honest men in L.A. It's the law."

The young man smiled and began to place the letters and photos lovingly in the glove box once more. A few empty containers from Chinese takeout and McDonald's meals littered the floorboards. I respected a man who respected junk food. He said, "I think I'm the first and last honest guy in Los Angeles. I got an award for that when I got here last year, I think."

"Where did you come from?" I asked.

"Labana, Cuba," he said. I figured "Labana" was Cuban for La Habana, which was Spanish for Havana, which was English for Cuba, which was Texan for exotic and forbidden land of hot men. "Where did you learn Spanish?" he asked me.

"In Texas," I said. He nodded as if this made perfect sense, which, if you'd ever been to Texas, it did—and I loved that, too.

"Texas," he repeated, only he said it "Tay-has," which is "Tejas," which is the Mexican word and spelling for Texas, which, by its very existence, scares the bejesus out of most non-Mexicans in Texas, my awesome daddy excluded.

"Well," I said. "I guess I'll call the police now."

"Yes, of course," he said.

I dialed 911 on my cell, and told the dispatcher what had happened. The

Cuban hottie parked his Jeep nearby, then returned. Daniel had not noticed any of this. He was still inside talking to Ross and Betty.

"Again," the young man said, his hand outstretched to shake mine. "I'm so, so sorry. It's such a nice car, too. And I crashed into it with my ugly Jeep. I'm sorry."

Drugged by coffee, I let my mouth go. "I must have made it happen by staring at you," I said.

Oops! Did I really just say that?

"Well, yeah, I noticed that," he said. He did not flinch. Rather, he grinned with one side of his mouth. He had the same sideways grin Daniel did, except that his teeth gleamed white and his lips were the kind you could nibble for hours. "I thought maybe I knew you, or I had food on me or something."

He took a long look at me and said, "I lost concentration because you look like someone I used to know. Your eyes. They're a lot like hers . . . So, why did you stare at *me?*" the man asked, lifting a brow suggestively, playfully.

"Like you don't *know.*" I slipped back into English. "You're a total hottie, *hombre.*"

He smiled warmly, and took a piece of paper and pen from his pocket. He wrote something down, and handed the paper to me. "This is my phone number. I forgot to include that before, I was so shooked up from crashing into your car." He smiled. I read his name: Vladimir G. Menéndez. I would let the "shooked" go; he had a nice butt, he had an accent, his grammar didn't have to be perfect.

"That's so weird," I said, staring at the piece of paper in my hand.

"What is?"

"I just got back from two weeks in vegetarian hell at the Ashram, and this old Russian man kept talking about some Vladimir friend of his. Then there was this guide called Vladimir there. And last week, my friend in Texas says she would name her second son Vladimir. I haven't heard the name Vladimir in a million years, and now here it is, four times in two *weeks*. It's a little much for me."

"It must mean the apocalypse is upon us," said Vladimir, his mouth solemn but his eyes bright with humor.

I giggled. How long had it been since a man—a super-cute man—had made me *giggle*, child? Years.

"The second coming of Saint Vladimir," I said, putting my Methodist education to use.

"Or Monomakh," he said.

"Lost me there, sugar," I said. "Who's . . . Mononucleosis?"

"*Monomakh*. The great Russian uniter," he said. "Twelfth-century ruler."

I rolled my eyes as if unimpressed.

"Hey, when your name is Vladimir, you know all the important Vladimirs for self-defense." He raised his hands like a karate master.

Did I know any Vladimirs in history? I had to. What was that one, who wrote *Lolita*? I concentrated and said, "Nabokov."

He raised his eyebrows. "Ah, right. The endearing pedophilic love story that would land a man in prison these days. So, you see? Vladimirs everywhere you look."

"Everywhere?" I asked.

"It's a common name," Vladimir said.

"Not really."

His mouth opened in mock frustration. "Everywhere I go, people tell me they know another guy named Vladimir. It really is very common, globally speaking."

"You said you're from Cuba?" I asked.

"Yes."

"And Vladimir is common *there*?"

He saluted and frowned. "My generation is all named after Soviet heroes," he explained, clicking his imaginary boots together. He thumped his chest with sarcastic abandon, as if he had little regard for Soviet heroes. "My dear, deluded mother named me after Vladimir Lenin." He made a doubtful face. "Anyway, I go by Goyo. It's short for Gregorio, my middle name."

"That's probably for the best," I said. I liked Goyo a lot more than Vladimir. I could not imagine a place in the world where mothers named their children after Vladimir Lenin. If anyone ever tried that nonsense in my hometown, they'd get a boot up the booty and a one-way ticket to Siberia.

Vladimir Goyo Hot-man walked to one of the outside tables, and motioned for me to sit. "Please," he said. "We might as well get comfortable while we wait."

"Thanks." I tried to squat midair in order to land lightly when he slid the chair under me. My quads quivered, sore from all that marching around in the mountains of the past week. I wasn't born for exercise. I was, however, born to have beautiful men slide in my chair for me.

"So," he said. "What did this man at the Ashram say about his Vladimir?"

"He's some fat old man singer from Russia. Nothing like you."

"No?" Goyo's dark brown eyes sparkled beneath his thick black eyebrows.

"Nah. He said he was missing an eye."

I realized after I said this last part that I had confused the conversation in the

Starbucks with the conversation at the Ashram, mostly because in both instances I'd wanted terribly to be somewhere else and was only half listening.

"Missing an eye?" Goyo recoiled. Then he wrinkled his lovely well-formed nose in disgust, held the table, and laughed, loud. He shook his head and said something fast in Spanish, a fluid, beautiful Caribbean Spanish nothing like the staccato Mexican Spanish I was used to.

I smoothed my hair back behind my ears and consciously lowered my shoulders, which tended to ride up to my ears when I was nervous, giving me all the sex appeal of a hibernating guinea pig. "Well, probably. He sounds like the kind who'd be missing an eye. Pulled it out with hot Russian tweezers or something."

"Is he good, this old man singer from Russia?" The Cubano spread his legs and leaned back, entirely comfortable in his own skin. His own incredibly creamed coffee skin that smelled of all the yummy kinds of things they'd never let you eat at the Ashram.

"Sorry?" I asked. I was so busy imagining him naked in whipped cream that I hadn't really heard his question. He repeated himself: "Is this one-eyed Vladimir any good?"

I shrugged. "I have no idea. I don't know. I doubt it, though. I mean, okay, *you're* a Vladimir, sort of. But even *you* go by another name, right? And I have to say you are the first and only handsome Vladimir I've ever met." I blushed at the xenophobic and inane compliment, remembered that I of all people ought to know better than this, and blamed the caffeine overdose.

"You think I'm handsome?" he asked. He sat there veritably glimmering in the sun, a jewel this one, and he asked a question like that? He really didn't *know*?

"Well, sure, sugar," I said, resorting to the female-friend friendly tone, the sisterly tone I used with beautiful men as a defense mechanism.

"Thanks," he said. He smiled and the chin dimple became more pronounced. Wow.

I gulped, and blinked, and tried to think of something else to say. I came up with this: "It's not, you know, well, *look*. If someone was going to write a romance novel, they wouldn't pick Vladimir as the name for the guy."

"It depends on where they're writing it," he said with a shrug. "Such a book would be quite popular in Novgorod. Or Drezna. Chernogolovka."

"Chernogolovka?" I asked.

He nodded. "And not just there," he said, talking as much with his hands as his mouth. "Poland, too. In Poland, Vladimir is a normal name."

"*Is* it now?" My tummy tingled with excitement that he had a brain *and* a body.

"Then again," he said, "I had a Polish friend named Wienczyslaw."

I giggled. It wasn't polite to laugh at people's names, but I couldn't help it. "Sounds like he'd go good with fried chicken," I said.

He spelled it for me. I traced the endless line of consonants onto the tabletop with my finger. "Poor child," I said.

He nodded and pointed at me, as if to say "see?"

"Okay," I said. "So you have a normal name. Sort of. But you know what I'm saying? If you wanted to be a pop star, or an actor, wouldn't you change it?"

"I never thought about it." He looked hurt. "But probably not."

"No. Most people don't think about things like that. I'm sorry if I insulted your name. It's a fine name for a normal guy like you. But for a celebrity?" I shrugged. "I don't know. At least in this country."

Goyo smiled. "You say that like you know something about celebrity. In this country."

I sat up taller, feeling important. "I'm a manager and publicist for music acts and actors."

"That sounds like a very exciting job," said Goyo. He licked his lips without, I think, realizing he had done so or that by doing so he had burst into my imagination—where I put him to work licking other things.

I sat forward in my seat, trying to get comfortable with all that dang tingling, breathlessness, and so forth. "Not really. What do you do?"

He smiled without losing eye contact with me. My body filled with hormones. He shifted in his seat as though thinking about a very difficult question. He ran the long, strong, and surprisingly graceful fingers of both hands through his thick, short black dreadlocks, and said, "I'm a writer."

He looked up at me through his eyebrows, flirty, guilty, and boyish, as if waiting for me to punish him for his poor career choice.

"That explains the Jeep," I said before I could stop myself. Me and my big mouth. I was in rare form today. I clapped a hand over my own mouth. The Ashram wasn't good for me. "Oops," I said. "Sorry. It's a lovely Jeep. No, really. A little errant, perhaps. But nice enough." I smiled.

"How does writing explain the Jeep?" Goyo asked. He seemed truly and innocently perplexed by my cynical comment. I was horrified at myself for insulting this man. Here I'd been lecturing poor little Marcella about exactly this kind of thing. Gosh, maybe that rude woman was wearing off on me instead of the other way around?

"Nothing." I sucked down the last of my melting latte and longed for another. "My friend is a writer and he has an old car, too."

"You mean a cheap car?" He laughed.

"You said it, not me."

Vladimir took in the designer cars all around us and shrugged. "Your boyfriend probably knows then that there's not much financial reward in writing. Money isn't everything. In Cuba everyone has bicycles and we still like each other. We still have lives of meaning. Without all this." He flicked his hand in the direction of the expensive cars in the parking lot, and continued, "There is reward in being true to your ideals and spirit. Your boyfriend must know that."

I thought of Daniel, and shook my head. I doubted he had either ideals or a spirit. "*He's* his own reward. Daniel. Who needs a nice car when you can drive your girlfriend's car anyway?" I gave a fake smile and blinked my eyelids quickly.

"Sounds like you picked a real winner," he said in English. His head cocked to the side and I totally, completely wanted to pounce. I rarely felt this way. I was feeling very ripe.

"No, he's a journalist." I laughed, hoping as I said it that this man was not also a journalist.

"I see," said Goyo. "They must be as bad here as they are in Cuba."

We shared a brief, awkward silence. I broke it by asking, "So, what do *you* write?"

Goyo paused as if he was weighing a decision carefully before answering, "Poetry."

"Oh, Jeez Louise," I joked. "I think I'd rather be with a journalist." I winked.

We cracked up.

A police cruiser pulled up at the curb next to us, lights flashing. We walked to the young, nervous-looking officer and introduced ourselves. Mr. Law took down the relevant information as a few curious people stared. Looking at the cop I tried to imagine Marcella blowing one, as she told me she had once done to get out of a ticket. I worried about that child, I truly did.

"You don't have to call the police for fender benders," the officer said. "There's not much damage here. You could just trade information. But I'll make a report."

"They think a drug bust went down," I said under my breath to Goyo.

"Two Latin people, in Calabasas, with the police," Goyo offered. Then, shaking his hands at the sides of his face, he added, "Oooh, scary." He smiled. "Run, hide."

The police officer gave us a curious stare from behind his sunglasses, but continued to write.

"So what were you doing listening to Pedro Negrete?" I asked Goyo.

"What am I doing listening to Pedro *Negrete?*" he repeated in astonishment, as if everyone in the world, given the choice, would also listen to my weird biological father at decibel levels great enough to deafen burros. "He's the greatest bolero singer ever!" His arms shot out to the sides with great drama.

"You think he's that good?"

"Yes," he said. "Don't you?"

"I guess."

"Everyone in Cuba loves Pedro Negrete," he said. "My mom and grandma are crazy about all the Mexican ballads."

"Wow. You sure you're not Mexican?"

Goyo laughed, and shrugged. "I'm not Mexican," he said. "But I like Mexican music. I'm . . . an open-minded Cuban."

"I've heard that's not very easy to find. At least in this country."

"The man who told you this was very wise," he said, tapping his temple with a delicious finger.

"What else do people listen to in Cuba?" I asked.

"Puerto Rican salsa, of course," he said. We both laughed. "They like Marc Anthony and India, Jerry Rivera, all that. But we have our own stuff, *timba* is the most modern. And rap. There's a *lot* of rap in Cuba."

"Rap? Nuh-*uh*."

"Yeah." He smiled as if he'd just told himself a joke I couldn't hear. "It's true."

Daniel finally made an appearance, limping onto the scene all gangsta foul, his faux-ghetto cool shattered by the police car. He started his journalist nonsense, where he tried to get the cop's name and badge number and acted like he knew how to do the officer's job better than he did. Then he started dropping the names of people he knew in the LAPD.

"He yours?" Goyo whispered to me in Spanish. "That your journalist . . . *friend?*"

"Unfortunately."

Goyo looked him up and down, whistled lightly and slowly through his teeth.

"He's gangsta fresh," I whispered.

Goyo took me by the arm and led me out of earshot from the shouting Daniel. "Tell me something," he said in English, urgently. Really, his English was perfect, just accented. "I know I don't know you, but are you settling?"

I loved how he said that last word: Eh-seh-teh-*leen*.

"Settling down? With him? No. I don't think so."

"No, *settling* settling, like you don't think you can do better."

"Me?"

"You." His eyes searched mine and it felt as if a box opened and my heart flew out.

"Look, he's the kind of guy girls like me get," I said. "I'm not like these babes around here."

Goyo observed the Calabasas constructions and shook his head as if unimpressed. "You're not bad, you know?"

My heart slammed back into the cardboard box and sank in my chest. "Gosh, thanks. Nothing warms a girl's heart more than hearing she's 'not bad.' If the whole poetry thing doesn't work out, you might consider diplomatic work."

"I mean, you're *cute*. You're very cute. You have beautiful eyes. I like your eyes. And a nice smile. You could do better than *that* guy."

"Probably."

"So you're settling then."

"Sort of. Yeah, I guess so."

"Don't," Goyo said with a smile. He placed a hand on my forearm. "No one should do that. Love is the most important thing in life. True love will not have a way into your life if the path is blocked by a journalist dressed like a, like a . . . what is he dressed like, anyway?"

"A rap star," I said.

Goyo threw his head back and laughed. "A *rap* star. That's good. I didn't realize that's what they looked like."

"That's cuz they probably dress better in Cuba."

"Don't settle," he repeated. "Love will find you."

I smiled and let myself enjoy the feel of this stranger's hand against my arm. "Only poets think like that," I said. "All that love will find you nonsense."

The officer left with a promise to mail a copy of the accident report to both parties. Daniel introduced himself to Goyo with as little charm as possible.

"You drunk, motherfucker?" Daniel asked, rolling up his sleeves as if he thought he might have to fight.

"I don't drink alone in my car, and I don't have sex with my mother, though I apologize that these are common enough events in your life to speak of them so quickly upon meeting someone," Goyo said in rapid, perfect English. "I was distracted."

"By what?" Daniel bounced like a prizefighter on the balls of his feet.

"Your girlfriend." Goyo looked at me and grinned. "She has beautiful eyes."

"Oh, really." Daniel was not pleased.

"Let's go, Daniel," I said.

"I didn't get your information," Goyo said to me.

"That's okay," I said. "I have yours."

Goyo nodded, saluted me with the couple of fingers to his forehead, and smiled as he walked backward toward his Jeep. What a walk! So graceful and easy and powerful. Daniel, meanwhile, pulled my keys from the pocket of his supa-fly Adidas pants and tried to spin them on his finger like a revolver; he dropped them by mistake. Smooth.

"What a hater," Daniel said as he bent over to pick up the keys, exposing his butt crack in the process. Oh, lordy.

"Here," I said, holding my hand out.

"Here, what?"

"The keys. Give 'em."

"You want to drive?" Daniel's voice rose in surprise.

"It's *my* car, Daniel."

"Fine." Daniel looked offended. "What a fucking morning."

We got into the car and I immediately removed his Tupac CD from the player, replacing it with my Thompson Twins. I sang along: "*Hold me now,*" imagining I sang it for the handsome Cuban who'd just said I wasn't bad. He said I was cute. He said I had beautiful eyes.

I pulled up alongside Goyo's Jeep on the way out of the parking lot. He looked over and gave me a thumbs-up when he heard the music. He flashed the most perfect, beautiful grin I had ever seen. He fiddled with his car stereo and soon blasted "She Blinded Me with Science," by Thomas Dolby.

"Eighties!" he shouted in that rolling, sensual Cubano Spanish of his. "Excellent! Tell me you'll call."

"I will," I said. I felt like a teenager again, like I was Lydia driving Daddy's Suburban past boys' soccer practice and the cute one just smiled my way.

"Tell me you won't settle," he cried as I started to pull away.

"I won't," I called.

Next to me, Daniel frowned and put his hands over his ears, incapable of tolerating my music the way I constantly tolerated his.

"I hate this shit," he said.

"Okay," I said. "What would you prefer?"

"Anything."

I inserted the most recent Chimpances record, knowing Daniel hated Mexican music more than he hated eighties pop. Oom-pah, oom-pah.

"This sounds like the fucking circus coming to town," Daniel moaned. He sank lower in his seat, as if to hide. "Turn this shit off. Please."

"No, I will not turn it off. The Chimps have a tour coming up, and I have to refresh my mind of their lyrics, for press questions. Besides, you seemed impressed enough with Mexican music to brag to Ross at Starbucks."

"What do they sing about?"

"Drugs, drug-running, illegal immigration, drugs, crime, and girls, sleazy girls."

"Good to know somebody's battling the Hispanic stereotypes," Daniel deadpanned.

Good joke. I laughed too, and for a moment remembered what it was I had actually liked about Daniel way back when.

"Yeah," I fired back. "Like your buddy *Ross* in there. He's a real crusader for racial and gender equality."

Daniel sat up, excited, and turned the stereo down as if it were his right to do so. He didn't even *ask*. Suddenly, I remembered all the things I *didn't* like about Daniel.

"So," he said. "What did you think of Ross's idea for the all-girl Mexican rap act? You're in Mexican music."

"I think it was offensive."

"You think?" He smiled as if offensive were a good quality, which, I supposed, it was, in *rap*.

"Completely." I pulled a U-turn and sped west down Mullholland Drive. "He doesn't know Mexicans if he thinks that's going to sell. We're really conservative about how women should dress and act. We want women to be sweet and innocent while *dressing* like whores. It's . . . complicated."

"You're going the wrong way," Daniel said. He shot panicked looks over his shoulder and pointed behind us. Daniel was a control freak. Not driving was the closest thing to being castrated for a man like Daniel. "The 101's the other way."

"We're not taking the 101," I said.

"Why not?"

"Traffic. I'm taking the PCH."

"I have to be at the office in an hour."

"And *I* have to pick up Juanga at the kennel. Trust your cabbie, this is the fastest route."

"I'm having a meeting with my editor at ten to talk about this story." Daniel fiddled with the mammoth Paleolithic-age cell phone again. It must have been pumping the car full of lethal doses of radiation.

"Good for you."

"You really don't think I should do it? You're worried about me. That's so sweet."

I glared at Daniel. My stomach turned. "Actually," I said, "I *don't* care." It felt good to be honest. I thought of the piece of paper in my purse, with Goyo the Poet's number on it.

"It's a great fucking story," Daniel said, confused.

"I bet." I turned up the stereo, sang along with the Chimps and hoped he'd stop talking now.

"It is. A great goddamned story."

I gunned the engine, cut off a Porsche, which felt better than I thought it might. "With you writing it, Danny boy, I don't see how it *couldn't* be great, do you?"

"That's nice of you," he said, smiling, puffed-up and smug.

"*Everyone* thinks you're great, you know that." I made myself want to throw up.

"Well, yeah. That's true—Hey, look out! You're driving like a woman. You trying to kill us?"

Not us, I thought. *Just you.*

Weaving in and out of traffic, grinning like a madwoman, I thought of the Ashram and chanted my brand-new mantra of the day: *nam-myo-ho-dump-his-butt.*

"What are you whispering?" Daniel asked as he popped a forehead pimple in the visor mirror. Charming.

"Nothing," I said, turning on the smile. "Just that I can't *wait* to read your amazing story."

He smiled and wiped the pus of the zit core on his pants. "Yeah, boo, you and everyone else in L.A.," he said, and he meant it.

Several hours later, after a refreshing absence of Daniel, I parked at a meter in Beverly Hills, and walked half a block to Beige, a small, chic shop on Beverly Boulevard, between Martel and La Brea, narrow and beautifully lit, like Marcella herself.

She was already there, waiting for me behind her gigantic sunglasses, her long hair tied up in a low, glamorous messy knot. She smoked. I didn't know that. Gross. She wore tight low-slung jeans, a white tank top, a long knit black sweater with fake fur at the sleeves and neck, and high-heeled black boots.

"Alexis Lopez," she said through a cloud of smoke as I approached. "My oddly forward, ballsy savior."

"Howdy, Marcella. How are you today?" I held my hand out to shake hers, and she laughed at me.

"What, you don't shake hands?" I said.

"I don't know what the point is," she said. "It's a weird ritual. Think about it."

"The *point* is that you show someone you are open and civilized." I picked her hand up, put it in mine, and showed her how it went. "Like that," I said. "Polite, nice. Civilized."

"Nice gets you nowhere," she said. "And I'm not open or civilized. I'm difficult and moody. Ask anyone."

"Sweetheart, you were waiting tables a month ago. Maybe it's time to try a new approach."

Marcella gave me a look that was half a snarl, and shook my hand again, too hard. "How's that?" she asked.

"Better, but you need practice," I suggested.

She looped her arm over my shoulders and tapped the tip of my nose with her finger. "I like you," she said before dragging me by the arm into the boutique. "But that could change any minute now."

The interior of the shop was sleek and modern through the window, almost Asian in feel, and my heart sank when I realized it was one of those places they only let you shop in if they knew you or knew you were coming.

I'd never been here, but I'd heard about it. Beige was a celebrity magnet, a trendsetting boutique popular with stars and stylists on the hip end of the spectrum, which pretty much discounted me and my bulk. We stood at the door, and I started to pull away.

"Can't we just go to Bloomies like normal girls?" I asked.

"Come on." Marcella pulled me behind her. "Live a little."

The attendant buzzed us into the boutique, and I immediately felt out of place among the bamboo vases and sixties-inspired metal sculptures. Marcella, not so much. She greeted the owners by name, and they hugged her and offered her champagne. I stopped her from taking the alcohol, reminding her that she had an audition in a couple of hours. She introduced me as her "new manager," which took some of the edge off the looks I got for wearing a tent-size I doubted they even carried there. And then, Miss Marcella was off, touching with longing the tiny lacy tops and flowing scarves, the miniature tight pants and tiny shimmering skirts. It was all perfect for her, and she piled the clothes high in her arms.

After a free and creamy cappuccino to loosen me up, I joined her in looking. There was no doubt about it, darlin', the clothes were luscious, every item like its own little work of art, with embroidered silk sleeves flared at just the right angles, jeans cut for bodies and booties like hers. The designers were not household names because most households couldn't afford them, but I recognized some of them: Seven, Strenesse, James Coviello, Lix. You read about them in *InStyle,* if you were most people, and wore them if you were Marcella.

I tagged along with her to the dressing room and balked when she asked me to come in with her. Marcella lacked self-consciousness about her body, and stripped down to nothing but a breezy little black thong before sliding into one funky, sexy outfit after another. The perfection of her looks was more depressing than I'd imagined. It must have been amazing to have a body like that.

"Why don't you try something on?" she asked. "Come on!"

I shrugged. "I'm too big," I said.

Marcella, to my horror, called out to Tina Webb, a designer and owner of the shop, and asked her to bring some clothes back in my size. And to my surprise, Beige actually had one or two things lying around. One, a kimono-like shirt-jacket in peach silk with red flowers, wasn't exactly my style, but I liked how it looked and bought it anyway.

As Marcella and I tried clothes on in the little room, she grilled me about the audition, and told me her version of the basics of her life. I'd Googled Marcella last night, to see if there was anything I ought to know. I discovered a couple of scandals involving nude beaches and huge credit card bills, but did not think it polite to bring it up.

She talked me into trying on some jeans, and asked me about my life and I told her the truth: I was normal, I liked my family, I enjoyed my job, I hoped to get married and have kids someday, I had a dog in the meantime. She listened in what seemed to be amazement and laughed in all the places I didn't think she should have, like when I told her I was in a sorority and had been a debutante.

"What's so funny about that?" I asked her.

"It's just very cute," she said. "And strange. Like your underwear."

"Excuse me?"

"Briefs? Honestly. No one wears those anymore, do they? Grandma drawers. The panty-line thing is truly disturbing." She ran a hand along my backside and chuckled. "I'd suggest a thong. Even with the excess of ass."

"I don't need to floss my enormous bottom," I said, blushing.

"Oh, but you do. You do. They're great. You don't feel them, or if you do, they get you horny. But you have to get the right ones."

"A word of advice," I said as I quickly changed back into my own clothes. "Insult me all you want to, that's fine. But in the audition, keep your very strong opinions and judgments about people and their underwear to yourself. Okay? I can't believe how rude you are."

She snorted in amusement. "Thanks, Miss Manners. I'll try to remember that."

Marcella continued to laugh at me and my apparently disgusting panty lines all the way to the counter, where she piled dozens of expensive items next to the register. The owner rang up the order, and Marcella opened her wallet, revealing dozens of credit cards. I knew plenty of wealthy girls in college, but I had never seen such a varied and excessive collection of plastic. She seemed to be thinking very hard about which one she wanted to use, a finger running along them as she bit her lower lip.

"Let's go with the check card," she said. "Why run up debt if you don't have to, I say."

"Good philosophy," I said, wondering if the Google articles I'd seen about her huge debt were true. Looked like they might be.

The cashier ran the card through her machine, and after a few moments gave a confused apologetic smile. "I'm sorry, Marcella, it's getting declined."

Marcella's jaw dropped. "Declined? That can't be right."

"You want me to run it again?" she asked.

Marcella nodded. And again, the same thing happened. "I'm sorry. Do you have another card?" asked the owner.

"Of course I do," snapped Marcella. She handed over a MasterCard. "But I don't understand what's happening with the other one. I've never had a card declined in my entire life."

The owner looked at me and shrugged, and exchanged cards with Marcella. The new card worked, and Marcella and I left the boutique carrying bagloads of tiny little Buzz Jones jeans and Vato and Jakes T-shirts worth forty-eight hundred dollars, more than most people spent on their entire wardrobe for a year.

"That felt good," she said, as we strolled into the bright sunshine. She dropped her Gucci sunglasses onto her nose, looking every bit the star I believed she could become. It was one of those rare days in L.A. with little smog and incredibly sharp blue skies. "Next stop," she announced, "Lisa Kline."

"Who is she?" I asked.

Marcella gaped at me.

"It's a store. *The* store?"

Lisa Kline, the *store*, was something I'd never enter because the sign featured those naked woman silhouettes you see on the tire flaps of semi trucks. It also did not carry sizes larger than six or eight. I hated it. And once again, Marcella charged up a fortune that made me wince. Before we left, she changed into a new outfit, for the *Bod Squad* audition, something embarrassingly skimpy, but appropriate.

"You must have a lot of money saved up," I said.

"Thanks for reminding me," she said.

She stuck the burning cigarette in her mouth, yanked a small silver flip-phone out of her bag and dialed quickly as we stood on the sidewalk. She started to speak—then shout—in half English and half French to a person I deduced was her mother. Pedestrians went out of their way to avoid coming close to us, and I could not believe a person could be shameless enough to rant and rave in a public place like this. I wanted to hide. From what I could understand, Marcella was learning for the first time that her mother had demanded her father stop secretly putting money into her checking account and paying her Visa bill and Marcella was furious.

"What a fucking bitch!" she cried as she hung up. "I don't *believe* this."

"What's going on?"

"My parents cut me off. I mean, they always say they will, but my dad comes through. Now my mom is making him stop because I fired Wendy. She can't do that!"

"You fired Wendy?" Silver lining?

"She was an idiot," Marcella said. "But that's no reason to stop supporting me! I have bills to pay!"

"With all due respect," I said, "I have supported myself since I graduated from college. How old are you now?"

"Twenty-nine."

"Ah." I wondered what kind of spoiled loser cried because her parents had cut her off when she was going on thirty years old.

"It's *my* money, Alexis!" she cried. "They still manage my trust fund like it's theirs. But it's my money. All of it. I don't even think it's legal for them to cut me off from my own money. *Fuck fuck fuck.*" She took her sunglasses off and wiped away a tear.

"Are you okay?"

"I'm fine," she snapped. "Everything's fucking *great.*"

I looked at my watch. We had an hour until the audition. "We should get going," I said. I started to walk toward my car, figuring we'd take it and come back later for Marcella's car, wherever it was. "Are you prepared?"

"Stupid motherfuckers," she fumed.

"Who? Darren Wells?"

"My parents."

We had reached my car, and I unlocked the passenger door for her. I couldn't be sure, but it seemed like she found my Cadillac amusing. As she stepped into her seat, I could swear the girl laughed at me. I got behind the wheel, and started the engine, but did not pull out right away. Rather, I turned toward my new client, and put a hand on her shoulder.

"Marcella, darlin', please try to stop thinking about your parents for a minute. I know what you're going through can't be easy." Yeah, right. Let her try to live my life for a day! "Try to think of it this way: You're about to act your way into the best job you've ever had, because you deserve it. You won't need money from anybody. But you have to be in control and prepared for this. Are you? If you're not, we can ask to reschedule. I'll make the call right now if you want me to."

"I'm always prepared," she huffed. "The real question is: Are *they* ready for me?"

Of course, they *were* ready for Marcella. I saw it the moment she walked into the luxurious whites and yellows of Darren Wells's bright Century City high-rise office. Mr. Wells was there, along with several assistants and producers for the new show, *Bod Squad*.

Without exception, everyone there, male and female, gay and straight, had to grab hold of their eyes to keep them in their heads as Miss Marcella strutted in, wearing her tiny black jeweled Lotta halter top and black-and-white-striped Corey Lynn Calter mini, a preening, pretty little peacock. Mr. Wells and his various assistants smirked to one another the way they do when they want to communicate without words, and I knew what it meant: She's the one.

Marcella didn't have to do much, other than be herself. I passed out copies of her résumé, videos, and an assortment of (flattering) Latin press articles to the six people in the meeting. I had slipped a few of the racier articles in, but on the bottom of the stack in case Marcella objected. It turned out Mr. Wells had done some digging of his own since we'd met at the Getty, and had come across a few samples of Marcella's soap opera work, which he had screened and apparently enjoyed.

"This is very interesting," said Mr. Wells as he absently leafed through the collection of material and unapologetically viewed Marcella's assets live and in person. "Very interesting indeed. Thank you, Alexis, for bringing this lovely lady to my attention." He turned to face Marcella. "You, my dear, are somewhat the answer to my prayers. We're very interested in having you start the *Bod Squad* season with us."

"That would be nifty," said Marcella, almost as though she were being sarcastic. I had never met a person with thicker walls of defense around her fortress. I wanted to kick her under the proverbial table, but we sat side-by-side on a long white sofa, without a table in sight.

"It *would* be nifty," I repeated, "assuming the *terms* are agreeable."

"Of course," said Mr. Wells.

"We start shooting next week," said an assistant. "I'll get the details to Alexis and you can discuss it by phone."

Butterflies, grasshoppers, tadpoles. I wasn't sure what was swimming inside my belly. But I was effervescent as a shook-up Pellegrino. I'd shot, and I'd scored.

As we gathered our things to leave, Mr. Wells stood up. Holding up his dark blue glass of sparkling water—we all had one—he proposed a toast.

"To a great new season," he said.

Marcella, quite possibly the oddest human being I had ever met, answered in what I would soon come to regard as her natural way. With a brainy, creepy quote.

"Well, ladies, gentlemen," she said. "I'd just like to say: *'To be interested in the changing seasons is a happier state of mind than to be hopelessly in love with spring.'* That's George Santayana."

Blank faces all around.

"The philosopher, poet, and fag?" said Marcella, with characteristic diplomacy. "He hung out with Bertrand Russell? You might know him as the Hispanic Tocqueville. Lots of people do."

Silence as everyone tried to think of something to say to this woman, who was probably *not* what they expected (she sure wasn't what I'd bargained for, I could tell you that) and who did not show any interest in becoming what they, or anyone, expected.

I cleared my throat and tried to clear the air, too.

"To a new season, Mr. Wells," I said, clicking my glass against his. "And to many more to come."

Winter

To change masters is not to be free.
—José Martí

MARCELLA

O kay, Marcella, do it again," barked Gabe, the director. "But this time do it with *feeling*."

"What am I supposed to be feeling, exactly?"

I slid the red Tommy Bahama Lycra bikini bottoms out of my crack with my index finger, as a makeup girl quickly ripped an errant coil of pubic hair out of the skin at my bikini line with rubberized tweezers, plucking me like a chicken.

I'd been starring in *Bod Squad* for four months now, and was no longer embarrassed by this, or by the way she smeared tanning makeup on my inner thighs when she was finished. I was more or less resigned to life as a piece of televised meat because it was *fun* and it was making me *famous*. Every tabloid in the land, it seemed, could not get enough photos of Marcella Gauthier Bosch, the actress they had all come to regard as "the new Carmen Electra."

I did what I had to do, thought about my big paycheck, and then I went about my life without thinking too hard about much else. And I was happy that way. Thinking too hard was the surest way to court misery. The quote popped into my head: *"Happiness is nothing more than good health and a bad memory."* Albert Schweitzer.

"You are *feeling* anxiety and lust," Gabe cried. "You want this man more than you've ever wanted a man in your *life*, and it looks like he might have just *drowned*. It's up to you and only you to save him. The usual shit."

"Right," I said.

As Gabe fussed with an assistant, I stood in the sand and squinted against the bright white sunshine toward Gabe's tall director's chair. His PUH (personal umbrella holder), an intern who had undoubtedly imagined her network job would be somehow more meaningful than *this*, looked like her arms were about to fall off; but at least she got to wear clothes, and a coat. It was now winter in Los Angeles, and even though this was a private patch of Malibu Beach, I was freezing my ass off.

They liked to shoot me cold because you could see big nipple that way. And puritanical America, for all its bitching about Janet Jackson's halftime Timberlake fiasco, loved a good, hard nipple. America, for all its complaining about pornography, in reality poured more money into the X-rated side of the film industry than they did into the "clean" version, meaning lowly Chatsworth was more profitable—and in more homes—than its slick and famous Hollywood sister. But we as a society would never collectively admit to our sleaze, because to *admit* to it meant losing the forbidden allure. To America, secret sin was beautiful, and the more banal the better.

Another quote came to my brain as I stood shivering, waiting for the next take: *"There is no excellent beauty that hath not some strangeness in the proportion."* Sir Francis Bacon. Oh yeah.

Almost five hundred years before, Mr. Bacon had understood it all quite clearly. That's why I didn't put too much effort into thinking about things, the way my sister Mathilde the feminist academic did, because people much smarter than I had figured it all out long ago and not a damn thing had changed. The best you could do in life was make good money, which meant freedom, and do something you enjoyed, which in my case was acting. And forget the past, just forge ahead with a vengeance.

If only the tabloid reporters realized how hard I *was* acting on this show, that I wasn't actually the vacant babe on the TV screen. If they understood how entirely unlike me it was to run vapid-faced down the beach, if they only knew, as I moaned in faux ecstasy, that I had never *once* in my life had an orgasm with a man, they might appreciate me and my work more. I was used to being unappreciated, however. And the public assumed I had been born to bounce on the beach; they made no effort to see anything more than that. That, and nipple, in the right light. Ultimately, this was fine with me. I was well used to hiding my true self behind a wall of silicone.

This is what none of the ruthless tabloid spawn understood about me: I had the true actress's memory for lines, a gift passed to me by my mother, Brigitte Gauthier, the renowned 1960s French cinema actress who still could not bring herself to be happy for me and my newfound, if limited, stardom.

Last time we talked, Mother let me know she thought my skills were being wasted on *Bod Squad* and she might have been right. It was, in fact, more or less the same plot every week. The very lusty, sexual predictability of it had made *Bod Squad* the most popular new program in Germany, parts of Austria, and Korea, where punctual predictability—and large breasts—were apparently of great value. I wasn't complaining.

The success of the show had provided me enough money to keep myself afloat without intervention from my parents, more or less. I was still living in my lovely little cottage in a quiet, wild, green, coyote-crossed pocket of Laurel Canyon, and I had an appointment at the Bentley dealer later today, to look over my new car for any last-minute adds. Yes, I was still juggling my credit card bills, paying one card off with the other each month, and I would have to finance the Bentley through a bank (the dealer did not finance, figuring, correctly perhaps, that if you couldn't pay cash you weren't a Bentley kind of customer) to the point it would cost more than my mortgage each month. But I was a star. I had to live like a star. And it made me feel good, at least for a little while, to buy shit. Lots of shit.

"Take four!" shouted Gabe. "*Rrrrolling!*"

Ian Cross, a handsome Australian actor who was now a star on a daytime U.S. soap opera, was the drowning guest star for this episode of *Bod Squad*. Each week, someone hot drowned on my show. I was glad it was Ian, who bore a scary resemblance to Enrique Iglesias.

Perched on one elbow in the wet sand near the water, he pushed his dirty-blond hair out of his eyes and smiled at me for a moment, then resumed his dead-man pose. Ian wore glasses, and I had caught him reading René Descartes in the dressing trailer earlier, just as I had finished rereading Balzac's *Bureaucracy* for fun. In other words, he was just my type. We'd been flirting all day and it looked like he had a hard-on beneath the floral Hawaiian surf-boy trunks. I was flattered.

It wasn't difficult for me to counterfeit lust for the man. Every woman I knew wanted him, except my mother. *Mère*, who now ran a gallery in Santa Barbara, found everyone on American television, including me—maybe especially me—vulgar. Though she'd made many false public proclamations of pride in me in the U.S. press lately, my mother often let me know she didn't *really* believe what I did in Hollywood and (gasp) on television (*vulgaire, vulgaire!*) was *acting*. *Mère* Brigitte believed, as did the media, that *she* was the only real actress in our family, and my starring role on a *Baywatch* clone did nothing to help.

Ian lay covered in seaweed, with saline water spilling from his nose, and looked great in spite of it. He had big biceps, and abs that were so strong it looked like his six-pack had a six-pack. Yes, sir. He'd look effing good on my arm walking through the door of Dolce or the Ivy. And what better way to get back at Ryan Fuckwad than dating a man who was richer, better-looking, more famous, and obviously more refined? Oh, and with an apparently (much) bigger dick. Not that the last bit was hard to find, or anything. Even my neutered male cat had a bigger one than Ryan Fuckwad.

It was the anxiety part I had trouble with. The pasty "death" makeup was so obviously makeup on the rosy, glowing life-form of Ian Cross. He didn't look drowned so much as he looked like a man who had been mugged in a dark alley by Blue Man Group.

Still and all, I lifted my implants skyward, sucked in my gut, and ran on my long legs and bare feet toward the water, the bright orange life preserver held high enough for the camera to get a good shot of my ass, my long brown hair with honey highlights tossed to the side for an unobstructed angle on my tits.

As extras oohed and aahed along the beach, I tried to imagine what the sound-track would bring to this week's touching scene. A little *wonka-wonka* porn guitar, perhaps? Cheesy synthesized violins that brought to mind the early days of *Charlie's Angels*? The possibilities were endless.

I reached Ian, and kneeled down, careful to toss my hair once more and squeezing my arms together for maximum cleavage. I checked his pulse. It raced, but I pretended it was absent. Then, honoring our time-worn tradition, I licked my lips and began to perform a disturbingly passionate mouth-to-mouth. Ian Cross's mouth tasted like mint and honey. I wanted more. But soon enough, he coughed and revived, blinking up at the cloudless sky like a miner freed from a coal-shaft disaster.

"Cut!" cried Gabe. "It's a wrap. Bagel break."

I lingered at Ian's side, and he offered a hand to help me back to my feet. I would have loved a bagel, but I was limiting all carbs and most other food with calories. A cigarette would have to do.

"Good job, lady," he said.

"Thanks, Ian. You too."

As assistants wrapped us both in thick, warm terry-cloth robes and offered cups of steaming herbal tea, we walked back to the trailer.

"I meant to tell you, I'm real sorry about the tabloids," he said, alluding to the fact that the U.S. tabs had come across all those topless photos from *Cristina* and my tits were now plastered all over American grocery lines with headlines that invariably compared me to a jalapeño or "hot tamale." "What a bunch of fucking wankers."

I nodded. "No matter what they say, I'm *not* a nympho," I said.

"That's a disappointment," he said with a grin.

"Everyone at that beach was nude."

Ian nodded, solemn. "The press is a bunch of fucking pigs and vultures," he said. "And I hate the way they can't think of anything else to call you except the new Carmen Electra. I don't see the similarities."

"I know! Why do they do that?" I smiled at Ian. He was smart, considerate, perfect.

"For the same reason they call me the new Mel Gibson. I'm Protestant! But I'm Australian. They don't know you."

I studied him. "Neither do you," I said.

He pushed his bangs back again, with a shy smile. "But I'd like to."

"Really."

He ascended the stairs to the boys' trailer, I to the girls'.

"I'll have my agent call your agent to set something up, if that's okay."

In my line of business, this was a man asking for a date.

"That'd be great," I said, ducking into my trailer.

"Hey, Marcella?" he called.

"Yes?" I peeked out at him again.

"You should go into movies, get out of this TV shit."

I smiled. "That's the plan. But first we have to find something that doesn't require a Latina actress to be a maid or a crack whore or Jennifer Lopez."

OLIVIA

'd gone to the doctor because Samuel swore he would leave me if I didn't. And why did he want to leave me? Because, after getting the last remaining copy of my horrible first screenplay in the mail from that Alexis woman three months ago, I had promptly burned it, and almost burned the apartment down, too.

And then, after writing the whole thing again, at his suggestion and because Alexis kept calling and visiting me and having lunch with me and telling me I needed to, I took Jack, went for a hike in the hills near our home, and burned it once and for all, last month. I'd made a little fire in a picnic area, and as Jack and I toasted marshmallows, I tore up the pages and fed them to the flames. I was convinced as I did it that I was the worst writer who had ever lived, and believed that if I burned the thing then maybe the nightmares would stop.

Of course, I wasn't that bad of a writer, at least I didn't think so when I felt better. Alexis, when she wasn't telling me to shorten parts and add other parts, said I was talented.

The nightmares continued to come, though, with me generally ending them by beating Samuel and scratching at his eyes. He had been bloodied and bruised more than we cared to talk about anymore, and he was, he said, sick of it. I didn't blame him. Even Jack seemed to feel the stress, and the once-happy child brooded more than I liked, and seemed like he was watching me in fear.

The shrink diagnosed me almost immediately. Post-traumatic stress disorder. I wasn't crazy, he said. There wasn't even anything wrong with me. I was a normal woman, he said, who had witnessed horrific and almost unimaginable violence.

The answer? To meet with him every week, or even a couple of times a week, to talk it out, and to take medication, something called Zoloft. And, he said, I should try writing about my experiences. Again. Alexis would like to hear that, I was sure. She seemed to think her new client, that gorgeous Dominican actress everyone was calling the new Carmen Electra, could pull off a great movie, but I wasn't sure she was that great an actress. I was even more unsure that I was a decent screenwriter, or even a screenwriter at all.

I told the doctor that I already *had* written about my experiences, that I had written two screenplays about it, both named after my mother. *Soledad*. I even told him that a woman who managed some bands and a fairly well-known actress had liked the first two versions, and that since burning the last one, I had written half of a third version all over again, working in an almost trancelike state during Jack's naps and in the very early mornings when I could not sleep. I told him the truth: I wanted to stop writing, but I couldn't. Writing, for me, was a compulsion and a curse.

Unlike Samuel, my doctor thought it was a very good idea to do it a third time, and he even thought it made sense that ever since I'd started writing the script the episodes had gotten worse.

"Things are working themselves out in your brain," he said. "When we worry is when PTSD patients don't dream. The sleeping brain has been shown to work on problems the awake mind can't deal with. It's quite amazing. Keep going with it."

The doctor had also asked if there was tension in my marriage. I did not have to think too hard for an answer: Yes. There were no overt fights, but Samuel and I were not as close as we used to be. He worked a lot, I was always tired, we didn't have sex anymore. The doctor suggested I start to spend some time on myself. He said that the lack of a personal identity or alone time can compound the problems I was having, and that I seemed to be focusing too little on my own wants and needs. He asked me what I liked to do, other than write, and the answer was easy: Run. I loved to run. But since Jack was born, I'd cut back on running because it seemed so selfish and because I didn't have anyone to leave him with.

"Heart disease is the number one killer of women," the doctor said. "I don't see anything selfish about prolonging your life. I think your son would appreciate having you around, don't you?"

I wasn't sure.

To that end, I was here in East Hollywood, on the border of Silver Lake, near Waterloo and Reservoir, on the block where I grew up. It was now a neighborhood in the throes of an identity crisis, with new Internet cafés and trendy antique shops rubbing up against the cheesy Mexican dress shop and unsanitary nail salons whose side walls bore graffiti stains. On second thought, it was less of an identity crisis than it was a glorious expression of the diversity of Los Angeles.

I was leaving Jack with Debbie, my brother Frascuelo's wife, for the evening, so I could go running.

After that, I was going with Alexis and Marcella to a photo shoot. Alexis had not given up on me. We'd met for lunch a couple of times, but I'd always had Jack with me and had not been able to fully concentrate on Alexis's advice. I'd given her the latest version of the screenplay and she had said she thought it was much better than the first two. I was sure she was lying, but she had reassured me just the same.

Frascuelo and Debbie lived in a small, rented, shingled house with bars on the windows and dark brown glass shards in the front yard from where people had driven by and thrown beer bottles out of moving cars. It wasn't ideal. But inside, the house was tidy and comfortable, and Jack enjoyed spending time here because his cousins had turtles and hermit crabs in aquariums, and those were about the neatest things he could imagine. I didn't want the responsibility of pets yet, so little animals were of great interest and novelty to my son.

Debbie opened the door wearing a black tank top with the word CHICA written in glittery pink script across the front, and jeans with black platform sandals too small for her feet. Her big toenails were long and yellow, like dog claws. Her long hair was styled the way it had been as long as I'd known her, flat down her back, with big bangs that curled under in a loop over her eyes. She wasn't actually Frascuelo's wife, but that's what we called her. She was his *woman*, the mother of his two kids, and they had been together since high school. He called her his wife, and she called him her husband, but to my knowledge they had never officially tied the knot. But in this neighborhood, "wife" was a frame of mind.

Debbie was a stay-at-home mother like I was, but she had barely finished high school. She did things to her children I would never do to mine. For instance: Debbie put thick blankets imprinted with cartoon characters over her baby carriers because she thought it would keep out germs and the evil eye. Lots of women around here did that. They'd been doing it since I was a kid growing up here, and they still did it.

I didn't honestly know how the babies survived in East Hollywood, with all the mothers covering them in suffocating blankets to keep them "healthy." Debbie also allowed her children to watch violent programs on television, and she seemed to think "cheese *stuff*" was a major food group best washed down with "orange *drink*." She used double-negatives with great frequency, as in: "I don't see no problem with cheese stuff and orange drink." Debbie also saw no problem in letting her children play with toy guns, and I wondered how Frascuelo, who'd lost a *foot* to guns and had been raised by our *mother*, a major opponent of guns, could justify the way his kids chased each other around saying, "Bang, bang, you're dead!"

Because of our differences of opinion in child-rearing, Debbie was my last choice for childcare. But she was all I had right now. It didn't ease my mind at all that she also had a teardrop tattoo under one eye from her days in a gang, or that the other tattoo, on her fleshy triceps, read LA SAD GIRL. Frascuelo had finished high school and college, and was now in his third year of medical school at USC, so I was confused about their relationship. I didn't know what they had to talk about, but I didn't pry. My brother loved Debbie, and liked to say she was his best friend. Now twenty-four, Frascuelo was devoted beyond reason to things. I think it was his way of dealing with the losses, to be loyal to a fault. Paz and I talked about it behind Fascuelo's back all the time, which wasn't very nice, I supposed, but was our way of puzzling it out.

Earlier, as I drove here, I'd called Samuel at work to say I felt guilty about leaving Jack with Debbie, but he told me to relax. It wasn't like I was leaving Jack to do something productive, like polish my screenplay. I was leaving him to go to a photo shoot with my famous friend. Samuel had this idea that it was a healthy thing to do. He said it would be good for Jack to get out and be with his cousins for a while.

"But what if she suffocates him with one of those thick Bugs Bunny blankets the way they do?" I asked Samuel.

"You tell her not to cover him up. She's free to cover her own kids, but not ours."

"What if he starts shooting things up with toy guns?"

"He'll never own a toy gun. We'll explain to him why they're bad, but teach him to be tolerant of kids who are different from him. It's not bad for him to be around different kinds of people, Olivia. You have to let him experience life."

Jack ran into the house to find the crabs. Debbie smiled awkwardly and I saw again that she was missing several back teeth. She invited me in, and started to remove the laundry she was folding from the sagging sofa. I thanked her, but said I had to run—and I did, literally. I was planning to jog five miles along the beach before I went home to shower and dress. I had a total of three hours to find the photo shoot. With L.A. traffic, that wasn't much time.

I called out to Jack that I loved him, gave Debbie a weak, obligatory hug, and went back to the van. As I opened the door, a familiar voice called my name.

"Olivia!"

I looked up and saw Chan Villar, a guy I'd known since childhood, standing on the porch of a house half a block away.

"Hey!" I said, waving.

Chan trotted to the van, smiling. "I thought that was you," he said. "Long time, no see."

Chan, who was half-Korean and half-Mexican, had been a fat, pasty kid who'd had a crush on me through middle and high school. I had all but ignored him, and lived to regret it senior year, when he grew six inches in one shot, lost the baby fat, and became one of the most chiseled, best-looking men I'd ever seen, in a block-ish, Dean Cain sort of way. But by then I was dating Samuel, and Chan and I lost touch. I'd heard from my mom, who was friends with *his* mom, that he'd married a beautiful Armenian girl named Katya who used to live nearby.

"What brings you to the neighborhood?" he asked.

"Dropping my son off with my brother's wife."

He smiled and nodded, and looked genuinely happy to see me. One of the bonuses of being an ugly duckling, I thought, was that once the duckling turned into a swan, he didn't stop being a nice guy. Chan had never had time to grow vain, and he carried himself as if he didn't realize he was handsome.

"You look great," he said. "How old's your kid?"

"Two."

"I've got a three-year-old girl," he said. "Melanie."

I blushed without meaning to as he smiled at me. He was even more handsome now than he had been the last time I saw him—broader through the shoulders, as if he'd been working out. "You still live around here?"

"Me?" He shook his head vigorously. "Oh, no. I live in Santa Monica. But my studio is here."

"Studio?"

"God, it's been that long, huh?" he asked. "I'm a photographer now."

"I thought you were going to be a dentist."

"I thought so too, but nah. I take pictures. And I do some cinematography. How about you?"

"I live in Calabasas," I said. He raised his eyebrows as if impressed. "I stay home with Jack, and my husband teaches at UCLA."

"Sounds nice and normal," he said.

"You still married to Katya?" I asked.

He smiled sadly. "I guess you didn't know," he said. "Katya had ovarian cancer. She died two years ago."

"God, I'm sorry, Chan."

"Yeah. That's when I got the studio here, so I could be close to my folks. It's good to have my mom help out with Melanie, you know? Give her the girl's perspective on life. Woman's. Sorry. See what I mean? She needs someone a little more sensitive than me."

"You doing okay?" I said.

He smiled artificially, brushed his hands together as if he'd just finished an important job and it was time to pack up. "I'm doing as okay as you'd expect, you know? Well, if you're ever around the neighborhood and you want to catch up, that's my studio right there, the purple house with the red door. Come by anytime." He turned and started back toward his studio with a wave.

"I'd like to see your work."

"Sure," he called. "Whenever."

I arrived ten minutes late to the shoot. At first I thought I had the wrong address, because the building was nothing but a warehouse. But Alexis was waiting outside the door for me.

Inside the warehouse, a corner was lit up and decorated with modern-looking furniture in bright primary colors. Marcella sat in a high director's-style chair as a man put makeup on her, another man fiddled with her hair, and two other men—both of them very good-looking—picked at the fruit and bagels on a foldout table and watched. A woman riffled through clothes on a long rack nearby, choosing outfits.

Alexis pulled me to where the actress sat, and introduced us. Marcella did not shake my hand until Alexis forced her to. I wanted to leave.

"Olivia is the screenwriter I told you about. She's got an amazing movie that I think you'd be good for."

Marcella stared at herself in the mirror and said, "Congratulations."

"Don't pay attention to her," Alexis whispered as she pulled me away from the actress. "She's a little unusual, but she means well. Big walls up. I don't know why."

Next, Alexis took me to the area where the furniture was set up and introduced me to a woman in a very fashionable tight red satin suit, whose name was familiar.

"Olivia," she said, "I'd like to introduce you to Rebecca Baca, the publisher of *Ella* magazine."

The petite woman with the short black hair smiled and shook my hand purposefully. I remembered the days when I used to shake hands like that. It had been so long, I felt out of practice.

"Nice to meet you," I said, feeling rusty.

Rebecca asked me if I lived here in L.A., and I said yes. Then she asked me what I did, as in what I did for a *living*. I blushed, and told her the truth.

"I'm a stay-at-home mom."

She nodded, but looked like she felt mildly sorry for me. "Most important job in the world," she said, but immediately she seemed to lose interest in me and started talking to her assistant.

It was a platitude, that whole "most important job" thing. People said it all the time, but I didn't think they usually meant it. If they meant it, then more men would be dropping out of the workforce to do it.

Alexis pinched my arm. "Rebecca? Olivia is a *screenwriter*. And a very modest one."

Rebecca regarded me anew. "Oh?" she asked.

I nodded and shrugged.

"She's very good," said Alexis. "Keep an eye out for her."

Alexis dragged me toward the table with the handsome men next, whispering in my ear. "You can't *do* that, sugar. You have to seem like you believe in yourself when you meet people, or no one else will believe in you."

"But I'm *not* a screenwriter," I protested. "Not yet."

"Did you write a screenplay?"

"Yes. But it's not published or anything."

"Did you *write* a *screenplay*?" she repeated. She sounded more like Dr. Phil, her favorite source of inspiration, every day.

"Yes."

"Okay, then."

The exchange seemed to have upset Alexis, because she pulled an inhaler out of her handbag and started to wheeze up the medicine. A stack of receipts and other papers tumbled to the floor. She scooped them up.

"I'm sorry," I said.

Alexis held a breath and shook her head at me. She exhaled, and said, "You see? Like that. You can't take blame for things that aren't your fault. Gosh darnit, Olivia, get some confidence, girlfriend! It wears me out."

She looked over the papers as she replaced them, one by one, in her bag.

Alexis pulled me up next to the men, a smile threatening to take over her entire face.

"This is Olivia Flores, she's a screenwriter," she said. The men smiled and held their hands out to shake mine. I tried to fight the urge to shrug and shrink, and Alexis watched me, beaming.

"That's better," she said.

The taller of the two men was a soap-opera star I recognized, Ian Cook, who was here with Marcella. Of course he was. She had glamorous boyfriends to go with her glamorous life. The shorter but still tall man was Marcella's brother. I could have sworn he was flirting with Alexis.

"I think he likes you," I whispered to her as we walked away from the men.

"Who, Nico? He lusts after power and thinks bedding me would be a challenge," she said, matter-of-factly. "He wants to convert me to a liberal."

"He's cute," I said, wondering to myself, again, what I was doing hanging out with right-wing fascists like Alexis.

"Too easy," she said. "Besides, I don't fraternize, or fornicate, with family of clients. Especially not liberals," she added with a wink.

Alexis settled me in a corner near a cooler filled with Penta bottled water, and excused herself to take care of some business. I stood there, with my water, trying to look like I belonged. So as the handlers fussed over Marcella, as Rebecca talked on her cell phone in hushed and blushing tones—probably to a boyfriend—and as Alexis flirted with Nico and Ian flirted with Marcella, I just stood there, clutching my tote bag. It was heavy with the screenplay, and I felt like a fool for bringing it. I wasn't a screenwriter, no matter how creatively Alexis introduced me. I wasn't like these people, important and interesting.

That I felt inadequate wasn't a surprise. That was precisely what I'd counted on. What I hadn't counted on, though, were the ghosts. I felt them, but thankfully didn't see them. I felt, rather than heard, the last words my father's ghost had spoken to me in the apartment. "They'll see you," he'd said.

Marcella finally took her position, on a chaise longue that was supposed to look like it was in a library, next to a high bookshelf. The photographer positioned me behind the bookshelf to keep me out of the way, but I could still see what was happening. Marcella preened and posed, pursing her lips, opening them, laughing with her head thrown back. The lei around her neck threatened to expose her breasts at any moment, but it was discreetly taped in place. The entire scene was absolutely glamorous, and would be excellent ammunition for a future screenplay.

I didn't feel envy, exactly, but I did wonder what it would be like to have Marcella's life. She seemed so comfortable there, in hardly any clothes, with more makeup than I'd probably worn in all my days combined.

Suddenly, I felt the floor lurch beneath me. I'd been through this enough times to know what it was. An earthquake. Before you had time to realize what was happening, in many cases it was already over. But this kept going. I looked up at the hanging lights, and sure enough, they swayed like pendulums. This would be a big one.

The shelf began to tip toward Marcella as the photographer and publisher shouted at her to move. Marcella sat frozen in terror, a pretty rabbit trapped in headlights. People ran for cover. Before I knew what I'd done, I dashed out from behind the bookcase and grabbed Marcella by the arm, pulling her away from the shelves moments before they would have crushed her. As I pushed her toward a safe spot, I heard the wood of the chaise longue splinter. Next, I heard glass breaking, and something that sounded like gunfire.

At the gunshot sound, I fell down and began to scream. I saw my tote bag slip from my grip, and watched almost in slow motion as *Soledad*, the screenplay, cascaded onto the floor. I heard the ghosts shouting, and the boots scraping the wooden floor, and then I felt a very distinct and very real thump on the head.

And then I blacked out.

When I came to, the earthquake was over and Marcella held my head in her lap while Alexis screamed into a cell phone that we needed an ambulance. We were in some sort of back room I hadn't been in before, and everyone stood around me like I was going to die. Ian Cook held my hand, which I found strange because he played a doctor on the soap opera and I had to wonder for a moment if I had just woken up in an alternate reality where I now lived in a television.

"What happened?" I asked.

"I think a piece of plaster fell from the ceiling on your head," said Marcella.

"We've got medics on the way," said Alexis.

"No," I said. I felt fine. I sat up. I had a small headache, but nothing worth going to the hospital over. I avoided hospitals whenever possible, as they were massive triggers for my disorder.

"But you passed out," said Marcella.

"I always pass out," I explained.

"So cancel the ambulance?" asked Alexis. I nodded. "Are you sure?" she said, brow furrowed with concern and indecision. I nodded again. She yelled into the phone that we did not need an ambulance, and then said to me, "If you're always passing out, you should get checked. I have a girlfriend back in Dallas who had that. It was low iron."

"I know what it is," I said.

Ian let go of my hand and started to pace the room with his hands stuffed deeply into his pockets. I looked for Marcella's brother, and found him seated on the floor in a corner, reading my screenplay with a half-smile on his lips.

"Hey!" I cried. "Don't read that!"

He looked up. "Why not? It's really good."

Alexis asked me what my condition was, the one that made me pass out, and I told her the truth.

"I have post-traumatic stress disorder. When I hear anything like bullets, it sets me off."

"Really?" Alexis's eyebrows shot up in surprise.

"That's deep," said Ian Cook. "What's it from?"

Nicolás answered for me. "If this is at all autobiographical, she has the disorder because she witnessed a death squad assassinate her father when she was a kid in El Salvador. Is Soledad your mom? I've heard of her."

"That's deep," Ian said again.

I stood up and walked to Nico. "Give me that," I said, groping for the document.

"No," he answered as he lifted it out of reach.

I thought he was joking, but he ran from the room with my screenplay. I was dizzy and didn't want to chase him. I sat back down.

"He's an asshole," said Marcella. She got up to chase her brother and came back with my screenplay. She kissed me on the forehead as she handed it to me, which I did not expect.

"You saved my life," she said. "The least I can do is give you back your work."

I blushed and stuffed the pages back in the tote bag.

The voices came then, soldiers and my mother, my Tata. "They'll see you, and they'll never forget."

I clutched my manuscript and walked out of the room into the warehouse. I took my cell phone out of the tote bag and called Debbie to see if Jack was okay. He was fine, she said, and had slept right through the earthquake. Nothing to worry about there. I walked toward the parking lot.

Alexis ran after me, clicking on her cute little pumps, panting. "Sugar, you sure you're okay?"

"I'm fine," I said. "Just a little late. Gotta go."

"When can we talk about this script?" she asked. "I want Marcella to read it."

"I don't know. I'll call you when I finish it. If I finish it."

Then, without saying good-bye to my strange and glamorous friends, I left, with ghosts trailing me.

ALEXIS

aniel sat with his legs splayed, elbows planted on the soft white arms of my overstuffed family room chair. He looked so wrong in that chair. It was a classic. He was . . . not. Not to be mean or anything, but I worried he'd stain it with his grit and grime.

Daniel had just come from playing basketball at a local park with a group of high school boys, and he'd gotten his butt kicked, of course. When Daniel had swaggered back to my house from basketball, cocky and breathless, covered with dirt from where, I could imagine, a kid with glasses and tuberculosis or something had knocked him over, bragging of his "mad b-ball skills, yo," I decided today was the day, now the moment.

Good-bye, Daniel.

"I'm sorry, sugar, it's just not . . . working out."

He grinned as if he'd just heard a joke, and laced his pasty fingers together like a sickeningly blue-white little igloo over his crotch. He must not be getting enough oxygen after all that physical exertion. Outside, in the backyard, Juanga yapped at Daniel; I'd locked her out, knowing she hated him and would sense that I wanted him gone. She might have been small, and she might have been wearing a pink rhinestone collar, but my pooch was *tough*. I couldn't hear her, but I saw the longhaired Chihuahua mouth open and close, the doggie lips roll back to reveal black doggie gums and sharp little teeth. Snap, snap.

"You think *what*, boo? I can't have heard that right, now." Daniel glowered at Juanga. "Fucking ugly-ass mutt," he said. Daniel growled with alarming accuracy, and lunged toward my sweet little puppy, snapping his lips like a turtle. Juanga responded by charging the back door, smearing poopy paw prints all over the glass. Nice to know someone had my back, even if that someone only weighed three pounds and danced uninhibited in her own excrement.

I stood at the pink granite island in the kitchen, and chopped a piece of Sara Lee frozen pound cake with a butter knife. "You heard me, Daniel," I said. "It's not working out. I need space."

Daniel laughed out loud. "You? Space? You *bouncin'*, chicken? Now I done heard it all."

I opened the door of my white refrigerator and removed a carton of whole milk. I knew I should drink low-fat milk, but I liked whole milk better, especially when I was under duress. So sue me. I poured a glass, took my plate of cake, and sat on one of the stools at the island.

"Yes," I said to the cake. I couldn't bear to look at Daniel. Even though I was sick of him and his faux gangster ways, it hurt me to hurt him. I didn't want to be mean, I was raised to make life as easy and comfortable as possible for people. "I just don't feel like I have the time for this right now."

"That's whack," he said. "Come let me put it down on ya. It's better when you're mad. Let's fight like weasels and do the make-up booty call thang." He stood up and tried to hug me. It felt more like he was trying to hump me, though, like a dog on someone's leg. Plus, I recognized his liberal use of dated LL Cool J lyrics, and was not impressed.

"Please," I said, shrugging him off. "I'm serious."

"You on the rag or something?" he asked. Okay, I thought. I'd tried to be compassionate, considering, but now he was starting to plain old tee me off.

"Daniel, just because a woman dumps you doesn't mean she's crazy or on the rag."

Daniel bristled. "Dumps me?" he asked. "You said you needed *space*. That's not the same as dumping someone."

I swallowed the milk, dabbed the corners of my mouth with a cloth napkin, and, finally, looked him in the eye. He had tears. Oh, dear.

"I'm sorry," I said, wanting only to be alone with my pastry.

"So which is it? Time, or *dump?*"

I hesitated, set my fork on the counter. Sighed. "Dump," I said softly. I shrugged an apology. I wasn't good at this. I was usually the one who got dumped, the one who got too clingy and started demanding engagement rings and baby names.

"I don't *fucking* believe this," Daniel said, his voice loud with rage. "You're out? *You* are bouncing on *me*? That right?"

His anger and profanity set me off. "Yes," I said, "I'm out. Bouncy, bouncy." I pantomimed bouncing a ball, and shooting a basket with nothing but net, which I doubted he'd done all day.

He flicked the plate of cake with one hand and it rattled and gyrated like a child's top against the countertop. "You can't dump *me*," he said. "Who else is going to love your fat ass? If anyone should dump anybody, it's me that should dump you. Look at you. You're starting to look like Rosie O'Donnell."

Ouch.

I stood up and walked toward the front door of my house. "Good-bye, Daniel," I said as I opened the door and stood, sentrylike in the soaring white entry, waiting for him to, as his cop "buddies" would say, remove himself from the premises. "It's been fun, but I think it's time for you to leave now."

Daniel stood in the kitchen doorway and fiddled with the large gold pendant hanging over the Fubu logo on his outsized T-shirt. "What is it? Is there someone else?"

"There is no one else, Daniel."

He snickered. "I bet it's someone else. Don't lie to me. I know how chickens be."

"Daniel, go." I pointed to the door. *"Now."*

"What? Why? What did I *do?*"

"Let's see," I said thoughtfully. "Oh, yeah. That's right. You just called me a chicken. That's one. You think you're a high-school rap star. That would be the biggest problem. You hate my dog. And you talk nonstop about yourself. You don't care about my job or my life. You are so in love with yourself there's no room for anyone else in a relationship with you, Daniel. And you think you're still a teenager. I guess I already said that, but it really gets on m'last nerve."

"What are you talking about?" Daniel honestly seemed stunned by the description of himself. I sighed. My neck and shoulders tensed and a headache started. "Can I at least get my toothbrush?" he asked.

"Feel free." *Even though you never use it.*

"It's another cat," Daniel said knowingly as he took the stairs two at a time. He called down from the master suite: "I never trusted you completely, you know that? I always knew you had a freaky-deaky side, always thought you'd be getting your freak on with another player."

"That's right, Daniel," I called with a roll of the eyes. "I've been getting my *freak* on with another *player.* You *happy* now?"

He bounded down the stairs with a raggedy blue toothbrush in his fist. "I knew it! You bee-atch! One of them banda dudes, right?"

"Right." I thought of me in bed with one of the beer bellies from Los Chimpances del Norte and wanted to laugh, but didn't. Rather, I nodded somberly.

Daniel shook a finger at me as he slid past. "You know, I'm not the violent type," he said. "You should be glad about that. Just be glad about that. But don't think I don't know no boys who might eff you up."

"Oooh, I'm scared," I said, stifling a laugh, a smile playing across my face. "What are you going to do? Sic your posse of copy editors on me?" I laughed and imitated hitting someone with a rolled-up newspaper. "Or maybe you can call your *good friend* Nelly and ask him to send the bad boys over. Oh, wait, I'm sorry. It's b-boys, right? Did I say it right?"

"You keep laughing, Alexis," he said, nodding furiously with his mouth wide open. It should not be legal to have that many fillings. "That's fine. You'll see."

Daniel stood on the porch facing me. I closed the door, but could hear him shouting on his colossal dinosaur of a cell phone, calling one of his *Times* pals to pick him up from "the whorehouse in Newport Beach;" his car was in the shop again, this time with brake problems. Just like Daniel, I thought, the Corolla didn't know when to stop.

I opened the door again.

"My keys," I said, holding out my hand. I had almost forgotten. Daniel dug in the pocket of his oversized Sean John jeans, and produced my extra set of house keys.

"Oops," he said as he intentionally dropped them on the ground. I had to stoop to pick them up, which he enjoyed. He laughed and pretended he was going to kick me in the head. Nice. It occurred to me that Daniel, wild in the bedroom, might have yet another side to him no one figured upon looking at him. A side I probably ought to actually worry about. I backed away without looking at him, shut the door, and locked it. Thudding sounds shook the condo, as if Daniel were outside kicking the walls.

I raced to let Juanga in. She scurried around like a miniature hyena, sniffing everything, snorting her disapproval. She had such fantastic people instincts. I gathered her in my arms and let her kiss every inch of my face. "Don't worry, precious," I said. "The bad man is gone. Now let's go get ready for work."

Twenty minutes later, I watched from my guest-bedroom window upstairs as Daniel's freckled, redheaded reporter pal, the one who looked like Alfred E. Newman from *Mad* magazine, pulled up in his Pontiac Grand Am, blasting the demented non-music of Tom Waits, as if that might impress someone. For some reason, all of Daniel's friends thought Tom Waits was cool and clever; I, on the other hand, thought he sounded like a man who only sang while barfing.

Daniel strode like a prizefighter with a load in his pants down the walkway, chuckling like he didn't care. He paused at my mailbox and kicked it repeatedly, until it fell over. I'd get Lydia's dad to come over and fix it later; he was one of those men I dreamed of one day marrying—handy, devoted, calm, steady, and re-assuring as a lighthouse.

I waited until Daniel had been gone for twenty minutes before leaving my post at the window. I didn't want him coming back and doing something crazy. I needed to take a shower and get ready for tonight's concert—the Chimps were playing at the Whittier Sports Arena—and I had this fear that I'd be scrubbing away under the water when Daniel showed up again with a butcher's knife.

I shook myself. "Okay girl," I said to Juanga. "Let's find some clothes."

I laid all of the clothes out neatly on my bed, a habit of mine. I supposed that if I hadn't been a publicist I might have enjoyed a career dressing mannequins in a fancy department store window. I loved clothes, playing with clothes, and lately, thanks to the generosity of my real father and my job, I had plenty to choose from. Had the concert been a normal kind of affair, I would have dressed up more, but being a Chimps show, at the Whittier, I chose something subdued that could with-stand walking through a pile of bull corn. Blue jeans, a T-shirt and blazer, and hot-pink cowboy boots, tucked into the pants.

I locked all the doors before leaving the house, then walked through and made sure they were locked, *twice*. I tucked Juanga into her new pink-and-white polka-dot Penelope pet carrier, with the white leather handles—I wasn't about to leave the poor dear all alone here with Daniel lurking around—and activated the alarm.

I was thirty years old, and I didn't want to live alone anymore. I really wanted a husband. And a family. I was starting to think it would never happen for me.

I arrived at the Whittier Sports Arena at five, three hours before the Chimpances' concert was scheduled to begin. I walked Juanga in the parking lot, tucked her back into the Penelope, and stashed her on the square pink snuggle bed in the cor-ner of my office. "Be right back, snookie," I sang.

I had paperwork to sift through, and my boss, Benito Tower, wanted to talk to me about a few things. That's how he said it on my voicemail. "I want to talk to you about a few things." Plus, I had to meet Patsi Robles, the local Univision en-tertainment reporter who was coming to the show. The reporter was particularly interested in Filoberto, the potbellied lead singer, whom she described as "cute." I almost laughed when she said it, but didn't, of course. I still couldn't see why so many women threw themselves at the Chimps. Rappers, maybe. Rockers, definitely. But polka artists? I didn't know.

Benito Tower, twenty-seven, was younger than me, worth millions, and married with children. He'd been a parking attendant at the sports arena back in the days when its owners tried to make money with country music acts and monster truck rallies. A lifelong resident of Whittier, Benito listened to the music blasting from windows of East L.A. cars, and realized the arena might make more money booking ranchera, banda, and norteño concerts, and said so to the non-Hispanic white men who owned the venue.

At first they laughed at Benito, who was still a teenager at the time. But he kept at them. Finally, they agreed to let him have one night, to see what he could do. Benito booked none other than Pedro Negrete, my biological father. He advertised the concert on Spanish-language radio stations all over Southern California. He contracted a Mexican caterer for the show, knowing the hot dogs, hamburgers, and popcorn normally served there wouldn't much satisfy an audience of Mexican immigrants the way an assortment of tacos, burritos, and churros might. He got Western clothing stores with Spanish-language names to sell the tickets for him. The owners of the arena advised him to sell the tickets cheap, because, they said, "Those people won't buy a thirty-five-dollar ticket." Benito sold the tickets for $65 apiece. The concert sold out in three days.

From that day forward, Benito was allowed to book bands the owners of the arena had never heard of. Within two years, Benito, by then twenty years old, had saved enough money to buy the arena outright. Seven years later—or now—he was worth an estimated $20 million, and had expanded his empire to include management and international concert promotion. I admired his drive, but his success story still didn't make him a nice person.

In spite of his wealth, Benito still lived in Whittier, blocks from his parents. He was the father of four well-groomed little girls who always, it seemed to me, sat quietly in chairs in the office in red velvet dresses and black patent-leather shoes, smoothing the synthetic hair of tiny toy horses with miniature pink plastic brushes.

Benito did not hide his contempt for me, even though I was required to hide mine from him. He found me loud and disagreeable, chubby and sloppy, and told me as much. No one had ever said this kind of thing to me before. I was hardly loud or rude, but Benito seemed to think women should be half-naked, stacked, smiling, and completely silent, like the women "hostesses" on *Sábado Gigante*, his favorite television show. He said he tolerated my "abrasiveness" because it was important to the company, and said he valued me because with my "university degrees and white stepfather" I would know how to maneuver the Anglo world better than anyone else who worked there. And, he reminded me, he was deeply indebted to Papi Pedro for providing him with his first opportunity to prove himself in the concert promotions business.

"He didn't have to come here," Benito often told me, sometimes with a tear glimmering in his eye. "But he did. He came here and that made me a millionaire."

Still, I had a sense that Benito's empire was doomed. Benito Tower was loyal, and worked, to my horror, without contracts with most of his artists. "I admire these people," Benito said of his clients. "They're men of integrity. And so am I. A handshake is enough."

Tonight, I found Benito in a starched white shirt and navy-blue-and-red-striped tie, seated behind his huge, shiny dark-wood desk, tapping numbers into a calculator. The sports arena was somewhat dumpy, a dusty, weed-riddled place tucked, like most things east of the 101, between three or four different freeways. Yet Benito's office looked as though it had been plucked out of Santa Monica. Gold records lined the walls. Plants grew strong and green. Oriental rug covered the floors.

"Come in," Benito said with a dazzling wave of his diamond rings. "Sit down." He looked up and smiled broadly. "Wow," he said. "You look great. You almost look pretty."

Gee, thanks, you jerk, I thought.

He puffed on a cigar. The whole room stank of it. My lungs closed in on me, and I wheezed, wishing I'd brought my Coach bag and inhaler.

I lied, as usual. "You look good, too."

He licked his lips.

I hated to admit it, but there was something undeniably sexy about Benito. He was fat. He was corrupt. He was a mean person. But he was confident, with beautiful brown eyes. He was like a Mexican Bill Clinton. And even though I'd worried he would have another complaint to share with me—the last few had involved me messing up in catering the Chimpances' Texas shows (they wanted Perrier, not Pellegrino, small flour tortillas for their tacos, not corn, blah blah blah)—I soon realized Benito wanted to congratulate me for the success of Lydia's European tour, from which he had collected five percent.

"I've been going over the numbers and the press clippings," he told me with a grin. "They're amazing. You should be very proud of what you guys did over there."

"Thanks," I said. I actually blushed because I suddenly remembered a recent dream I'd had where Benito and I were having sex in a car wash. Why hadn't I remembered it until now? And what in tarnation was my subconscious doing *doing* Benito in a car wash?

"I just wanted to tell you I appreciate what a good job you're doing," he said.

"Thanks." I tried to push the sex dream out of my head. I was going to miss Daniel's body if not much else about him. Already I was obsessing about sex. Maybe I should have kept Daniel around for a while, like an old vibrator. No. No I shouldn't have.

Benito stood and held his hand out to me. "Again, good work."

As he had already shaken my hand minutes before, I grew suspicious. "Anything else?" I asked. He was hiding something.

Benito paced the office in his too-small, too-shiny tasseled loafers. "Actually, yes. One last thing."

"Okay."

"I got a call from a guy I know at the LAPD," he said. "He's a good friend from childhood, we grew up together. He said he heard something about the cops having a tip about Los Chimpances drug-running . . . or something . . . ridiculous like that."

I pretended to be surprised. Benito feigned shock as well. The Chimps? Selling drugs? The guys who sang, "*I ran from the cops across the desert, carrying the coke straight to your heart,* mujer"? No way!

"I know," he said. "It's ridiculous. They think that just because the guys sing about the drug life that they're involved in it. They're just out to persecute us Mexicans. I don't see no one arresting rappers."

I didn't think reminding him of all the rappers who'd gone to jail in the past year would make an impact.

He continued, "You know that, I know that. But my friend wanted me to let you know that the LAPD and the FBI and I don't know who else is following the boys."

I nodded solemnly. "Good to know. But they're wasting their time, aren't they?"

"Of course." Benito could not for the life of him make eye contact with me. He was lying.

"Everybody's out to get the Mexicans," I said. I didn't believe this, of course, but he did, and the situation called for a frontal assault.

"It's the truth," he said. "Especially if we have money, like me and you. They hate that."

Having been raised by a non-Hispanic white man who was the most wonderful human being I knew, I didn't share Benito's tendency to lump "gringos" all together in one neat, evil category. I smiled and listened. Best policy.

"They hate that we can have more money than them. I can tell you that from personal experience. They think that just because we have a lot of money it must have something to do with drugs. That's what they think of us Mexicans, that we're all low class. But they don't know shit."

"Ah." He was nothing if not high class, that Benito.

Then, he dropped the bomb. "If anything happens with them, you have to swear you knew nothing," he whispered, his eyes darting frantically around the room.

I balked. What was he trying to tell me? "You think something will happen, Benito?"

"I didn't say that. I said *if*."

"Okay." My heart began to race. "Honestly, Benito, I don't want to know. Please, sugar, don't tell me nothin' else. Okay? I don't want to be involved. Whatever it is, I don't want to know."

"Good girl." He inspected some of the trophies on a shelf for dust. "So, you ready for the show tonight?"

"I am."

"Are the boys ready?"

"I just called Filoberto at the Bellagio, and they're on their way."

"Great. I'll probably stick around for a while, but my oldest has a soccer game I have to go to." I had never known him to be an overly involved dad before.

Benito seemed really nervous, and shook my hand a *third* time. That was a record. His palm was damp as a car-wash rag. He guided me to the door.

"Remember," he said, putting a finger to his lip in the "shh" gesture. I shook my head and put my hands over my ears.

"Don't," I said. "Please. Keep it to yourself."

I trotted to my own office down the hall with a definite lump in my gut, and slammed the door.

"Pookie," I said to Juanga. "What we gonna do, sugar?" Her ears perked up and her tail wagged.

I sat at my desk, dropped my head into my hands, and resisted the urge to cry. Something bad was going to happen, and I didn't want to be around for it. I thought about things the Chimps might have said over the years that alluded to possible drug trafficking. Once, when Rafael, the bass drummer, was drunk and tired, he told me flat out that they ran a drug ring that brought them triple the money their music career brought them. That blew my mind at the time, as they had sold more than 10 million albums to date and consistently sold out large arena shows.

"But how much money do you really need?" I'd asked. "Is it worth the risk?"

He laughed and pretended it was all a joke. That had been my big mistake. I'd believed it was a joke, even though he kept talking and told me that the drug business came first, before they hit the big time musically, and that they had just sort of never given it up. "Once you're part of the family, you can't really leave," he'd said with a sad shrug. He'd laughed then, and given me a brotherly shove, like it was a joke. I'd looked the other way and pretended I hadn't heard a word.

I lifted my head and looked around the office. My voicemail light flashed on the phone. I made a few phone calls, including a new one to Filoberto, to make sure everything was running on time. The boys had just had dinner in the hotel restaurant, and were about to pile into various limos. I reminded him of the Univision interview, and tried to see if there was anything different in his voice. There wasn't. Same old Filoberto, pompous and cracking homophobic jokes like they were going out of style, which, in Mexico, they most certainly weren't.

The sun was starting to set. All concerts at the Whittier started no later than eight P.M., in order to accommodate families. And in fact almost all of the people who attended concerts at the venue came in large familial clusters that included grandparents and babies. That was part of the Mexican music equation that people like Daniel's fat bastard friend Ross, who were forever trying to tap the market, failed to grasp. We Mexicans traveled in family packs, and we rarely used babysitters. Children were welcome everywhere. Benito had recently purchased a small series of animal pens for a petting zoo inside the arena gates, and I was fairly certain the Whittier was the only concert venue in Los Angeles equipped with a full, modern playground.

Patsi arrived exactly at the time she had said she would arrive, dressed, as I had anticipated, in the sort of bright, tight, revealing clothes worn by newswomen on the Spanish-language stations.

The camera crew set up their equipment in the green room while Patsi primped and preened in front of the mirror, bending over the small makeup table, it seemed, with the intention of revealing just enough of her admittedly spectacular rear end to give the men in the room heart failure. The guys from the band showed up several minutes later. The Chimps were dressed in the clothes they wore when they weren't on stage: jeans, T-shirts, and Nike sneakers. Several of them were reasonably handsome, I thought, in spite of giant moustaches and belt buckles bearing their names. Dilberto. Dagoberto. Norberto. I imagined taking one or two 'bertos into one of the arena's bathrooms and getting it on in a stall. The fantasy was fleeting, and I laughed at my own dirty mind. What was going on? I had *never* fantasized about a 'berto before. Must be the new freedom from Daniel, I thought. The ovaries were celebrating.

Assistants carried the Chimps' concert attire in clear plastic bags. It was the usual, humiliatingly cowboy baroque. Tonight's outfits—the boys always matched— consisted of turquoise skin-tight designer jeans, gold snakeskin cowboy boots, and black leather jackets with long red fringe. Oh, and big Mexican belt buckles, of course, and white cowboy hats.

Patsi flirted with the men in the band, who enjoyed the attention in the weary way of married, oversexed men who are constantly propositioned by women with ulterior motives involving money or drugs. She asked fun, harmless questions, such as, "Which of you is the sexiest?" or "What do you look for in a woman?" In-offensive, classically Mexican entertainment-reporter questions. Nothing hard-hitting, ever, and certainly nothing about drug-running. I believed this type of reporting was in fact classier in its way than the kind of "journalism" done by Daniel and his ilk. I couldn't imagine how Patsi could not have heard the rumors about this band. But she didn't think it mattered, ultimately, because their main purpose in life was to play music for parties. The Latin press in the U.S. was not hell-bent on knocking celebrities off their thrones the way the English-language press seemed to be. In fact, they were more hell-bent on complimenting the beje-sus out of them, no matter what.

When the interview ended, I left the boys to dress in peace, even though I would have liked to stay and watch them take their clothes off. (What was wrong with me?) I climbed the back stairs to the press box and looked down on the sta-dium, which was quickly filling with families typically headed by men in black Wrangler pants and white cowboy hats. I looked out over the parking lot at the as-sortment of immigrant-mobiles, mostly older cars lovingly tended to and with at least one infant car seat in each one. Because there was a uniformity to the vehi-cles driven by fans of the Chimps, I immediately noticed the four black Ford Tau-ruses parked together near the back of the lot. The glass was dark in them, and they had large antennae.

Police. Undercover police.

I strained my eyes on the surrounding streets and saw several patrol cars, more than was normal for this area. I noticed a couple more of the black Tauruses, too. My heart raced. Had Benito warned me for a reason? Had he suddenly decided to be a great soccer game–going dad tonight, or was he avoiding something he had been tipped was about to happen? And if he knew, why didn't he tell me? Did he think I'd take the fall?

I ran back down the stairs to the green room, hoping to warn the Chimps, to see if they could prevent any trouble, but I was too late. They'd already headed out into the outdoor, hay-strewn "backstage" area behind the makeshift stage on the rodeo grounds. I walked quickly past the Univision crew, hoping not to raise suspicions with running, and caught the guys just as they opened the gate to head out to the stairs leading to the stage. The crowd roared as they caught a glimpse of the famous bad boys of norteño music.

"Filoberto," I called. I motioned for him to come back to where I was, out of sight. Filoberto turned to face me. *"Que quieres?"* he asked. Annoyed. Filoberto was always annoyed by me. Like Benito, he did not believe they needed an Americana, as he called me, publicizing their affairs. He allowed me to do so because Benito, who he viewed as his real manager, insisted.

I pushed my way through the Chimps and whispered in his ear, in Spanish, "We're surrounded by cops."

Filoberto smiled. "Why would we care if we were surrounded by cops?"

"Are you kidding?" I asked.

Filoberto affected the macho face and stance I had seen so many times. "No, I'm not kidding. Los Chimpances del Norte have nothing to hide," he cried with a pointed, nearly matador-like flourish of the hands. "Let them come. What do I care? We are Chimps." He pounded his chest like an ape.

"This is no time for manly denial, dear," I said.

"And what could we do, anyway?" he hissed, his breath hot and smelling of beer. "Run? That's not suspicious, right? The best thing we can do is carry on as normal."

He turned from me and walked through the gate to face the cheering masses. The other Chimps followed behind him, unaware of the conversation their leader had just had with their manager, who now muttered, *"Cabrón, hijo de la gran puta."*

I skulked back to the green room, only to find it filled with men in DEA uniforms and business suits, some with guns displayed, others rifling through assorted instrument cases belonging to the beastly boys in the band.

"Can I help you?" I asked, smiling as if there were nothing unusual about this situation. "How's everybody doing tonight?" I did my best good ole girl.

The tallest one with, I figured, the deepest voice, produced a badge and a search warrant. He identified himself as an agent with the Drug Enforcement Agency and asked who I was.

"My name's Alexis López," I said, still smiling. "I work for Tower Entertainment."

"Do you work with the Chimpanzees de el Norte?" he asked. He had a strong Texas drawl, so we had something in common. I watched as another agent broke open Dofiberto's accordion case, removing several large foil bundles and two smaller clear plastic bags full of white powder. Another agent located a pistol inside a drum case.

"Sometimes." My jaw dropped in horror as he pulled a machine gun from the case. "I handle press conferences and stuff like that. What's going on?"

"You mean to tell us you worked with this band, heard their lyrics, and had no idea they were involved in drug trafficking?"

"Well, my Spanish ain't that great," I lied. "I'm from Dallas. I just came out here a little while ago to work in the office here. I work with a lot of artists, and they sing about a lot of things none of them actually do. I never thought about it, honestly." I opened my eyes in wide innocence.

The agent in charge checked a notebook. "Your name is here," he said. My heart pounded. He looked at me and, it seemed, smiled slyly to himself as I squirmed. "But . . ." He paused, with a half-smile. But? But? I waited, strained smile on my face. "But, it's on the innocuous list."

"The *innocuous* list?"

"We have a list of names a reliable source provided us with," he said. "We have names of people in the organization who probably know what's going on, and names of those who probably don't have a clue. You're one of the ones they think won't have a clue."

"Gee, thanks."

He laughed. Were drug enforcement agents supposed to laugh? He was cute, too. I imagined, for a split second, what it would be like to be on my knees in front of him, his fly down. Marcella had done it. Why not me? Down, libido!

"Who's on the *non*-innocuous list?" I asked.

"Can't say," the agent said. "But I would advise you to remove yourself from the premises, if you can. And don't come back. Ever."

"What about my job?"

The agents laughed. The deep-voiced one asked another agent, "Yo, man, did we get Tower yet?"

"Yeah. They got him on his way to Mexico, at the border. Bart's on his way back here with him."

I gasped. "Benito? He said he was going to his daughter's soccer game!"

"Unless his daughter plays for the Cruz Azul, I'd say Mr. Tower lied to you," said one of the agents.

"Miss Lopez," the head agent said. "I'll tell you what's about to happen here. We're about to go out on that stage after this concert and arrest your boys for coke trafficking and a whole list of other offenses relating to money-laundering, prostitution, firearms, and a bunch of bad stuff."

"The boys did all that?" I asked.

"Yes, ma'am. We've been following them for a while. We've also got your boss coming back here in a few minutes, and we're going to have a few questions for him, too. A lot of questions, actually."

"Holy cow."

"Right. But you seem like a nice young woman. We have no reason to think you had anything to do with any of this. So, if I were in your shoes, I think this might be a good time to quit."

"Quit?"

"Quit your job. Skeedaddle. Look in the Help Wanteds, find something else. Quit hanging out with Mexicans."

My skin crawled. *I'm a Mexican,* I wanted to say. But I smiled, as usual, and nodded as if he'd said something quite sensible. "Are you serious about leaving?"

"Well, if you want to stick around and defend these clowns, be my guest. If you want to get tangled up in something complicated—and I am here to tell you it ain't pretty—go ahead. Knock yourself out. But if you want to get on with your life, you know, get yourself good and out of here."

"Now?"

"Yep."

"Is this a setup? Can I get in more trouble if I leave or something? Because I swear to you I didn't know anything about any of this." I opened my eyes as wide and innocent as they'd go, and blinked as if I was fixin' to cry.

"No setup. Just advice, Miss."

One of the other agents looked up from where he'd found a supply of ammunition stashed in the body of a guitar. "You should go, miss," he said. "We're not joking around. Am-scray. Va-moose. Adios."

I looked around. "Can I get some stuff out of my office?"

"Later," the head agent said. "This is a bad time to do that."

"Golly."

"Bye-bye now."

I ran to my office and grabbed Juanga, her tote and bed, my photos and plants, then hurried down the long hall to the box-office area. Where security guards had been, drug agents sat. A fleet of black Tauruses sat outside. I tiptoed past, half expecting them to stop me and slap on the cuffs. But they didn't. They didn't give me or my doggie a second look. Even in those pink boots! I made no impression?

Not a good recipe for getting a husband.

It didn't hit me until I pulled onto the freeway that I was out of a job. Benito was probably in handcuffs. My main moneymaking band was on its way to prison. And Lydia was officially on the Tower roster, and I, stupidly, had signed Marcella to the Tower roster, even though I was her sole manager and agent, so I didn't know what this would do to their careers. Basically, I might have no income. Papi Pedro gave me things, but rarely cash. My daddy and momma didn't think it was right to provide financial assistance to children older than twenty-five. Papi Pedro would probably help if I asked, so I'd never starve. I knew that much. But still. It was disgraceful to be thirty years old, with an MBA, and be taking money from a parent, even an estranged and famous parent who wouldn't notice the money was gone.

I thought of calling my Dallas friends to tell them what was happening, but I didn't think they'd understand why or how I'd become involved with such unsavory business partners. I dialed Marcella on my cell phone, and told her what was going on. I tried not to sound panicked. She did not seem concerned for me, or for herself, and told me to take what was happening as a sign, and use this opportunity to start my own business.

"You don't need Benito around to be my manager," she said. "From the little I saw of him, we're better off without the fat fuck."

"Marcella!"

"Sorry. No, wait. I'm *not* sorry. We *are* better off without the fat fuck. Start your own company. What's stopping you? You talk shit about it all the time."

"Marcella! I can't just *do* that."

"Why not? Benito did it, and he had a high school education. You have a master's, in business. I don't see the problem."

"I don't know. I can't just start a business. You need money for that."

"You know people with money, Alexis. Don't you? You get investors, you make their money back. It's not brain surgery."

It made sense, what she said. The entertainment business was almost completely male-dominated, and this led to stupidity at just about every level you could imagine. But starting your own business required a lot of organization and confidence. I told her so. She reminded me that I had all of those things. I reminded her that I didn't.

"Yes, you do, dumbshit," she said.

"Watch your language," I said. "You really think so?"

"Fuck yes, you dumbshit."

"Thanks."

"You should manage all sorts of artists," she said. "Not just Mexican polka bands. In fact, I'd recommend you get out of that shit altogether. What about actors? I know some."

"But I don't know anything about acting," I said.

"This is where your little Miss Manners act comes to an end, okay? You have to have balls in business, Alexis. You've got the brains, now you need the fucking balls, man."

"Please watch your language, Marcella. You're giving me an asthma attack."

"Hey, where are you? What are you doing right now?"

"I'm about to get on the 60. I'm going home. I'm so tired. I broke up with Daniel today."

"Thank God."

"Yeah. I just want to rest."

"Okay, focus on the road, and call me when you get home. We'll figure this thing out. Nico can handle all the paperwork for your new business. He's good."

"Really?"

"You do a business plan. You know how to do a business plan, don't you? I mean, after an MBA you better fucking know how to do one, or you should get your money back from SMU."

"I can do a business plan. Please stop cursing."

"Great. Do one. Talk to your people, I'll talk to some people. We'll get the money. It's not like we need a lot of equipment, right? A space, phones, computers, fax, copier."

"I can do it out of my house."

"You should have an office."

"I guess so."

"Let's have coffee with some people. How about Lydia? She'll need you, with or without Tower. So there's two moneymaking artists already. We'll get you a business of your own, up and running."

Marcella hung up on me, as usual.

I was starting to almost like it.

pulled onto the 60 and began zooming westbound. Traffic was light, for Southern California. I turned on the AM news station, paranoid, to listen to the top stories. National news about a school sniper in Michigan, Martha Stewart in trouble for something new. International news about possible U.S. military action in Pakistan. Then, local news. Gang shooting in East Hollywood, broken sewer line off Venice Beach. Nothing about Tower Entertainment.

That was another bonus of working for Latino companies in California; the mainstream media more or less ignored you, no matter how much you misbehaved. To chronicle a Hispanic company's criminal activity would be seen as racist in the modern English-language media, which preferred to run feature photos of five-year-olds in Cinco de Mayo costumes.

I took the interchange to the southbound 5, and listened as the news repeated itself. Then, as I was about to take the 710 westbound to the 405, which would take me home, the traffic report informed me of a "sig alert," or complete backup, on the 710. A tanker truck had overturned and spilled olive oil across the freeway, the reporter shouted through the whacking of helicopter blades, and there was no telling when the mess would be cleared up. I thought briefly of running into the middle of the spill and licking up as much grease as possible, but decided against it. The distraught announcer advised that no one attempt to take the 710 at all for the rest of the night.

"Great, just great," I fumed aloud.

Maybe it was bad karma for my bad attitude. Whatever it was, I would now be stuck in slow-moving traffic on the 5, all the way into Orange County. I'd have to drive all the way down to Laguna Hills before I could head north again on the 405. It was only eight P.M.; I figured I'd get home by midnight. I fished for doggie treats in the glove box and let Juanga slurp a few out of my hand. "It's gonna be a long night, baby."

The traffic grew even slower once I reached Anaheim. In fact, it hardly moved at all. The repetitive news was starting to give me a headache, so I turned it off. That's when I noticed that I was surrounded by cars with their windows down, with rap music blaring from them. Rap and some kind of conga music with trilling flutes. Some cars had Cuban flags—I think they were Cuban, either that or Puerto Rican, I got them confused all the time—waving from them. Others had Mexican flags. I saw a few flags I didn't recognize. What was going on here?

Young, fashionably hip people hung out of the windows of the cars, singing to one another. I rolled down my window to get a better sense of the music. The kids looked like they might be Mexican, but the music didn't sound Mexican at all. It sounded Caribbean, and also hip-hop. I liked it, but felt a little ashamed that, as a Latin music publicist, I didn't know who it was or what this concert was—and it had been on a competing night with mine.

I checked the rearview mirror, and couldn't believe my eyes. The flags waved from cars for miles, it seemed. What the heck was going on? And why wasn't the traffic moving? Was it some kind of holiday, or a parade? Gosh, just my luck, right?

I craned my neck in search of the fastest lane. It was the far right. I nudged my car through the singing, joyous masses, almost running over a man who stood on the shoulder of the freeway holding a big piece of cardboard with red-marker words scrawled across it. I read the sign, then read it again, to make sure I got it right.

"VLADIMIR TICKETS $100"

A *Vladimir* scalper? *Another* Vladimir? Or was this the *same* Vladimir the hairy Russian had talked up at the Ashram? Did that mean the flags I didn't recognize were Russian flags? Holy cow, I thought. All these people are going to see *Vladimir of Glendale?* That couldn't be, could it? He was Russian, wasn't he? And old?

It *had* to be the same guy, right?

I dug through my handbag to find the tickets. I still had them, a miracle. I tilted them into the light from the dashboard and read. Vladimir was playing tonight, at the Arrowhead Pond. He was opening for Cypress Hill, a hugely famous rap act, and Orishas, a trendy Cuban rap group I had heard before.

I was so embarrassed. I'd been so snooty-pants I'd never bothered to look at the tickets. This Vladimir was opening for famous people. And Marcella thought I had what it would take to be a good manager? I thought not. Lydia was looking to make a move into hip-hop and R&B, and here was a guy wanting to record with her and he was doing well enough to open for Cypress Hill at the Arrowhead Stadium. Oops. I had assumed this Vladimir, whoever he was, would be performing at some Podunk belly-dance bar in an out-of-the-way corner of the town; I'd never imagined he would be playing at the largest concert arena in Orange County.

I checked out the Vladimir fans in the cars around me. I rolled down my windows to get a better sense of the music. Juanga stuck her head out the window and panted her approval. A car zoomed past with a Vladimir poster taped to the side window. He didn't look old at *all*. He didn't even look Russian. And, come to think of it, he looked familiar. Really familiar. I strained to see the poster better, but the car was gone.

My Cadillac joined the throng of automobiles exiting at the Arrowhead Pond ramp. What did I have to lose, I asked myself. I had tickets. I needed to do something halfway fun. I was scared to go home and the traffic sucked anyway. Burian had said Vladimir needed a manager. He had a lot of fans, apparently, and his music wasn't that bad, if that was the music I heard coming from the cars. Maybe he had some money. And suddenly I couldn't be picky about clients. He wasn't as old as I'd thought, and now, shoot, now I didn't seem to have a job of any kind anymore. I would have even considered an old Russian singer. A young one had all sorts of possibilities.

I parked in a rapidly filling lot at the stadium, left the window open a crack for Juanga after letting her pee in the grass, kissed her and promised I'd be back soon, and got out of my car to join the mass of perfumed and excited young bodies moving toward the arena. I was dressed all wrong, a riding-class preppy in the middle of a rap show, and got the dirty looks to prove it. The front windows of the Pond were full of posters featuring Vladimir's face. I stopped in my pink cowboy-booted tracks and stared, and my jaw dropped for the second time today.

It was *him*. *Him*, him. The gorgeous guy from the Starbucks, the sexy Cuban poet guy who crashed into my car! Vladimir! He stared back at me from the posters, seductive and gorgeous as before, but more so because he was on a poster and that meant he was famous or at least sort of famous. Vladimir, the guy's name had been *Vladimir*. Of course. I should have been able to put two and two together, as my momma would say, but I hadn't. I'd even told him about the guy at the Ashram telling me about some awful old Russian singer. He'd had such an amused look on his face when I said it! Now I knew why. Oh, gosh, how embarrassing. This was the kind of gaff not even an apology card could fix. The Boris guy told me Vladimir was a big star, that he loved Mexican music. But I didn't listen.

I stared at the sexy poster, and remembered how Goyo had told me he thought I was cute. He'd even asked me to call him, and I never did, thinking I couldn't face his rejection if he hadn't meant it. I had completely convinced myself that he had flirted with me as a way of getting me not to demand too much of him as far as repairs, which might have still been true, I didn't know. I'd let the insurance company deal with the whole thing.

"What in tarnation is wrong with me?" I cried, standing and staring at Vladimir, the Cuban musician.

"You gonna move?" someone asked. I turned to see a long line of people shifting and jockeying behind me. Oh, dear. I was blocking one of the entrances, standing in my trance, staring at Vladimir/Goyo.

"Sorry," I said. "Pardon me."

"Just go," someone else shouted. "We don't have all night! The show's about to start."

The ticket-taker ripped my ticket and I soon found my body moving in a giant pulsating stream of bodies, toward the open doors of the arena. My seat was very good, close to the front. The one next to me remained empty, as I held the ticket in my glove box. However, three seats down sat another familiar man. Burian.

"Alexis López!" he cried, delighted.

"Hi, Burian," I said, embarrassed. He was seated with two young men and a young woman, presumably his children, and his kind-eyed wife, a woman shaped like a gerbil, with gerbil hands.

"I am so glad you got un-busy," he said.

"Well, I thought," I stammered, and didn't finish the sentence. I didn't know what to say.

"You see? Many peoples here!" Burian shouted over the din of the crowd. I turned to look at the stadium, and it was full.

"I'm sorry I doubted you," I managed to stammer.

"Not at all," Burian said. He then introduced me to his family, all of whom were very warm and nice, even though he identified me with, "This is the woman I told you about from the Ashram. She real American-style bitch!"

The lights went down, and blue lasers lashed the stage. A heavy reggae beat started to pound out, and the crowd roared, as if they recognized it. The reggae mixed with a classic Cuban beat I recognized but couldn't name, and flutes fluttered out over the top. A man's voice roared out, faster and faster, chanting: *Libre, libre, libre!* Percussion, flutes, it was like classic Cuban music, but with incredible modern hip-hop and rap mixed in. I'd never heard anything like it.

Then, there he was, rising out of the floor with his arms spread wide at his sides. He wore the cowboy hat and everything. He wore jeans with a large white T-shirt bearing the words CUBA LIBRE in large black-and-red letters. He was as cute as I remembered, and then some, because I could see he had an inner charisma, a natural ability to glow from the stage, that few people possessed. He was cuter than Timi Martinez, the big Puerto Rican crossover star. Vladimir. He was flanked by dancers with sexy little bikinis, and when he shook his hips with them, during a thrilling conga solo, I wanted to faint.

"Thank you," he said simply. Then, in Spanish, "*Grácias, mi gente!*"

Then, rather than launching into whatever it was he was going to do, sing or rap I supposed, he stepped to the side and an older man with a large, two-headed drum strapped around his neck took the spotlight, beating the drum with sticks. The band segued into an African-sounding beat.

"The *batá*," Vladimir said into the microphone. He held his hands in prayer before his chest. "The holiest drum in the Afro-Cuban tradition."

As the drummer played, a large image of a beautiful woman with laughing green eyes appeared on the screen behind him. She held the same kind of drum, and appeared to be playing it. Her eyes were the same color as mine.

"This concert is dedicated to Caridad Herédia," he said. "She's the best *batá* player I've ever known. In Cuba, they still say women shouldn't play the *batá*. But she plays anyway. She stayed behind in Cuba, playing with boys, and the government is after her for it, and for being associated with me. I ask everyone here to pray for her safety."

The band started to play very softly, and the images changed, showing more pictures of Caridad Herédia. She had dark red hair, perfectly straight, and long. Her skin was dark, almost black, but her features looked Chinese. Her eyes were green, like mine. She was the most stunning and unusual-looking woman I had ever seen, other than Marcella. I recognized her from the collection of photos in Vladimir's car. My heart sank as I realized this man's heart was heavily occupied.

The music slowly began to gain volume, and it sped up. The reggae came back, and it got louder and louder until Caridad's photos were replaced on the big screen behind the stage with an image of the island of Cuba with a white dove superimposed over the top.

"*Libre, libre, libre,*" Vladimir began to chant, again. The crowd screamed and joined the chant. The dancers broke into a complicated routine, with Vladimir joining in every so often. He danced well, moved well, and I couldn't help feeling incredible excitement. I felt sexual excitement, but also managerial, business-in-the-making excitement. This man was a gosh-darn star, in every sense of the word. He could be a superstar.

I leaned over to Burian and asked, "How long has he been in this country?"

"About one years," Burian yelled out. "My brother fight with his uncle in Angola war."

"Wow," I said.

Vladimir began to sing, and rap, combining the two. The song, in Spanish, was about freedom—religious, political, and social freedom. The words came in clever, incessant waves, rhythmic, hypnotic, the rhymes distant and surprising at times, words that made me laugh out loud. He was a poet, just as he'd said, but a hip-hop, Cuban poet. A rapper. He'd laughed when I seemed surprised that there were rappers in Cuba, and when I'd said Daniel dressed like a rapper. It made sense now.

The first song ended, and he stood at the edge of the stage smiling. An American flag unfurled over his head from the stage, and next to it, a Cuban one, with the red triangle for the star. Red, Cuban; blue, Puerto Rican. I would never forget that again. I fell in love with him, right then and there. Even if he was taken, even if he loved that annoyingly brave, maddeningly talented, infuriatingly stunning woman in the photographs. We had no control over what our hearts did, but I sure wished we did.

"Long live freedom," Vladimir shouted as the piano broke into a montuno pattern for the next number and people began to dance in the aisles.

"*Que viva Cuba libre!*"

MARCELLA

t was my birthday and my heart pounded so hard I felt dizzy. I snatched the keys from the towering, lanky delivery boy—a butterscotch Labrador of a youth with gleaming white teeth—and smiled.

"Thanks," I said.

I yanked up on the spaghetti straps on my black Cosabella baby tank, making sure too much of me wasn't hanging out.

"I saw you in the paper," said the delivery boy to my breasts, with a smile that said he really and truly thought I might drag him inside and suck his little dick. "A *lot* of you."

The idiotic *Cristina* magazine photos of my boobs were literally everywhere. Alexis thought it was ultimately going to help my career—and the *Bod Squad* producers agreed. The ratings for the show had shot up as soon as the photos came out. But I didn't need this shit. Especially literally in my own front yard.

"Listen, asshole," I said. He stared in shock. "Those pictures were *personal*, sold for a shitload of cash as a parting fuck-you by Ryan Fuckwad, my idiot exboyfriend, a self-loving man whose conceit was so epic he simply could not believe he'd bored me nearly to death."

"Sorry," said the delivery boy. "I didn't know."

I did a loop of the car, making sure surf-boy here hadn't scratched it on the drive over.

"I think you need to chill," said the boy. "You'll have a heart attack stressing so bad."

"Yeah, thanks, Freud, everyone thinks they've got good advice."

"My name's Lance," he said, confused. The quote came onto the cue card of my brain before I could stop it: "*It is dangerous to be sincere unless you are also stupid.*" George Bernard Shaw, one of my favorite minds.

"Well, *Lance*, how about you stop talking and let me look the merchandise over, okay?"

Advice. Even Nico had weighed in on the tittie shots, and tried to comfort me by reminding me that sexcapades and scandal had made Paris Hilton a major-league star. I took no comfort in this whatsoever. I wanted to be vapid Paris Hilton only slightly less than I wanted to be vapid Carmen Electra, and I wanted to be either of these ladies only slightly less than I wanted to be tortured.

"Looks fine," I said to the boy, about the car.

"You sure do," he said, thinking he was clever.

I hadn't worn a bra today, which is not unusual on a Saturday morning at home for most women, but which butterscotch the human puppy seemed to have taken as an invitation of some sort. I wanted him to leave, as is the usual course of action with delivery boys who've succeeded in delivering, but he stayed, staring, panting.

Then, zap, just like that, the prep school memory popped up, a line from Socrates, of all things: "*The dog is a watcher, and in this point of view is not the noble youth very like a well-bred dog?*"

Dogboy lingered. What did he want? A tip? Hadn't I given the dealership enough money already? Though *non*-paternal male attention was *usually* a positive thing in my life, right now I wanted to be alone. It was my *house*, after all, my *sanctuary*—and a Saturday morning. But butterscotch lingered, hoping for a peep show. Fuckwad. Instinctively, I checked my belly button ring, made sure the black low-riding crop terry pants hadn't slipped too far down, you know, *plumber*-crack down. Nothing was showing that shouldn't have been, but he gaped and gurgled as if I were nude. He just couldn't get over his great luck.

"It's an awesome car," he called out, ever hopeful.

"I'd like to be alone with it now, if you don't mind," I said.

"Yeah," he said. But he didn't budge.

The hot white Los Angeles sunshine flashed off his teeth, and he stuffed his giant hands, ogre hands, into the pockets of his wrinkled, baggy cargo shorts, no doubt bought at a store where angry-boy music blasted, posters featured models wearing nothing but goose bumps, and teenagers, the world's most susceptible and unforgiving market, routinely got ripped the hell off. He took his hands out again, fiddled with the bleached hairs on his tanned knuckles, like he expected something. Because he *did* expect something; they all did, men. Sex, compliments, more sex, more compliments, the occasional backrub, the frequent blowjob, a woman who didn't think too much of herself or too little of him. A woman who laughed, even when the man's jokes weren't funny.

"I'm not giving you a tip," I called out. "So you can go surf now."

"Why not?" He looked crushed.

"Why not? I'll tell you why not. Because you talked to my tits instead of my face."

He shrugged.

"Sign here, please," he said. He shoved the clipboard at me fearfully, but still could not take his eyes off my boobs. Fine. I didn't care. Today, of all days, I could live with it.

"Thanks, Dulcinda," he said.

"That's the name of my character on TV," I snapped. "I have a real name. It's on the form you just asked me to sign. Try Hooked on Phonics. Worked for me."

"Bitch," he muttered as he shuffled away toward the curb.

" 'Talk sense to a fool and he calls you foolish,' " I called out. "That's Euripides."

I smiled. Nice, like college, was overrated. Nice, as any sweet little squirrel knew, got your sweet little ass run the fuck *over*.

I turned to face my gift. Ohhhh, *yeah*. She *was* beautiful, shiny and black, a work of art, two-door, rounded like a woman's body, turbo-charged, a 552-horsepower machine. And it was the car voted most beautiful in all the world, by the French, no less. Even Mère might have approved.

A Bentley Continental GT. And we weren't talking those old, stodgy, boxy Bentleys. We were talking smooth, sleek, sexy as a Porsche in a *thong* Bentley. A woman's Bentley. Mine, all mine.

After all the upgrades, I'd paid almost $175 grand for this baby. Or, rather, I had financed that much. So my debt was quickly approaching that of a small nation. I knew I could have built a condo for a homeless family instead, or I could have started a foundation. That's what Alexis said. She thought I should have settled for a Lexus or Mercedes, put the rest of the money to good use that would have brought in good press. She didn't see the sense in a Bentley, when people were going hungry. But a *Bentley*. A *brand-new* Bentley. What did Alexis know?

With her humanitarianism, I didn't know how the girl could continue to call herself a Republican. And with my selfishness, I didn't know how I could continue to call myself a Democrat.

As I often did when I didn't want to feel guilty about something, I called my sociopathic brother Nicolás, who worked as a defense lawyer for Belgian Ecstasy dealers, tobacco magnates, eerily attractive Icelandic serial killers, and other assorted fashionable, high-profile international riffraff. I dug through the Prada bag for my phone, flipped it open, and hit speed-dial number one.

"*Dímelo,*" he answered, trying to sound like a street tough. Since when did little Nico sound so authoritative?

"Where are you?" I asked.

"San Pedro de Marcoris, hey *princesa,*" he replied.

He was back in the Dominican Republic, where our father was born and raised, where our grandparents still lived, where we'd summered since childhood, and where the Belgian Ecstasy lords were at the moment based, probably because it was warmer than Belgium and had better baseball.

I heard ice cubes rattle in a glass near the mouthpiece, heard him blow air out of his mouth as if smoking, which he likely was. He said he wanted to quit, but he never really tried. We shared this particular vice, Nico and I, smoking. Hearing him smoke made me want to, so I rummaged through the Prada bag for my Capris and lighter. As I lit up, I heard the tinny plucked strings of a *bachata* guitar churning in the background on the phone. I inhaled deeply, savoring the instant jolt of nicotine to my system. Nico and I had both hated the workingman's *bachata* growing up, but both rather enjoyed it now, with something bordering on nostalgia, especially when we've had a glass or two of Papa's homemade, sun-brewed Mabí.

"Tell me something good about my beautiful Bentley, *hermanito,*" I said. We'd grown up with three languages, my brother and I, but we didn't usually use French with each other for some reason. Some reason named Mother, to be precise. She was no less dismal toward him than she was toward me.

"You got it?" He gulped and chomped ice.

"Uh-huh."

"Congratulations." I heard him kiss someone. Sloppy, slurpy. Guh-*rohs.*

"*Mira,* Casanova. I just need a quote," I said.

It was a game of ours, remembering things we'd read or heard. Our father and mother were both great book lovers and both had incredible memories; all three of us kids were the same way, for better or worse. Photographic memory was a mighty fine attribute to help you ace tests, and a *terrible* attribute in a family of hotheads who held grudges like Swiss bank accounts.

He continued chomping on ice as he talked. "Okay, here: '*Living with a conscience is like driving a car with the brakes on.*'"

"Who said *that?*" I asked with a laugh.

"Budd Schulberg."

"Who the fuck is that?"

"Budd Schulberg, the writer. I gotta go, *princesa,*" he said. "Duty calls. Don't crash. *No te chóques.* I'll call you later."

And he hung up on me.

I slid my body into the driver's seat as if the car were a pool of cool water. The beige interior smelled of fresh, clean, expensive leather. I flicked the ash from the end of the Capri out the window, and took another drag. The wood shone like glass. All felt cool and smooth to the touch. Who else did I have to be happy for me? Collis, my former best friend, did not return my calls anymore.

I called Alexis and sang, *"Do you wanna ri-ide in my Bentley, girl? Tell you what I'm gonna do. If you wanna ri-ide in my Bentley,* chica, *you best have your Texan ass ready by two."*

Alexis laughed. "I take it you got the car?" Was that a fake laugh? I couldn't tell. Alexis was a good actress, I decided. Almost as good as me.

"Yes, ma'am, I did." Ma'am was one of the many Texan words that popped into my mouth when I spoke with Alexis.

"That's terrific, sugar," said Alexis. "Did you remember that you invited *Olivia?*" Alexis panted in a hoarse whisper.

Olivia, Alexis's newest project. Alexis collected pals like she collected hand-bags. She was too nice, in some ways. In exchange for her having saved my life during an earthquake, Alexis expected me to take Olivia cruising in my new Bent-ley, so that we could all be good friends. But for all her confidence in Olivia, I was not sure I wanted her around. Olivia struck me as morose, boring even, and Alexis, like most literary critics, seemed to mistake morose and boring for genius.

Alexis apparently didn't realize everyone and their grandmother in L.A. be-lieved they were screenwriters. Alexis, rather, believed Olivia was "grounded," which she thought would be a good thing for my psyche and my image. That was the word. Grounded. To Alexis, grounded meant stable. To me, it meant unable to leave my room.

"Alexis," I whined. "Do I haftooooo?"

"Olivia needs to get out, and you need to be around more normal people. I'm sure she's looking forward to it. She's not from big money like you; she's probably never been in such a nice car. But it's entirely your choice."

"Yeah. Okay, Alexis. Bye."

"Wait, Marcella?"

"What?"

"I know you don't like her, but Olivia is special."

"So are Jerry's kids, but I'm not bringing *them*."

I hung up. My phone rang instantly. It was Alexis.

"You wait for the other person to say good-bye," she stated. "It's basic manners, Marcella."

"I know."

"Okay, hon'," she said. "Good-bye, Marcella."

I hung up on her again.

While I waited for Alexis and Olivia to arrive at my house for an afternoon of high-style So Cal cruising, I called *Mère* at her gallery, to brag a little and, I hoped, glean at least a semi-compliment from her, some sense from her that she recognized I'd done well at last.

"So, I got my Bentley." I paused. Even through the phone I could feel her eyes close in icy disapproval. "Guess I'm a real star now, huh?"

"Star," she snorted into the phone, a laugh. "What is that word, 'star'? *Tu me fais chier.* 'Star.' Please. It is so *American.*"

She spat out the last word like rotten foie gras.

"But *you* were a movie star," I reminded my mom.

"I was an *actress*," she corrected me. "Actresses have no need of this *stardom.*"

Of course. *Her* movies had been deep and meaningful, even when she, you know, took off her *shirt* and wore huge fake eyelashes and these awful patchwork floppy hats that made her look like a cartoon sunflower. *Her* films were directed by men like Jean-Luc Godard, films that dealt with politics and utopia and got seen in the U.S. mostly on college campuses. Boring-ass movies, in other words, pardon my . . . French.

"You *were* a star, *Mère*," I insisted. "Don't deny it." I thought that last bit might cheer her up, make her like me, but it didn't.

"*Peut-être*," she hissed. "But you see? Even that comes to an end, and then what do you have, *mon amour*? Nothing."

She sighed mightily and I wondered what they'd been: Vicodin? Or Demerol, for headaches and other imagined pain? Xanax for the never-ending depression? An occasional hit of Dexedrine to get going in the morning? All the brightly colored pills in *Mère's* medicine chest made it like a candy store for woeful has-beens.

What did she *have*, she asked? You had *me*, I thought, and two other amazing kids who loved you (more or less) and a husband who adored you to the best of his ability, and a big house near Santa Barbara, and a ranch in Jackson Hole, and a hacienda in the lush green hills of Portillo, in the Dominican Republic. Guess that wasn't enough. I might have listed these wonders, but there would be the small issue of an overdose, the jimmying of her bedroom door lock as she wailed and threatened self-destruction on the other side, or another afternoon talking her down from the cliff's edge as the sea lions barked on jagged rocks in the distance.

We all tiptoed around Mademoiselle Brigitte.

"No one in this family has ever failed," I reminded her. "Don't worry about me."

"*Oui*, no one has failed. Yet. You have come quite close."

"Believe in me?" I'd asked. "Is that so hard, *Mère*? It's a really nice car."

She sighed. "So you are broke now? Do you need money again? Is that it?"

"No, I don't need money. I have plenty of money."

"Well, good."

"Okay, bye."

I hung up. Did I need money? What a thing to say to your kid who has become a star and bought herself a Bentley! She did it on purpose, of course, to insult me.

For *years* I *did* need her money. (Try living in Santa Monica on two bucks an hour plus tips, thank you.) And she always gave it to me, even for the implants and the porcelain veneers on my teeth; *Mère* might have found Hollywood vulgar, but she understood perfecting one's beauty.

Still, for almost ten years I'd been looking forward to the day I could say no, I didn't need any money, to the day I could ask my parents if *they* needed anything, even though I knew with Papa's millions they never would.

Today was that day.

And *Mère*, aloof, artistic, and superior as hell, didn't notice.

By two o'clock, Olivia and Alexis had both shown up at my little 1920s yellow Spanish-style cottage in Laurel Canyon. Blocks from Laurel Canyon Park, my place was entirely hidden from view, down what appeared to be the driveway for the house closest to the street. I waited in the car in a black, short-sleeved J.Lo terry-cloth sweat suit, tight-fitting, with Puma Californias. I'd jammed my girls into a pushup bra, opened the zipper on the little jacket for maximum cleavage. After the run-in with my mother, I needed attention.

I wore little makeup; I wore so much of it during the week when I was shooting that it was a tremendous relief to be rid of it on the weekends. There was something about running on the beach in thick stage makeup that made me feel dirty and clownish. Well, actually, there was something about my job in general that made me feel dirty and clownish, but that was beside the point. My pores held parties on the weekends, gasping and heaving like nearly drowned creatures pulled onto jagged rocks. I wore my hair pulled back in a ponytail, with a Dodgers baseball cap on top.

Large silver hoops dangled from my ears. My skin, which was naturally light brown, glowed deep golden brown with help from the weekly spray-on tanning session I'd had at the salon yesterday; in my line of work I had to look like I spent most of my time in the sun, even though I actually spent most of my time in my car, in a TV studio, or in the gym. I wore my Gucci watch, a collection of gold and diamond rings, bracelets, and necklaces. My black Prada bag rested on the backseat. I never put my purse on the floor—in the D.R. it was considered bad money mojo to do that. It was one of my father's many strange superstitions that finally seemed to be working out for me.

I was good to go, and I looked damn fabulous—it wasn't vanity that made me think this about myself but rather a sense of accomplishment for all my hard work and discipline. Britney Murphy and Lara Flynn Boyle made it *look* easy, sure, but starving was hard effing work.

Olivia came first, in a congested, dented, old gray Ford Aerostar minivan with one of those dated, yellow, diamond-shaped BABY ON BOARD signs stuck in the side window. I couldn't say why, but that sign made me unspeakably sad for her. The interior of her van was a plasticky maroon, giving the vehicle all the matronly allure of a Kmart tennis shoe. Like there'd be anything *but* a baby on board, right? She rolled the window down and whistled through her teeth, smiling peacefully. How could you be so placid in such a miserable car? I would have have been in agony being a passenger in a heap like that, much less being the name on the vehicle registration.

"*Híjole*," she said. "That's a nice ride, Marcella! Is it okay if I park here in the driveway?"

I wanted to say no, but didn't. She was tentative around me, wide-eyed with wonder. I hated when people looked at me like that, as if I were somehow far superior to them. But in this case, it might have been true.

She wore sunglasses and had her chin-length dark hair pulled back in something like a ponytail, with *bangs*. Nobody did bangs anymore, did they? Except maybe Valerie Bertinelli and Eddie Van Halen, who were entirely indistinguishable these days, them and those women on the *novelas*, and that one singer who was shacking up with Oscar de la Hoya—what was her name? Millie. *Those* kinds of people had bangs, but no one *I* knew. She wore black Levis jeans with all the style and grace of Jerry Seinfeld, and I was surprised to see she wore sandals instead of the red Converse sneakers I thought were required of a black-jeans look. She had a plain black T-shirt that appeared to be stippled with baby vomit, and awful dangling wooden earrings my former dumbshit agent Wendy would have called "ethnic" because my former dumbshit agent Wendy was a fucking moron and didn't therefore realize that French and German were as much "ethnic" as Kenyan or Guatemalan. Upon closer inspection, Olivia appeared to have a very pretty face with a strong chin. She had thin arms. It's too bad she was so short and had apparently never come within shouting distance of a good facial.

She got in the car, complimented it, and then our discussion came to a raging halt. We sat in silence for a minute or two, with her slouching and looking over her shoulder every second, as if someone were following her. She smelled of sandalwood oil, like a hippie. Finally, she said, "So, how did you decide to become an actress?"

"It wasn't a decision. I just obviously *was* one."

"I'm sorry. It was a dumb thing to ask."

"Uh." She seemed to be waiting for me to ask about *her,* as people do, but I wasn't in the mood.

She blushed, and started talking, too fast. "I still haven't really seen your show. I don't have time to watch TV, well, other than the *Wiggles,* and *Caillou.* Jack loves Caillou. He's supposed to be four, but he's still bald. Caillou, not Jack. Jack's only two, and he has *tons* of hair. He was born with all this hair, people couldn't believe it. They were all, like, 'Wow, your son, he has so much hair, we can't believe it.' You know?"

She laughed, nervously. I could tell my celebrity made her uneasy, but I didn't have the energy to comfort her. I just wanted to drive my car. Without Olivia in it.

She went on, "I can't figure that out. Is Caillou supposed to be in chemo or something? It'd be nice to have a show about a boy with cancer, I guess, if he recovered. Not if he died, even though the parents always die in those Disney movies. I don't know. It's good when kids learn about kids who are different."

I stared blankly at her.

"So," she said, trying to break the silence. She sighed. "But Alexis told me you're very good. As an actress, I mean."

"That was nice of Alexis," I said. "But considering that she's my manager, I think she has to say that, it's in our contract."

"It is?" Olivia looked at me with wide eyes, horrified at the possibility of having to compliment someone under contract.

"No," I said. "It's a joke."

"Oh," said Olivia. "Sorry." She smiled too little, too late.

A quote came to me, something from Mel Brooks: "*Humor is just another defense against the universe.*" Olivia, I realized, was completely defenseless.

lexis, a card-carrying member of the Wham! fan club, pulled up to the curb,
blasting that eighties crap music she adored. At least it wasn't the St. Elmo's Fire
theme like last time. Her car, a shiny Cadillac coupe, brand-new, was nice, in a red-
meat, fascist kind of way. Who bought Cadillacs anymore, except rappers with gold
teeth who spelled hundred "hunerd," and people who belonged to rotary clubs?

Because I'm honest with people, I'd asked her about this, and Alexis assured me
plenty of young, fashionable people drove Cadillacs—in Texas. She had taken me
for drives in the damn thing, and I had to admit it was comfortable, and smooth, and
fine—if you liked big steaks (which she did) and White Diamonds perfume (which
she did). But I was starting to like Alexis and forgave her the whole bad-taste thing.
I did. She was the reason I was living my dream and not waiting tables anymore, and
I could never forget that. It's like Nico always said—you might not *like* Republicans
or *agree* with them, but they made the best accountants and the best managers.

Alexis tiptoed with great deliberation and delicacy across my small patch of
lawn toward the Bentley with a big old grin on her cute little round face. She had
one of those Julia Roberts smiles that took over the whole face and made you smile
back even if you didn't want to. She wore the usual Alexis type of ensemble, an outfit that went with her car. Today that meant conservative white cropped pants, cotton, with a large pink floral pattern across them, a matching pink short-sleeved
sweater set, and pearls. She had another new handbag, and perfect nails. I had not
yet seen her use the same purse twice. She had joked with me about her "handbag
habit," and I wondered how many she had. With fat girls, it was all about shoes and
bags, right? They couldn't shop for normal sizes in any other area, and so they
stocked up.

Alexis had straightened her thick, wavy, shiny brown hair and curled the ends
into a stylish flip. She looked like a Mexican *That Girl*, or a flying Señora Juana
Inez de la Cruz.

"Oh, m'gosh!" Alexis cried, her down-home twang ringing sweetly as usual. I
hated her politics, but loved—*loved*—her accent. It was cute, like Alexis, who, even
though she was a little chubby, was the kind of woman men always seemed to feel
at ease with—unlike me. Even her big square teeth were cute. Her skin glowed,
flawless and healthy. And even though her chest was entirely flat and her butt entirely huge, men always approached her in public, and seemed to shy away from me.
And, in the short time I'd known her, Alexis, prim and proper though she was,
shared stories of sexual escapades that made me cringe. There was the guy who
loved to lick her dirty underwear. The one who put peanut butter on his privates so

his dog would lick it off. Etcetera. Alexis enjoyed experimenting and felt no shame about it, yet still vibed like the sweet, innocent girl next door. Incongruous.

She also had beautiful eyes, these huge, smiling dark green orbs of an uncommon shade. Purple eyeshadow didn't work on everyone, but it worked on Alexis. They were almost jade, her eyes, magical. If she'd been thinner, she would have put me to shame.

"It's *gorgeous*!" She stood next to the car, giggling her approval. "Gorgeous" for Alexis had three syllables, like go-ohr-gis.

"Climb in," I said.

Olivia, smaller than Alexis by about four dress sizes, opened the passenger door, and catapulted into the backseat of the Bentley, making room for Alexis. As I eased the new car out of my driveway, afraid to break it, I asked Alexis how the ride compared to her Cadillac. She opened her eyes with contrived innocence.

"Oh, m'gosh," she said, hand over her chest, big mascaraed eyes bat-bat-batting like Scarlett O'Hara's. "This is *way* nicer, woman. Psh. Please."

One hand on the wheel, I hit play on the stereo. Up bumped the thumping bass and happy *modern* beat of Pink's "Get the Party Started," the best party cruising anthem of all time. My chin rose, my nostrils opened, and as the blood coursed through my veins I shout-sang the words. I pointed my toe into the accelerator and whooped as G-forces pressed my lower back into the seat. I zipped past a white Cadillac Escalade packed with handsome hoodies head-bobbing inside, probably to a moronic rap by Mister Foschizzle Snoop Dog.

"See?" I said to Alexis, nodding toward the Cadillac. "What you people think is fine in Texas is flat *ghetto* in L.A."

Alexis pretended not to hear me.

I felt inordinately pleased when the windows of the Escalade slid down and the men's bright brown eyes flashed and winked our way. I waved at them out of habit—never disappoint a fan—and peeked at Alexis. "I hear hoodies give good head." Olivia gasped in the backseat, but Alexis was unmoved. She pursed her lips toward one of the boys in the car and winked, dissolving into giggles right after.

"*Loca!*" screamed Olivia. "What if they're *dangerous?*"

"Dangerous make the best *fucks*," I said.

"Except for Mystikal," said Alexis.

"Who?" I asked.

"The rapper. Convicted of rape. I know this because of Daniel."

"Oh, please," I said. "If you're a woman in America, you've been raped."

Alexis gave me a quizzical look, and I looked away.

"What if they have a gun?" howled Olivia.

"It's just a *game*, Olivia," Alexis cried out, loud. "It's called *flirting*. It's just playing! With *boys*."

"Don't worry. My gun's bigger," I said, toying with Olivia. I didn't *have* a gun, of course, but she didn't need to know that. She gasped again.

I drove faster, sang louder, shimmied my shoulders in defiance of my mother's indifference, my crushing debt, and my tanking love life. If I didn't think too hard about the circumstances of our meeting it almost seemed like we were three old friends, out for a good time. I almost felt like I *had* friends.

I was going to enjoy this afternoon cruise. Out of the ashes of my screwed-up, Televisa-recovery life I was going to create the scene I wanted, right here, right now: me, a flush Hollywood starlet, with two close amigas and a fun car, having a great and easy life. A life like Alexis had, with loving parents who believed in you and sent you smiley-faced e-mails just because they adored everything you did, and an unquestioning faith in things like God and football. A life like Olivia's, with a husband and kid and a fear of danger and normal things like that.

The kind of life you saw on television, portrayed by hopeless fuck-ups like me.

OLIVIA

Jack pouted and it didn't seem like I could do anything to make him happy. He sat at the edge of his toddler bed, on top of the bright blue *Bob the Builder* comforter, in his *Bob the Builder* T-shirt and *Bob the Builder* shorts, swinging his almost-three-year-old feet in their tiny red socks. His lower lip jutted out and his brows caved in on his tiny perfect nose.

"No," he said. "I don't *want* shoes."

"Please?" I begged.

I'd been taking the prescription antidepressant Zoloft for two weeks. I felt less jumpy than before, less guilty, too. It was almost like magic.

Before, guilt had pushed down on me at all times, for no obvious reason. Now I didn't have as many negative thoughts during the day, but I was far more exhausted. I could sit through one of Jack's tantrums without feeling I'd lose control, or crying, but I'd lost my appetite, and I'd been sweating a lot, staining my shirts. Samuel called it a trade-off, and I had to agree it was a good one.

Through the door of my son's bedroom I caught my reflection in the floor-to-ceiling mirror in the hall. Who was that old woman with runny mascara coagulating in her crow's-feet? Why did it look like she stored food under her eyes? I wondered if getting old would just be a long journey of increasing exhaustion like this. I couldn't remember ever feeling so completely weak and tired. I used to fantasize about a husband and kids; now I fantasized about naps and daytime talk shows. How nice would it have been to be able to spend a day watching Lifetime movies? Rest. I wanted rest.

White hairs invaded my shoulder-length black bob. I didn't have time to color them; *that* was a personal indulgence and the only personal indulgence I allowed myself anymore was using the bathroom with the door almost closed, and *that* happened only when Jack took his afternoon nap. The books said moms should nap when their children napped. But if I did that, my writing would never get done. And if I didn't write, I'd die.

Sometimes, if Jack was still napping when the chores were done and I'd written as much as I could for the day, I let myself flip through a magazine. After going to the photo shoot with Marcella, I bought a copy of *Ella* at the grocery store. It was glossy, with Jessica Alba on the cover, and not something I would ordinarily buy. The articles on beauty and fashion got me thinking about those days when such things used to matter to me, back at Pepperdine, when my roommate and I used to put mineral masks on our faces, and even back at Immaculate Heart, the all-girl Catholic school I went to, when we young ladies used to get as creative as possible with our socks and hair ribbons—the only nonuniform things we were allowed to wear—in the name of self-expression.

I looked at my reflection, the tired woman kneeling in khaki shorts and white Target T-shirt, tiny white *Bob the Builder* sneakers with Velcro straps in my shaking hands. I was still physically fit, but I was starting to look a lot like my mother anyway: spent, tired, used up.

Samuel and I hadn't had sex in almost five months. He was interested, all the time; but I wasn't. We used to have a pretty good sex life, nothing earth-shattering, but decent. But ever since Jack's birth, I had only really wanted to have sex a handful of times. The birth was so painful. To me, now, sex was a loaded gun. There was so much that could go wrong. So many ways a mother could die. Samuel said he understood, but he didn't really understand. He had never lost a parent. He didn't know how empty life would be for Jack if I died. Sex might mean death, so I didn't see the point. I had a sex drive, sort of. I looked at porn on the Internet now and then, when Jack was asleep and Samuel was at work—though I'd never admit it to anyone—and got excited by it and dealt with it on my own.

Alexis, who was oddly becoming a good friend, had this idea that porn was healthy, and she talked about it like there was nothing shameful about it. She even bragged about how she watched it with her ex-boyfriend, Daniel. I told her it never crossed my mind to look at it, that I thought it was made for men, but that was a lie. There were some things I didn't think I'd ever be able to admit to people, and this was the biggest of them all. I was distanced from sex with Samuel, though. I just couldn't go through with it anymore.

Samuel, gentle, never pushy, asked me this morning if it was him, if I found him ugly. "No," I'd said. If anything, *I* felt ugly. I looked again in the mirror and wondered why Samuel would even want to touch me. I looked washed-out, gray, lifeless.

What happened to me? I knew the answer to that: Motherhood happened to me. And marriage. And now Samuel had his chance at a career. I'd had my career already, it was only fair. It was my choice, staying home. I reminded myself of that. It was my choice, because I wanted my child to be the most important thing in my life. But you had to have energy to make someone feel important. I didn't.

I smiled at Jack. "You *know* you can't go to the playground without your shoes on." I leaned toward him to plant a kiss on his hot little cheek. How was it possible for children's cheeks to be so pink, so perfectly beautifully pink? They had such warm, soft, beautiful skin.

"No! I want to go in *bare* feet," he said. He kicked me in the jaw. It hurt like hell but I stifled the shriek. Seeing Mommy panic only made Jack panic, and with him teetering on the edge of toddler breakdown, panic must be avoided. I shook my head like a dog with something stuck on its nose.

"*Mommy* doesn't go to the playground in bare feet," I offered calmly, sweetly. "Look." I pointed to my own feet, in their Asics running shoes. The shoes were worn and old, hundred-dollar sneakers that spoke to the life I had before I left work to be a full-time mommy, back in the days when I bought what I wanted and didn't agonize because every last penny wasn't going into the 529 plan for Jack's college education. I needed new shoes, but on Samuel's salary that was months away. I'd have to wash these again, and make the best of it.

I thought of Alexis and her never-ending flow of shoes and purses, Marcella and her photo shoots and magazine interviews, and that publisher of *Ella*, Rebecca what's-her-name, who was one of the richest Latinas in the country. I bet she never worried about affording new shoes. I wanted a life like that, only I would appreciate it more than they did. I sighed, and remembered the way my heart had felt light when I finished tackling a pile of paperwork and had a clean office when I used to work, that sense of accomplishment. I used to love walking to the bank and depositing my check, and taking myself out for lunch on payday, or shopping. I loved that feeling of the workday ending. Everything was different now. Work never ended.

"See? Mommy wears *shoes*. Mommy *likes* to wear shoes. Jack likes to wear his shoes, too."

"No!" he screamed. His face twisted up, red, and tears filled his big brown eyes. "I *don't* like shoes. I don't want to!" The wail rose from the tiny, trembling red bow of his mouth. The breakdown began.

"Oh, no, *cariño*, please," I stammered. "Please don't cry. Mommy doesn't like it when you cry. Mommy likes when Jack is happy."

He cried harder. He flung himself down on the bed and started to kick the mattress with his stockinged feet, the Baby Gap rubber logos on the bottoms of his feet blurring white through the air. He got his socks at the Gap; I got mine at Target. "I don't want to," he shrieked. "I don't want to! I don't *want* to!"

Samuel was forever coming home from his job as an assistant professor in UCLA's Chicano Studies Department with new clothes for Jack. I tried to do the math in my head, to figure out where all the money was coming from. Samuel, a Mexican-American with little Spanish but a great instinct for money, handled the finances, because he was better at math than I was, and he told me not to worry about it; he told me his parents, both physicians, sent him money to get clothes for the baby.

I wished his parents would send him some money to get clothes for *me*. My mother thought I should never have married such a "spoiled" young man, a man who, as she said, "never had to work for anything his entire life." She never tired of reminding me that Tata was the hardest-working man she had known. But she didn't see the good in Samuel like I did. Samuel was handsome, and gentle. He was the gentlest man I'd known, other than Tata, and he cared about the struggles of our people.

"Okay," I said, giving in again. I knew I wasn't supposed to. He was two years old now, so I was supposed to set limits, to let him know that he couldn't always get his way. "Jack doesn't have to wear shoes."

He stopped crying long enough to sneak a look at me. His eyes were heavy with doubt, unconvinced, as if he had been tricked before—which, of course, he had. That was the unspoken nature of parent-toddler relationships—constant trickery and manipulation on both sides.

"I don't *want* to," he repeated, for the record.

"I know," I said. "Mommy knows Jack doesn't want to wear shoes." I put a hand gently on his soft little arm and stroked it. "You don't have to wear shoes if you don't want to. You can sit in the stroller on the way to the playground."

He sniffled and seemed to have trouble catching his breath after all that effort, the air catching and catching. He sized me up out of the corner of his eye. Somewhere along the way in his two short years of life he had decided I was not to be trusted. How was that possible? Maybe he was tired; maybe he didn't hate his mother already. Maybe I only imagined that he wished he were bigger and stronger so that he could pummel me and take the car keys. He must have been ready for a nap. He was inconsistent with the naps these days, and I could never tell if he would sleep or not. I prayed he would; I loved nap time, the minuscule scrap of solitude it provided.

He rubbed his eyes with little fists. *Yes!*

"I want to go to the playground," he said. *No!*

"I know," I said. It was three in the afternoon, playground time. We did the same thing at the same time, every day, and Jack, somehow, kept time like a Swiss watch.

"I want to go to the playground," he repeated, suspicious, whining. He looked at me and his face screwed up, the big brown eyes filled with tears again. The breakdown began anew. I had no idea why. I had told him what he wanted to hear, said he didn't have to wear shoes. I said he could go to the playground anyway, which was against the rules. But the chemicals must be flowing through his tiny bloodstream, sadness in his cells.

"Oh, *cariño mio,*" I said. "No, it's okay. Mommy's here."

He pushed my hand away. "Want Mommy to left," he said. Ouch. He already wanted me out of his life. I had not imagined it. That's what the obsession with dinosaurs was; he wanted to be big, with fangs, to do away with me. I knew he didn't mean it, but it hurt.

"Okay, baby," I said. "I'm going to go in the other room and get the stroller out, okay?"

I didn't know why I always asked Jack if things were okay. It was toddler policy to tell me things were *not* okay. And I was the adult. I didn't need his permission. I knew this constant challenging from him was normal. I knew this was how he asserted his fledgling independence. But knowing these things didn't make smiling through his tantrums and wallops any easier.

"Nooooo," he wailed. "I don't *want* to." I wasn't sure what it was Jack didn't want anymore. I knew, though, what I didn't want anymore; I didn't want to be awake anymore. I wanted to sleep. For about a year, straight.

"I'll be right back, sweetheart," I called. My feet dragged along the carpet, my back hunched in on itself. My body curled instinctively inward, protective, as if to say "enough," begging for rest.

Jack sobbed so hard it was tough to make out what he said. It sounded like "swings," or "slide," or both. He wanted to go to the playground, but he *needed* to take a nap. My only hope was that once I got him into the stroller he might fall asleep on the walk to the playground. Motion lulled toddlers to sleep, and I couldn't imagine what mothers did before strollers or automobiles.

I tried to block out the wails, sniffles, and thrashing as I unfolded the Maclaren stroller. But then a loud thud came from the baby's room, followed by a blood-piercing shriek.

"*Achis!*" I screamed, lapsing into Salvadoran Spanish, my language of panic. I dropped the stroller with a clatter and sprinted to Jack's room, convinced I'd find him lifeless in a puddle of blood. I knew better than to leave a toddler alone, even for one minute, but I was so tired I hadn't thought about it. They were bound to stick tiny fingers in sockets, fall out of windows, slam their heads in closet doors, set themselves on fire. How could I do this? What was going on with me?

I flew into the room and located Jack, sitting beside a pile of Lego shrapnel. He looked frustrated, for a moment, but when he saw me, and the look of terror on my face, he lit up. He giggled. Then he picked up the plastic toy box that held his Legos and flung it against the closet door. Thud. He did it again. Thud. He looked up at me to see if I'd look terrified again. He hoped so.

"Mommy looks funny," he said, laughing.

I felt my body slide down the wall to the floor until I slumped next to Jack and his discombobulated pile of blue, red, yellow, and green plastic blocks.

"Oh, Jack," I said, exasperated, exhausted, spent. I felt as if I carried a boulder on my shoulders. The meat in my head pounded from the inside out, inflamed with sleeplessness.

"Oh, Jack," he mimicked, laughing. He did a pretty good imitation of me, the little brat.

"Are you ready to go to the park now, kid?" I asked. I mussed his hair.

"Want to go to the playground!" he said with great enthusiasm. He pushed himself to his feet, toddled to the bed, and picked up his sneakers. "Want Mommy to put them on Jack," he said. Apparently, he had forgotten all about our battle of eight minutes before.

"Okay," I said. Quickly, I strapped the shoes on his feet. "Let's go get the stroller."

Jack pawed through a wicker toy basket in search of Little Blue Jack, the dinosaur puppet he had named after himself and without which he was convinced he could not survive. "Take Little Blue Jack to the park," he said. "Play in the sand. He's walking." He placed the puppet's limp clawed feet on the carpet and moved them. The puppet staggered forward like a drunken soldier.

Together, we walked to the vestibule, me, Jack, and Little Blue Jack. Jack allowed me to pack him into the stroller without much of a fight, busy talking to Little Blue Jack about the slide. I dug my keys out of the entry-table drawer full of unpaid bills and late notices, stuffed them into the pocket of my shorts, and out we went at last.

The street was busy with cars, but no people. Calabasas was supposed to be wonderful, a rural mecca in the midst of L.A. county, perfect for raising kids, but it was so different from everything I was used to. Calabasas felt sterile and insincere to me. In East Hollywood, where I'd spent the latter half of my childhood and most of my life until I met and married Samuel four years ago, the streets teemed with people out walking, chatting, shopping. East Hollywood was a neighborhood most people around here would never experience, thanks to the news media's constant overblown, racist reports on gang violence. To me, East Hollywood, with its greasy smells of food cooking and constant guitar strains and rolled Spanish Rs, was home.

My cell phone rang as I walked down Lost Hills Road, toward the pastoral tranquility of De Anza Park, a national park at the edge of the Santa Monica mountains. It was Samuel.

"Hi there," he said. "How's Jack?"

"He's fine. We're on our way to the park."

"Sounds pleasant."

I shrugged. "Yeah, I guess."

"How are you? Still weirded out from the Zoloft?"

"I'm fine. How's your day going?" I asked him.

"Pretty good," he said. "I think it sounds like you need a break."

"I do. When are you going to give it to me? I'd love to go running tonight, by myself. I can't run with Jack anymore because he spends the whole time screaming to go whatever way I'm not going."

He sighed. "I'm sorry, baby. That's why I'm calling. There's a panel discussion tonight and they want me to stay to moderate the last part."

The meat in my head swelled double, pressing on the brittle bone of my skull. "Do you want me to bring dinner by or anything like that?"

"Oh, no," he said. "Don't worry about that. I'll be home as soon as I can, unless they want me to stay to talk to the panelists afterward, which I think might happen."

"No problem," I lied. "Have fun. Hey," I said, remembering that my mother had called earlier. "Nana called. She wants us to come to East Hollywood this weekend for a cookout at Frascuelo's with my brothers and their families. What do you think?"

My mother still lived in East Hollywood, which she called "Little San Salvador," but which was increasingly becoming Little Korea, in a crumbling four-bedroom house with a large vegetable garden, near the border with Silver Lake. She could have moved to another neighborhood, but she didn't want to. She was just a few blocks from Debbie and Frascuelo.

Samuel sighed. "You *know* what I think," he said. He feared Jack would absorb a bullet in my old neighborhood. But he liked my mother; they had a lot in common, politically. He also got on well with my brothers, especially Paz, the poet, who was his age and shared his sense of humor. "Why don't you see if they can all come to our place?" he asked.

"It's too small," I said. "Paz's wife just had twins, remember?"

"Right."

"And Frascuelo's family. They're four."

"Right," he said. "We'll go to Nana's."

"Thanks, *amorcito*."

"I love you, Olivia," he said, with great drama. Sometimes Samuel was melodramatic. I was the opposite, opting for cool distance and numbness.

"Love you too. Bye." I hung up the phone and tried not to think too much about Samuel. I didn't want to get angry with him for having a career. But I couldn't help it.

As I'd hoped, Jack leaned back in his stroller, with one more block to go to the park. His head lolled to one side, and his eyelids began to flutter. The sun blasted his eyes, so I put the stroller hood down over him. *Yes!* I thought. *There is a God!* He might take a nap today. I might get an hour or two to chop vegetables for dinner without having to entertain him at the same time. I might get a chance to check my e-mail without fear of tiny fingers pounding the keyboard and deleting something important.

I headed toward the park out of obligation, but I went slowly. I would have loved to have someone pushing me around in a stroller like this. I'd have loved the chance to fall asleep in a big stroller. Or a bed. I'd even have slept on the sidewalk, I was that tired.

A bleached-blond white woman with a child in a stroller approached from the opposite direction. I smiled as we were about to pass, noting that her child was asleep, too. She wore the usual Calabasas mom outfit—hip-hugger cargo pants, trendy sneakers, and a clever tank top with a distressed hooded sweatshirt. A white paper Starbucks coffee cup stood in the stroller's cup holder.

"Excuse me," she said, reaching out to touch my arm with a huge smile. "Do you speak English?"

"Yes," I said, hoping our voices would not rouse Jack.

"Does your employer live around here?" she asked.

"Sorry?"

"Well." She shrugged and smiled again. "I'm new to the area and I'm looking to hire someone. I thought I'd ask the nannies in the area for recommendations. How did they find you? Do you know any girls who need work?"

It took a moment for me to understand that she had assumed I was my own son's caretaker, because of how I looked, and where we were.

"This is *my* child," I said. "And we live in the area. And I don't have a nanny. Have a nice day."

I walked away without looking to see the expression on her face. As I moved along the sidewalk, numb, I looked at Jack in his stroller. His eyes were closed, and I marveled again at how long his eyelashes were. He had his father's wide face, broad jaw, and strong cheekbones. In the dappled shade of a large tree that spilled over the cement wall of a backyard, I leaned over my son to kiss his soft pink cheek. His breathing was regular and deep. He was asleep, and I loved him with a guilty sadness I couldn't name. I loved him desperately. My exhaustion was more than loving him, it was lifelong, a pain he had never placed in me that I needed to clear from my soul for his sake.

"It's not your fault," I whispered.

I turned and started for home again. I would place Jack gently in his bed, remove the dreaded shoes, and tuck him beneath his *Bob the Builder* comforter. And then I would be free again, if only for a few minutes, to be Olivia Flores, the human being. The writer. Not Olivia the mommy, Olivia the wife. I would write, and write, and time would pass so fast I'd not notice it passing at all. And when I finished writing, I'd look up Salvadoran newspapers on the Internet, just to see what was happening in the place I'd left, imagine the life I might have had if I'd stayed. I would read *I Can't Get Over It: A Handbook for Trauma Survivors*, the book I'd been trying to get through for a month; Marcella read about five a week, which you could do when you didn't have kids. I'd pluck my eyebrows, finally. I'd look over the screenplay again, even though I'd all but memorized it by now. I would be alone, blessedly alone, for a few minutes. Was it wrong to savor these moments so much? Was I weak for being so tired? For longing for so much more than I had, when I had so much?

I stopped at the metal row of mailboxes in the downstairs vestibule and retrieved the newest flurry of bills. There was something from the UPS store. I tore open the envelope and found a statement charging us—me and Samuel—for a rented mailbox. We didn't have a rented mailbox. I dialed his office on my cell phone and in a whisper asked about the bill.

"That's a mistake," he said quickly. "Remember when I sent your mom that vase for her birthday?"

"Yes," I said. He had sent her a nice piece of pottery from Oaxaca he bought from a graduate student.

"Well, that's the bill for it. I asked them to bill me because I didn't bring my wallet that day. I forgot it and they let me send it. They must have punched in the wrong charge key or something. I'll call them and straighten it out. They're always screwing things up over there. It's probably because of the changeover from Mailboxes Etc."

"Okay," I said. I stuffed all the bills in the pouch beneath the stroller and tried not to agonize about them. There wasn't enough money. That's all there was to it.

I pushed the stroller into the elevator, praying the sound of the doors closing would not rouse my sleeping child. He stayed asleep. But as I turned the key in the apartment door, Jack's eyelids popped open. I hadn't walked long enough to lull him into a deep enough sleep to withstand the clicking lock. He was up. And he was unhappy about it. His eyes began to dart around. He recognized where he was, and stared at me like a man promised a warm meal but led instead to the guillotine.

"Jack wants to go to the playground," he whined. "Don't *want* to go home."

"Okay, precious," I sighed. "Don't worry. We'll go to the park." I leaned over and kissed him on the cheek. He sat up. His hair stood straight up in the back, damp with sweat where he'd leaned against the plastic stroller back.

"Want to go to the park?" he asked sweetly.

"Of course," I said. "Mommy wants to go to the park with Jack."

I plodded back to the elevator and swallowed the urge to cry, filled with loss and mourning. I loved my son.

But I missed *me*.

CARIDAD

Forwarded mail from Chicabata@cubalinda.cu
To: Goyo528@rappermail.com
From: JulindaLinda@cuny.edu
Subject: New address

Goyo!! Buddy!! Here she go again bro. I attached a pixture of me for you to see. ;-) Big KISS right atcha brothaman! Li'l Juli

Mi querido Goyo,
I was happy to hear from Francisco that you've been getting my e-mail. I'm writing to let you know I've moved with my mother and grandmother into my uncle's apartment in Luyanó. The government kicked us out of our house so a party member could live there. My mom is hardly speaking to me anymore. Goyo, she's so upset. We are barely scraping by and I don't want to think about what I might have to do if things don't get better. Goyo, I don't know why I write to you except that I miss you and wish I went when you left. I was too afraid to go somewhere new. I didn't know any of this would happen. I have started selling cakes I bake with my mom. Do you remember that corner where the blind guy used to sell oranges? I spend my days there on the other side of the street with the cakes trying to keep the flies off. They aren't much but the money lets us buy a few more ingredients on the black market and we

make more cakes. It's so hot in that apartment when we have the oven on all day. I don't know how long we'll be at it. Someone already came by and told us we'd be jailed for selling contraband. This is what has happened to Cuba, Goyo. Cakes are contraband. But every day I see little girls, young girls barely out of pigtails, lined up on the Malecón in their cycling shorts and lipstick with those too-big quinceañera shoes they got from the government, waiting for men to buy their bodies. It breaks my heart and I don't know what to do. I want to talk to you about the crossing. Were you afraid on the raft, Goyo? Goyo, give me the courage to do this. Sometimes people leave in airplanes, don't they? I love you and miss you. Please don't forget to call on Sunday.
—Caridad

MARCELLA

Ian Cross lived in a small dark blue house in Encino, a few blocks from Ventura Boulevard. He'd offered to pick me up to take me to Santa Barbara for brunch with my parents and Nico, but it didn't make sense to do it that way. His place was on the way for me, so I was supposed to meet him there.

I parked my Bentley in the driveway and clomped in my black Prada mules to the back door, as he had advised me to do. We weren't top-tier celebrities yet, but there was a certain kind of loser paparazzi who stationed themselves outside our houses from time to time, hoping something exciting might happen. And me showing up at Ian Cross's house would probably cause some excitement somewhere. For this reason, I wore large sunglasses that I hoped would make me harder to identify. With any luck, they'd think I was Carmen Electra.

Because Mère would likely criticize me for showing up too casually dressed if I wore pants, I wore a skirt today. Roberto Cavalli, black, with an asymmetric hem that fell jaggedly and randomly, more or less at the knee. I also wore a cream-and-black bustier top, with my hair down. I had a light jacket in the car because even though it was late March and unusually warm, I couldn't show up in a bustier at my father's house without him complaining that I ought to dress more conservatively.

I rapped lightly on the screen door, admiring the clean little pool and neat square patches of garden. His lawn was freshly cut, and very green. The scent of freshly dried laundry steamed out from a vent near the back door. Ian Cross, it seemed, knew how to take care of things.

He opened the door a crack, peered out at me, and before I knew it grabbed me and pulled me in.

"God, you look amazing," he said, planting a large, wet kiss on my lips. We hadn't slept together yet, though we might have the night of the photo shoot if the earthquake hadn't left everyone rattled and dazed. We had kissed pretty passionately, groped a bit, and we'd talked on the phone every night since then, for at least a half hour. Things, I thought, were going very well.

Ian wore beige pants and a black stretchy short-sleeved shirt. We matched—a good sign. He smelled of cedar and mint. His hair, newly styled, fell adorably over one eye and when he smiled I felt bubbles invade my bloodstream.

" 'Anyone who keeps the ability to see beauty never grows old,' " I said. "That's Kafka."

"You're crazy," he said.

"No, I'm trying to impress you. *And* flirting with you."

Ian laughed and lifted me up. He started to carry me through his house. I didn't know what to make of it. He kissed my neck and I giggled. It was all so easy with him, it almost seemed too good to be true. I hardly knew the guy, but he smiled and seemed playful, so I relaxed in his arms and allowed myself to be whisked away.

His kitchen was neat, decorated in chromes and pretty bare; the dining room, which whirled quickly past as he hauled me through it, seemed to be more of the same, with a mammoth and somewhat jarring painting of Ian's own face dominating the largest wall. Ian dumped me on the sofa in the living room, and stood over me, grinning. Another portrait of Ian hung over the sofa, and I spied no fewer than four mirrors in the room. Not good signs.

"Just humor me, okay?" he said, unbuttoning his fly.

"What are you *doing*?" I scooted away from him, and he followed me.

"It's like we talked about the other day. We should strive to be totally honest in life, all the time, just to see what happens. You're right about that. You inspired me."

Then, his dick was out, *boi-oi-oing*. Just like that. No questions asked, bobbing blindly there in front of my face, one big uncircumcised and hooded shaft of expectation. I looked up at Ian's eyes to see if he was laughing.

"Is this a joke?"

"Please? Suck it."

I got up and walked away, flooded with horrible memories. He followed, zipping up his fly but without a hint of embarrassment.

"It's me, being honest with you," he explained, hands out to the side in demonstration of his innocence. "I want a blowjob."

I'd been left speechless only a few times in my life, and this was one of them.

"I can't stand the thought of being around you all day without getting off first. I'll embarrass myself. I won't be able to concentrate. I could have taken care of it before you got here, but I wanted you to do it and I thought you would understand. Since you like honesty so much."

"Sorry, Ian," I said. "I don't like it *that* much."

He apologized, and blushed. I gave him points for trying something new, and let it slide, because the alternative involved remembering, and that was something I did not like to do.

Ian drove my Bentley toward Santa Barbara.

He had a Bentley of his own, as it turns out, used, but understood that I wanted to show mine to my parents. But, he said, he really wanted to *drive*. And I let him, because I thought I owed him something for not, you know, blowing him back at the ranch.

"There's something about driving a beautiful car with a beautiful woman next to you that is so fucking exciting," he said. I didn't have a problem with that. I was glad he thought my car and I were beautiful. We were.

Ian opted to take Pacific Coast Highway. "It's longer," he said. "But prettier."

"It's a nice drive," I agreed, still scooted away from him, inside the car.

"Hey," he said sweetly, scooping up my hand and kissing it softly. "I'm really sorry about what happened back there. I must have misunderstood what you were trying to say to me the other night. So I'm sorry. Okay? I was an ass. I'm not usually that stupid. Honest."

He grinned over at me, and I had to forgive him. How could I stay angry at something so beautiful? I had to admit, he looked good driving my car. He looked good from every angle, too. Ian Cross did not have a bad angle. And he knew all the weird, wadded-up English-language lyrics to my latest Cherie CD, spinning in the stereo. Nobody knew Cherie, this incredible French singer, at least not many Americans I knew. Reckless demands for fellatio aside, Ian Cross was interesting, and I thought I might be falling a little in love.

"So what are you reading these days?" I asked, expecting something along the lines of the last book I saw him read on the set, the Descartes.

"Reading?" he asked, confused.

"I took you for a reader," I said. "Descartes in the trailer? Very impressive."

"Oh, *that.*" He laughed. "I read for work, when I have to. I had to say some lines from that garbage on the show."

I felt my heart squeeze a size smaller. Garbage? "Really?"

"Hey," he said, unwrapping a piece of chewing gum as we sped through Malibu, "do me a favor?"

"Sure."

"Lift up your skirt."

"What?"

"Lift it up and play with yourself."

"Right here?"

"Right here."

"Ian, that's stupid."

"Oh, come on. Just stick your fingers in so I can see."

"Are you insane?"

"You're beautiful, baby. That's why. I want to see it."

"You're being honest again, right?" I crossed my legs and leaned a little closer to the door.

"Don't be a party-pooper," he whined. "You're hot, Marcella. Any red-blooded man would want to see your pussy."

I remembered a recent conversation I'd had with Alexis where she told me about how offended she was by that word. I'd argued, at the time, that it was a nice, soft, girly word, perfect for what it described, but she'd insisted that it was only used by men who didn't respect women. Again, it seemed, Alexis the un-worldly debutante might have been right.

I turned up the stereo, stared out the window, and hoped he wouldn't talk anymore. I got my wish, but with a catch. Halfway to Santa Barbara, Ian Cross, the sexiest doctor on daytime television, unzipped his fly again and beat himself off. I think he looked at me as he did this, muttering, "Fucking bitch, wow, wow, wow, fuck," while driving, but I couldn't be sure because I did not dare look at *him.*

"If you stain this car, you sick fuck," I said to the window, "I'll kill you."

"Don't worry," he panted. "I always use my shorts."

N ice place," said Ian, almost sounding normal, as he pulled my Bentley past the security gate, onto my parents' long, curving driveway on Campanil Drive. He'd zipped up again, and apologized again, and tried to explain his behavior by saying he was a sex addict and getting treatment for it. "I mean well," he said. "I really do. And I guess I thought after what I'd read about you that you might understand."

"I told you none of that shit was true," I said.

I stared out at the estate where I'd grown up. Big lawns, big trees, birds everywhere, puffy white clouds. So peaceful and quiet, if you listened very carefully you might hear whales spouting off the coast, or my mother sobbing into her pillow at night.

"Wow," he said.

"It's okay," I said. But it was a lie. My parents had an incredible house, for which they had paid an incredible sum—close to eight million dollars. Perched high on a hill, overlooking the Pacific Ocean, it was a gray-and-white stone mammoth, with nine bedrooms, nine bathrooms, a pool, spa, guest house, tennis courts. The backyard was laid out in grass and flowers down a hill toward the sea, and was sculpted like an English garden. The air seemed cleaner here than anywhere in L.A.

"Wow," said Ian.

"Wow is a very useful word for you, isn't it?" I said as I opened my door and stepped into the mottled shade of the cobblestone driveway. Nico's Land Cruiser was already here.

"Wow," said Ian, standing and staring up at the house. "This rocks."

I took off my shoes before entering the house, and Ian did likewise. It was not required of guests to do so, but with wall-to-wall white carpeting in every room that didn't have marble floors, I did it out of habit as a precaution. Why did Ian's socks have holes in them? Didn't he earn enough to have good socks? And why did he take his shoes off if he knew he'd worn socks with holes in them?

Mère swept to the door with a rustling swoosh of layers of flowing natural fibers, all corals and pale yellows, and the jingle of expensive, artsy jewelry, all squares and triangles. She pinched a long, thin, burning cigarette between her fingers, and smiled like a cat, not exactly a happy smile but more like a ready-to-kill grin.

I watched Ian as he took her in with his eyes, his expression one of pure unadulterated "wow." Mère had long, dyed blond hair, cut in layers to flatter her pretty, round face, and still wore false eyelashes that made the stillness of her surgeried eyelids all the more stunning. She'd painted her lips the palest of pinks. She held her chin up high, probably to stretch the skin she feared was sagging on her neck, giving her a snooty air. She looked, in every way, like what she was—an aging French film star who loved smoking, drinking, and drama.

"*Bonjour*, Marcella," she said with light, insincere kisses to both cheeks. "How good to see you. And your friend. Come in." She smelled of tobacco, alcohol, and the cloves of dusky perfume.

As I stepped into the bright, spacious expanse of white carpet and black furniture that was the living room, she looked me up and down with a sniff. The shades had all been opened, and the midday sun gleamed off the dark blue ocean that filled the windows.

"Wow," said Ian.

"*Que vous! Etes belle,*" said Mère, complimenting my looks. It was more for show, I figured. If I didn't have a guest, I doubt she would have said something as nice and motherly as "Gosh, you look pretty."

What I didn't understand, however, was why she chose to do so in French, a language my guest probably didn't understand. Probably trying to impress and intimidate Ian all at once. Mère was fluent in English, but she resisted speaking it for the same reasons she resisted television, chain groceries, and McDonald's. She hated America. She lived here, and benefited from the country's freedoms, and it was very likely that she would never be able to live anywhere else again simply because life was so easy for her here, but she hated my country nonetheless.

"Mom, this is Ian," I said, thinking, *He's a crazy masturbating psychopath with cum dripping down his leg into his repulsive old sock.*

"Nice to meet you, Ian," she said. They shook hands, he using the masturbation hand, which of course he hadn't had a chance to wash.

"How do you do, Mrs. Gauthier?" He sounded stiff and fake as Keanu Reeves in a Shakespeare production. "I'm a fan of your work."

"Please, call me Brigitte." Mère looked him up and down with another sniff. "What a handsome man. Come in. Please. We're so happy to have you join us."

We followed Mère through the living room to the kitchen, where Nicolás and my father sat at a counter, playing chess and drinking Dominican coffee. The kitchen was very large, with light granite counters and stainless-steel appliances. My parents' cook, Georgina, stood with her back to us at the stove, sautéeing something that smelled of onions and cream. Here, like the living room, wraparound windows gave an incredible, unobstructed view of the sea.

"*Princesa!*" cried Nico, standing and smiling. "Hey, Ian. Buddy."

My father looked up, so I knew he saw me, but as quickly as he'd looked up, he looked down again, scowling at the rooks and knights. I pulled the sides of my jacket closer together, hoping I hadn't given him reason to think me a whore again.

"*Hola,* Papá," I said.

He held a hand up, as if to put me on pause. "Marcella," he answered, without looking up. "I'll be right with you."

Mère walked over to my father and whispered in his ear. I saw her fingers pinch the skin of his arm with force. He looked up again, and my mother spoke.

"Papá, this is Ian, Marcella's boyfriend."

"He's just a friend," I corrected her.

My father stood up and scowled, which was what he usually did upon meeting the men in my life. He wore gray trousers and a silk shirt, and radiated power and money. He lowered his voice a few tones and strolled over with his arm out-stretched.

"Hello, Ian," he said. As he shook Ian's hand, I saw Ian wince in pain. My father was a powerful man, even if he was five-nine, and he didn't mess around. Since I'd first dated in the ninth grade, my father made it clear to the boys and men that he was top dog. "Do you play chess?"

Ian looked at me for help, but it was Nico who saved him.

"They just got here, Dad. Why don't I give Ian a tour of the house, and we'll finish our game later?" Our father eyed my brother admiringly.

"Fine," said Papá.

"I might even let you win this time," joked Nico. He was expert at diffusing Papá, a skill that helped make him a hell of a lawyer.

With a bored expression, *Mère* sat at the counter to watch Georgina preparing brunch. I figured my mother was drugged, but what did I know. Papá strode to the refrigerator for a beer.

"You do what you like, Nicolás. You always do," he said, popping the top of the dark brown bottle.

Nico glanced at me with knowing—he knew I disliked the stress of being around these people as much as he did. "Hey," said Nico. "Why don't you come with us, Marcella? Show Ian where you grew up."

"Sure," I said. Relief.

"We'll be right back," said Nico.

Ian wowed his way through the house and backyard, and asked if he could use the bathroom in the guest house. While he busied himself with the facilities, do-ing God knows what, Nico and I talked about him outside, next to the pool.

"So, you *like* this moron?" Nico scowled in disbelief.

"I thought I did," I said. "But he's a little weird."

"I got that sense." Nico lit a cigarette. He pointed with his chin to the main house and blew the smoke out thoughtfully. "You up for this shit? Mom and Dad?"

I helped myself to one of his cigarettes. "Not really. You?"

"Fuck no. Every time I see them it's weirder than the last time."

Ian exited the guest house and walked toward us, smiling. I wondered what he'd been up to in there.

"Who's hungry?" Nico asked, trying to get excited.

"Wow," said Ian. "That's a really nice bathroom."

As brunch was served, Nico finally spoke the obvious that neither parent had managed to mention. "You guys should go see Marcella's car. Wow. It's really nice."

"What did you buy again?" my father asked. I had told him two or three times already. I told him again. He nodded approvingly and watched a slab of fatty duck flap onto his plate from Georgina's serving fork. I hated duck.

"Good choice," said Papá. I could not remember the last time he'd complimented me. It felt really good.

"She's doing well," said Nico. "I'm proud of her."

My mother and father smiled at me. Not to be outdone, particularly not by one of his own children, my father began to list his own accomplishments for the week. He'd met with important people, come up with important ideas, done important things. Mère's head bobbed along as he spoke, admiring and protective of his delicate ego. It was the dance they did. When he was finished bragging, Mère spoke.

"Your father is wonderful."

We ate the rest of the meal in awkward silence, broken only when Nico asked Ian all the sorts of polite questions my parents did not find necessary. At one point, Nico asked how we had met, and Ian told him about the episode where he guest-starred, and how we hit it off.

"You offered a strange man your number at your place of employment?" Papá asked, stern and disapproving.

"He wasn't a stranger," I said. "He's an actor, too. I knew about him. He had his agent call my agent, it's how we do it."

"But you didn't *know* him, correct?" Papá wanted to fight. I could always tell when he wanted to fight. He'd say it was just in his nature to question, his lawyer's nature, but the truth was, my father loved to fight, especially if he'd been drinking.

"Not exactly," I said. "But it turned out fine. We get along fine."

"They get along fine," said Mère, trying as usual to deflect my father's temper. "It's normal these days for women to approach men."

My father stabbed a piece of duck with his fork, then pointed the food at Ian.

"And you?" he asked, popping the meat into his mouth. "You like it when women approach you?"

Ian didn't seem to know what to say. He smiled and shrugged. "When they're as beautiful as your daughter, sir, I don't have a problem with it."

Mère winced, and I imagined she was remembering when she used to be beautiful. It was a preoccupation of hers.

"Beauty fades," said my father. *Mère's* mouth tightened and she swallowed. "Marcy should have gone to college, so she'll have something to fall back on when *her* tits hit the ground."

My father shot a look at my mother, and Nico and I shook our heads at each other. The games had begun.

Ian's eyes widened at my father's graphic image.

"Marcella is fine, Dad, lay off her," said Nico.

Mère stared at my father, I thought with loathing, and probably would have narrowed her eyes if she were still capable of such expression after so much Botox. "Are you trying to say something about my breasts?" she asked calmly.

My father went on as if my mother had not spoken, pointing the fork at me this time. "If she'd gone to college like her brother and sister, she wouldn't be an embarrassment to this family with the pictures and the articles." He looked at Ian. "If I were you, I would stay away from her. She's my own daughter, and I love her, but she's not marriage material. My other daughter, she's not as beautiful, but with a brain in her head."

"'*Beauty is truth and truth is beauty*,'" I said. "That's Kafka."

Mère sniffed, and left the table in a dramatic whirl of citrus skirting, muttering softly in French in defense of her breasts. This was what she usually did at mealtimes. Ian watched her go with fascination and discomfort, and leaned toward me.

"'*Death is the mother of beauty*,'" I called after her. "That's Wallace Stevens."

"Should we, like, leave or something?" he asked, low.

"Probably," I said.

"Come with me a second," said Ian. He stood, and my father stared hard at him for it. This was against the rules, getting up before Papá. But I wasn't exactly pleased with Papá, so I followed Ian with a bewildered shrug at Nico, hoping he'd understand that he should send the police to find me if I wasn't back in ten minutes. Ian took me back to the guest house and opened the refrigerator in the kitchen.

"I saw this earlier," he said, holding a bottle of barbecue sauce. "I thought of you."

Ian pulled me by the hand into the small bathroom and dropped his pants. Before I could understand what was happening, he was pouring thick brown goop on his rock-hard dick.

"For you," he said with a playful grin. "Yum, yum."

I stood and stared at him, and my heart shrank until I couldn't feel it anymore.

"You are one sick motherfucker," I said. I turned, and left him there, dripping hickory-smoked pre-jiz onto Mère's plush hand-woven rug.

Back in the dining room, I grabbed Nico. "Come here," I said. Our father continued to eat as if we were all still seated around his table. I dragged Nico out of Papá's earshot and told him about Ian being a freak and possibly dangerous.

"I can't take him home," I said. "And I don't want to stay here anymore."

In the distance, Mère wailed in French that she was going to kill herself because no one loved her since her tits had hit the floor.

"You go," said Nico. "I'll deal with Mom."

"What about John Wayne Gacy out there soaking his güebo in Corky's special sauce?"

"I'll deal with him, too."

I didn't want to, but I started to cry. "Why do they hate me, Nico?"

He smiled softly and placed a hand on my shoulder. "You remember the first time you asked me that?" I did. We were still in grade school. I nodded. "And what did I say then?"

"You said we should forget about them and take care of ourselves."

"Was I right?"

"Yeah."

Nico wiped a tear from my cheek and hugged me. "Forget about them. They're damaged goods. They mean well, but they don't have the tools, right? Just go home and sit in the hot tub for a while. Go shopping. Do something fun. Call your friends."

I nodded, and gathered my purse and keys from the living room.

"What about Ian?" I asked Nico at the door. "How's he going to get home?"

"Is he smart enough to hitchhike?"

I laughed. "Not unless the driver wants to blow him. He's so cute, too. It's sad."

" 'Beauty fades, dumb is forever,' " said Nico, as if standing at a podium, which alerted me to our favorite game.

"Who said that?"

"Judge Judy. Don't worry, princesa. I'll take Ian home."

"You sure you want to do that?"

"Oh, hell yeah." Nico's gentle expression faded to darkness. "I'll take care of him."

ALEXIS

Olivia looked out at the small waves off Laguna Beach and sipped her espresso.

"I shouldn't have left Jack with her," she said, for the hundredth time. "Her" referred to Olivia's apparently heinous sister-in-law. This was one of my very favorite waterfront cafés, and she didn't appreciate it.

I swallowed a bite of chocolate chip cookie and washed it down with a gulp of hazelnut latte. At my feet, Juanga whined in her carrier. I gave her a bit of cookie. "Please stop worrying about it," I said. "He'll be fine. Let's talk about this movie, okay?"

"What do you want to talk about?" she asked. She stared at Juanga. "Do you take your dog everywhere?" I ignored the question.

"Well, we already talked about how darn good it is. Let's think about where we're going to get the money to make it."

I'd already tried going to the major movie houses in town with the script, but they all told me basically the same thing: No one in Hollywood had interest in original screenplays anymore. The big companies were all about money these days, and as such they only took on projects that involved little risk, and little risk, in Hollywood, meant that they were all in a big hurry to be the first to do something second. I'd spent weeks trying to convince people in the ridiculous and myopic film industry that Olivia's movie could do for Latino audiences what *The Passion of the Christ* had done for Christians. In Hollywood, no one had been willing to take on *The Passion*, because they didn't believe Christians like me were a real market, that's how arrogant and isolated they were. But after the movie kicked much Christian booty at the box office, these same executives who refused to take it the first time around started running all over the place trying to make their own version of it. Well, I told them, you are also wrongly assuming that people will not go to see a movie like this, about a Salvadoran woman who also happens to be an American hero. I was met with yawns and exit doors everywhere except Columbus Pictures, where one enlightened producer told me that if I could get the movie made, and if the movie got good reviews at smaller film festivals, then she would agree to distribute it across the world. I explained this all to Olivia.

"They hate me," she said.

"No," I insisted. "They don't. They like it, er, you, they all think it's a fine script. But they're all scared, Olivia. Nobody in Hollywood wants to do anything new because this place is full of cowards."

"So what do we do?"

I had crunched some numbers, and figured out how much money we would need to produce a high-quality version of Olivia's movie. It was a lot of money. When I told her the sum, she whistled and shook her head.

"That's crazy," she said.

"No, it's not. We can do it. We just have to find the money somewhere."

Olivia finished her espresso and stared at me. "Why do you believe in me so much?" she asked.

"Because you deserve to be believed in."

"I don't know any rich people," said Olivia.

"That's okay," I said. "I do."

"Should we get going?" she asked.

I left a tip on the table. Olivia stood in the sun and smiled. "I'm so sore," she said, rubbing her lower back. "I've been running a lot, trying to get back in shape, and, man, it's taking a toll on my back. I'm getting old, Alexis."

"Let's go sit in the association hot tub at my condo," I said. Olivia looked at me like I might be hitting on her or something, so I put her at ease. Nobody trusted anybody in SoCal. "We can have some wine coolers and talk about the movie some more. I'm really excited about it. We've got to do something with it."

S o, with Olivia following in her minivan, I pulled up to my condo, only to notice that my biological father's black Lincoln Towncar with the bulletproof glass was parked out front. What on earth was he doing here? He had not called to warn me. What if I had been home, and had been with a man? Thankfully, that would probably never happen again, right?

I parked the Cadillac and explained the situation to Olivia as we approached. Juanga growled at the smell of Papi Pedro. Olivia looked like she had just won the lottery.

"Pedro Negrete? Your dad is Pedro Negrete? Wow! I can't believe I'm going to meet Pedro Negrete."

"I guess it's just your lucky day," I said, with a hint of sarcasm. I was starting to think Marcella's bad attitude was wearing off on me.

Papi was waiting inside the condo, as usual. He'd bought it for me, and kept a key. It was part of the way he dealt with the guilt of never having been there for me. He was essentially a good man, and it really wasn't his fault no one told him about me until I was grown up already. He did not try to deny me, as so many celebrities might have done.

And even though with Daddy's work in sales and Momma's work for Avon we had never been poor, I had never known money at the level Papi Pedro had it. He'd bought me the condo in cash. He'd also purchased the Cadillac for me, for my birthday last year. Who was I to ask for privacy under such circumstances?

"Alexis," said my father, dipping his head as a greeting and sipping his mineral water with pomp and ceremony. He swore by mineral water. I introduced him to Olivia and watched as she blushed and stuttered. He smiled, but the thick black *Magnum, P.I.* moustache gave him all the jubilance of a depressed, sleeping walrus.

Papi took his place again on my overstuffed sofa in tight black jeans, baroquely decorated cowboy boots, and a silk shirt with green and orange swirls, the buttons open almost to his navel. The usual assortment of gold chains hung around his neck. Two enormous bodyguards with mirrored sunglasses stood sentry on the tiles of my small foyer, hands clasped in front of them in the kind of black leather gloves favored by O. J. Simpson, pistols ready at their sides.

There was little risk Papi would be kidnapped in Newport Beach, but he was in the bodyguard habit because so many of his rich friends in Mexico had been sacked and held for ransom—it was rather a Mexican pastime to kidnap the rich and famous, and rather a status symbol to tote your guards everywhere, even, I imagined, to the potty.

"So, how are you?" Papi Pedro asked, coming to hug me awkwardly, like a robot. He spoke perfect English, but his deep, purple, manly man voice boomed operatic off the peach and white of my walls, as if he never knew when to stop singing. He left smears of husky, soapy cologne on my hands and cheeks.

"Good," I said, heading to the cabinet for a glass. "If you'll excuse me, I'm a little thirsty. Smog."

I walked to my white refrigerator and instantly noticed it was gone. A new,

shinier, silver refrigerator stood in its place. I looked back at Papi with my eyebrows raised high.

"I thought you'd like it." He crossed his arms and smiled proudly. "She's Sub-
Zero. The best money can buy."

"The other one was fine," I said weakly, feeling violated. And it had matched
the dishwasher and stove, white, my favorite appliance color.

"I know it doesn't match," he said, once again seeming to read my mind. "I've
got the rest of the appliances coming next week."

Papi Pedro liked to spoil me, but only on *his* terms. I didn't want or need a new
refrigerator, particularly not in this masculine color, but he thought I did and here
it was. He was used to controlling people and their lives and expected to be adored
for it. He usually was.

"I got rid of the ice cream," he said, patting my tummy, "because, Rosalba, you
shouldn't eat too much."

"Alexis," I corrected him. Both of us froze for a moment, and couldn't look at
each other.

Papi frowned and stalked out of the room, embarrassed to have been caught
once again calling me by his other daughter's name.

"What was that about?" asked Olivia, gingerly taking a seat at the counter. I
explained to her that Rosalba was Papi Pedro's official daughter, the product of his
marriage to a neurotic heiress, and she'd died in a fiery BMW crash one year before
Papi Pedro found out I existed. He'd loved that girl. She'd had the same green eyes
as me and Papi. "He's transferred a lot of his love for Rosalba to me," I said. Papi
Pedro was so emotionally transparent, even an amateur psychologist would have
found it boring. Olivia seemed impressed that I had family drama, too.

I unscrewed the top on a bottle of water and joined Papi Pedro in the family
room, where he once again sat on the sofa, pointing a shiny silver remote at another
something new, this time on my entertainment unit. A stereo. Olivia did not join us.

"The best stereo money can buy," he said, as the room filled with the strains of
his own voice singing over a sea of violins. "My new album," he said with a self-
satisfied smile. "I wanted you to have a copy first, *mi vida*."

"Thanks," I said. "Where's my old stereo?"

"I threw it away," he said, as if this were the only option in the world.

"Why?"

He ignored the question. "You listen to this record, and maybe you'll name
your little puppy after me instead of that *pendejo maricón*."

Papi was competitive and saw Juan Gabriel as his main foe.

"Thanks for the stuff, Papi," I said, furious he'd thrown something of mine away without asking me but not sure how to bring it up, and sick that he'd use a derogatory slur against the wonderful Juanga. "I'm sorry, but Olivia and I had planned to go soak in the hot tub for a while. You're welcome to join us." I knew he'd never do such a thing.

"Are you doing okay?" Papi asked, as if I weren't trying to leave the room. He stared out the window and sang along with himself, his hands circling as he conducted an invisible orchestra.

"Yes," I said. "Why?"

"I sound good, eh?" he asked of the CD. "You like it?"

"Uh-huh," I said. Daddy Stiffler had never been a needy man, and I couldn't believe how often I had to compliment Papi Pedro. Weren't his millions of fans enough? What must life be like for his wife?

He stood up, beaming with pride at his own voice, and hooked his thumbs through his belt loops. "I've still got it, eh?"

"Yes, you do," I said. "We're going to the hot tub now."

I called out for Olivia, and she appeared meekly in the doorway.

"So you're okay?" he repeated.

"What do you mean?"

"With money. You lost your job. I've been worried about you."

Olivia looked at me as if she expected something wonderful. "I'm starting my own business, Papi," I said. "I'm going to do everything I did before, but for myself."

"You know," he continued, as if I hadn't spoken. "My wife and I haven't slept together in ten years, not since Rosalba . . ." His voice trailed off. Olivia shot me a stunned look. I didn't want to hear the rest. "I think of how good life would have been with your mother instead."

"I'm sorry," I said. "We're off to the hot tub. It was good to see you, Papi. Thanks again. Have a great concert tonight. Wish I could be there."

"If she hadn't been so easy, I might have married your mother," he continued. "Did I ever tell you that?"

"Yes," I said. I grabbed Olivia's hand and started up the stairs.

"Don't be like her," he called out. "Keep your pants up, Alexis. Your mother is wonderful, but don't be like her."

Don't worry, I thought. Momma was happily married, and had a relatively normal father.

There was no chance I'd end up like that.

"Alexis," he called. "Come here." I told Olivia to wait in my master bedroom and returned to the family room.

"You weren't involved, were you?" he asked.

"With what?"

"Benito, the drugs."

"No! Gosh, Papi Pedro! Please."

Papi stood to leave. "If you need anything for this new business, you're my daughter. I want you to remember that. I think of you as if you were my own child. If you need anything, anything at all. Ask me."

"Thanks."

"I'll see you soon," he said. "Do you need anything?"

"No, thanks," I said, thinking, *My old refrigerator full of ice cream, please.*

"Let me know if you do," he said, holding me hard and dramatically by the shoulders and locking eyes with me intensely. "Anything I have is yours. You know that."

The *Los Angeles Times* followed Papi Pedro's business affairs as if he were Harrison Ford, which, in the Los Angeles music world, he might as well have been. They recently estimated his wealth at close to $500 million. I knew he meant it when he said he'd get me anything I needed.

"Here," he said, stuffing a folded check into my hand with great ceremony. "For you. Buy yourself something nice. Some of those pretty purses you like so much. And remember," he glared from beneath bushy eyebrows, "keep your pants up."

I didn't dare unfold the check in his presence. He bowed, ever on stage, and exited the condo in a cloud of something expensive but nonetheless quite Aqua Velva, trailed by guards.

Once I heard the door click shut and lock, I ran upstairs and uncrumpled the check as Olivia squeezed my arm.

"That was like something out of a movie," she said, bouncing on my bed like a kid.

He'd given me five thousand dollars, on a whim.

"I guess you can live with the refrigerator," said Olivia.

We changed into swimming suits, Olivia in the bathroom, probably still scared I'd ravage her, and headed to the association pool and hot tub area across the parking lot to soak in the warm, soothing water.

"I guess you know where you can get the money for the movie," Olivia suggested.

"I can't ask him," I said. "It wouldn't be right, would it?"

"He's loaded, Alexis, and he wants to help you. Just do it."

I looked up at the lying sky of Southern California, and realized it was probably the only way *Soledad* would ever get made.

"Okay," I said. "I'll ask him."

MARCELLA

Alexis and I were always doing this. I had just punched her number into my phone, and as I listened to it ring, the call waiting beeped. I hit flash, and sure enough, it was the sunny, shiny-haired debutante herself.

"Hey *mujer*, how did you know I was trying to reach you?" I asked.

I lounged in the Jacuzzi under the pergola in my sweet little green mess of a backyard, sipping a tangy glass of chilled Pinot Grigio. Somehow, the tabloids had gotten what they *thought* was a photo of me *blowing* Ian Cook in his living room, but which was really just the side of my head and him with his fly down, shot from his front yard through the window by some psycho paparazzo who needed to get a fucking *life*. Poor Alexis was doing overtime denying the picture was me, and I was doing overtime trying to figure out why my sex life interested people so much.

I tried to tell Alexis that Ian was a sex addict and that nothing had happened, and that if anyone needed to get reamed in the tabs it was *him*, but I don't think she really believed me. I think she thought I actually blew the guy. She didn't think that was so bad, either. "I love sucking dick as much as the next girl," she said innocently. "But you should do it where people can't see you, sweetie." She'd wanted to know if he was big, like that mattered, which it did, but I was insulted by the question anyway.

I needed this drink. I'd run the calories off tomorrow.

"Me?" she asked. "Is that you beepin' up my other line?"

"Yeah," I said. "Would you please try to stop proving Jung right about synchronicity?"

"Sure, whatever, sugar," she said.

"Hang up and I'll call you right back. You at home?"

"I'm driving, but the traffic is hardly moving. I can talk. No, wait, it's speedin' up. Give me five minutes?"

"Okay. Call you right back."

I hung up and took a sip of the wine as I admired the wild green curves and twirls of my garden. Tipsy, the whole nightmare with Ian didn't feel so sharp and loud. It almost seemed funny. Did he really think women would want to slurp barbecue sauce off his dick? Shit. I toasted the crisp, salty evening air, and inwardly recited one of my favorite lines from Walt Disney the man, not the corporation: *"I don't like formal gardens. I like wild nature. It's just the wilderness instinct in me, I guess."*

Though I spouted Walt Disney, I was feeling very Walt Whitman, and wasn't that oh-so symbolic? My Whitmanness was only natural, as I'd been reading a book of poetry sent my way by my little sister Mathilde, who appeared to be undergoing some sort of Latino reclamation at Stanford, on top of her feminist awakening. Suddenly, she was sending me "Latino literature," where global, universal literature had been good enough for her before. This was one more reason I was glad I'd skipped college; modern "multiculturalism" looked more like modern *segregation* to me. But what did I know, right? I was just a tittie actress, oppressed and victimized, not to mention self-hating, as demonstrated by my constant pitiful displays of sexuality and skin, blowing soap stars because I had nothing better to do. Mathilde said so herself.

This time, it was a local Salvadoran-American poet from L.A., named Paz Flores, which, translated into English, meant Peace Flowers, so I figured it was a pseudonym. The poems were pretty good, but depressing, about revolution and gunfire and remaining true to the 'hood, whatever the hell that meant. I was getting dewy in the hot tub and didn't want to ruin the paperback and so I tossed it onto the table and lowered myself into the water to think, all alone. That was dangerous.

Blades of grass and wildness instinct. Blades of grass and wilderness instinct. I liked the sound of that. I had plenty of wilderness instinct. That's what got me into so much trouble. I tried to use that quote to save myself after I got caught with one of the parent chaperones on the trip my class took to a Tijuana orphanage junior year at Cate; Papá and Mère didn't buy it. In fact, they threatened to send me to Bishop Garcia Diego High as punishment for having made out with

Jon Roth's dad. He wasn't a bad-looking guy, for a dad, handsome in that Sean Connery way, and we hadn't had sex, unless you counted what Bill did with Monica. He'd been so excited by my youth and imagined virginity he just let me touch him in his hotel room and explore and explained it all to me so carefully.

I was old enough now to recognize that it was displaced parental yearning and mental illness caused by being nearly molested by an uncle, that I was a neglected child in search of a father figure. Why didn't my parents get that part? Why had they blamed me? I needed love, like any kid needed love. Fuck it. I still did.

I loved my backyard. It was small, and backed to a hill, so there wasn't a terrific view or anything. But it was wild, this yard, untamed and filled with living things that chirped and fluttered, tangles and complexities ever changing. I tended to it when I had time, but mostly I just let it be what it wanted to be, and that worked for me. I preferred this secluded, nurturing space so much more than the expansive, world-dominating vistas of my childhood home. Here, I found safety. There, I'd felt exposed, always so exposed.

My house was set back from the street, down a long, narrow black private driveway I shared with a couple of other houses. I had three bedrooms and a remodeled gourmet kitchen I hardly ever used, for the simple reason that I rarely had guests or ate. But it was the backyard that had sold me on this place. It felt like my own secluded private jungle, and my cats loved it almost as much as I did. Both of them spent most of their time out here, hiding and trying to catch birds and insects, whose putrefied, mangled body parts showed up on the back doormat with alarming regularity.

I knew I ought to keep the cats indoors, as every veterinarian and wild bird aficionado had implored me—but I couldn't. They'd tasted freedom, and as was the case with most creatures, they weren't going back without a fight. I agreed with Adlai Stevenson, who said, "It is in the nature of cats to do a certain amount of unescorted roaming." That other human beings did not recognize cat nature, the wilderness instinct in cats, peeved me. I was not going to imprison them, mostly in deference to their wanderlust but in part because, imprisoned, they passed the hours endlessly screeching and scratching at the door, ever hopeful and demanding. What halfway decent actress could memorize her lines in that sort of chaos?

My backyard! Even when the rest of Los Angeles boiled with dry heat, my oasis was always cool and shaded. Every inch seemed draped in vines and exploding with pink bougainvillea blossoms. That was my favorite flower, because it was like me. No matter what obstacles you threw in its path, bougainvillea always found a way to grow and show off.

I dialed Alexis again.

"Hey girl," she said. "How are ya?"

"I'm in the hot tub with a glass of wine."

"At *your* house?"

"Uh-huh. It's called *relaxing*. You should try it. Hey—what do you mean 'at *your* house?' Who else's house would I be at?"

"I'm really close by," she said, ignoring my question. "I just finished up a meeting with the people at the Hollywood Bowl. How about I stop by? Are you up for company? I want to talk about Olivia's movie."

"Sure," I said. I didn't want to talk about Olivia's movie, but I wanted company; trade-off. "What was your meeting about?"

"Oh, it's the best darned thing! I'm trying to get them to book Lydia for the fall on a double bill with Juan Gabriel."

"Gee, think they could invite Liberace and Wayne Newton, too?"

Alexis refused to take my bait. I could usually get her on Juan Gabriel. "Look, I'll be right there. Give me ten minutes, sweetie?"

"Okay." I hung up and she did not call back to chastise me. She was learning I was hopeless.

The heat from the whirlpool was starting to make me dizzy, so I got out of the Jacuzzi and wrapped myself in a large white towel. I dried off, went inside, and poured myself another glass of wine. The toaster gleamed because the cleaning service had been here today. I loved coming home on the days when the cleaning service had come. Everything felt just right. It almost felt like I didn't live alone on those days, like someone cared about me.

I walked to my closet—one of the best things about this little house was the gigantic master closet with the built-in dresser in the middle. I stood in front of the full-length mirror and noticed my inner thighs looked a little loose. I could go in for lipo, but that would take a long time to heal. I just needed to stop eating so much. No more milk in my coffee, not even skim. No more wine.

That idiotic movie with the Hispanic Stripper Number One was in production, and I'd seen in the trades that they'd gotten Paulina Rubio to play the stripper. It was almost funny, the way the same Mexican woman could be sort of a snooty, snobby, white fashion girl in the Mexican media world, and a lowly brown hooker in the English one. The trades said she would be the "next Jennifer Lopez," even though Paulina was not an American and would never speak English convincingly. The press made no class or nationality distinction between any of us, and with Paulina, everyone was buzzing about how she had agreed to do full-frontal nudity in her next movie, opposite Owen Wilson.

I looked at the body I worked so hard for and wondered if maybe I wasn't bringing some of this Hollywood frustration upon myself. Maybe it had been silly for me to resist the roles Wendy had lined up for me, like she said. After all, it wasn't like Latinas were the only women Hollywood liked to show as strippers. They did it to *all* women, didn't they? All women except those who starred in artsy French flicks from the sixties. And even the fragile Mère was obsessed with her weight. I could have been the Hispanic Stripper Number One, getting press and on my way to film stardom with Owen Wilson. Instead, I was a bouncing boob girl on the beach show on TV. What was the difference? Maybe I'd been better off with Wendy than Alexis. After all, Alexis wasn't exactly hurrying to start her own business officially, and she wasn't a known entity in town. She hadn't landed me a single gig since *Bod Squad*, and I kept telling her I wanted movies.

I hummed an old corny clichéd striptease song to myself and tried to gyrate my hips like a stripper. The wet bikini froze onto my skin with the air conditioner on full blast. What would I do if I eventually got a movie and they wanted me to do a nude scene? Mère had begged me never to take nude scenes. She told me it would kill my grand-mère in Paris if I did that, that none of our "friends" in France would tolerate it. But I had no friends in France. She did. And I liked how I looked naked. If I could make money off it, so what?

"Nudity in French film is not vulgar," said Mère. "But in the American film it is rapacious and disgusting, imperialistic dominance of man over nature."

Typical. This from the same people who smash McDonald's restaurants but smother everything in butter and cream, the same people who march in the street against war but have the world's fourth-largest nuclear arsenal—just in case. I loved my French tribe, but sometimes we could focus on the wrong shit.

Shivering, I stepped into a tiny thread of lime-green thong underwear and stuffed myself into a matching bra. Then I pulled on a cozy pair of cream-colored baggy, cropped exercise pants by Cosabella. I loved these pants. Not these exact pants, but this cut and style. I lived in them. I finished off the outfit with a baby tank top in the same color as the pants.

The house felt quiet, too quiet, and, as I knew, an actress cannot stand to be alone—even as long as it takes a friend to drive over—because she always needs an audience. I called Mathilde in her apartment in Palo Alto. Her boyfriend answered. I was surprised she hadn't turned lesbian yet. I hadn't met him, the boyfriend, though Nico assured me he was as complete an ass as Mathilde herself. That's how long it had been since I saw my baby sister. I asked for Matty, and he called her to the phone.

She sounded tired.

"Studying hard?" I asked.

"Arguing with Tim, actually," she said in French, which Tim didn't understand. "He thinks Ayn Rand was right about the altruists."

I hung up. Of course she was fighting. That was Mathilde's primary mode of communication.

Still, I thought, it would have been nice to have someone to fight with, other than my sister.

The doorbell rang. I usually left the door unlocked when I knew Alexis was coming over, but I'd forgotten. Alexis stood on my front porch holding two things: Juanga, the accursed longhaired Chihuahua dog, dressed in a tiny four-legged velour jogging suit with a pink plaid collar and a matching bow on top of her small head, and a bouncy little potted plant.

Bougainvillea.

The dog I could live without, but the plant was a nice touch. Very thoughtful. I wondered, again, why Republicans seemed to take better care of their dogs than they did those children who had to attend public school.

"For you," she said with a smile, handing me the plant. "Because, you know, you don't have enough of the dang stuff clogging up the backyard. And I thought you could use some cheerin' up."

"Why, thank you, Miss Alexis." I smiled at the dog, who, in spite of her cute outfit, still smelled perfectly like a piece of rotten meat. His eyes ran, leaving dark smears down its cheeks. Yuck.

I didn't understand dogs, the way they cowered and lied all the time. Cats were honest, even if they killed things in their free time. That's why I loved them. Dogs could not be trusted. They did what you wanted only to get what they wanted. Dogs were very Hollywood that way. *"Artists like cats,"* Desmond Morris once said, *"soldiers like dogs."* I appreciated having a soldier for a publicist and manager; after all, bullets and war cries were rather what you wanted in a publicist and manager. But I did not appreciate her overdressed dog in my house. It looked like a bat.

"Hope you don't mind," Alexis said, tilting her head toward Juanga. She scratched behind the beast's ears, releasing even more of Juanga's offensive perfume into the air. "She was home alone all morning and I couldn't bear to leave her in Orange County." She slipped into baby talk. "Could I, woof-woof? I couldn't weave you aw awone!" She allowed the dog to lick her on the lips and I almost threw up.

I coughed and squinted. "You know Juanga is always welcome here, especially when she dresses like Christina Aguilera."

Juanga growled and snapped in the air next to my head. I did not get along with the damn dog.

"Hey," I shouted at the dog. "I'm your mommy's *friend*. Remember me?"

"She probably smells the cats," Alexis said. As *if*! My cats didn't smell—not like Juanga, anyway. "Can I set her down?"

"Of course," I said, but I wished the dog would stay in the car or something, maybe with the windows rolled up on a really hot day.

I shut the door and Alexis set Juanga down on the tiles of the foyer. The dog began to sniff and snort, turning in little circles, looking like it wanted to pee.

"You look great," Alexis said. *"Como siempre."* She batted those eyelashes with great meaning, meaning she did not think she was as pretty as me. Mostly she did this to tease me and make herself feel comfortable around me.

I knew that Alexis *thought* she envied my body and looks; she'd told me so many times. But she didn't really. At least I didn't think she did. She carried her body with confidence. I wasn't so sure she realized she was pretty, though. I'd told her so, but she always accused me of charity when I said it. Today, she wore a crepe-textured, knee-length navy blue dress with a matching navy-and-white short-sleeved jacket, very proper and sorority. As always, she wore her pearls. Unlike the mutt, she smelled fabulous.

"Let me see your feet," I said as we walked to the living room. She kicked up a heel, playful.

Today's selection was navy, like the dress, slingbacks, with buckles on the toes. "What are those, matte leather?" I asked.

"No, cloth," she said. Her quads trembled as she held a foot up for me. "See?"

I ran a finger over the surface of the shoe. "Very nice," I said. "You know, if you come over here in one more cute outfit, I'm going to have to skin you and keep it."

"You're not feelin' that low, are you, darlin'?" She placed her handbag neatly next to her on one of my two sage-colored, kidney-shaped velvet sofas, which faced each other over an imported dark-wood Bergman coffee table.

"I'm okay," I said.

"Good. Just remember, if you can survive the bad press, it'll probably help you out in the end."

"How so?"

"The resurrection, sweetie," she said as if I should have known this already. "The press, the only thing they like more than destroying a star is building them up again after a beatin'. They gotta sell papers, and what sells is movement, from good to bad, and back again."

Rounding out the room I had a black baby-grand piano I never played but which my designer had convinced me to use for displaying flowers in interesting vases, several large works of original folk art with a Spanish theme, a small white-seated Kerry Joyce chair for balance, which I also rarely used, and a thick Persian carpet in muted honeys, purples, and reds. The walls were a soothing cream, with three arched doorways leading to, in order, the kitchen, the entry, and the back hall.

What a handbag. Alexis had brands I'd never heard of, from designers all over the world. Her mother apparently shared this obsession with her and they had a little unofficial competition going to see who could outdo the other. Alexis was winning because she had more money.

"What designer is this?" I asked, and picked the unusual bag up for inspection. It seemed made out of what looked like crocodile skin, in the palest blue, sort of clunky but feminine at the same time, angular.

"Nancy González," said Alexis, beaming. "She's a new Colombian designer."

"Oh, my God!" I cried. "I just read about her in *Ella* magazine. Where'd you find it?"

"The Beverly Center. I read that piece, too. I just *had* to have this."

"Is it new?"

"Of course," she said. "What do you think?"

"I think you should have gotten two of these bags. Where's mine?"

Alexis smiled. "You know you can borrow it any old time you please."

"I don't want to *borrow* it," I said. "I want my own. What kind of a manager are you?"

"I got you flowers. Be happy about that," she joked.

"You know I am," I said. I sat next to her and resisted the urge to hug. There was something about Alexis that demanded hugging. She was like a mother, or a Teddy bear, or a combination of the two, even if she *was* a Republican. Or maybe it was because she was a Republican. My parents were Democrats, and they still sucked. It seemed to me that Republicans made better parents, but worse citizens.

"You want a glass of wine?" I asked.

"No, thanks." She pantomimed to holding a steering wheel with her hands. "Driving."

"Just a *glass*. You're not driving *soon*. It'll be out of your system by the time you leave and if it's not then you'll just have to stay here."

"Okay."

I went to the kitchen and poured some wine into one of my 1930s English carven uranium glasses for Alexis. Because I so rarely used the kitchen, it was perpetually charming. I'd had it done in an Art Deco style that more or less matched the age and tone of the house, but modernized with new appliances that just *looked* old—sort of the opposite of the practice in my business where people got old but looked young, or tried to.

I had wanted the kitchen to have the feel of *Grand-Mère's* Paris apartment kitchen, where I'd spent some of the coziest moments of my childhood. She was thin, and aloof, but otherwise rather predictable in that she baked. But she didn't just bake. She baked in French. *Grand-Mère* could have been a pastry chef with her concoctions, delicate shells with rum cream and apricot filling, things like that. Because I couldn't eat those things anymore, I wanted at least to remember them in my kitchen. In that spirit, I'd had the designer come up with a mostly white backdrop, cabinets and backsplash included, with my red-and-green glass-ware, plates, and jars displayed on walls, shelves, and counters to great impact. The black-and-white checkered floors looked original, but weren't; ditto for the frilly pink-and-red curtains above the sink. I even had vintage dishtowels in burgundy and lime.

Alexis joined me in the kitchen, taking a seat at the 1940s chrome table I'd had painted a dark chocolate brown. The red seat cushions were custom-made. "I adore, *adore* this room," she said. "Let's cook something."

"No," I said. "I'm not in the mood."

"Oh. That's right. I forgot. You only eat once a week."

"Let's go out back." I handed her the glass. "It's nice out."

"Sure. Just keep the cats off me."

Excuse me? I wanted to tell her how I really felt about that little rat—oh, right, "longhaired Chihuahua"—of hers, but I kept my mouth shut, for once. I was starting to doubt the intelligence of being polite. It simply wasn't my style. As I pondered this, a quote from Aristotle flashed through the brain: *"Wit is educated insolence."*

It wasn't Alexis's fault she detested my cats. Alexis had allergies and asthma and could not bear to be near them. If she so much as touched them her eyes puffed up and she started to wheeze and sneeze.

The three of us—me, Alexis, and the stinky Juanga—traipsed through the kitchen door to the backyard. We humans took seats at the wrought-iron table. Juanga scampered after the cats, her painted toenails ticking over the redbrick patio floor. The cats scrambled to safety on top of the walls or in trees, and hissed down at the dog. It was so much easier to be tough when you were out of reach.

"Can't we all just get along?" I asked, Rodney King–style.

Alexis laughed. That was another thing I liked about her. She laughed at my bad-taste jokes and she really seemed to think they were funny. She picked up the book of poetry I'd been reading and looked it over.

"Did Olivia give you this?" she asked.

"Olivia? No. Why would she?"

"Hello? Her *brother* wrote it."

"What?" I snatched the book from her and looked at the cover photo of Paz Flores again. I could see the resemblance now that I knew. "Mathilde sent it."

Alexis nodded as if this made sense. "He's good, no? The whole family writes amazing. I've been trying to tell you."

I tapped a cigarette out of the box on the table and lit up, without a word. "Amazingly," I corrected her.

Alexis scowled at me and said nothing, disappointed. We both sipped our wine, and sat in silence for a minute or two. Alexis looked very pretty and clean. I had a brief, odd fantasy about kissing her. I had no idea where it came from, I really didn't.

"Did you lose weight?" I asked her finally.

"Uh, I don't think so, sugar."

"You look good," I said.

"Yeah, right," she said.

"Hey," I said. "I'm serious. You look healthy."

Alexis laughed to herself, said, "Thanks," and downed her wine in one gulp.

"You look great," I said again. Again, the image of the kiss. I would have liked to kiss Alexis. I don't know why. Too much wine.

Alexis dove into her story about pounding the pavement in Hollywood and coming up with almost nothing. "None of the major studios will touch an original script about a Salvadoran-American heroine," she said. "Not even Miramax. It was amazing. You'd think after *Frida* they'd at least be a little open-minded, no?"

"Miramax is an *independent* film company," I corrected her. "Not a major studio."

Alexis giggled with a hand over her mouth. "I'm sorry," she said. "I just get a kick out of the fact that Miramax wants us all to believe it's an independent film company."

She had a point, but I wasn't about to say so. Instead, I said, "Even if Miramax were a mainstream company—which it isn't, but I don't feel like arguing—*Frida* would still be the exception. Salma had to fight really hard to get that movie made. No one in America will ever make or see a commercial mainstream movie about Latinas, Alexis. They're probably right."

"What about *Y Tú Mamá Tambien*?" Alexis asked. "I saw that in a regular theater with stadium seating. I love stadium seating, don't you?" She was trying to make me crazy, I could see that now.

"Lex, that was a *Mexican* movie, not an American movie. It was an art film, too, just like the other ones. And it was in Spanish, with English subtitles—that's not commercial or mainstream *at all*. And on top of all that, the woman, the lead female character, she was a *slut*. Her character, I mean."

Alexis gasped and pounded the table with one hand, smiling but not wanting to. She liked it when I stepped out of bounds with things, mostly because, I assumed, she probably thought these things but would never be rude enough to say them. "She was *not* a, a, what *you* said!"

"Sssssslut," I said. I repeated it just to see her blush.

"Stop that right now!" Alexis demanded, her eyes sparkling with delight. "She was *dying*! She wanted to have a last *fling*! Her heart had been broken! That's not sleazy, that's beautiful and *sad*."

I shook my head. "She was a hussy," I said. "Sssslut."

"You're *bad*, Marcella. You're such a bad influence on me sometimes. I can't *believe* you'd say that about a dying woman!"

"So she *dies*," I said with a bored shrug. "That makes her less of a slut? Everyone dies eventually. Even the sllllluts."

Alexis cracked up. "Stop it!"

"Sorry. *Not*."

Alexis gathered herself sipped her wine and asked, "So, listen, seriously. We have to raise the money and make Olivia's movie ourselves."

I stared up at the green creeping vines that wove themselves up and across the slat roof of the pergola. I bit my lower lip. I looked back at Alexis and shrugged.

She said nothing.

I looked at the hot-pink flowers climbing the wall. The sun was starting to set and the automatic outside lights came on, soft and soothing. Juanga licked herself under the table with a disturbing, repetitive wet sloppy sound. She must be enjoying herself, I thought. If I could lick my own crotch, I probably would, too.

"You don't look like you think it's a very good idea," said Alexis.

I rubbed my thumb and fingers together in the air in front of me. "Here's what I think would be a good idea. Something that would make money, dear. That's the only reason we should do anything in life."

I lifted my elegant Deco glass, sipped the expensive wine, looked through the window at my home with all its designer furnishings and original art. Other than the dog in my yard, I really *liked* my surroundings, all this *stuff*. I didn't *want* to give it up. If anything, I wanted *more* things. And I didn't think a crappy little indie film about Olivia's mom was the best thing for me. "I should have done the Hispanic Stripper."

"That's bogus," said Alexis. "There's more to life than money."

"Like what?" I asked.

"Like love."

I cackled. "Puh-lease."

"Artistic fulfillment?"

"Okay," I said. I leaned forward across the table and met her eyes with mine. "Who planted *that* crap in your head, Miss GOP Business Major?"

"A Cuban poet named Vladimir. I want to sign him as a client. Then sleep with him."

"Vladimir?"

"He's smart and pretty and so he'll never go for someone like me."

"Oh, Christ, not that again," I groaned. "You're pretty, too. But you shouldn't sleep with clients."

"I need a man," she said. "I'm actually thinking of calling Daniel just to fuck him."

"I think you can find another man to fuck," I said.

"Oh, right. It's real easy for me to do that. Hello? I'm not you. I'm not Miss Perfect Body."

I shrugged. I didn't *feel* very perfect. My implants hurt. My thighs jiggled. I felt hungry. All the time.

"Read the script," she said. "Before you decide against it, just read it, Marcella."

I tipped the wine bottle toward her glass. She covered it with her hand. I moved her hand out of the way and poured. She smiled and continued to drink.

"Can you watch Juanga a sec while I get it out of the car?"

I nodded and watched as Alexis tiptoed in her delicate way to the door of the house. A few moments later, she was back, with a manila envelope. She dropped it in front of me with a thunk.

"I figure, you're reading her brother, why not give *her* a shot?"

I turned the envelope in my hands and pulled the little metal tabs to open it. "I don't know, Alexis. I'm thinking bigger budget, you know? Established people."

Alexis smiled condescendingly. "We have connections."

"So you'd be the producer?"

"Pretty much. Me and whoever gives me money."

"How much of a budget?"

Alexis shrugged. "Big."

I looked at the cover page. *Soledad*, by Olivia Flores. It looked professional enough.

Juanga, twig in jaws, clawed up my leg for attention. It hurt. I fought the impulse to punt her across the yard.

"It would be really nice, and I hope you don't take this the wrong way, Marcella, but it would be really nice to see you play a different kind of character. I mean, I've learned a lot about you recently. I'm not sure I went the right route with you the first time out, with the *Bod Squad* and all that. Olivia's screenplay is really deep, Marcella. I'm talking *Frida* kind of deep. That's not exactly what you're known for. But it's what you *should* be known for."

I stopped talking and read about ten pages of Olivia's screenplay. By page nine, I had tears in my eyes and felt like an idiot for dismissing Olivia as boring. Far from it.

"It's not bad," I said.

"I tried to tell you. But you didn't listen. You ought to listen better, sweetie."

I read another ten pages, and then it occurred to me that I was being sold a story about U.S.-sponsored death squads by one of the perkiest cheerleaders on the Republican team.

"Alexis," I said, tapping out another cigarette and lighting up. "How the *fuck* can you be friends with Olivia and know her life story and still support people like Reagan and Ollie North and Dubya?"

Alexis frowned at the cigarette and made a big show out of sucking on her purple inhaler. Then she stared into her glass of wine with an expression that almost seemed introspective.

"I don't know," she said, shaking her head. "I really don't. I can't explain it in any way that makes sense to you. I don't feel like fighting. Let's just agree to disagree."

"It's such *shit*, Alexis."

Alexis stared at me with a look I had never seen before, with pain and confusion. "Can I tell you the truth, Marcella?"

"Don't give me that shit," I said. I tended to overuse the word "shit" when I was drinking. "I hate it when people ask if they can be honest with you, as if you would ever want it any other way. As if I'd *want* you not to be honest with me. Just talk to me. Go."

Juanga scrambled up into Alexis's lap, and she pet the stinking mutt as she spoke. Juanga opened her mouth and smiled with her tongue hanging out. Dogs.

Said Alexis, "I didn't know about all the other things our country did. I knew bad things happened, but until I read the screenplay I didn't ever really think about it. I didn't want to."

"So you agree they're evil?"

She shook her head. "I wouldn't say that. I know so many conservatives and they're mostly all really nice people. But I don't think I knew as much as I used to think I did. Liberals hide things, too. Look at Clinton. All he did was lie. They're not blameless. That's all."

I laughed out loud. "Okay, Olivia's dad was killed by men your favorite president of all time paid to be there. How can you justify that?"

"I'm not a bad person, Marcella. I didn't kill her dad."

"Not directly."

"I was in grade school."

Alexis had tears in her eyes, and I didn't know what to say. She finished off her glass of wine, and laughed. "Would you look at us, talkin' politics like a couple of lobbyists? And to think I thought we were nothing more than a couple of shallow girls who liked handbags and shoes." She winked at me. "Can we just agree to disagree, sweetie? I'd really like that."

She'd never winked at me before. This was a new Alexis, a drunk Alexis, and she radiated pure heat and power. I wanted to bite her. She had no idea how powerful she could be, if she just let herself.

"Yeah. No problem."

Alexis stood up and came to hug me. I hugged back, and caressed her arm. She didn't seem to notice that I ran a finger along her shoulder. I stopped. I wasn't a lesbian. "Olivia's screenplay is so good," she said. "And it's so perfect for you." She staggered a little, under the weight of the wine. "Plus," she whispered. "I think I might know where to get the money. My dad's Pedro Negrete. I never told you that. But he is."

"Are you drunk?" I asked, even though I knew the answer. I scooted away from her.

"No, he is! I mean, yes, I'm drunk. A little. But my dad is Pedro Negrete. He and my mom had a one-night stand and here I am."

I remembered hearing about this about ten years ago, that the mariachi king had an American daughter and how he wasn't ashamed of it. She was in Texas. I had never guessed the daughter would be Alexis, however.

"You're shitting me?"

"Nope."

"Well," I said. "This puts things in a different light. Maybe it wouldn't be the worst idea, to do this movie."

Alexis looked at me and giggled. "I used to think you were the rudest bitch I knew, but now I understand you. You're honest, and angry, and you have an amazing brain." She raised her glass. "To your brain," she said.

"To my brain," I echoed, clinking my glass against hers. Not since high school had anyone but my parents said anything so nice about my brain.

"And . . . to . . . my boobs," she concluded. She looked down at her chest as if searching for something she couldn't see. "Wherever they are. They're here somewhere, I could have sworn I just saw them. Hey," she shouted to an imaginary crowd. "Has anyone here seen my chichis? Could you tell them to phone home, please? They're late. I've been waiting on 'em goin' on about twenty years now."

I laughed. "You could always fix that problem," I said, joking. "I know a really good doctor in Beverly Hills." I brushed my hand across her chest, and she gave me a short, puzzled look.

She slugged me on the arm. "Death before implants! God did all right by me."

"Never say never."

She grinned and poked my boob with a finger.

"Oooh," she said. "Like jelly."

"They can be yours," I said. I gave her a look that made men melt, but she didn't get it.

"Well, maybe. Give me his number. Is he single? Is he a Cuban poet rap star with a big lump in his pants?"

"I'm not sure about that," I said. "But there's one thing I'm sure of."

"What's that?" she asked.

I pushed her toward the house. "I think you better stay in the *guest* room tonight. I don't want you driving all the way to Orange County like this, *borrachona*."

"Like what? Flat-chested?" She searched again for her breasts, pulling her shirt away from her chest and giggling. "I just *knew* they'd make that a crime in Southern California eventually. Driving while flat, go to jail. Do not pass go. Do not collect two hundred dollars." She stumbled and caught herself.

"They need to update that game," I said. "Who the fuck can get excited about two hundred measly dollars anymore?"

"Not me," she said.

"Not me," I said.

"I can drive," she said. "Just give me a little coffee. Some menudo."

"Bullshit," I said. "You're sleeping here."

I pushed her all the way to the guest room, removed her clothes, dressed her in my biggest T-shirt, removed her makeup for her, and by the time I'd dabbed away her mascara and kissed her softly on the cheeks, and then once on the lips, she was fast asleep on my guest bed, with Juanga curled at her feet.

I cleaned up our glasses, and settled into my bed with Olivia's screenplay. I started reading with the intention of finishing the first act and going to sleep. But I kept reading, until the end—and then I read it again.

By the time I was finished, the sun was up. I fished the receipt with Olivia's number from the bottom of my handbag, and neatly entered her name and information into my Pocket PC.

Then, I called her in the middle of feeding her son, to tell her how fucking talented she was, and how fucking sorry I was for not noticing sooner.

Spring

*The first duty of a man
is to think for himself.*
—José Martí

GOYO

G oyo, spent and sore from his performance to a sold-out crowd in San
Diego the night before, put the cordless phone back in the charger in his
father's office, folded his arms, and lay his head down on the desk to
think. Caridad had sounded so scared when he called her on the phone, so down.
He'd reached her at Francisco's house in Havana, they'd talked for twenty minutes, and now she was gone, again. Why didn't she just come with him when he'd
asked her to? They'd had their problems, and they'd argued the night before he
left, but she was too damn stubborn sometimes. She should have let it go. Look
what was happening to her now. They would kill her if she didn't keep her mouth
shut, and he knew Caridad—she would never keep her mouth shut. He almost
couldn't stand to think about it. He loved her. He had to get her out.

Goyo had called from the back office of Libreria Alabár, his parents' Spanish-
language Christian bookstore in Glendale. Since coming to the U.S., they had
finally been free to do the things they'd had to do in secret in Cuba. Goyo's father was now officially an ordained Baptist minister, and his mother was a
Christian children's-book author with an agent. In Cuba, these were hanging
offenses, and so his father had earned a degree in archaeology and pretended to
be a scientist, while his mother had worked as a librarian for the university and
cried into her pillow at night when she had to ban religious books, including
the Bible.

His father had run an underground church out of their house, which is where
Goyo had learned the art of hiding your ideas from the government. It was nothing

new in Cuba, the notion of masking your beliefs as the beliefs of others; that's where Santeria came from, from African slaves putting Catholic saints' faces on the gods and goddesses of the Yoruba pantheon. The government taught this last bit of history with pride in the schools, but pretended it wasn't still going on all over the island. People pretended to be communists, but they weren't; they were scared. Their hypocrisy was enough to drive a man insane if he thought too much about it; the government of Cuba was proud of Cuban religion, even as they outlawed it.

As he'd gotten older, Goyo had been less and less able to hide his opinions. Through the Internet and visitors to Cuba, he saw how much he was missing in the world, and hated it. He studied the true meaning of the words of José Martí, shoved down the throats of Cuban schoolchildren, and he'd realized that the very words being used to defend the Revolution argued for its overthrow. The communists had promised freedom but they had failed the people, and broken promises were the crippled backbone of contemporary Cuban society. He'd grown more brazen in his lyrics and concerts, in his critiques of Castro and his cronies, in his analysis of the numb despair of his people, until he could only hold a concert fifteen minutes after it was announced, because otherwise the police would raid his shows and shut him down. They'd gotten into the habit of locking him up, roughing him up, and it was getting more violent each time. Goyo loved Cuba more than he could express, but he did not love it enough to die in a prison under an unjust regime. After he was jailed for the first time, he made the decision to leave. Maybe he could do more, he thought, by telling the world what life was like in Cuba, than he could have ever done by staying there and living it.

The whole family had come to the U.S. on the same small raft they had built with their own hands and launched in the middle of the night, praying to God and La Caridad del Cobre to deliver them safely to Key West, which they did. Goyo's family got some resettlement money from the Cuban American National Foundation in Miami, and now Goyo lived in a spacious apartment above the bookstore with his mother and father. They had a microwave, an air-conditioning unit in the window of each of the main rooms, and cable television, more than he'd ever had. But now that several record labels were interested in what Goyo did, and now that he was making friends with big-time rap stars, he realized life could get even more comfortable. A lot more comfortable. More comfortable and open and free than he'd ever imagined.

The guys in Cypress Hill and Orishas had houses that looked like palaces to Goyo, with three or four cars sometimes. It was only a matter of time before he had the same for himself. And when he started to really make money, he'd do with it what he did with it now, and give half of it to his parents for raising him with a strong faith in God and a strong desire to express himself, in spite of the illegality of both these things in his country.

Goyo walked out of the office into the soft golden light of the bookstore and told his parents about the conversation he'd just had with his girlfriend in Cuba.

"Ay, *niño*," his mother said. "I think you'd be better off just forgetting about her. I know you love her, but there's something I don't like about her. You might never see that woman again. There are lots of beautiful women here in Los Angeles. Find another one. Get on with your life."

"I don't want another one," he'd said.

"You *need* another one, but let me meet her first."

Goyo took a deep breath. "I don't think any woman I ever meet will ever be good enough to meet your qualifications, Mamá."

Goyo's mother laughed and handed him the pink feather duster with instructions to dust the colorful rows of quiet tomes in the cozy bookstore. Goyo obliged, but watched the moody sky out of the front window. He thought of Caridad, suffering in the stench and heat of her uncle's apartment, barely surviving. Here he was, in his parents' store, living in a freedom he'd never imagined possible. Life was so unfair.

Today was unseasonably cool for spring, almost cold, and Goyo's father had the corner fireplace going, and the Persian cat—a permanent resident of the shop—snoozed contentedly on one of the plaid armchairs near the hearth. It was the sort of day other people used as an excuse to curl up like the cat, inside, with a book, safe. But that is not what Goyo preferred to do on this kind of day. Days like this were perfect for surfing, conjuring windy, churning, furious waves from the soul of the earth. Big waves. Life-altering waves. He had done this in Cuba, and he still did it here. That was one thing Americans really missed out on, he thought, by not being allowed to travel to Cuba: phenomenal surfing when the wind was right.

Goyo's mother looked up from her seat behind the cash register, her bifocals riding low on her long, delicate nose, their silver chain draping delicately around her neck. Gently, she set the Spanish-language newspaper she read on the counter, next to her cup of strong Cuban coffee. She shivered, as she always seemed to; since moving to Los Angeles, she could never seem to get warm. After spending all her life in Cuba, the dry air and cool evenings of Southern California were a difficult adjustment. She pulled the open sides of her gray cardigan sweater together over her heart, and spoke.

"Vladimir Gregorio," she said, using his birth name. "I know what you're thinking." She smiled and pointed a long, pink fingernail toward him. "I see it in your eyes."

"You do?" he asked. As usual, they spoke in Spanish.

"Let me guess," called Goyo's father, a balding man with the same handsome features of his son. He stood on a wheeled wooden ladder attached to the back wall of the small bookstore, stocking the newest titles in the travel section. Goyo got goose bumps thinking about his father handling all those faith-based travel books; not one year ago they all lived in a nation where it was forbidden to travel or openly worship God. In English, his father said, "Gnarly tubes," adding, in Spanish, "am I right, or am I right?"

Goyo laughed. It always amused him to hear his father attempt California surf slang. The words sounded incredibly funny spoken by a bookish Baptist minister in his sixties.

"Go," his mother said kindly. "Today is slow. We'll manage fine."

Goyo's father smiled down at his son. "Go on," he said. "You're only young once. *Diviértate.*"

Goyo thanked his parents for their empathy—really they were the best parents a man could want—but finished dusting the store anyway. He pet the cats until they purred. He really wanted a dog—they'd had to leave his Welsh Corgie with friends in Havana, and he missed her. But the apartment was too small for a dog, especially with four people living in it. When he got his own house, that was what he wanted to do first: Find a dog.

He walked behind the front counter and wrapped his arms around his mother's shoulders. He kissed the top of her head, which smelled of Chanel perfume, the old, musky kind. She had always loved perfume, and it was one of the things Goyo bought for her every time he got paid. In Cuba, perfume had been in short supply. Alcoholics on the island drank it out of desperation. Caridad had given Goyo's mother everything the government-run Suavitel brand came out with, but most of it stunk from cheapness; now, of all the things she enjoyed about her new country, perfume was one of her deepest pleasures.

"*Bueno, Mami.* I'll have my cell," he said. "If things get busy, call me. I'll come right back."

Goyo's father frowned as if he were insulted. "We can manage," he said. "You think just because we're old we can't manage without you?" He winked.

"Will we see you for dinner?" Goyo's mother asked.

"Of course," Goyo said. His mother made a savory, oniony *vaca frita* every Sunday and he never missed it.

"That's my boy," his mother said, patting her son on the cheek. "Be careful out there."

"*Niño?*" called Goyo's father. "*Qué va.* Give the man some respect, *por favór.* He's a man now. You coddle him too much."

Goyo's parents smiled at each other with great love and affection, as they had done all his life. They embraced, and kissed on the lips, still as much in love as they were thirty-five years ago, on their wedding day. Goyo knew how lucky he was. In every way except love, that is.

In love, he was the unluckiest man in the world.

Goyo kept his black O'Neill wet suit and his baby-blue Becker LC-3 surfboard in the back of his Jeep, all of it clean, waxed, and ready to go at a moment's notice. Next to Caridad, singing, and composing, surfing was Goyo's greatest passion.

He'd first surfed at the age of ten, off the blue-green coast of Matanzas, with a cousin five years older. He'd shown a natural aptitude for it then, coasting through whitewater to the shore, standing effortlessly, his first time out. He'd been hooked, in love with the roaring silence of the sea and the soaring views of the earth from atop the water. His parents—supportive to the point of selflessness, he now realized—had hooked him up with homemade, crude miniature surfing equipment his father built himself. They'd stood offering endless applause and cheering from beneath their big red polka-dot beach umbrella, fashioned out of a tablecloth his mother bought at a street fair in Havana back in the good days, when people could get things like that.

Wearing his usual workday outfit—jeans, T-shirt, and sneakers—Goyo climbed into the driver's seat of the topless rusty blue Jeep, which was parked in the usual spot in the alley lot behind his parents' shop. He turned the key and the engine and stereo simultaneously ignited. Today he listened to Pépe Aguilar, by Goyo's estimation the finest vocalist working in Spanish, and contemplated once more his idea for a mariachi-rap-timba album that could cross over all Latin music genres borders. If someone could figure out how to do that, he thought, that someone would be very wealthy.

Goyo adjusted sunglasses onto his face, checked the darkening, churning sky—promising, promising—and backed out of the alley into the street.

He had to get out in the water. He had to forget about her. Or rescue her. Or die trying, as they said in his new country.

Goyo took the usual route to Santa Monica—the 5 to the 110 to the 10—

charging instinctively toward the ocean, in the fast lane. The 10 ended at the beach, turned into Pacific Coast Highway, which Goyo took north toward Malibu. As he drove on the narrow, curvy stretch of road, he took in the blue expanse of water to his left. The waves crested white and high, maybe fifteen feet. They were like breasts, waves like this, soft and curved when you were inside of them, brushing their solid walls with your hands.

Goyo drove directly to Surfrider Beach State Park, at the southern tip of Malibu. He was not surprised to find a dozen or so of his hard-core peers already here. He knew most of them by name, and recognized their cars. Most of us, he thought, would have made a lot more money by now if we didn't feel the call to disappear into the ocean every time the wind stirred. Surfing was like an illicit lover who threatened to ruin your life. You could not live without her, but you would never be in charge of the relationship. She would control you until you died, and you would submit to her abuse willingly, lovingly, constantly. You would try to learn her well enough to please her, but she would be ever unpredictable.

Goyo parked the Jeep, and, like a couple of other guys in the parking lot, stripped to his underwear and shimmied into his tight black wet suit standing directly behind his car. With waves this awesome, there was no time for modesty. People expected this sort of devoted display along this stretch of highway, and, with the exception of curious gawking teenage girls, no one paid the naked surfers much attention.

"Looks good out there!" a young man with a black goatee called to Goyo.

"Yeah," Goyo answered with a grin. He tried to remember the guy's name.

"Diego," the guy said, holding his hand out for Goyo to shake. "El Mejicano Loco."

"Right," Goyo said, shaking. The self-described "Mexican" who was really an American and spoke no Spanish. Goyo had been meeting a lot of these guys since moving to California. "Goyo."

"Well," Diego said, grabbing his board and heading toward the sandy hill at the edge of the parking lot. "See you out there, dude!"

Goyo rolled the reluctant wet suit up over his shoulders at last, and zipped himself in. He found his Adidas Jasper surfing sunglasses in the backseat of the Jeep and adjusted them over his eyes; even though it was overcast, he needed them. He smeared sunblock across the exposed parts of his face and arms, then locked his wallet, Caridad photos, and CDs in the small metal safe welded in the back of the Jeep. He sat on the bumper and pulled the split-toe O'Neill Freak Socks over his feet, stuffed his fingers into the strict compartments of O'Neill surf gloves. He considered wearing a hood, but didn't think it was cold enough; as a musician, he relished the music of the sea, and hated the way hoods blocked it from his ears. Finally, Goyo grabbed his board, waxed and gleaming, and followed Diego's footsteps.

There was an official path at the other end of the parking lot, but the surfers rarely used it, preferring to risk their luck stumbling down the hill and onto the beach—it was the quickest route. When Goyo first got to L.A., he was so excited about "gnarly waves" that he'd actually run down this slope. Today, however, Goyo felt mellower, almost melancholy. Today, Goyo felt lonely, and for all its spectacular beauty, surfing was an activity that reminded him in no uncertain terms of the enormity of the universe and the puniness of himself. And feeling small, today, Goyo thought, would amplify his pangs of loneliness.

The pale beige sand darkened underfoot as he grew closer to the water, becoming dark brown where the sea washed over it. Goyo waded boldly into the angry water, holding the board over his head, feeling the pulse and surge of its rhythm pushing his body. There was undeniably something sexual about the pulse of the sea against a man's hips, he thought, something wanton and careless about it, something vicious and loving. When he was waist-deep in the ocean, he dropped the board, and lay on top of it, on his hard, toned belly, using his hands to scoop and paddle, kicking with his feet. The sea fought for a moment, spit him back toward the land, but yielded as Goyo's board and body became one with the rocking water. Or maybe, Goyo thought, it was *he* who yielded. Yes, that was it. *He* allowed his body to be sloshed and slammed in the waves, happily accepted saltwater slaps across the face. The living, bitter taste of the water, he thought—and not for the first time—was identical to the taste of blood. *We are made of ocean*, he thought, paddling faster and faster to reach the strangely calm deeper water where a few other surfers waited, silent, for mother earth to sling them across a wave.

Goyo reached the glassy, dark blue water, the proverbial calm before the storm, he thought. Like the others, he rested on his belly, bobbing in the deceptively gentle water. Nearby, a woman surfed, the only female here today, her long brown hair tied up in a tight knot. He had seen her before, her tight body tanned and powerful as his own. She was spectacular, this woman, gorgeous in the wonderful way of those who are not concerned with beauty because they are concerned with things greater and more beautiful than that. Part of him wished he could speak to her. But he might fall for her. He avoided that kind of woman. His body was young, strong, and it had needs. He needed a woman, craved a woman.

He thought of women constantly, found the curves of their bodies magical, hypnotic. He hadn't officially dated since coming to the United States. He couldn't. His heart belonged to one woman, and one woman only. He'd broken down exactly three times and had sex since coming to Los Angeles almost two years ago, but it was just that: sex. They'd been gorgeous American women, fans who'd thrown themselves at him, and he'd been curious and horny and done it, then regretted it. They called him, but he never called them back. Love and sex confused Goyo, tied his spirit into a knot as tight as the hair on the surf goddess's head.

Goyo stared at the swelling water along the horizon, and thought, again, of aging, and of death. For him, these were the natural thoughts that followed thoughts of love and sex. He wasn't in his twenties anymore. He was thirty, the age when a man should consider having children, starting a family, settling down. He wanted to. But how on earth would he be able to allow himself to fall in love, to start a family, with his heart in red, bleeding shreds for Caridad? How could he love another woman while Caridad still lived in his heart? It would not be fair to the woman. It would be unfair to any children he would ever have with any woman other than Caridad, and he didn't want to raise children who would hate him for his love of a woman other than their mother. He had begun to forget her, but then she wrote to him, and it all came back. He thought of Caridad constantly, of her poems and her eyes. Those electric green eyes. Cuban eyes. He had never found eyes like hers, in all his searching.

He'd found beautiful eyes, brown eyes, solemn eyes, joyous eyes, but none with the sparkle and ferocity of Caridad's, none with the determination and tragedy of hers. Some men liked rear ends, others liked hips or breasts, chopping women into meaty parts like *carniceros*. But Goyo was an eye man. The eyes were, truly, windows on the soul. And the soul, he thought as the wave gathered strength, was the only part of a human being that really mattered. And no one, no one, had eyes like hers. There was that one woman he'd accidentally crashed into in Calabasas months ago, after visiting his friend Fantasma, the Puerto Rican songwriter and former child star with Sancocho. She'd had beautiful eyes, too. But he didn't have her number, and she hadn't called him. Of course not. He'd let her think he was a struggling poet. An attractive woman like that didn't want anything to do with a struggling poet. It was a big city. He'd probably never see her again, which was good because she had a cuteness to her he'd find hard to resist. She didn't look like Caridad, but she *felt* like Caridad. Something about her had felt, if only briefly, like *home*.

Goyo and the other surfers, feeling the tension building in the water as the wave moved steadily toward them, turned their boards and bodies toward the shore and began to paddle furiously to keep up with the tide. As the water swelled and rose beneath them, they curled their legs against the boards, toes searching for the place on the board where they would be most secure, like fetuses waiting to be born. One by one, they released their hands from gripping the boards, and stood, and balanced. Goyo, too, unfurled his body. On his feet, he crouched, teetered, regained control, humbled by the power of the planet, electric through his body with the life-force he connected with nowhere so much as here, on the gigantic, indifferent water, wanting to sing and cry and scream all at once. The wave was fast, and strong. Goyo synched his body with the movements of the water, like a lover eager to please and placate, selfless atop this body, his eyes moving from the sand of the beach in the distance to the water beneath and next to him, attentive at every moment to the needs of a sea that cared not whether he lived or died.

One by one the surfers challenged the huge, hissing wave, and one by one they fell, splayed against her spires and spumes, all of them except Goyo. The percussive torture song in his broken, desperate heart matched the smooth drumroll of the ocean, and he moved with its crescendo, one with the planet and all the pain a human could find here, all the pain and all the beauty, life and death linked inexorably, dancing together here on the tip of a wave. For Goyo, there was hardly any difference anymore. He lived, but without Caridad he might as well have been dead, most alive only on the stage, where the muse of her danced with him.

Quickly, almost too quickly, the wave closed round and delicate over the top of him, and he was inside a tube of ocean, riding through a concealed, secret, private tunnel of air. Inside her. The light inside the tube was a color unlike any other Goyo had ever seen, a green-blue light that seemed to emanate from the center of his soul, or the ocean's soul, or Caridad's soul. His board sliced through the water with a soothing sizzle. It was beautiful here, and unnatural, and frightening. His heart pounded with the thrill of this moment, the glory of it, and the terrified certainty that the aquamarine peace of this instant would end, brutally, dizzyingly, and dangerously in mere moments, when the sea decided to teach him a lesson about his own human arrogance. Surfing, Goyo realized, was a form of masochism.

Finally, horribly, the wave burst, exploding into Goyo's body and board, separating them and pulling Goyo down and down, in great, violent underwater circles, turning him again and again, like the adult hands against the shoulders of Mexican children he'd seen beneath piñatas in public parks, until he could not recall which way, if any way, led to the air. Panic cut through his belly in a shock. Relax, he told himself. When you become disoriented under the water, he reminded himself, the best thing you can do is relax and let the ocean win. Let her rage and rail until she is spent and guilty and calm, until she releases you from her death grip and you float, like a spirit, toward the light. Toward life, which was love, which was Caridad, which was impossible, which was pain, which was death.

Alone, more alone than he had ever been, in the dark green light of the ocean's heart, Goyo held his breath, and waited.

ALEXIS

Marcella's brother Nicolás sat at a back table at Hugo's, sunglasses still on, waiting for me. The restaurant looked deceptively normal, the kind of place where you might expect to get a big old omelet with greasy home fries. But, like everything else in West Hollywood, looks proved to be deceiving. Hugo's was actually a favorite breakfast spot for Hollywood elite, probably because it looked like a movie set of a Texan diner. But there wasn't a diner in Texas, I was darn near sure, where your eggs came with things like "turmeric rice." Except Austin, maybe.

I didn't like the smell of the "tantric veggie burgers" any more than I liked the way everyone's eyes inspected me as soon as I walked in. Yes, I wanted to scream, I'm chubby, and I'm wearing a pale yellow suit with heels. I'm not wearing what you're all wearing, I wanted to shout. And what they were wearing were sweats, pajamas really, all manner of them, with expensive shoes that barely hid their feet. Slobs, every last one of 'em, and I didn't care how much money they had in the bank.

Nico saw me and waved. In a gray long-sleeved T-shirt and jeans, with his hair jagged with gel, and his cell phone ringing on the table, he fit right in. The sunglasses were a dead giveaway that he had money, too, and more than one wannabe had her eye on him. You could tell the legit from the fake in these places by their body language. The truly honest-to-God powerful folks seemed to be the least threatening. It was the ones who fronted and fretted who probably couldn't pay their mortgage—or rent—that month.

I waved back and made my way through the crowded restaurant to Nico. He'd ordered a pot of herbal tea and I swore it smelled like hay, straight from the farm *hay*. He stood and helped me into my seat before offering me some of the evil brew, saying something about how healthy and fashionable it was.

"No, thanks, sugar," I said. "I need coffee. Real coffee."

Our tall, tanned waiter wheeled into view fast enough to overhear me, and after grilling me about what *kind* of coffee I wanted—he had a list an arm long with the usual pretentious variations—he promised to be right back with a plain old simple cup of Joe.

I scanned the menu and decided on toast and fruit salad, the same thing Nico was having. It never felt right to eat more than a man during a meeting. I'd eat later.

Nico said he liked the business plan, and gave me a copy of his edited version. He'd changed a few things, but left most of it intact. "All you need now is to come up with the starter cash," he said.

"I know," I said.

"You have anyone in mind?"

I looked around and realized more than one person was listening a little too intently to our conversation.

"Yep," I said, emptying almost the entire contents of the little white cream pitcher into my plain old boring coffee. "I have a plan."

I flew Southwest Airlines to Harlingen, Texas, and marveled as the plane came down at both the pale blue and green beauty of the Gulf Coast of Texas from the air, and the way this flat, rural-looking region seemed completely desolate but was actually home to millions of people on both sides of the border.

Papi Pedro was spending a few weeks at his ranch near McAllen, and had agreed to meet with me there about my new business, this afternoon. I landed in Harlingen, got my rental car, a white Mitsubishi Montero, and found the hotel where I'd be parked until tomorrow. Papi had of course invited me to stay with him, but I avoided that when I could, because it was exhausting complimenting him and listening to his albums, which was all he wanted me to do when I visited him. I preferred room service, and a night of channel-surfing, but had told Papi I had meetings and an early flight the next day—neither of which was true. When the time came to head to the ranch, I put on my jeans, boots, button-down shirt, and pale pink cowboy hat, and drove to Papi's.

My biological father's Texas ranch, Rancho Paraiso, was everything its name implied. Two hours' drive from McAllen, it sprawled across two thousand acres near Randado, Texas, close to the Mexican border and the ocean. The ranch had originally been founded in the late 1800s, and Papi purchased it from the founder's cash-strapped great-grandson twenty years ago, and immediately set about tearing down the existing house and building a shining palace for himself. I'd been here a few times, and every time it took my breath away and made me wonder what kind of woman I might have become had I known about all of this years ago. I'd grown up in a subdivision of simple brick tract homes, going to public school, Girl Scouts, and church.

After having my car inspected by Papi's armed guards at the gated entrance to the compound, I was allowed to take the rental car over the bumpy dirt road onto the massive estate. From the moment I passed the gate, the landscape grew lusher, greener, and, it seemed, quieter. The long road to the house was flanked on the left by seemingly endless grassland prairies, dotted with grazing longhorn cattle and the prickly paddles of short cactus patches. I rolled down the window and listened to the light wind in the long yellow grass, the soft murmuring of cattle, and the chirping of what seemed to be a million birds. I smelled earth, and sea salt, and longed to have the kind of job that would allow me to live somewhere like this. As it was, however, I had really only one city that matched my job description: Los Angeles.

Though Papi didn't need the money a working ranch might bring in, this was, in fact, a working ranch because raising prize-winning cattle and bulls with enormous testicles made Papi proud. A functioning windmill whirred high above the top of a grove of mesquite trees on a small rise to the right, postcard perfect. I knew that tucked somewhere behind the trees were Papi's high-tech stables, horse pools, and training arena, where his twenty or so thoroughbred horses were tended and groomed by an experienced staff that numbered near a dozen.

When the pastures ended, ponds and lagoons took over, some fenced off because they were stocked with alligators that my father's wife enjoyed observing in their natural habitat from tripods hidden in the trees. My father's wife had interesting habits. In the southern and western corners of the ranch, wild mesquite savannas rolled clear to the Gulf of Mexico; Papi swore these parts were littered with so many peyote plants he had to have his guards chase "collectors" from nearby Nuevo Guerrero, Mexico, away. Papi had a boathouse at the water's edge, and a heavily guarded shelter for one of his yachts.

Papi Pedro had been given awards by the Monte Mucho Audubon Society for his tireless efforts to preserve the ecosystem and wildlife in the area. After 'gator-gazing, his wife loved nothing more than bird-watching, and so Papi made sure Rancho Paraiso was filled with the three hundred native birds she had memorized.

The main house was enormous, probably ten thousand square feet, two stories high, made of white stucco with bright blue roof tiles. The windows of the house spilled over with bright flower planters, and towering electric-green palm trees looked out over a variety of pools, fountains, and sculptures. Many of the sculptures were of Papi Pedro himself, in one or another ecstatic singing pose, commissioned by Papi Pedro, primarily for Papi Pedro's enjoyment. The house itself sat in a small valley in the center of the ranch, with sentries posted in towers to keep watch over the self-proclaimed king of Mexican music and his adoring wife.

One of Papi's pretty young maids answered the door in her white uniform, and led me to the plush, beige-and-brown media room, where he sat watching footage of one of his own concerts on a television screen that took up the entire wall. I gasped at the sight of Papi Pedro's mouth open, the size of a pickup truck, as he sang from the screen. The usual block-bodied bodyguards stood at the door, and Papi's wife sat nearby, smiling with her knees tightly together and her hands clasped on top of them. She greeted me with a tepid hug and immediately left the room, saying she had a watercolor to finish painting. It was hard for her to admit her husband had a child from another woman, and I figured she thought it was unfair that I had lived while her own daughter with Papi Pedro had died.

"So," Papi said, patting the sofa next to him for me to sit. "Tell me what you need."

"Well, I told you I was starting my own company," I told him. He nodded, solemn and serious. "And, if you let me, I'd like to handle your bookings in the States, the way Benito did, but with written contracts this time. Benito had a good roster, but he wasn't dealing with American rules, and that's why he lost. I know how to handle the American marketplace and media."

Papi nodded, and I knew that he knew the U.S. was not his primary marketplace. "It's fine," he said. "I trust you." This was no surprise. I had been unofficially handling his bookings since Benito went to prison, and would continue to do so, with a contract.

"But that's not all," I said.

"Well, go on," he said, smiling as if he were proud of me.

I grinned, excited to share my dream with him. "I want to produce movies, too. Or one movie. It's an incredible opportunity."

I told my father about Olivia and Marcella, and he listened with a dark look on his face.

"I don't know," he said. "Managing and publicizing music is one thing, producing movies is something else. You have a degree in business, not in film production."

My heart sank. "But I know how to surround myself with the right people, the way you do when you have a show. You don't play every instrument yourself, but you know how to pick the best people for the job. That's what I can do."

I handed Papi the copy of my business plan, including projections for earnings and market analysis. He asked for more information about the movie, and I told him about it. But his enthusiasm had faded. He seemed only mildly interested. In fact, he seemed much more interested in a piece of lint on his shirt than in anything I had to tell him.

"You'd have to know how to get our people to the theater," he said. "In the States, Mexicans don't go to the movies as much as they should. I read that in the L.A. *Times*."

So it must be true, I deadpanned in my mind. "I know," I said. "I can get people to the movie. Plus, it's not just for a Mexican audience, this movie. It's for a general audience. It's about a Salvadoran woman who made this amazing journey to the States and became a famous union leader."

Papi Pedro shrugged again. "I just don't know. How much money are you talking about here?"

I told him. It was probably close to what he'd paid for this house, which, in spite of its splendor, was just one of five houses he owned, and the least opulent. I reminded him it wasn't a gift, but an investment. "You'll make it back and then some."

He drew a sharp, deep breath, and exhaled, slowly, dramatically. He frowned. I reminded myself not to feel guilty asking for this much money because Papi Pedro had it, and he didn't know what to do with it.

Papi whistled through his teeth and shook his head. "I can't do that," he said.

I felt crushed. "Why not?" I asked. "The plan is solid. I have the skills. I know what I'm doing. It will work. I know it will."

He shrugged again. "And if it doesn't?"

"But it will."

Papi Pedro stood, smoothing his jeans out of his crack. "I'm sorry, Alexis. I wish I could help, but at my age . . ." He shrugged an apology. "I just don't know how much longer I can keep touring, and I have to be very careful about what I invest in."

"But, sir," I protested. He dumped a fistful of peanuts from a dish on the coffee table into his mouth and smiled as he chewed.

"You'll be fine managing acts," he said. "We'll do some big tours this next year, yes? You've got your condo, and your car, and once you get married you'll have your husband to take care of you. Don't you worry."

"But I'm your daughter," I said finally. Husband to take care of me? What the heck was he talking about?

I did not feel like it was the truth, that I was his daughter, but neither did I feel like it was a lie. I didn't want to be a sap and cry about this, but it happened.

Papi Pedro stared at me. "We're going riding in a few minutes," he said. "You're welcome to join us."

"No, thank you." I was full-on sobbing now, in spite of myself.

"This," he said, pointing to me and my tears, "is why women shouldn't run their own businesses. Too emotional."

I stared in disbelief at him, and realized, finally, that it had never been a disadvantage not knowing this man.

If anything, it had been a blessing.

He continued to babble: "Females are too weak to be in charge of something like making a movie. Take a look around. No women do it, and if you take a look at yourself right now, you'll see why."

And then he left the room. I stood, not knowing what to do with myself. I hadn't planned on him rejecting me. I had planned on him giving me the money I needed. I was his child, his blood relative, and he was filthy rich. He had promised to help me in any way I needed, and he had let me down. I had a good idea for this movie. For my company.

But I still didn't have the money.

I had not planned to stop in Dallas on the way back to Los Angeles, but I needed to see my momma and daddy. I was a mess, and I didn't know what to do. They always knew how to make me feel better.

Daddy picked me up at the airport and held me in a long embrace. "Don't worry about a thing, sweet pea," he said. "It'll all work out."

After Papi's ranch, the modest house I grew up in seemed pitiful.

"We could try to take out a loan," said Daddy, after reading through my business plan and the script. "Doesn't that seem about right, Mary?"

Momma nodded. "How much do you need, Alexis? We'll do our best. We can refinance the house, maybe."

My daddy nodded, and I burst their well-meaning bubble by telling them how much I needed: more than $10 million. They gasped in unison. "The most we could get is a couple hundred thousand," said Momma.

"I'll do it somehow," I said. "I don't want your money. Save your money."

"I wish we could do more," said Daddy. "And I don't agree with the politics of this movie. But I believe in you, Alexis. I always have."

"Thanks, Dad," I said, hugging and thanking them both. "I love you guys so much."

MARCELLA

I wasn't used to people coming to me in times of crisis. We didn't have times of crisis in my family, at least none that we'd admit to. Or else crisis was the only mode we functioned in. And when there were times of crisis, no one came to me. I was the reason for them, usually.

So I didn't know how to handle this, a teary-eyed Alexis on my doorstep with her equally sad-looking dog.

"He didn't give me any money," she said. "He told me women couldn't handle it. Oh, but he wants me to keep managing his affairs in the U.S. for him, because apparently I'm good enough at making him rich, here."

"Come in," I said. What else was there to say?

Alexis and her dog sat on my couch. I would have ordinarily asked the dog to step down, but this seemed to be a special occasion.

"We can't do it," she said. "I'm sorry. I wanted to make the movie. I wanted you to star in the movie." She began to cry harder. "I've been bad for your career. I'm sorry."

"What are you talking about?" I asked.

"My biological father wouldn't give me any money for the business," she insisted.

"So?"

"So we're doomed."

"No," I insisted. "That just means your biological father is an asshole. We're not doomed. Never doomed. Don't say 'doomed' in this house. We'll find the money."

She wiped her eyes and laughed. "Oh, right. The way *you* find money? With credit cards and self-deception? Right. Let's just charge the whole movie to your credit cards, shall we?"

"Whoa," I said. "Don't take it out on me."

"I'm not," she said. "I'm sorry. Maybe I am. But Marcella, you don't manage money well. I know that. I see what you do. You can't hide it from me."

"I take what I need," I told her. I decided we'd need some alcohol and went to the kitchen for a bottle of wine and two glasses.

"We'll think of something," I said as I poured her glass. "We always do. You always do. You're enterprising, remember?"

"Shut up," she said.

We went through the list of potential investors we knew, and figured out that combined, they would still come up short by a couple million. We tried to brainstorm about cutting corners on the production of the movie, but there was only so much cutting we could do without all of us going broke, or without compromising quality.

"We could try to find new investors," I suggested.

"Nobody in this town is going to give us money," said Alexis. "It's all corporate now, and all anybody cares about is making money. They don't even take original screenplays at the major movie companies anymore, Marcella! Unless we're doing a remake of some stupid seventies sitcom, or a sequel to a cartoon movie, we're doomed."

"There's that word again," I said. "Stop saying that."

"Doomed." She stuck her tongue out at me.

I got up and paced the room. I was angry. Very angry. This shouldn't have been happening. But it was. And it was happening because a male relative who had never given a shit about Alexis was continuing his fine tradition. My parents would likely do the same, because they still remained unconvinced that I would be able to do anything with my life, even though I was starting to become a household name.

"Wait here," I told her. I went to my guest bedroom closet and opened the door. I stood for a full five minutes, staring at the cardboard box with the geometric shapes on it, thinking about the videos of Uncle Hubert they contained. I'd been a strange teenager, making a tape like that, and an even stranger adult, keeping it. But I'd suspected the time would come when I would need it, when I wouldn't have the strength to lie to myself about it anymore, when I'd need revenge and closure—and money.

I took the box down and brought it to the living room.

"Here," I said to Alexis. I opened the box. Inside were the old-fashioned video-tapes. Fuzzy, grainy, but they were real, and they were horrible. Scene one: A man puts a video in a machine in his office, after making sure the shades are drawn and the doors are locked. Scene two: Man plays video of teen girl picking zits naked in front of her dresser mirror. Scene three: Man beats off.

"What is this?" she asked. "Turn it off, please."

"It's our money," I told her.

Alexis looked at me with a question in her eyes, and so I told her. I told her everything I could remember. And the expression on her face changed from self-pity to shock to sympathy to sickness.

"Oh, Marcella," she said. She ran across the room to me and took me in her arms. "I am so, so sorry that happened to you."

I shrugged. "I should have gotten at least scale, you know?"

She didn't laugh at my joke.

And then I broke down. At last, I broke down. I'd forgotten how hot tears felt. It had been at least fifteen years since I'd cried.

"This uncle, is he very wealthy?" asked Alexis.

"He's loaded," I said. The tears stopped as quickly as they'd come. "And fa-mous. And he'd do anything to hold on to that."

"It's blackmail, that's illegal," she said.

"Not the way I see it," I said. "The way I see it, he owes me. And if anyone asks where the money came from, we say it was his attempt to keep me from going public."

"You'll go public?"

"Maybe I won't have to."

Alexis frowned. "I'm so sorry it happened."

I tried to smile. "Hey," I said. "If I do go public, just think about all the press this will generate for the movie."

"God, Marcella," she said. "How can you be so glib about everything all the time?"

I looked her deep in her eyes and asked, "How the fuck do you think I've sur-vived?"

OLIVIA

It was Thursday, and that usually meant only one thing in my world: playgroup. But today it meant two things: Marcella and Alexis coming over for coffee, to talk about my screenplay in the morning. And playgroup after that.

Who said women couldn't have it all?

I dressed and readied with such energy and happiness, singing as I brushed my hair, dancing my way to the closet and back to the bedroom, that Jack noticed. He looked up from where he pushed a toy car across the carpet, and he smiled at me. I had not realized until that moment, when I was singing and dancing and brushing my hair, when he started singing and dancing with me, how much Jack needed to see me happy.

"Come on, kid," I said, carrying him to the living room with such a bounce in my step that he laughed out loud.

We danced to a Wiggles video and drew shapes with crayons and paper until my friends arrived. Jack was as excited to see them as I was. He liked having people over. Especially Alexis. She scooped him up immediately, covered him with kisses, and fussed over him. She'd brought her little dog and Jack loved her. Marcella stood off a bit, but Jack was smitten with the actress anyway. Already he was showing an interest in women, even if it was just to look at them. He knew she was beautiful, and stared. How had he already figured that out?

Though I didn't usually like to, I planted Jack on the couch in front of a video, *Finding Nemo*. He'd seen it a million times, and never tired of it. Marcella joined him on the sofa for the opening scenes, as Alexis and I prepared coffee and toast in the small galley kitchen. Marcella was used to having people wait on her, apparently.

"This movie is amazing," Marcella called. "I can't get over the animation. It's like you're really underwater. It's incredible."

Jack mimicked her. "It's *incredible*," he said, with precisely her inflection. We all laughed. Jack's eyes lit up at the attention, so he repeated the punch line. Again we laughed, and again he said, "Incredible." Jack liked telling jokes, making people laugh—he was like his father that way. I figured he'd be saying "it's incredible" for the next six months, to anyone who'd listen, hoping for a reaction as great as the one he'd just gotten.

As Jack continued to watch the video, Alexis and Marcella joined me at the small round dining table from Ikea. I lived in an Ikea catalog. We couldn't afford anything else. Ordinarily, I would have been embarrassed about my modest apartment and its cheap furniture, but today I didn't care. Today, I was more than the sum of my *stuff*. I was more than a mommy and wife whose husband hardly had time for her. I was a writer, and these women I respected and admired took me seriously.

"We love it," said Alexis. "It's a great script. There's nothing like it out there, and the market is ready."

"And we want to make it," said Marcella. "I mean, I want to."

I didn't know what to say, so I tried this: "Okay, that's good. Right?"

Alexis and Marcella looked at each other and cracked up. "That's it?" said Alexis.

"I don't know what to say," I told her.

"It's *incredible*," cried Jack, as if on cue.

"I know I don't look Salvadoran," said Marcella.

"It's a nationality," said Alexis. "You can't 'look' like a nationality. Anyone born in El Salvador looks Salvadoran, *technically*."

Marcella rolled her eyes at Alexis and continued to speak as if Alexis hadn't said a word. "But I love this character, and I'm an actress. It's my job to turn into the character."

"My mother would be thrilled to know she was being portrayed by Marcella Gauthier Bosch," I said. "I think you'd be fine."

"Fine?" Marcella looked offended.

"No, you'd be perfect," I said. "Seriously."

Alexis chimed in, "That's what I think. We want a Latina actress, who's fluent in English and Spanish, and who is well known enough that people will go to see her but not so well known that it becomes about the celebrity and not about the movie."

"Right," said Marcella.

"What do I need to do?" I asked.

"Right now, nothing," said Alexis. "We'll get started. But I need you to look over these papers, and sign them if you approve. I can be your manager if you want. But I'd still advise you to take them to a lawyer to make sure things are on the up and up."

"A lawyer?" I asked.

"We're your friends," said Alexis. "But as your friend I'd say never trust *anyone*, not even your friends. Business is business." She looked at Marcella and smiled. "And in business, you can't be polite. You have to . . . have balls."

"Nico could recommend some, if you don't know any," said Marcella.

"Lawyers," said Alexis. "Not balls."

"Actually, I'm sure he could recommend balls, too, if you were in the market for some. Big, hairy ones."

I took the papers from Alexis as if in a dream. But a good dream. There were stacks, contracts, and proposals, technical jargon and patterns of language I recognized from the tedious medical writing I used to do. "I'll take a look at it later," I said, "when Jack is napping."

Alexis suggested that she and Marcella take Jack to the park for an hour or so, while I looked over the papers. "I think you'll like what they say," she said. "We can't pay as much as the big studios, but I think what we're offering will help out."

Samuel was out of town on a business trip, an academic conference in Florida, and wouldn't be back until after the weekend. He'd already been gone for two days, and I needed a break from watching Jack. The offer was very tempting, but I didn't want to impose upon my friends and—could it be true?—business partners.

"You sure you can handle him?" I asked.

"It's incredible!" Jack cried.

"It's much harder than it looks," I said of watching a toddler.

"I love kids," said Alexis. "A bunch of my girlfriends back home have kids. I'm used to them. I can handle it."

"I can't make any promises," said Marcella. "I'm not the kid type."

"I'll keep her away from Jack," joked Alexis. "And I won't let her smoke near him. Now where's your stroller, sugar?"

From what I understood of the contracts, Alexis had formed her own management and production company, called Talentosa, Inc., which had scored a very tentative distribution deal with Columbus Pictures after they saw the script and learned Marcella would star. Columbus would distribute the film in "Latino markets" such as El Paso and Los Angeles, with the understanding that if it did well there, they would consider opening it in a wider range of cities.

That they had done all of this behind my back upset me at first, but I thought about it and realized why they'd proceeded that way. If they'd asked me, I would have been too shy and scared to say yes. I wouldn't even have let them read the script, in fact.

Alexis's company wanted to purchase the rights to my screenplay, for—how much? I squinted to make sure I hadn't misunderstood. For more than Samuel made in two years of work? Was that right? In addition to the purchase amount, I would get a certain percentage of whatever the movie made in theaters, assuming it made it to the theaters.

What would it be like to have money like that? I knew that was a lot of money, but what did it mean? How did you live with money like that? What did it feel like not to have to juggle bills—or, worse, ignore them—and what might it feel like not to worry where you'd scrounge up the cash for new shoes? I had no idea.

I looked down at my beat-up Asics and wiggled my toes with glee. I wanted to call Samuel and share the good news with him, but it was better to tell him face-to-face. I'd wait, and tell him in person once he got back from Florida. Honestly, I wasn't sure how he'd react, knowing that I'd be making more money than him. I hoped his ego was up for it. With men, you never knew.

When Alexis and Marcella came back, I had the Internet up to a runner's equipment page, looking at shoes. Samuel called my bad habit of window-shopping online "Olivia porn." Alexis noticed the shoes instantly.

"It'll be nice to see you spend instead of just looking for once," said Alexis.

MARCELLA

It had taken five minutes to copy the videos to a DVD, two days for the package to be shipped to New York, and a matter of hours for dear old Uncle Hubert to wire several million dollars to the newly established corporate bank account for Talentosa, Inc.

Because Alexis thought it only fitting to make me a co-owner, I'd been able to make up the financial shortage by hiring my own brother as a lawyer and looking into the matter of the trust fund. Turns out the money was mine, legally mine, and my parents were, in fact, trying to keep it from me because, as we knew, my parents were shits.

So I took what I needed, and the rest, as they say, was history. *Bod Squad* would keep the bills paid until the movie was made, and then I would never have to worry about money again. I was banking on it. Literally.

Alexis and I rented a small office space complete with wood-paneled walls and an antiseptic smell, in Sherman Oaks, and began to put together a real company, with a real Mr. Coffee in the corner and a real office-looking telephone. Nico was our contracts guy and legal source.

Of our company, Alexis was president and CEO; and I was the queen artist whose very name would entice other artists to join.

Step one? Finding new clients.

Because no woman in her right mind can be expected to hit the Santa Monica and Venice boardwalk for an afternoon of in-line skating and networking without being properly caffeinated, Alexis, Lydia, a friend named Sidney, and I met in the best place in L.A. to caffeine and be seen, a neo-Gothic masterpiece called the Chateau Marmont Hotel on Sunset, in West Hollywood. Olivia said she couldn't make it because she had promised to take Jack to the children's museum. Strange as it sounded, I would have liked to join them. I didn't suddenly want to be a mother or anything like that, but I enjoyed Jack's presence. He was a funny, good guy. A person in a very small package.

I figured Alexis could do magic for Sidney, a pretty and promising young actress I knew through a friend at the gym. Both of them needed a manager, and Alexis needed clients. I didn't want to be the only one officially signed to her firm. I felt good, like the fairy godmother bringing everything together. All I needed was a tiara, and wings. Saint Marcella. It almost seemed like I was doing something nice. *Mère* might approve, but probably not.

I wore a black terry sweat suit with a bikini top underneath. Alexis wore something I'd never even considered, a cross between a miniskirt and shorts, in black. A skort, she called it. At first I thought she was saying the word wrong, Texan, but she wasn't. Very cute. She wore a simple T-shirt, pink, with a black sweater tied preppy around her neck. She had sunglasses and the ever-present pearls, these ones small and simple.

Lydia dressed—or *undressed,* as Alexis liked to call it—pretty much like me, all in black, revealing, cute, which was no surprise; Alexis told me Lydia idolized me, and from the constant questions she kept asking about acting and beauty, I felt that was true. What I did *not* believe, however, was that Lydia would ever come close to being anything like me. If I truly thought she had Marcella potential, I would not have encouraged Alexis to sign her up again—after all, someone with Marcella potential might have taken jobs from me. Lydia was too innocent, and too stupid. I didn't mean to be snide, thinking the poor girl was dim, but it was obvious she was some sort of idiot savant, able to sing her ass off but unable to understand compound sentences. By her age I was living on my own already. Lydia's eighteen was more like my twelve.

Sidney, an Israeli girl who grew up in Venezuela and might as well have been a Latina, wore Daisy Duke jean short-shorts with the word SINGLE printed on the butt, and a tiny bustier—but she was new in town and still trying too hard. She was gorgeous, but she didn't need to be so obvious about it. She'd learn. In fact, that was the kind of advice Alexis could give her. I hoped *she* didn't have Marcella potential. Hmm. I hadn't considered that. I was so excited to find a beautiful young artist for Alexis I hadn't even considered that she might be more beautiful and younger than I was. This line of thinking made me feel dangerously like my mother, so I stopped.

The four of us sat on the patio, sipping *café con leche* from large white pottery cups. We'd already spotted three celebrities, including Salma Hayek. Salma smiled and waved at me, and I was so flattered! I had met her at a party once, but I didn't think she'd remember me. She even came over and asked about the TV show, which was sort of humiliating, and congratulated me for having taken so public a stand on all of the issues of gender equality in the *novela* business. She was behind me completely, she said. I took it all as a sign, a sign about Olivia's movie. Alexis laughed.

"There you go with the Jung stuff again, sugar," she said.

"When things work out, you know it. The universe lets you know. Like now. Here we are, talking about your business."

"Ah, slick change of conversation," Alexis said.

At that moment, another strange coincidence blew in the door. "Uh-oh," I said to Alexis. "Your ex-gangster Mac Daddy piece of shit is here."

Alexis turned and saw Daniel stroll through the lobby in baggy jeans and a large hockey jersey. Sidney and Lydia looked at him, too.

"What's up with that old guy?" Sidney asked, laughing, as so many people did, at the fake limp and snarl that characterized Alexis's weird ex. He stared at Alexis coldly, like a wolf, and made some sort of gesture with his hands that I think he intended to seem scary. He wasn't alone, either. Next to him was a young guy in long shorts and long white socks, a prototypical *vato* from an East L.A. movie produced by Edward James Olmos, complete with a shaved head and a tattoo of the Virgin of Guadalupe on his arm.

"Oh, m'gosh," said Alexis. She looked worried. "I could swear he's been following me."

"You should, like, call the police," said Lydia.

Alexis smiled and shrugged as Daniel disappeared around a corner. "Oh, I dunno. He talks big, but I don't think Daniel would ever do anything stupid."

"Fubu jeans," I said. "That's pretty stupid for an old man."

Alexis considered my statement and nodded, immediately breaking into a cheerful grin. "Let's talk about something else," she suggested. "Like business!"

Alexis asked the two young women what they thought about signing on with Talentosa, Inc. Sidney asked what the name of the company signified, and I explained that it was a nod to the male-dominated entertainment industry and Alexis's desire to change that. I spoke the concept so clearly and meaningfully I wished Mathilde were there to hear me. It was almost like I cared.

"I can't think of anyone I'd rather have represent me," Lydia said. She put her head on Alexis's shoulder and closed her eyes, revealing sparkly silver shadow. "You're still, like, totally my best friend."

I looked at the ground to avoid meeting Alexis's gaze. I knew how Alexis felt about having been claimed as the best friend of a very immature, if exceptionally talented, eighteen-year-old. She thanked Lydia and complimented her, without returning the claim to best buddyhood. Amazing. What a pro.

"What about you, Sidney?" I asked.

Sidney, who was at that moment being pointed at with great interest by a couple of Hollywood executive types in the shadows, sat up and flashed her big, flawless, megawatt smile.

"I've heard nothing but great things about you," she said to Alexis with her slight, and hard to place, accent. She spoke four languages fluently. Of course. Not only was she a younger, prettier version of me, she was one language more lingual as well.

Alexis asked each of the women what their long-term goals were, and wrote the answers down on a yellow legal pad she'd brought. She told them how much she cost.

"Plus, we get to be best friends," said Lydia. Then, speaking to Sidney, she said, "You'll see. Alexis is, like, totally *fun*."

Again, I looked at the ground.

"Well," I said, once the women had signed on the dotted lines of the contracts Nico had drawn up. "I'm glad this all worked out. Now what do you girls say we go have some fun?"

"I *love* fun!" Lydia cried.

Sidney stared at Lydia with a polite but curious gaze and said nothing.

"Did you all bring your skates?" I asked. Everyone nodded. "Great," I said. "So how should we get to the beach? My car's too small." I smiled at the thought of my little Bentley. "Do we take separate cars?"

"I have a big car," said Sidney.

"What are you driving?" I asked. Alexis cringed as if I had asked an intrusive question, which I realized in retrospect I had.

"A Volkswagen bus," she said with a blush. "An old one. I painted the outside. It's sort of funky and retro, but it'll get us there."

I wanted to refuse, but didn't.

"I think that will be fine," Alexis said. She opened her eyes wide at me, the same way my mother did when she wanted me to agree with her. "It sounds cute, doesn't it, Marcella?"

"It sounds fun!" Lydia said, looking at Sidney with new interest. "I love fun stuff!" Sidney looked back at Lydia and I could see the sparks fly. These two would be great friends. Good. Maybe then Lydia would forget about Alexis being her best friend and move on.

The bus smelled like gasoline, and backfired as if it had a bad case of indigestion. It needed shock absorbers. But it had a great stereo, and Sidney had good taste in music. Better taste in music than Alexis, anyway. If I had to suffer through her Cyndi Lauper or Sheena Easton collections again, I'd have to kill myself.

"Who is this?" I asked. The music ground out dirty and hip, part salsa, part hip-hop.

"It's a new rapper, from Cuba," she said. "Vladimir."

I immediately hit Alexis on the arm. "Hey," I said. "Synchronicity."

She glowered at me. "Pshaw."

"No," I said. "Isn't that the guy you saw in concert? The cute one you told me about who ran into your car?"

Alexis nodded. "I wasn't going to say anything," she said.

"He's so good!" Lydia said. "This is really fun! Is this the guy that Russian weirdo told you about?"

Alexis looked embarrassed. "Yeah."

"Oh," said Lydia, looking disappointed. "I wouldn't mind making a duet with him. I thought you said he was an old Russian guy. You said—"

"I didn't *know*," Alexis said. Suddenly, I was sorry I'd brought it up, because Alexis was starting to look like, well, like a bad manager. Which she wasn't.

"That's okay, sweetie," Lydia said. "You'll just have to introduce me to him now."

Maybe, I thought, Lydia had more going on than it seemed?

"Okay," Alexis said, with a nod.

"Did you call him yet?" I asked. I'd been on her case about it ever since she told me how great the concert was, how cute he was, and how he had told her he thought she was cute, too.

"I haven't," she said.

"Well, what are you waiting for?" I asked. "It's been months, Alexis. You need to get in touch with him."

"I don't know," she said. "I keep forgetting. Sorry."

But I knew why she hadn't called. She didn't think he'd remember her, or she was afraid he wouldn't want to talk to her, all the things Alexis thought when she tried to psych herself out of the good things in life, especially the good things involving men. Normally I would have lectured her at a time like this, but I didn't want to make her look bad in front of her new clients.

"Well, you'll call him soon, right?" I asked. "So he can do a duet with Lydia? That would be a good move, manager woman."

"Sure," she said. She smiled, but I could see the worry in her eyes.

"Can you turn it up, Sidney?" I asked. "Shit rocks."

The beach was crowded, as usual, but when people saw us coming, believe me, they cleared a way. We were four hotties on wheels.

Alexis would have disagreed, but that girl needed to get a better mirror. Sure, she wasn't ever going to be anybody's centerfold, but that didn't mean anything. I worked with women (and men) who were beautiful on the outside but didn't have half the inner spark Alexis did. I was starting to realize spark was just as important as boobs, but unlike boobs, you could not buy or cultivate spark. Either you had it or you didn't. And she did.

Lydia and Sidney were excellent skaters. I was pretty good, too. But poor Alexis had a hard time staying upright. She was a little slower than we were, and had a way of skating where her knees touched but her feet were as far apart as humanly possible. She reminded me of that scene from *Bambi* where Thumper tries to teach the lanky doe how to ice-skate. I kept stopping to wait for her. She had a couple of really bad falls, and finally just sat down on the cement wall next to a playground, near one of her favorite beach snack bars. She panted and her face glowed red.

"Come on, manager!" Lydia teased from several yards away. She clapped like a drill sergeant. "Let's go! Earn your keep!"

Sidney, who, it turned out, had taken figure skating pretty seriously as a young child (of course she had) rolled in figure eights on one foot on an empty basketball court, and sang beautifully at the top of her lungs. It was rare for men's eyes to land anywhere but on me when I made a public appearance, but I'll be damned if they weren't all staring at *her*.

Huh.

I thought: I better learn to do something else in Hollywood, and quick, because even with endless surgery, I was nearing thirty. There was always going to be someone younger and prettier coming along, doing perfect figure eights on one foot, babbling in a million languages, and I found fewer things more pathetic than aging stars who did everything they could to hold on to their sexy images. I thought of Olivia's film. I had wanted to do it before, but now I *really* wanted to do it. If I got critical acclaim for something like Olivia's movie, then there was a chance I could cross the boundary from sexpot to serious actress, and that meant a lifetime of work. I could be Diane Keaton instead of Loni Anderson.

"Get up," I said to Alexis. "We've barely started."

Alexis gasped for air and pulled an inhaler from her pocket. I'd forgotten about the asthma. I should have left her in the van.

"You okay?" I asked.

She nodded, but took another puff from the inhaler. "Go ahead," she gasped. "I'll wait here. Don't let me ruin your skating."

I motioned for Lydia and Sidney to come over.

"Don't," Alexis said. "Just go on ahead." She seemed upset, an emotion I rarely detected in her. Her eyes focused on two young couples with babies in strollers, out exercising together. She stared at the babies with despair and envy.

"What's *wrong*?" I asked.

"Nothing," she said.

Lydia and Sidney skated over, arm in arm and giggling, fast becoming good pals.

"What's wrong?" Sidney asked.

Alexis looked up at us standing there, and she laughed bitterly. I had never heard her laugh bitterly before.

" 'What's wrong?' " she asked. I swear, she looked like she was going to cry.

"Yeah," said Lydia. "What's wrong?"

"Well, let's see," Alexis said. Tears formed in her eyes and started to leak onto her cheeks. "I'm ugly and fat, and all three of you are completely gorgeous. I'm out of shape and can't breathe, and you three are out there doing pirouettes. Men stare at you guys with their tongues hanging out, and they can't even see me. Even though I probably weigh more than the three of you combined, I'm invisible. It's amazing! And I'm about to have a heart attack."

Lydia, Sidney, and I looked at each other. I sat on the wall next to Alexis and put my arm around her. "What are you talking about?" I asked. "You're so pretty, Alexis."

"Please," she sniffled. "Don't patronize me right now. I know what I am. I have a mirror. I have six mirrors, in fact."

"Hey," I said to Lydia and Sidney. "You guys go on ahead. We'll catch up with you later. I need to have a talk with Alexis."

"Okay," Lydia said. They skated off, to catcalls and whistles from the now-occupied basketball court. To my relief, they didn't seem to think Alexis's break-down spoke poorly of her potential as a manager and businesswoman. They were young.

"Alexis," I said. "Look at me."

"No. That's just it. I am *sick* of looking at you. I *hate* looking at you."

I didn't know what to say. "Please don't say that," I said.

"But it's true," Alexis said. She had stopped crying and managed to pull herself together. She looked up, smiling, the perfect little debutante again.

"I had no idea you felt this bad about yourself, Alexis," I said.

"I've told you," she said. She was still smiling. "I don't want to bother you about it. I don't know what's wrong with me. I guess when you need to lose thirty pounds, and you kick out your boyfriend and lose your job, and your new best friend is only, like, the most beautiful woman in the world. It can be a little depressing."

Did she just call me her best friend? "Come with me," I said.

"What? Where?"

I pulled her up and off the cement wall, and dragged her, wobbly on her unstable skates, to the nearby women's restroom. There were no real mirrors here, probably because there were so many crazy people on the beach they didn't want anyone breaking them and attacking people with the shards. But there were fake mirrorlike things, metal, on the wall.

"Come here," I said.

"No."

"Yes." I pushed her in front of one of them. "What do you see?" I asked.

"Nothing. It's all blurry. It's better that way."

"Alexis. Stop it. Look at yourself. You're so pretty! Why do you do this to yourself?"

"Can we just go?" she asked. "I'm fine. Really. It's okay."

"If you want, we can go," I said. "But I really want you to know that I think you're pretty."

"Sure, whatever you say."

"Say it, then."

"What?"

"Say I'm Alexis Lopez and I'm beautiful."

Alexis laughed. "I'll say it later," she said. "How's that?"

"Say it now. I want to hear you say it."

"I'll call you when I say it later in the privacy of my own home."

I laughed. I realized it was fairly ridiculous to demand that she stand in a public restroom full of people complimenting her semi-reflection. "Okay," I said. "But I'm serious. I don't want you beating yourself up anymore. It's really unhealthy."

"Okay," she said. She smiled. But then again, she almost always smiled.

"Is anything else bugging you?" I asked as we left the bathroom and started to skate, arm in arm, slowly.

"Sort of," she said.

"What?"

"I can't stop thinking about him."

I looked at her. She blushed. "Who?" I asked.

"Vladimir. That rapper."

"Ohhhhh. *Him*."

"I got some of his songs off the Internet and I'm totally obsessed."

We skated into the light.

"Oh, shoot," Alexis said, and she tried to hide her face in my shoulder. She tripped on her skates and clutched at my arm to keep herself up.

"What?" I asked. "What's wrong?"

"It's *him*." She pointed at the boardwalk. Two young men walked along holding surfboards. One was incredibly handsome, with little dreadlocks on his head, and the other was plain old weird, with bright blue hair and miserable piercings everywhere.

"Which one is he?" I asked, hoping Alexis did not lust after the freak. I didn't need any more freaks in my life.

"The cute one," she said. "Hide me! Do you think he heard me? Talking about him? Oh, gosh."

They were pretty close to us, but I didn't think they'd heard anything. Then again, the cute one was staring at us with a huge smile on his face.

"Maybe," I said.

"Oh, Jeez Louise," Alexis yelped. "Help!"

I pushed Alexis up straight and dragged her to where the men were.

"Hi," I said, while Alexis wilted in fear next to me. The men grinned. "I'm Marcella," I said. I held my hand out to shake theirs. They leaned their boards against the cement wall and shook my hand. "This is my friend Alexis," I said. "I think you met her already, Vladimir?"

He smiled beautifully. "Yes, we met." He spoke the cutest accented English I'd ever heard. "I crashed into her expensive car with my inexpensive car." He stared at her. "It's good to see you again," he said to her. He didn't even know I was there—a sure sign that this guy dug Alexis. I was thrilled for her, which surprised me. Maybe I was developing empathy and kindness after all.

"Thanks," Alexis said.

"I was hoping you'd call me, but I never heard from you. Burian told me you came to my concert, so I hoped you'd at least call to tell me how awful I was."

"Sorry," she said.

"You know," I said, "Alexis just opened her own management and publicity company, and I heard you were looking for a manager, Vladimir."

"I am, actually," he said. Then, looking directly into Alexis's eyes with that spark I had seen so many men give her but which she never seemed to notice, he said, "I'd love to hear more about it."

"Okay," she said.

"Here, sit down," he offered. Nice guy, I thought. And freaking fine. And, I noticed, he scarcely gave me a second look. Obviously, he wasn't the fake boob type. The best guys never were, unfortunately. He liked Alexis. I could see it. She could see it. And they needed some alone time.

"Hey," I said to the other guy, whose name, I learned, was Fantasma, which meant what it sounded like and wasn't at all a normal name. "I need some help with these skates. Can you help me?"

It was stupid, my excuse. But it worked. I got Fantasma to go with me to the other side of the basketball court, leaving Alexis alone with Vladimir.

Fantasma helped me with my invented skate problem, and as he worked, I noticed that in spite of the heavy gothic makeup and crazy hair, he *was* in fact a handsome man. Very handsome. He looked smart, and soulful. And familiar.

"Where do I know you from?" I asked.

"I don't know," he said, with a grin that told me he did, in fact, know, but was going to make finding out as hard on me as he could.

"You look really familiar," I said.

"Do I?" he asked. "That's too fucking bad."

Yikes. I stared for a while, but couldn't place him.

"And you," he said. "You're Marcella Gauthier Bosch, the big TV star."

"You watch the show?"

"Occasionally. I think it's a piece of shit, though. Waste of your talents."

"No, please, tell me what you *really* think." I tried to convey an Alexis sort of shock at his lack of manners, but the truth was I admired his honesty. Too many people who hated the show lied to me, and it was usually obvious. I wasn't a fan of the show, and if I weren't on it, I would never have watched it.

"Sorry," he said. "But I try to say what I think when I think it. I don't lie."

"That's my line," I said.

"Pardon?"

"I always say the same thing. That I don't lie."

"Good."

"But here's something I've learned. You can tell the truth creatively. You don't have to be rude."

"*Lying* is rude. Presenting a false self is rude. There is no ruder person than the super-polite."

I liked this guy.

He continued, "And the show is stupid. It was stupid when it was *Baywatch*, and it's even stupider when it's ripped off. But you do a good job, considering the limited material."

"You think?" I asked.

He looked me square in the eye. "You are smarter than people think you are," he said. "I can't explain it exactly. I always thought that, but seeing you now makes me believe it more."

I kept staring as he tried to adjust a wheel. He started humming, with a secretive smile on his face. I knew that song! It was an old Sancocho song. He started to sing the words, and gave me a crazy, wild look. He put the skate down and started to do a little dance I used to watch the boys of Sancocho do back when I was a huge Sancocho fan. I even had a notebook with the boy band on the cover.

"Oh, my God," I said. "No way! You're Chiquito! From Sancocho!"

He laughed. "That was my stage name." He made a cynical stupid face and said in a high, high voice, like a little boy, "Chiquito! Hey!"

"I used to love Sancocho," I said. "I loved Chiquito! Timi was my favorite, though. Sorry to say."

"You and everyone else," he said. "Fucking Timi. He looked like a girl then and he looks like a girl now. What's the big deal?"

"But you were cute," I said.

"Chiquito was a piece of shit," he said. "My real name is Carmelo Hernández, but they thought Carmelo was too grown-up for a little boy and gave me Chiquito. People who know me now call me Fantasma." He bared his teeth as if he had fangs, and hissed. Weird guy, but I liked him.

He held his hand out again to shake mine. But rather than shake it, he kissed it. I remembered hearing stories about Chiquito, about how he went crazy when he was fifteen and defected from Sancocho. I'd heard that he just walked away one day, in the middle of Paraguay, and went off into the jungle or something to find himself, with a guitar. He had come back a changed young man, and started writing incredible rock songs, heavy metal. He was supposed to be writing lots of hit songs these days for other artists, like Timi Martinez. I asked him if that whole thing about walking away in the middle of Paraguay was true.

"Yeah," he said. He sat next to me. His eyes scanned the horizon.

"Why did you quit?" I asked.

He sighed and stared into my eyes like a vampire.

"I wanted to write my own songs," he said. "And they wouldn't let me, the stupid shits. So I quit."

I gulped, hard. "How did you find that kind of courage at fifteen?" I asked, thinking, *I don't have that kind of courage and I'm twenty-nine.*

"Courage?" he asked.

"Yeah," I said.

"I just felt the spiritual call to do what I needed to do, the way I wanted to do it. And I did. I didn't know I had a choice."

ALEXIS

Nothing worked. Not the twin sets. Not the linen pantsuits. Not the little pleated chiffon skirts. It was all too prissy, too Dallas, too *me*. I didn't *want* to be me tonight. I wanted to be someone prettier, hipper, thinner, better. I wanted to be someone Goyo the rap star wouldn't be embarrassed to be seen with, and as I stood there in my closet, clothes strewn at my feet in chaotic, pastel, sensible clumps, it hit me: He would never fall in love with a woman like me.

He was a rapper, which meant he was trendy, expressive, outspoken, tough, and contemporary. I was a debutante, which meant I was stodgy, reserved, insincere, wimpy, and, by Los Angeles standards, bass-ackwards. It would never work. Unless I had some serious help in the hipness department. I only knew one truly hip woman, and I realized I had no choice but to call her and beg for assistance. I picked up the white cordless phone from the island dresser in the middle of the closet and dialed her cell number by heart.

"Marcella?" I asked into the phone. I stood in front of the mirror in my big fuzzy yellow bathrobe with the blue duckies on it. I looked terrified beneath the cucumber mask and eye cream. I looked like one of those chubby girls in high school movies, where the other girls try to fix her up and make her look better but only end up throwing pig blood on her as she runs sobbing through the night.

"Yeah, hey Alexis. What's up?" I could hear the sound of her car engine droning along. She was in the Bentley again. I swore that girl was always driving around in that car of hers. She needed a life.

"Where you goin', girl?" I asked. I tried to sound cheerful, even though I felt like crawling in a hole and hiding for a thousand years. "Sounds like you're in the car again."

"Just around," she said. "I think best when I'm driving fast. I've got a lot on my mind."

"You're going to wear that Bentley out," I said. "Be careful. Don't speed."

"It's three o'clock. What do you want me to do?"

"Sorry?"

"It's like Jean-Paul Sartre said," Marcella explained. "'*Three o'clock is always too early or too late for anything you'd want to do.*'"

"I need *help*, sugar," I said. "Please hold off on the quotes for now."

"Yeah, well, it's not news you need help," she joked. "What can I do for you?"

"I'm going to dinner and clubbing tonight," I said.

"So?"

"It's a hip-hop club. I'm going with Vladimir, you know, the rapper."

"Uh-oh." Marcella laughed. "What time is your date with the delicious Vlad? You know what? That boy is fine. You got a fine man, at last. Just as I lost one, you got one. Life's fair."

"It's not a *date*. I'm going to see if he needs a *manager*. And don't worry, your prince will come."

Marcella snorted a laugh. "Did you ask him out, or did he ask you?"

"He asked me."

"Do you want him?" she asked.

"Pretty much. Yeah."

She cackled. I hated when she cackled. "Then it's a date."

"But he only asked me after you told him I was starting my own business."

"Oh. So it's *not* a date."

I felt disappointed. I'd hoped she'd convince me it *was* a date. I wanted it to be a date. I sighed. "No. I guess not."

"But you want to *look* like you're on a date?"

"Right."

"What time is he picking you up?"

I sat on the floral ottoman. Everything in my life was floral, or pretty. It's like I lived in an old woman's house. "He's not. We're meeting at Asia de Cuba."

"Oh, you're *meeting*. Huh."

She knew I thought men should pick the women up and be gentlemen. But that was for dates.

"It's not a *date*," I reminded her.

"That's a nice place, Asia de Cuba," Marcella said. "You ever been?"

I'd been there with *her,* and couldn't *believe* she'd forget. "Yes," I said. "I've been."

"You never told me," she said, as if I'd hurt her.

Honestly.

"It's really not a good thing to go there looking bad," she said. "You have to look good or they might not let you in. So what time are you meeting?"

"At eight."

"So you have some time. Meet me at the DKNY store in Costa Mesa."

"South Coast Plaza?" I asked.

"Yeah. In an hour. We're shopping."

"I thought you hated mall shopping."

"I make an exception for South Coast Plaza."

I did not feel like shopping right now, which was nothing short of astonishing because I could not remember another single time in my life when I had not felt like shopping. I felt like sleeping, so I said, "But I don't have a ton of money to go shopping. I'm saving everything for the business, remember?"

"Listen to me," Marcella said. She was losing patience with me. "You have a business to run. You have to dress well. It's a business investment. Jesus H. Christ, Alexis. You're not poor, so stop acting like it."

"Fine. But I don't want you to spend any money. I'm worried about the way you spend, Marcella. We should talk about that."

"Okay, look, there's a hot cop pulling me over. I gotta blow him to get out of the ticket. Bye."

"Puke," I said.

"I won't swallow," she said.

"You are *so* disgusting!"

"What a wuss! I'm only *kidding,* silly. A cop could never afford a Marcella BJ."

"What is *wrong* with you?"

"I have a sense of humor, my dear. That's what's wrong with me. An hour. DKNY. Don't be late."

I hung up and dressed in my usual gear—linen cropped pants and a silk tank with slingbacks. I looked at my reflection and it hit me again: I would never suck a cop. I would never even *joke* about sucking a cop. All I wanted was to spend my free time pushing a kid on a swing, like I'd done with Jack.

I was hopelessly, endlessly boring.

I didn't usually use valet parking at the mall. It always seemed like the laziest, most pretentious thing in the world to me that there would be valet parking for a *mall*. For me, the words "mall" and "valet" didn't belong together. But I didn't have much time. The traffic on the way to Costa Mesa had been a nightmare thanks to yet another fiery rollover, and Marcella was already in the mall waiting for me— and calling me every two minutes on the cell phone to say she'd found something perfect. I'd asked if she was spending money, and she'd said no, then explained that she was running up debts on plastic. I was two steps from an intervention.

Incidentally, I'd been horrified by the first six or so fiery rollovers I'd seen upon moving to Los Angeles. But by number seven, I was over it. Fiery rollovers were now routine in my life. I think L.A. was wearing off on me. And I was about to use the valet. At the mall. Because I was in too much of a hurry to park, because I was heading out to a trendy restaurant and night of clubbing with a rapper. Lordy.

All of this meant only one thing: I had finally adapted to life in Southern California. There was no turning back.

I drove up to the curb, stopped in front of the two young men in white shirts and red vests who stood beneath the canopy in front of a podium. Why did valet guys stand behind podiums? It wasn't like they'd be giving speeches anytime soon. Why not benches for them to sit on? I mean, it was hard enough work, wasn't it, running to the parking garage all day long, driving in dizzying circles underground for mean-spirited people who rarely tipped enough, if at all. A podium? Jeez Louise.

The whole valet thing seemed strange to me. I mean, here were these guys— and they were always guys, weren't they?—making a few dollars an hour, and they got the keys to cars worth more than they made in a year. What was to stop them from driving to Mexico and selling them? I never understood that. I didn't like the concept of giving my keys to a stranger, much less to a stranger in a polyester red vest, but here I was, doing it. It was like using credit cards. There was entirely too much trust going around.

In Texas, trust had seemed the most natural thing in the world; but after seeing my employer implode on drug charges, after hearing about soap stars who dribbled barbecue sauce on themselves in guest houses, I didn't like it. You really couldn't trust anyone at the end of the day, now could you? Except Vladimir Goyo. I trusted him. I didn't know why, but I did.

"Welcome to South Coast Plaza," said the valet. Poor thing sounded like a robot. I was pretty sure they made him memorize this stuff. There was probably even a hidden carmera somewhere, with an evil boss watching to make sure he said that line every time someone in a nice car pulled up.

"Thanks," I said. I stuffed a five-dollar bill in his hand, just to make sure he treated the car with care. He handed me a paper ticket.

"Pleasant shopping here at the South Coast Plaza, ma'am," he said.

Ma'am? Oh my gosh. Things were so much worse than I thought! Lately, I'd seemed to have crossed from the Miss world into the Ma'am world, and I didn't like it. Ma'am was for ladies whose breasts sagged, with bellies like backpacks, and varicose veins and wrinkles. I needed to go on a diet and start working out, I really did. These thirty pounds added ten years to me, I was sure of it, which meant the valet probably thought I was forty.

"Thank you, darlin'," I said.

"Where are you from?" he asked. "If you don't mind my asking."

"Texas," I said.

"I love your accent," he said, and smiled. Was he flirting? But he'd just called me ma'am. You couldn't call someone ma'am and then *flirt* with them. That wasn't allowed, unless you had, you know, *issues*. I was already so confused and nervous I didn't have time to think about whether the valet was flirting with me. I barely had energy to think about whether he would drive off in my car and never be seen again.

I smiled and waved, nice and friendly-like, the way I'd been raised, and walked down the red carpet—yes, this mall has a red carpet from the valet stand to the mall entrance—and entered the shiny, air-conditioned paradise of South Coast Plaza. We had nice malls in Dallas, that was for sure. But nothing compared to South Coast Plaza. It was a huge mall, but filled with only the finest boutiques and shops.

I found the nearest map and scoped out the DKNY store. I called Marcella on her cell and said I was in the mall, on my way to meet her.

"I found the perfect thing while I was waiting for you," she said. "But it's in the Dolce & Gabbana boutique. I couldn't believe they carried it in your size!"

Charming, as usual. "I'm on my way to DKNY," I said. "You told me to meet you at *DKNY*."

She couldn't believe they had it in my size? She was so rude, I could hardly believe it. I sounded panicked. I didn't mean to, but I was nervous. Nervous about my career, nervous about Vladimir. Nervous about being a ma'am thirty pounds overweight. Nervous that the valet was on his way to Mexico with my Cadillac.

Marcella coughed. She needed to stop smoking, that's what she needed. Then she said, "That's fine. I'll meet you there. I just think we should get you what I found at Dolce."

"I don't wear Dolce," I said.

"You will," she said.

I looked up and saw her inside the DKNY store. We looked at each other with our phones on our ears and laughed, hung up our phones.

"It's about time!" she cried. She gave me a hug. She smelled good underneath the vile notes of tobacco. That was the way with her, I decided; there was great beauty in Marcella, but it was smudged around the edges by her character flaws. Some people might say it made her interesting, but I was starting to think it just made her difficult.

"Traffic," I said, though I should have learned by now that blaming the traffic was hardly an acceptable excuse for lateness in Southern California, where traffic was a way of life. You were supposed to factor in traffic disasters when calculating your commute time. I kept forgetting about that part.

I looked around and noticed that Marcella had already collected a few bags of clothing for herself, and more than a few *fans*. People stood around gawking and pointing shamelessly, as if she weren't human and couldn't see them, as if she were standing there on a TV screen instead of in the flesh. A saleswoman stood nearby with a giant phony smile on her face, hoping, I imagined, that the TV star would drop a wad of cash and she'd get a good commission.

"How can you stand all these people following you?" I whispered in her ear. "Doesn't it make you feel strange?"

"No," Marcella said. She picked up a T-shirt and held it out for inspection, held it against her huge breasts in the mirror. "I like it. That's why I wanted to be a movie star. I'm needy and attention-starved, remember? And I have you to thank. Thank you."

She looked around to make sure people were watching, and planted a big wet kiss on my lips before singing, " '*Let's give 'em something to talk about. . . .* ' "

"You're going to need a bodyguard one of these days," I said.

"Nah. I'll fight them off." She circled her arms like a karate expert and made a ridiculous noise, like someone making fun of someone making fun of a karate movie. As before, at the Getty, she reminded me of Angelina Jolie, someone really gorgeous who carried herself like a fighter, ready to lunge and a little unhinged, almost tomboyish. Then, she patted me on the rear end.

"You're so weird," I said. She made me laugh. I couldn't imagine being as beautiful and famous as Marcella and still being so, well, so darn confused.

"Me? Weird? Remember, honey, it takes one to know one." She looked me up and down. "Now let's go get you some clothes." She grabbed me by the elbow and dragged me to the dressing room, where a pile of clothes in my size—a fourteen—

waited. I'd worn my granny panties, and once again she complained. But I didn't get the whole thong thing. Marcella was convinced I should buy them all. I bought two items. Then she, to my horror, bought the rest on her own credit card and stuffed them into my bag. The rest, for the record, cost more than two thousand dollars.

"I'll just return them," I told her as we left. "You can't waste so much money, Marcella."

"I've got it to waste," she bragged.

I stopped her and turned her face toward mine so she would have to make the eye contact she so rarely made with me. "I am your manager and your agent," I said. "I am the only person in the world who knows exactly how much you make."

She tried to get away, hiding her anger with an amused grin. "Let's go," she said.

"And as your manager, I am here to warn you—you don't make enough for all the stuff, Marcella. The Bentley, the clothes. You have to be careful."

"I'm fine," she said as she tore out of my grip. "Shut up."

We hit the Dolce & Gabbana boutique, where Marcella convinced me to buy a miniskirt and sexy tank I knew I'd never wear. I dragged *her* into the Escada store and Burberry, where I loved everything, and she dragged me out with an exhausted sigh.

"You're hopeless," she said. "You're not going to play *golf* with Liz Claiborne, Lexi. You're going clubbing with a *rap* star."

"He's not a star yet," I said. "That's what I'm for."

"Whatever."

We passed Lane Bryant and I looked longingly at the baggy fat-girl shirts and elasticized pants in the window. They looked so comfortable, so perfect for pushing a baby on a swing.

"No!" Marcella cried as she shoved me away from the store at top speed. "Don't even think about it!"

I followed Marcella into Emporio Armani, Christian Dior, Gianni Versace, Chanel, Gucci, Hermes, and all other manner of shops where everything seemed too flimsy, silky, *silly*, and small to do me any good, and where all the anorexic workers fawned over Marcella as if Jesus himself had just walked in the room with a Platinum Visa card.

In the end, she had spent close to nine thousand dollars that I knew she didn't have to spend, on clothes she didn't need. And me? Marcella had picked out clothes that I couldn't imagine wearing more than once, if at all, and I bought only a few things and still cringed at the fact that they cost me nearly fifteen hundred bucks.

"How do you live like this all the time?" I asked as I carried an armload of bags. "I'm not Catholic, but Jeez Louise, I feel s'guilty! It's more than my daddy makes in two weeks of work, Marcella. It's so wasteful!"

"You'll make it back hundredfold with Vladimir," Marcella assured me. "He's got the goods."

"And what about you?" I asked her. "You're going to end up as broke as MC Hammer."

She shrugged. "If that happens, I'll just start my own show on the Christian Broadcasting Network and rip off retarded born-agains."

"I take offense at that," I said. "It's not okay to make fun of Christians."

"I'm not making fun of all Christians," she said. "Just the retarded ones. I don't think you fall under that category."

"You don't *think*?"

"The jury's still out," she said. Then she bit my cheek. "Ouch!" I cried, slapping her away.

"Yum," she said, wild-eyed. "I knew you'd taste good."

"If I didn't think you were too dang broke to afford 'em, I'd swear you were on drugs, woman," I said. And we laughed. In spite of our crazy differences, we laughed.

"I like you," she said with an almost seductive look. Was she crazy? "I'm glad we're friends."

We waited for the mall's delivery service to bring our bags to the valet stand. The car jockey who I thought had flirted with me earlier ran to meet us. As soon as he saw Marcella, he forgot I existed. Story of my life.

"Here, miss," he said. Miss. He called her miss, and called me ma'am. Did I look like her mother? Jerk. "Let me help."

As he stacked my things in the trunk of my car, Marcella told me she'd meet me at my house after stopping for an iced latte.

"You don't have to do that," I said.

"Yes I do," she said. "I want to make sure you look hot, woman. I will not, repeat *not*, let you out of the house in a madras plaid mumu."

I pulled into my driveway and saw a manila envelope taped to the front door of my house. I rarely used the front door, and there had been times when FedEx had come and left something on my front step and it had stayed there for days before I noticed it. I didn't understand why they even *made* homes with front doors in Southern California, where everyone lived in their cars and where the garage was basically everybody's foyer.

I parked the car in the garage, and left the garage door open so I'd have natural light to work with in unpacking all my new clothes. I walked through the yard to the front door and took the envelope down. I recognized Daniel's scratchy, anemic handwriting immediately, and tore the package open to see what horrible thing he might have left inside.

It was a news story, one he had written but not yet published, printed out from his work computer, which I could tell because his work printouts—which he had always been happy to show off—had this crazy text at the top, codes and numbers and things like that.

I started to read: "The players in the Tower Entertainment scandal have all been caught and locked up. Or have they? Sources say the real ringleader in the drug-running Mexican music scandal might still be at large. Sources also say the woman—yes, woman—suspect is none other than the illegitimate daughter of famed mariachi singer Pedro Negrete, Alexis Lopez. The Dallas-born debutante seems an unlikely drug trafficker, but sources say that beneath her sorority-girl act lies a calculating businesswoman who stops at nothing. . . ."

The story was about *me*. Daniel had written a story accusing *me* of being involved with the drug bust at the Whittier Sports Arena. It was complete fiction. Attached by red paper clip was a handwritten note from Daniel that said, simply, "I thought you'd like to know what the world is going to know about you next week. Watch yourself. You never know who's out there, boo, watching you, or what they're capable of. Peace out."

My pulse surged. He couldn't do that! Daniel was always bragging about what an ethical journalist he was, and here he was concocting a lie just to get back at me for dumping him. All I had to do was contact his editors at the paper and tell them what he was up to. Not only could they not run a story like this because it wasn't true, but they couldn't run it because it was a conflict of interest for Daniel to write about his ex-girlfriend. I took a deep breath and calmed myself with the promise that I would deal with this matter first thing the next morning, at the *Times*.

I hurried back to the garage and shut the door. I had a sick sense that Daniel was somewhere nearby, lurking, watching me. I felt exposed. I flipped on the overhead light and began to unpack the trunk, carrying the bags and boxes up to my bedroom with Juanga yapping at my heels. She loved shopping, too. It took three trips for me to get everything.

I took the clothes out of the bags and laid them out on my bed, side by side. It was a favorite ritual of mine. After shopping I liked to look at everything I had bought. I loved the way new clothes smelled, the perfect way they hung on the hangers, before my body had a chance to crease and wrinkle them into oblivion. It didn't matter if I steamed them, took them to the dry cleaners, whatever, there would never be a way to replicate the perfection of new clothes.

I matched a few items, then scrambled them up and matched them a different way, trying to get just the right outfit for tonight. Finally, I decided to go with a simple pair of tight tangerine cropped jeans, a white shirt, heels, jewelry, and sassy mules. Understated and casual, but cool.

I hopped in the shower, and tried to stop my mind from imagining Daniel creeping around my house with a butcher's knife. He was crazy. And dangerous. I decided as I shaved my legs that I would have to contact the police and get a restraining order against him.

Marcella, true to her word, showed up a half hour before I had to leave and adjusted everything so that I looked just right.

"Thanks," I said.

"He's crazy if he doesn't fall in love," she said. "You're beautiful." I could have sworn she wanted to kiss me.

"Yeah, whatever," I said.

"Stop the modesty shit," Marcella said. "You really are a pretty girl."

"But the valet boy called me ma'am and he called you miss," I whined.

"That's because he respects you," said Marcella.

I wasn't a fan of driving, not the way Marcella was anyway. But as I flew toward Los Angeles to meet Vladimir, smelling clean and expensive, I felt free. The rush of excitement was something I thought I'd lost the ability to feel after two years of Daniel. But here I was, with my favorite Boy George CD blasting, feeling very full of my own potential. I liked it. "'*I know you missed me,*'" I sang. "'*I know you missed me-ee, I know you missed me bu-lie-i-ind.*'"

I couldn't remember the last time I felt so good.

Asia de Cuba was located in the groovy Mondrian Hotel in West Hollywood, and it was one of those places where people went to be seen, the kind of place favored by Marcella and fastidiously avoided by me.

Vladimir was already there, waiting for me in the entry. My chest contracted when I saw him, and the air felt sucked right out of the room. He wore dark jeans, baggy, with a tank top and a Hawaiian type of shirt over that. He wore Santeria beads and work boots, the camel-colored kind all the rappers wore. The straw hat was back, and he looked adorable in it. He had earrings in both ears, small silver hoops. He stood with a smile and reached out to hug me, as if we were old friends. People turned and stared at him because he had that certain thing, star quality. Lydia had it. Marcella had it. And this guy had it. That was good, from a business standpoint, and bad, I thought, from a romantic standpoint. What would a guy like that want with a woman like me?

"Alexis," he said, full of affection. *"Oye, pero te ves muy bella mi amor."* He told me I looked very pretty, in that Cuban Spanish of his, and I wanted to collapse in his arms. He smelled like coconuts and grapefruits again. I'd never known a man to smell so good.

I hugged him back and felt my belly twist in delight. He felt so good. I didn't want to let go. He pulled away first.

"They're holding a table for us," he told me in Spanish. "You ready?"

"Yes, of course," I said. The hostess led the way, and Vladimir motioned for me to go first. A gentleman, too. If anyone had asked me a month before if I thought rappers could be gentlemen, I would have laughed in their faces.

The table was hidden in a quiet corner, with a great view of the city lights from a nearby window.

"They have the best pork sandwiches here," Vladimir said. "Do you eat meat?"

I nodded and wondered why he couldn't tell from looking at me that I ate everything, in excess.

As we settled into our respective seats he explained, "In Cuba, we love pork. But there are hardly any pigs left."

I laughed, thinking it was a joke.

"I'm serious," he said. "There's so little food anymore."

"I'm sorry," I said. "I didn't mean to offend you."

"You didn't," he said. He looked surprised. He stared at me, and I felt something pop in my heart. We connected. I swear we did. He had a hungry look, as if he wanted to get to know me better, a lustful look. I didn't think I was imagining it. After all, he'd told me I was cute, that I had pretty eyes, the day he crashed into my car.

"That color really looks good on you," he said. He flashed a seductive little smile and leaned back in his chair, all man.

"Thanks," I said.

He blushed. I saw it. He looked like he wanted to say something but wouldn't let himself. I smiled. It seemed like that was all I knew how to do.

The waiter brought menus, took our drink orders—he ordered club soda with lime and even though I wanted alcohol, I followed his lead—and we spent a few moments in silence, reading.

We ordered, and began to talk. Or, rather, he began to talk. I asked questions, so I suppose it was my fault that it was all about him. I said, "Before I give you my pitch on why I want to represent you, I'd like to get to know you a little better. Tell me about yourself. Your life."

He told me, in Spanish, about growing up in Cuba, about his parents, who were very religious but had to hide it all his life there. Apparently, they were Baptists, but I wouldn't hold that against them. Some of my best friends were Baptists.

"That's terrible," I said, thinking about all the things I had taken for granted in my life, including the right to grow up attending boring Methodist services with my momma and daddy every Sunday. I felt guilty for all the times I'd complained about it when I realized freedom to worship God was a luxury not offered to everyone.

"It was a hardship," he said. "But it made me who I am. So in retrospect, I don't think I'd change anything about my life."

Retrospect. It was rare, I had discovered, to find a *native* English-speaker in Los Angeles who knew words like retrospect—I think there was a law in L.A. against using words with more than two syllables in public—but a man for whom English was a second language? "Really?" I asked. "Not a thing?"

He seemed to be thinking hard about the question, which I hadn't really meant for him to think about this much. "Well," he said. "There's one thing I'd change."

"What's that?" I loved the way he was looking at me, warm and seductive, like he wanted me, really wanted me, just wanted me to reach out and touch him, hold him, brush my hand along the side of his face. I wanted to get close enough to smell the coconut and grapefruit again. I wanted to drink him in, taste him. I felt the electricity between us, and braced for what he might say next, how maybe he regretted not getting my number when we crashed—or, rather, when he crashed into me—so that he might have gotten in touch with me sooner. It was coming. I looked at the way he held himself, the way he scooted ever so slightly closer to me. I held my breath.

"I regret allowing myself to fight with Caridad the day before I left for the U.S.," he said. "She was the love of my life. She is. I miss her."

I didn't want to feel tears building up beneath my eyes, but I did. *Stop,* I told myself, *don't cry. You got yourself worked up over nothing. You fantasized yourself into a frenzy about this guy and you knew this already, you dressed like a moron in tangerine pants—who wore tangerine pants?—you already knew he loved that woman.* I blinked hard, and smiled as hard as I could.

"You fought?" Blink, blink, blink. Gulp. "What happened?"

"It's stupid. It's not worth going into. The thing that matters is that she was supposed to come with me and she didn't."

"You really love her," I said. Smile, smile, smile.

He nodded. "More than anyone in the world," he said. "Other than my parents, of course."

"That's . . . wonderful." I tried to keep smiling. It was hard.

"She writes to me all the time," he said as the waiter delivered our meals. Goyo lowered his voice to a whisper, and I realized he was not used to the freedom to speak your mind yet. He was still used to hiding his politics and plans. "E-mail. She wants me to get her out."

"Could you?" I asked, hoping he would say no. No. *No.*

"Probably," he said. "But I'd have to plan it carefully."

I picked at my food. As sadness washed through every molecule of my body, I started to inhale the food like medicine. I shouldn't have eaten so much, I knew that, but there was no hope for me. I might as well enjoy my meals. They were my only company, my only pleasure.

"So," he said brightly, as if he hadn't just broken my heart. "Tell me more about *you.*"

I told him everything, about my dad, the biological one, and watched his eyes grow large. I could tell he wanted to talk more about Papi Pedro, but I quickly moved on to tell him about my degrees, how I went to work for Tower, what happened there. I told him about my new company, my roster, my goals. I told him about the work I'd done for Lydia in Europe. He listened carefully and nodded. I told him about the movie plans.

"That's great," he said. "Very impressive."

I fought the urge to play my accomplishments down, reminded myself not to shrug. Marcella was right, there was no room for obsequiousness in business. That was her word, obsequious, not mine.

"What do you want out of a manager?" I asked him.

He answered right away, so I knew he'd been thinking about this for a while. "I want someone who understands the Latin market and the American market, who can take me and my career to the next level, and then to the next level after that. I don't want to be like Proyecto Uno, only playing on VH-Uno until I get too fat and lazy to make records anymore. I want to be like Nelly and 50 Cent, everywhere, on *TRL.* I want to reach that level of media exposure."

I nodded. "You want to do a crossover."

He made a face. "I *hate* that word, but if that's what you want to call it, yeah, that's what I want."

"Crossover? Why do you hate that word?" I asked.

"Because people are people and music is universal. I don't like the imposition of irrelevant borders between people, especially as far as art is concerned."

"True," I said.

"So what do you think it would take to get me to that next level?"

I thought about it for a while. I'd listened to his music, seen him perform. He was unquestionably talented enough—and handsome enough—to be a superstar. It would take a good plan, though.

And then, just like that, the answer came to me. I didn't like it, but it came to me.

"You could rescue Caridad," I said. "And it would get a ton of press for you. We could use the press to get certain executives to listen to your music."

He licked his lips and I almost passed out. I was recommending the man I had fallen in love with rescue the love of his life from Cuba, and that I would be arranging for press coverage of the whole thing. What was wrong with me? I was too dang nice, that was what was wrong with me. And nice people really did always finish last. It was true. There I was, chubby, overeating, and coming in last.

"Brilliant," he said. "It's a really good idea."

I shrugged. "All in a day's work," I said.

"I know some people who could help arrange everything," he said.

"So do I." I thought of my father, and of some of the criminal types I'd met through the Chimps. "We could get her false documents pretty easily, get her tickets to Mexico. You said she was a musician, right?"

"Yeah. She plays percussion, the batá, and she's a hell of a rapper and singer herself."

This time, I lowered *my* voice. You just really never knew who might be listening to your conversations.

"Well," I whispered. "Then we could ask my dad to bring her over the U.S. border from Mexico as part of his band. That would be easy. He goes back and forth all the time. She could just defect at that point. Don't all Cubans who reach American soil have instant asylum here?"

"Yes," he said. "Dry foot policy." His yes glowed with the image of his lover returning to him.

I wanted to cry, but did not break.

"So it'll be a piece of cake," I said in English, cheerful as can be.

"A what?" He looked confused.

"It's a saying. A piece of cake. It means something will be easy."

He laughed to himself and popped a piece of buttered bread in his mouth. "That's weird," he said.

"Why?"

"Because that's how Caridad is trying to support herself these days, by baking cakes."

"Honorable living," I said, not knowing what else to say. I hated her, and her stinking cakes. I secretly hoped the documents wouldn't work out, or that her plane would crash.

"It's *not* easy," he said with such heavy sadness I wanted to wrap him in my arms and protect him. "You have no idea how hard it is to make a cake in Cuba, how difficult it is to find the ingredients. Piece of cake. *Coño.*" He laughed sadly, shook his head.

"What?" I said. "Did I offend you?"

"No, *mi amor*," he said. He reached a warm hand across the table and touched mine. His eyes were so warm and kind, so full of passion and longing. I didn't understand the mixed messages. Was it all my imagination? He said, "You didn't offend me. Your *country* did. Your culture of privilege. The sayings. The way Americans think. The world is starving, and here you say a piece of cake is easy. It's just funny to me."

"I can see why," I said. I loved the way this man made me think about things I had never thought about before. "Are you a communist?" I asked.

He laughed so hard the table shook and people turned to look at him as if they might need to call 911. "That's funny," he roared. "Me, a communist."

"I just thought, Cuba and all."

"Why would I have left if I was a communist?" he asked. I shrugged because I couldn't think of a good answer and the more I thought about it the stupider I felt.

"I'm a Republican," I said. "So I've never met a communist."

"In my experience there are only good people and bad people," said Goyo. "And every political affiliation has many of both."

"Huh." That made sense, didn't it?

"But that's not really the point," he said. "The point is you have a good plan, and I think it might work. So where do I sign? To make if official and everything. To make you my manager."

"You said you have e-mail?" I asked.

He nodded.

I handed him one of my own business cards with a pen, turned the card over to the blank side. "Write your e-mail down for me and I'll send you a contract tomorrow. You print it out, sign it, and send it back to me."

He grinned. "I have a better idea," he said.

"What's that?" I asked. I hoped he'd say his better idea involved forgetting about Caridad and coming home with me right that minute.

"You ever surfed?" he asked.

"I'm from Dallas," I said.

"So?"

"Landlocked? Hello?" The whole smile thing was getting really difficult to maintain. I was getting cranky, and my cheeks were starting to hurt from all the effort.

"Land what?" Again, he didn't know what I was talking about.

"No ocean? You say landlocked if there's no water around."

"Right. But you live here now. You've never surfed?"

"No," I said.

"I'll take you. We'll go this weekend, and you'll give me the contract then. You can come have dinner with my parents. You said you wanted to meet them, and I'm sure they'd love you." He paused and smiled. "I think they're Republicans, too."

I smiled and fought the urge to tell him I didn't want to surf, that I wanted to kiss him instead. But the thought of surfing, of being in the big ocean with him, alone, where I could feign—or not—complete lack of coordination so he would be forced to touch me, well. "I'd love to," I said. There were worse things than Vladimir in a bathing suit, right?

"Thanks for listening to me. You know, talk about her."

"Sure," I said, with a bigger smile than the situation warranted. But that's the problem with me. I am always making people feel good—everyone, that is, except for me. My face muscles started to quiver.

"You're really easy to talk to," he said. He scooted even closer to me and planted a nice, friendly little kiss on my cheek. I hated him for that.

I shrugged. "Thanks." That's me, I thought, the nice older lady every guy wants to make his best friend. Whoopee.

"I think I'd like it very much if you were my manager," he said. He leaned back and put his hands behind his head. He was so gorgeous I wanted to attack him. "I have a good feeling about you."

I had a good feeling about him, too. But not of the client kind. And he had no idea. I wanted to hold him, memorize the lines of his hands. I wanted to breathe him in. I wanted to kiss him so badly it literally made me drool. I stanched the leak with some bread.

"So," he said. "What do you say? Let's do it."

Oh, God. Yes, let's.

"You got it!" I said. I clapped my hands together like a kindergarten teacher.

"I think we could be good friends."

"Great," I said. But inside, my heart sank. Another beautiful, funny, talented, wonderful man who wanted to be my friend. They all wanted to be my friend. It was the extra thirty pounds. I knew it. I knew I had to lose it, if I was ever going to land a guy like this. But I was so depressed I didn't have the energy to think about it. I didn't want to go clubbing. That would just make things worse, seeing him dance, feeling uncoordinated. I just wanted to go home.

The waiter stopped at our table. "Can I get you two dessert menus?" he asked.

"Not for me," Goyo said. "No piece of cake for me tonight." He laughed to himself.

"Yes," I said with great energy. I hated myself as I said it, but smiled like there was nothing wrong. "I'd love to see the dessert menu. Please."

OLIVIA

I blew air slowly out of my mouth, the way the therapist had taught me to do in times of stress. Samuel told me he had to work late again, this time helping organize a student roundtable about the role of indigenous uprisings in the anti-imperialist movements of Chile and Argentina.

I'd planned to have dinner with him tonight, at home, to tell him about my movie deal. Columbus Pictures wanted to distribute my film! I hardly believed it myself. He got in late last night and was too tired to talk, and then he rushed out this morning. I hadn't had a chance to talk to him about it yet. And now, tonight wouldn't work, either.

I watched as Jack picked up the red plastic cup of water he'd been using to clean his paintbrushes, and ceremoniously dumped it onto the carpet. The white, not-ours, rented apartment carpet. Purplish, murky water spread everywhere, like a bruise. Jack laughed and said, "Jack paint the floor with water!"

My head pounded, but I resisted the urge to rub my temples, because that's what I remembered most about my mother growing up, the way she always rubbed her temples, as if I gave her the worst headache in the world. I needed time with Samuel. I felt like we didn't even know each other anymore. I couldn't stand the thought of another night doing everything alone, the dinner, the bath, the stories, listening to the whining when bedtime finally came. I needed help, and adult companionship, and Samuel didn't seem to care.

"Okay," I said. "But Samuel, you're going to have to talk to the department head about all this extra work. You have a *family*. And we need you."

"I know," he said. He sounded as flat and emotionless as I felt. "Why do you think I work this hard? It's for you guys. I hate this, Olivia. I didn't think it would be like this. I'm sorry to do this to you guys. It won't last forever."

"Okay."

"I'll call you if anything comes up," he said. "Give the little guy a kiss for me. I should be home by eleven. And we can talk then, about whatever you wanted to talk to me about."

Sure, I thought. I'll give the kid a kiss for you just as soon as I clean up this mess, make tamales in a steaming hot kitchen, and wash another three loads of stinky, crusty miniature clothes in the shared laundry room down the hall, all the while trying to keep a toddler amused and out of harm's way. Oh, and while keeping an eye on the crazy old Filipino lady in the muumuu downstairs who was known to steal items out of the washers mid–rinse cycle.

"Okay," I said. "I love you."

"I love you, too," he said with great emotion. I felt sorry for him. This was as hard on him as it was on me, I was sure of it. He loved Jack so much. He was a great father. It was hard to be home all the time, but it would be even harder, I thought, to be gone from home as much as Samuel was.

"Don't worry," I said. "It's okay." But it wasn't. It wasn't okay. My life wasn't okay. I had just gotten the best news of my life, and I was *still* miserable. What was the point of a dream coming true if you didn't have someone you loved to share it with?

He sighed. "I know," he said. "I just feel so guilty. I love you so much. The only place I want to be in the world is home with you."

"Work is work," I said.

"Right. Okay. I'm glad you understand. See you later then."

"Bye."

He made a kissing noise into the phone, but I didn't have the heart to return it; it would feel like lying.

I hung up and grabbed the paper towels. The trash cans in our apartment always overflowed with diapers and paper towels. It seemed I was single-handedly stuffing every landfill in Southern California. You try to be PC, I thought, until you have a child. I sopped up the water, and tried to be patient with Jack, who had moved on to tossing the paintings he'd spent the past hour making up into the air, watching them fall like autumn leaves all over the living room. Wet autumn leaves. Facedown. I guessed we wouldn't be getting our security deposit back.

"Please don't do that," I said, as one of the paintings landed facedown, on the old white leather sofa, staining it. This sofa was not long for the world. Nothing was ever clean in my world. I felt like crying.

"Please don't do that," Jack mimicked. He laughed and ran to his room.

After cleaning up, and washing paint off Jack and wrestling him into yet another new outfit—his fourth of the day—I decided I couldn't bear to cook. The heat, the sweating, the mess, all for a meal I was fairly certain my son would refuse to even taste—no. No *way*. Not tonight. Tonight, we'd get fast food. McDonald's. It was politically incorrect, unhealthy, horrible in a million ways, but it was fast and cheap and I needed the drive to at least pretend I was alone for a little while, with the car stereo on—and *not Toddler Favorites* or *Shake Sugaree*, I couldn't take it any more with those—and the kid so interested in passing cars and buildings that he sat quietly and didn't bother anyone, anyone being *me*.

I thought of my mother for a moment, and for the first time I could remember, I saw things from her point of view.

Maybe she hadn't meant to neglect me; maybe she'd been busy having a life of her own.

A s I stared at the menu of the drive-through, it occurred to me that Samuel would probably not have time to get dinner for himself. And even with his politics, he was a fan of the Big and Tasty burger; it used to be one of our guilty pleasures to get fast food and eat in the car while we listened to Phil Hendry's hilarious show on AM radio. I ordered a meal for him and decided to stop by his office to surprise him with dinner before the event. He'd appreciate that, and we'd at least have a little bit of family time before the roundtable began. Maybe I'd even have time to give him the good news. I was nearly exploding inside with the excitement of it, and I couldn't wait to share it with Samuel.

That's what I needed to do, I realized—put more effort into my relationship with my husband, remind him that I loved him and thought about him.

"You want to see Daddy?" I asked Jack.

"See Daddy!" he shouted. He began to kick his little feet with happiness. That settled it. We were going to see Daddy.

U CLA was a five-minute drive from the McDonald's, and I parked in the faculty lot thanks to the pass Samuel had gotten for the Aerostar. "Let's go, *amor*," I said to Jack. The thought of seeing Samuel, of doing something spontaneous with him for the first time in I didn't know how many years, lifted my spirits. Since realizing people liked my writing, I was a different woman, a happier woman. More spontaneous. The Zoloft helped, too.

I unbuckled Jack from the car seat, situated him on my hip, and cinched the white paper bags of poison dinner in the circle of my arms. "Let's go surprise Daddy." My son giggled, his mood, as usual, feeding off of mine. If only I were a happier person, I thought, my son would be happier, too.

The Center for Chicano Studies was still open, and the receptionist greeted us by name.

"What brings you guys here?" she asked.

"We thought we'd surprise Samuel with dinner." I grinned and lifted the McDonald's bags. "Nothing gourmet, but you know, I'm a busy woman."

"Samuel?" she asked. She looked confused. Then she looked uncomfortable.

"My husband?" I asked, with that annoying "duh" tone to my voice. "The busiest assistant professor in the department?"

She smiled. "No, I know," she said. "It's just that he's not here."

"Oh," I said. "He must have gone to get dinner for himself."

She looked worried. "Actually, I haven't seen him all day."

"What?" I explained that he'd just called and told me that he had to work late on the student roundtable. She shook her head and shrugged.

"We don't have a roundtable tonight," she said. Jack squirmed, so I set him down and he started to run around the office, hiding in the stacks of books in the corners.

"Are you sure?" I asked. Then, to my son I said, "Don't touch."

"Very sure," she said. "But I'll check again."

She lifted the receiver and called the director of the center to ask about a roundtable. "There's not?" she asked the phone. "Oh, okay. Thanks. I was just checking, because Samuel's wife and kid are here looking for him. She said he told her he had to work late tonight. Uh-huh. Okay. Sure. I'll send her right back."

The receptionist told me that Dr. Garcia, the director, wanted to see me in his office. "I'll watch the little guy for you," she offered. "I love kids."

I headed back to Dr. Garcia's office. He sat at his computer with a serious look on his face. The expression did not detract from the fact that he was a handsome, intelligent man.

"Olivia," he said. "Come in, sit down."

I did.

"How's Samuel feeling?" he asked.

"Fine, I think. Why?"

"He called in sick this morning. Said the flight from Florida did him in."

I shook my head. "He worked all day," I said. "I mean, I saw him this morning, before he left for work."

Dr. Garcia, a distinguished-looking man of about sixty, with kind eyes and a handsome face, looked uncomfortable. "Actually," he said, "he didn't come to work. He really did call in sick."

"Sick?" My heart started to race.

"He's called in sick quite often these past few months. I thought maybe there was something happening with his health."

"What? He's never been sick. He doesn't *get* sick."

"Uh-oh," he said, hands up. "Not my business."

"No," I said. "That's not possible. He's been working so much! He's been working late almost every night. He said you had a lot of extra work for him."

Dr. Garcia's eyebrows shot up. "He told you that?"

"Yes," I said.

"Well that's very interesting. Maybe it is my business. I don't like being used as a false alibi."

"He hasn't *been* here?" I asked. I didn't want to believe what I was hearing.

"Nope." He watched me and shrugged and it was hard to tell what he thought.

"*Achis*," I said. "I'll have to ask him about it." My stomach began to hurt with fear.

"I've been meaning to ask you or Samuel about your mother," he said, his eyes softening. "I have admired her work for years and I'd really love to ask her about the new developments with labor parties in El Salvador."

I smiled weakly. "Sure," I said. "I'll see if she can come by."

"She's an outstanding scholar and writer," he said. "I'd be honored to have coffee or tea with her, her schedule permitting."

I got the sense he admired more about my mother than her work. It might be good for her to date. Come to think of it, she had never dated, not that I knew of. Not since my father was murdered.

"Sure, I'll pass it on."

I stood up and said, "I'm sorry, Dr. Garcia. But I have my son with me, and he's hungry, and I really have to be going."

"Don't let me keep you," he said. He stood up and touched my shoulder with his hand. "And Olivia?"

"Yes?"

His eyes searched mine. "Take care. Be careful."

"Thanks," I said. I didn't want to believe what I saw in his eyes, that he was worried about me because Samuel had been lying. I hurried out the door. He watched me leave, his eyes sad. I ran down the hall to the bathroom and locked myself in a stall until I felt in control of the fear. I washed my face and hurried back to the lobby, where the receptionist lifted Jack over her head, tossed him in the air with the kind of fun and energy I had lost long ago. Jack squealed with delight.

"Thanks for your help," I said to the receptionist. "I'm sorry, but we have to go now."

"Okay," she said. "It's been fun. Bye-bye Jack!"

My son started to scream and squirm in protest. He wanted to stay here all night, getting thrown into the air. I didn't blame him. But he had the bad luck of being my son and that meant he'd have to go with me, wherever I was going—and I really had no idea where that would be. I only knew I couldn't stay here.

I gathered up the McDonald's bags and rushed to the car with Jack shrieking in my ear.

"Want to eat!" he cried. "Jack hungry."

Right. I'd forgotten to feed the child. Oh, God. I slowed down, took a deep breath. *Be strong for the boy*, I told myself. *No matter what is going on here, be strong for the child.* I kissed him on the cheek and tried to compose myself.

I walked to a green, open space on the campus, found a bench, and sat down. I tried to hide what I felt, which is to say fear, betrayal, horror, pain. Jack, intuitive and smart like most children, saw through my deception.

"Mommy's *not* sad," he said, as if saying so would make it true. He looked frightened. I tried to smile, but it only made him more afraid. "Mommy's *happy*," he said. "Mommy's happy." He started to whine, then cry.

"No," I said. Honesty was the best policy. "Mommy is a little mixed up right now. But Mommy loves you, and Mommy wants you to sit right here on the bench next to her and eat your dinner."

"No," he said. But as I opened the box of chicken nuggets, he opened his mouth in anticipation. I placed the food in his mouth, as if he were a tiny baby again. I felt the sting of tears in my eyes.

Jack looked up at me in confusion. But his eyes were the eyes of a full human being, not just a little child; he watched me from his soul and I felt like the worst mother on earth. Cursing, crying, feeding him McDonald's. Terrifying my son. The worst mom ever.

"You want some milk?" I asked. I tried to smile again.

"Want milk," he said, pouting. "Mommy's *happy*."

"Mommy is *not* happy," I said as I opened the little paper carton of hormone-filled white poison. "But Mommy will be happy soon. She's a little mixed up right now, that's all. Mommy needs to talk to Daddy." I flinched as I realized I was telling Jack too much. A mommy wasn't supposed to share her emotional turmoil with her child, was she? It bordered on child abuse.

"Noooo!" he shrieked. "Mommy's happy. Mommy's *not* sad!"

I stuck a straw in the carton and held it to his lips. He drank, and watched me with those eyes.

"Look, Jack," I said. I ruffled his hair to lighten the mood. "Sometimes mommies get a little sad, just like Jack gets sad. But it's not the end of the world. Mommy is fine. We're fine. Okay?"

He said nothing, and gulped down the milk with that sweet, almost cartoonish swallow sound he made. What a small person, I thought. His feet barely dangled over the edge of the bench. A small, defenseless, innocent human being, so perfect, so beautiful. Complete love washed through me, and I felt a panther's instinct to protect my young. Whatever Samuel was doing to this family, I knew one thing: I had to protect my son. I hugged him, planted a dozen kisses on the top of his head, his cheeks, his forehead. I wanted to clutch him to my breast and run away, go somewhere safe.

"Mommy loves you so much," I said. My voice quaked. He stared at me with intelligence, and intensity, trying to figure it all out. *God help me if he remembers this for the rest of his life,* I thought. I said, "Mommy will never hurt you."

"Want French fries," he said, opening his mouth like a baby bird.

I fed him the fries. I fed him the chicken. I fed him the milk. Even though he was old enough to feed himself, I fed him.

And he didn't cry, or complain; he watched my eyes for a sign.

Back at the apartment, unsure how I'd gotten there, I planted Jack in front of the television, strapped tightly in his high chair, with a Wiggles tape rolling, and I started to sort through all the papers I'd ignored. I found the one that had struck me as odd a week before, the bill from the UPS store. I called the number.

"Yes, are you still open?" I asked.

"Yes, ma'am, we sure are," said the helpful woman on the other end of the line. "This branch is open until midnight."

I weighed my options. I told her the truth.

"Look, I've discovered some weird things about my husband, and I was wondering if you could tell me whether he has a mailbox there. I have a bill here for it, but I don't know anything about it." I gave her our names and waited while she tapped on a computer keyboard.

"Samuel Reyes and Olivia Flores," she said. "Yep. You've got a box."

"My name's on it?"

"Well, it looks like he used a joint checking account to rent the mailbox, so your name went on it automatically, off the check."

"Does that mean I can get a key?"

"It says here we issued two keys."

"He never gave me a key."

"I can give you another one. There will be a five-dollar charge."

"Fine."

I hung up and called Alexis. She didn't answer her cell, so I called Marcella.

"I know we don't really know each other that well," I said. "But I don't know who else to call." I supposed I could have called one of the playgroup moms, but I didn't really want them to know about this, and their kids were probably getting ready for bed, too.

"Not a problem," she said. "Where do you live?"

I told her, and she said, "I'll be there in half an hour."

The mailbox contained exactly five items. A bill from AOL for an Internet account I didn't know Samuel had; it listed his screen name: *principemoreno,* and four love letters from a woman named Lisa Benavidez, with the return address in South El Monte printed clearly and lovingly in loopy purple ink on the envelopes.

"Oh, my God," I said. I sat in the driver's seat of my car and read the letters. She was a graduate student ten years younger than Samuel. They had been to Tijuana together to see her dying grandmother and she thanked him for the ride. They'd had sex in his car in the UCLA parking lot. She knew he was married but had the idea he was planning to leave me as soon as I got over my depression and "post-traumatic stress disorder." He told this woman about that? He *told* this woman about *that?*

The *ceróte* was *cheating* on me?

I began to shake. I called Marcella at my apartment and told her what I'd discovered, and asked her to do a MapQuest online to give me directions to Lisa Benavidez's house.

"Are you sure you want to do this?" she asked. "Think about it."

"Yes," I said.

"Breathe, Olivia."

"I'm breathing."

"Do you want me to go with you?"

"No," I said. "Just play with Jack."

"I've been doing that," said Marcella. She sounded surprised and pleased with herself. "He's actually funny. He's like a little person."

"Children are people, Marcella."

"I know, dumbshit. I was just saying."

"Please don't curse in front of Jack."

"Right. Sorry."

She asked me to hold on and I could hear Jack laughing in the background, repeating "dumbshit" over and over as she shushed him. Jack loved learning new words. She came back to the line with directions, and I wrote them on the back of one of the letters.

The worst mother in the world.

As I drove, my stomach felt as if someone had a fist around it, squeezing. My blood ran cold, and my bowels felt loose, as if I'd been poisoned. I couldn't find air. How could I have been so *dunda*, so stupid? This wasn't happening. This couldn't be happening. He loved me, and he loved Jack. We loved each other. Why would he do something like this?

I arrived at the house, and sure enough, his Sonata was parked in the driveway, covered with bumper stickers: "THINK OUTSIDE THE FOX"; "RUSH LIMBAUGH REPUBLICAN STONER"; "WORLD PATRIOT." Next to it was what I assumed was Lisa's car, an old, rusted Datsun, mustard yellow. The tiny house was nothing special, either, just one of those cheap stucco squares from the 1960s, with a pitched roof and a dying patch of lawn in the front. Bars covered all of the windows, and hunks of stucco had fallen off the walls into the shrubs. Somehow, this upset me. If he was going to cheat, at least do it in a good neighborhood. He was jeopardizing our relationship for a hood rat? Why? It didn't make any sense.

"Oh, my God," I said. I watched the front window. The thin cotton curtains were drawn closed, but I saw movement inside.

I parked the Aerostar on the street in front of the house and walked to the front door. The buzzer sounded sickly, in keeping with the smell of the street.

It all happened so much faster than I thought it would. The door opened, and she stood there, smiling friendly as if I were a solicitor she'd have to blow off. Seeing her, I understood with a wave of fear and envy why Samuel might risk it, and risk it in a crappy part of town. She was beautiful, taller than I was and with very long brown hair. She wore sweatpants rolled down low over her belly, which, I noted, did not bear the stretch marks mine had from the pregnancy. She also wore a clingy tank top over perky young breasts I was sure had never nursed a baby.

"Are you Lisa?" I asked.

She smiled and nodded. She had large, intelligent brown eyes. She smelled of sex. I knew that smell.

"I'm Olivia, your boyfriend's wife."

Lisa's smile sagged. "Oh," she said. "Hi."

Hi? That's it? She didn't move out of the way, look surprised, or close the door. She just stood there with the door open a crack, looking at me.

"May I speak to Samuel?" I asked.

"Let me see if he wants to talk to you," she said. She shut the door. I couldn't believe it. She was going to *ask* him? As if he was supposed to be there and I wasn't? As if she had more claim to him than I did.

The door opened again seconds later, and Samuel peered out with sorrowful eyes before slinking through the crack onto the porch.

"Olivia," he said. He looked at the cracked cement of the porch floor. "I can explain this."

I couldn't speak. I felt nothing. It was part of the disorder, that's what my psychiatrist told me, the numbness in the face of pain.

"I was planning to end it with her," he said. "She took a class with me, and she—" He stopped and sighed as if he hated himself. He ran his hand through his hair. "I'm sorry," he said. "I'm a shit."

I looked at him and tried to feel something, anything. Nothing happened.

"She came after me. I know that sounds stupid, but she really did. This was back when we hadn't had sex in seven months or something, back when you didn't even want me to touch you," he said. "I didn't do anything for a long time, but then I went out for a drink with her and it just . . . *happened*. I felt bad. I felt so terrible. But it was like we didn't have a marriage anymore, it was like we were good friends and that was it, you and me."

"Friends?" I asked. "*Puchica!*"

"You know we didn't have a real marriage."

"You mean we didn't have sex," I said.

"Right."

"So you had her. Your student. *Chuco.*"

He nodded. "But you were getting better with the medication and the new friends and things were getting better with us and I was ready to end it with her. I was going to do that tonight. I swear. I know that sounds like the biggest lie in the world, but—" He stopped again. "Oh, shit," he said. "I sound like such an ass."

I glared at him. "She's cute," I said. "Much cuter than me. How old is she? Twelve? Thirteen?"

"Don't," he said.

"Where were you today?" I asked.

"What?"

"I went by your office. They said you called in sick."

He stared at the ceiling of the porch this time and sighed. "I'm sorry," he said. "I was with her."

"Lisa."

He nodded.

"Where'd you go?"

"She wanted to go hiking. So we went hiking. We just got back."

"How nice for you."

"Where's Jack, Olivia?"

"He's fine."

"Where is he?"

"Home with a friend."

"What friend?"

"I don't think I deserve the interrogation here," I snapped.

I could hear the pounding of my heartbeat as if it were something outside of my body, and the numbness spread. "So," I said. "I have something I've been wanting to tell you." He flinched as if he expected me to spit on him or something. "I sold my screenplay. Marcella is going to star in it, and Columbus Pictures will distribute."

He smiled sadly and nodded. "That's great. Congratulations."

"I've wanted to tell you for days now, but you've been busy babysitting your student."

I turned away from him and started to walk toward the Aerostar.

"Olivia," he called. "Where are you going?"

"Home," I said.

"Can I come back?" he asked.

"I don't know," I said. "I don't want to talk to you right now."

All I wanted, in that moment, was to be as far away from this new Samuel as possible, to be home with my son, to protect what was left of my little family.

Jack was so excited by his new playmate that he hadn't gone to sleep. I walked in to find them chasing each other around the dining table, growling like monsters. Marcella was a convincing monster, and I realized actresses would probably make fun moms. Marcella looked embarrassed to be having such a good time in the company of a child.

"Time for bed," I announced. Jack screamed and immediately fell to the ground, crying.

"Mommy's dumbshit," he said.

"Marcella!" I shot her a glare.

"Sorry. He'd learn it sooner or later," she said.

"Jack, let's go." I picked him up. "Time for bed."

Jack started to wail louder, his face pinched up and bright red.

"What are you doing?" Marcella asked. "Why is he crying?" She stared at me as if I were an abusive mother. "You're hurting him!"

"It's called setting *limits*, and it's something parents have to do but babysitters don't," I said. "He's not hurt, he's learning he can't always get his way."

"Don't make him cry," she said. "We were having fun."

"It's past ten," I said. "And he needs to go to bed. Kids' brains only grow when they're asleep."

I grabbed him against his will, put him in his bed, and sang the usual songs. Soon, he sniffled the tears away and was snoring with a peaceful smile on his face, unaware that his world was falling apart.

Marcella stayed and made a cup of tea for me.

"I can't believe I'm not a total fuck-up with kids," she said, smiling. "It was actually cool spending an evening with your little man."

"Good," I said. I felt numb, and barely heard what she was saying. I staggered to the sofa and lowered myself with the care I used when I was pregnant, as if my bones would crack under my misery.

"I'm sorry," she said. "Let's talk about you. You want to talk about it?"

"Not really," I said.

"Were they there?"

"Yep."

She nodded and sat next to me on the sofa. She grabbed the remote controls and turned on the television.

"Moms are supposed to be good about this kind of thing. They come cook for you and stuff."

"Yeah," I said.

"I'd let you borrow mine but she's not that type. On the other hand, if you feel suicidal, she'll have just the right drugs for you. She might even have a how-to manual."

"Uh-huh." I didn't know what else to say to her.

Marcella stopped the remote at a nature program with humping mountain goats.

"Hard-core porn," she said. "You usually have to pay for it."

I wondered how the goats stayed on the sheer face of the cliff without falling off. Marcella changed the channel to Fox News, another fascist posing as a newsman.

"I think I'd prefer the animal porn," I said.

Marcella laughed and put an arm around my shoulders and squeezed. "O'Reilly is the devil."

"Pretty much," I said.

"What's up with Alexis and all that Republican shit?"

I shrugged. "She's Alexis. She means well. But she's ignorant."

"I'm sorry," Marcella said as she flipped to a Spanish-language music-video channel. "It must really suck being you right now."

"Thanks. I feel *much* better now."

"Was that *sarcasm?*" she asked. She put her head on my shoulder. "You bad girl."

I watched the television for a minute and said, without looking up from the screen, "She was pretty. His girlfriend."

"Well that's good," she said. She grabbed my hand.

"Why is that good?"

"Well, it would really suck if she'd been ugly, right? That would mean you were less than an ugly chick."

I was numb. I knew I'd have to cry at some point, but I didn't know when that would be.

"I can't believe it," I said.

"You know what? It's fine. You're at a good place, you don't need him. Financially, anyway. You're free now. That's one good thing."

"What if she had a disease?" I asked.

"You have a good doctor?" Marcella asked.

"Yes," I said.

"First thing tomorrow, you make an appointment," she said. "And you get every fucking *test* under the fucking *sun.*"

I nodded. This was sensible.

"I wasn't good enough for him," I said.

"Bullshit," she said. "It has nothing to do with you. It's all him, okay? He's got problems."

"What am I going to do?" I asked. "What about Jack?"

"You're going to take some time to yourself and figure this thing out. Jack will be fine no matter what. He's a smart little boy."

"I don't have anything to figure out. I have to leave him. Right?"

Marcella flipped the channels and cleared her throat. "Not necessarily," she said.

"What?"

"Do you love him?"

"Yeah. I don't know. I think so. I loved who I thought he was, but he's not that person anymore."

"Do you think he loves you?"

"I did. I don't know."

"Then maybe it'll work out. Sometimes these things happen like an alarm to get a marriage back on track."

"I can't believe that," I said.

At that moment, the front door opened, and Samuel walked in. His eyes were red from crying, and he seemed out of breath.

"I'm a shit," he said. He shut the door and slid to the floor. "I'm sorry, Olivia."

"Samuel, this is my new friend Marcella," I said.

"Hi," he said. Even as he tried to prove he wasn't a dog, he gaped at her as if she stood in our apartment nude. "Congratulations, on the movie. That's great."

"Nice to meet you," said Marcella. She got up and pretended to look at a watch she didn't have. "Oh, look at the time," she said. "Gotta run. You okay?"

"Yeah," I said.

"You want me to stay?"

"No," I said.

"Call me if you need me," she said, and she was gone.

Samuel tried not to watch Marcella's rear end as she left, and failed. Bastard. Then he staggered to the sofa and sat down. "We need to talk," he said.

I took a blanket down from the linen closet in the hall and threw it at him. "I don't feel like talking," I said.

"We have to," he repeated.

"I need to sleep right now," I said. "If we ever talk again, it'll be on my terms. You got that?"

MARCELLA

I lay on my back on the black velvet comforter and stared at the lilac walls of my bedroom with one thought: Stupid Samuel. Olivia was smart. Pretty. A great mom. One of the best screenwriters I'd ever read. She'd survived unspeakable shit in El Salvador, and was amazing just for being alive. She had given up her life for him and his child. And he didn't appreciate it.

I punched one of the geometric cream-colored pillows. I aimed the remote at the stereo hanging on the wall and blasted Juan Luis Guerra. So much of merengue was obscene, which in and of itself wasn't necessarily bad; but it was usually stupid, too. Juan Luis Guerra was the one exception. That's how it was with love, too. With men. Too few exceptions to the idiot rule. What *was* it with men? If they weren't vindictive assholes, they were gay. And when they weren't assholes, or gay, they were sex addicts. When they weren't those things, they were weird and full of nails and wires and had blue or purple hair and kissed your hand and made you feel tingly and excited even though they were rude and obnoxious. My life was slowly filling with oddballs.

I slathered Cellex-C body-smoothing lotion across my legs, torso, and arms, checked to make sure the salon wax job had rid me of every trace of hair. I liked being smooth and hairless, especially when I was heading to the gym, which I was.

My little sister Mathilde had this idea that the whole thing with women shaving or waxing off all their body hair was a patriarchal conspiracy to strip women of their rights as adult human beings. Mathilde became more idiotic the longer she went to college. Smooth bodies were nice to touch and look at, male and female, and when they were more than five feet tall and menstruating there was nothing childlike about them, even when bald. I pitied any woman insecure and weak enough to have her humanity and adulthood hinge on whether or not she had body hair. I called Mathilde to discuss this.

"Hello?" she answered.

"Hey," I said, "if body hair is an indicator of a woman's humanity, does that make Greek women more human than Japanese?"

"Marcella?"

"When you get the answer, call me back."

I hung up. I would always hang up on my family members without saying good-bye, and that's all there was to it.

My phone rang.

I answered: "*Quoi*, you feminist dumbshit."

Not the nicest greeting, granted, but I wasn't in the mood for a lecture from my little sister. Plus, I was ravenous, having practically starved myself for a week because Gabe had commented that it looked like I was "puffy" during last week's taping. To put it mildly, I hated the fucking world.

"Marcella," said a low, sexy voice. Definitely not Mathilde. Even with her feminist awakening, she had yet to sound like Janet Reno.

"Who is this?"

"Carmelo, el Fantasma," said the voice. " 'Feminist dumbshit' is one of the finest descriptions of me I've heard in a while. Thank you."

"The ghostly Sancocho boy!" I said, lightening my tone significantly. He hated the world, too. I was happy to hear from him. "How are you?"

"I'm calling to say I wrote you a song," he said, as if I hadn't just asked how he was. He was almost as rude as I was. I liked that.

"You what?"

"Can I play it for you later?"

"I don't know," I said. "I'm late. Bye."

"When will you be back? I want to bring you the song."

"I don't know."

"Where do you live? I'll leave it for you."

I looked at my reflection in the mirror above my dresser, with a question in my eyes. Should I give this strange, somehow sweet, but decidedly unstable man my address? Well, he *was* rich. I mean, he had to be if he was writing all these hits for Timi Martinez and everything. And how often did a man write a song for me? Well, let's see, uh, *never*.

I gave him my address.

"It'll be there when you get back," he said.

"Okay," I said. He sounded so odd, just a bit off.

"It's called 'The Blood in Your Brain,'" he said. Suddenly, I had visions of Billy Bob Thornton and that vial Angelina Jolie used to wear around her neck, and regretted giving him my address.

"Bye, Count Chocula."

I hung up and went off to the gym, to try a new exer-ball class called "Ball Busters."

When I returned to my house, I checked the mailbox and found a CD inside, with what looked like a card with a dried blood thumbprint on it, inside a scrawled drawing of an open mouth with huge dripping fangs.

"Great," I said to myself. I looked around to make sure the little psycho Sancocho man wasn't lurking in the trees with a hatchet. I checked the ceiling of my porch to make sure he hadn't shrunk down to bat size and hung himself by the toenails from the rafters.

Inside, I put the CD on the stereo while I prepared a snack for myself—rice cakes with seltzer and lime. Soon enough I had to stop munching the crackers, however, because they were too loud inside my head and I was overtaken by the beauty and brilliance of the song. He might be weird, he might look funny, but I was damned if Sancocho boy wasn't a phenomenal songwriter. And singer. And programmer. And keyboardist. The notes on the inside of the CD told me he had done everything. What a voice. He sounded like Timi, but harder. His voice growled and pleaded with me, and the song spoke of the importance of following your heart in life. Come to think of it, he sounded like Kravitz.

When the song was over, I played it again. I did this fifteen times, and by the end, I could not believe a man who had known me for only a few minutes could have read me so well. I looked again at the CD jacket, and sure enough, his phone number was scribbled at the bottom in blotchy red ink. Or scratched in blood with a toothpick? I called.

"It's beautiful," I said.

"Come with me to a party," he said.

"When?"

"Saturday."

"Okay."

"I'll pick you up at seven and we'll have dinner," he said. "I bet you like French, and sushi. But only the vegetables. No flesh for you."

I stared at the CD case. Who was this guy? "Yeah," I said. "Did Alexis tell you?"

"Who?"

"Alexis, my friend. Goyo's manager?"

"No one told me. I saw it in your aura."

"Oh. Right. Ye olde sushi aura. Smells of seaweed."

"It's baby blue."

"Gotta run, Count Chocula," I said.

"See you Saturday, bluegirl."

"Bye."

"Bye."

I pressed the phone off and played the song again—about a hundred times. I let pierced Carmelo, the creepy wayward Sancocho, sing me to sleep.

CARIDAD

Forwarded mail from: requetechica@cubalinda.cu
To: Goyo528@rappermail.com
From: JulindaLinda@cuny.edu
Subject: can't wait

Goyo, dog, whats up. I understand you're not available and yes I do know how to spell and I apologize for flirting. Peace out. Li'l Juli

Mi querido Goyo,
Guao! I can't believe I'm actually going to see you. Thank you so much, and thank your manager. I just have one last favor to ask of you, Goyo. And if you don't want to do it I understand. Do you remember my cousin Amado? The one from Pinar del Rio? He moved to Havana right after you left. He's gotten into a bit of trouble, Goyo, and I mean serious trouble. He's a writer and a dissident and he says I'm the only one he trusts to ask for help. Goyo, blood is thicker than water and I don't know what to do with a cousin asking me to save his life. I don't know where else to turn. Un abrazote y besos,
—Caridad

ALEXIS

So, okay, it probably wasn't the sort of thing a manager was supposed to ask a new and promising client to do, but I asked Goyo go with me to the *Los Angeles Times* building downtown while I confronted Daniel's editor about the letter he had left on my door. Anyway, L.A. was wearing off on me. Two years ago, I would never have used my profession to force a guy to spend time with me. Now, I was starting to think and act like a real Hollywood manager, looking out for number one, which meant me. Sad.

I had told Goyo about Daniel's letter, and he suggested I confront Daniel's boss in person rather than on the phone, so that they could see his handwriting with their own eyes. Why I hadn't thought of that I could not explain other than to say that whenever I talked to Goyo my brain cells became dormant and my sex cells took over. It was downright disgraceful.

I'd made an appointment with the editor, who, like every other newspaper editor I had ever met, was named Bob, but I did not want to go alone in case Daniel was there and wanted to do something crazy to me.

Goyo met me downtown, at the Briazz café in California Plaza, where we had iced cappuccinos and watched children splashing in the fountain. August was the hottest month in L.A., and these li'l critters were making the most of a good thing. I near about wanted to join 'em.

"This," Goyo said, lifting his coffee, "is the closest thing to Cuban coffee you can get. And it's still too weak."

"Oooh," I joked. "You must be a real he-man to hold your coffee so well." I pretended to pinch his biceps as a joke, but I really just wanted to touch him.

He laughed. I loved his laugh. He seemed to laugh at everything I said.

"They're so cute," I said, watching two little girls with matching purple rompers run squealing beneath the spray of the fountain. Goyo's eyes warmed at the sight of the kids.

"I can't wait to have my own," he said.

My heart jumped up like a cheerleader and did a round-off. I had never in all my years of dating, or hearing about my friends' dates, heard of a man who volunteered his desire to be a father.

"Is that some kind of joke?" I asked. He looked at me with hurt in his eyes and shook his head.

"Why would I joke about something like that?"

"I'm sorry, sugar," I said. "I just don't hear too many single guys talkin' about how much they want t'be daddies."

"I'm not single," he said with those dream eyes. "Caridad is so good with kids. She'll be a great mom."

He looked at me with what I could have sworn was wanting, which sent my little brain bouncing around in my head because had he not just waxed poetic about his stinkin' girlfriend?

"I think you'd be a great mom, too," he said. He scooted closer and touched my hand with his finger, light and playful, as he stared into my eyes. My pulse surged and I pulled my hand away as if I'd touched fire.

"You'll be a great daddy." I just wished he would father *my* children, and not the offspring of that she-devil who'd be here any minute now, but what could I do? The paperwork was nearly completed, and we'd already lined up a Mexican businessman who went to Cuba frequently on business and would be willing to smuggle the papers in for a reasonable fee. If things continued as planned, Caridad would arrive in less than a month, along with her cousin, Amado. Goyo was ecstatic about it, of course, and I was happy for him. But it hurt anyway. Who knew? Maybe Amado would be my type. As long as he wasn't communist.

"You think?" he asked.

"Absolutely, babe," I said. "You're a gentleman. You're fun. You're talented as the dickens. You're going to be rich. What's missing?"

He looked at me with sorrow and patience. "The most important thing a father can offer a child is a moral compass," he said. "I want to be strong, and good. And I want to teach my children right from wrong. That's the most important thing."

"Well, the fact that you're thinking about all that tells me that you'll do just fine," I said. I looked off toward the smoggy skyline. A Chinese jetliner flew low over the tops of the buildings; Daniel had once explained to me that the Asia-bound flights came in low over downtown when they took off because they were so full of fuel it took a while to gain altitude. Reporters were full of nifty information.

"You okay?" he asked. Again, he touched my hand.

"Sure, darlin', why?" I asked.

"The more I get to know you the easier it gets to read you," he said. He pushed a chunk of hair behind my ear and smiled. I melted as he said, "What's wrong?"

I had to think of a lie. I couldn't tell him I loved him, or that I oddly missed Daniel, a man I didn't think it would have been possible to miss. "I'm worried about this meeting with the editor," I said. "And Marcella and Olivia are inter-viewing a couple of directors today about the movie."

He shook his head. "Don't," he said. "Don't worry about it. We'll get this all worked out. Daniel can't frame you, Alexis. You didn't do anything wrong. He, on the other hand, should be worried about his job. And the thing with the movie—it's going to be fine."

I nodded. "You're right," I said. "Shall we go?"

"Yeah," he said. He looked like he was thinking about something else—he *looked* like he was thinking about kissing me. I know it wasn't just fantasy on my part. He looked at my lips and leaned closer. I knew that look. I did.

"Alexis," he said.

"Yes, sugar?" I tried not to betray my nerves.

Goyo looked away, suddenly embarrassed. "Never mind," he said. "Let's go."

The decrepit Times Building, which seemed to believe it existed within a war zone in the Middle East, was in reality just a short walk from California Plaza, down a steep hill that ended in a slew of Korean barbecue restaurants, trashy al-leys, and scary warehouses. For some reason, growing up I had not quite pictured Los Angeles to be a city full of hills and interspersed with wild green spaces, but here it was. It was nothing like Dallas. The thick, choking smog was a pulsating, living thing you could see for dang near a mile in every direction, or at least that was the case on the days when visibility was more than the usual two blocks.

The old building had been updated with state-of-the-art security, and a bored-looking guard stopped us in the lobby. They phoned Bob the Editor to make sure we were who we said we were. We showed our identification cards and got passes.

We took the elevator to the third floor. Bob's assistant met us on the elevator landing and guided us through the sunless chamber to his office. I had been here

ALISA VALDES-RODRIGUEZ

many times and found the newsroom as depressing as always, a place of fluorescent lights and overweight, stressed-out people. As we walked through the newsroom, an attractive but furious-looking young lady who didn't seem to know where she was going bumped into Goyo. She walked next to a tall man, who held a clipboard.

"Uh, excuse *you*," said the young lady.

Bob's assistant smiled at the man with the clipboard, and he greeted her. He introduced the pretty young woman, who had wild curly red hair and freckles, as "our top candidate for the Metro columnist opening, Lauren Fernández. She writes up in Boston, and she's in L.A. for a couple of days making the rounds."

"Nice to meet you," said Bob's assistant. "Good luck."

"Thanks," said Lauren, still staring at Goyo. We all shook hands and smiled, but I was relieved when she left.

Bob stood cheerfully at the door, wearing khakis and a striped button-down oxford shirt. I had met him casually a few times, but we had never been together without Daniel around.

"Alexis," he said. "How are you?" He shook my hand. To Goyo he said, "I'm Bob Turner."

"Vladimir Menéndez," said Goyo, shaking his hand.

"What can I do for you two?" Bob asked. He motioned to two chairs at a round table on one side of his office. "Please, sit," he said. He still smiled.

I looked at Goyo. He nodded and smiled his encouragement, and his eyes said I could do this.

"You know I dated Daniel for a while," I said.

"I was aware of that, yes," Bob said.

"I don't know how much you know about Daniel outside of work," I began.

"I don't socialize with Daniel. I just know he's a hell of a reporter, one of the best I've ever worked with."

"Yes," I said. "There are times when Daniel is very impressive. But I think you should see this."

With a shaking hand, I took the manila envelope with its letter and article out of my tote bag, and laid everything out on the table.

"I'm not usually one to bring a man's private life to the office," I said. "And I'm not a vindictive person. I would never come to you with this just to hurt Daniel. I want to make that clear."

"What am I looking at?" Bob asked.

"I'll let you read it," I said.

Bob read with a furrowed brow that grew more creased the more he read. He finished and whistled low through his teeth. He looked worried, and upset.

"When did he give this to you?" Bob asked.

"He left it on the door of my house," I said. "I don't want to get Daniel in trouble. I just don't think I should be slandered by your paper because my ex thinks I deserve to be punished for leaving him."

Said Bob, "You'll have to understand that this is a bit of a surprise for me."

"Of course," I said.

"And I'll have to hear his side of it."

"Right." I frowned. I didn't want to know how Daniel might try to get out of this. There was no way.

"It raises huge, I mean huge, questions for me," said Bob. "This paper prides itself on accuracy."

"I'm sure," I said.

"Well, just, *wow*." Bob blew air through his mouth, sat back and ran his hands through his hair. He seemed embarrassed, and angry. "Maybe he put it in *Times* format just to scare you. He didn't file this story."

"Is Daniel here?" I asked.

"No," said Bob. "But I promise you as soon as he gets back from reporting the story he's working on we're going to sit down about this."

"I invite you to have any reporter at this paper look into allegations he's made here against me," I said. "They're not going to find anything."

"I appreciate you coming by," said Bob. "And we'll let you know what the resolution is."

Goyo spoke for the first time. "He wants to frame her because she broke up with him."

"Like I said, I'm glad you came by," said Bob, gesturing with one hand toward the door, as in *get out now*.

"So what could happen to him?" I asked.

"Well, right now it's a he-said, she-said situation. I can't make predictions without facts." He shrugged and moved back so we might have better access to the door he so desperately wanted us to use.

Goyo spoke again. "That didn't stop Daniel."

"We'll take a look at the situation," Bob said. "I'll be in touch with you as soon as I know what's going on."

I handed Bob my Talentosa business card, we shook hands, and Goyo and I left the Times Building.

"See?" Goyo said. "There's nothing to worry about."

"Yeah, right. Like they're going to look into anything!"

He stopped me and gave me a hug. A long, close hug. I gasped, in shock.

"Hey," he said. "It's okay. I know in this country people don't hug much. But where I'm from, we hug all the time. This is for you, for being so strong and doing the right thing."

I felt his body against mine and wanted to melt into him. I didn't want to let go. I closed my eyes, and clung.

When I opened them again, I saw Daniel walking toward us on the sidewalk from the *Times'* parking garage.

"Oh m'gosh," I said. "It's Daniel."

Goyo released me and strode confidently toward the garage. As Daniel saw us, his face hardened and his pace quickened.

"What are you doing here?" he sneered.

"You'll see," I said with a smile. The thought of Bob confronting him made me very, very happy.

"You fuck with my job, you fuck with your life, bee-ahtch," he said.

Goyo gently moved me to the side and placed himself squarely in front of Daniel. Goyo was so much stronger, taller, and powerful than Daniel it was almost pathetic. And exciting.

"What did you say?" Goyo asked.

"You heard me." Daniel seemed to back off and tried to turn to get past Goyo. So Daniel wasn't a gangster after all. Goyo grabbed the collar of Daniel's butt-ugly Fubu shirt.

"Don't fuck with her," Goyo said. "You hear me? Do *not* fuck with Alexis." He didn't sound right cursing. His raps didn't use foul language, and I'd never really heard it come from his mouth.

"Goyo," I said. "Don't."

He ignored me. "If you fuck with Alexis, punk, you'll have me to deal with. Me and my friends. And I've got lots of friends. And we're not from here. I'm from Cuba, and in Cuba we deal with things a little differently."

"I've got friends, too," said Daniel.

"I find that hard to believe," said Goyo.

Daniel tried to be brave, but I could tell that he was scared. I had never seen Daniel scared. Goyo moved himself so that he invaded Daniel's personal space completely, and he spoke calmly, smack dab into the middle of Daniel's sickly old face.

"Do your friends have the ability to make people disappear, Daniel? Because mine do."

Daniel trembled. Watching Goyo defend me turned me on in some primeval way I didn't know I had in me. *My hero*, I thought. *He's my hero.*

"That's what I thought," said Goyo, with a triumphant grin, watching as Daniel nearly peed in his teenager's pants.

"What? Is he your boyfriend now?" Daniel asked me. "You're shacking up with a hoodlum? I thought you had more class than that."

Goyo walked toward me and left Daniel cowering on the sidewalk.

"We said what we have to say," Goyo said. "What Alexis does in her private life is not your business. Remember that. I don't want to see you, hear about you, nothing."

Daniel tried to laugh, like he wasn't afraid, but he was visibly shaken. Goyo put his arm around me, and together we walked the rest of the way to the parking garage.

"Goyo," I said. "Jeez, I had no idea you could be that tough."

"There's a lot you don't know about me."

Inexplicably, Goyo nuzzled the top of my head. Without wanting to, I hooked an arm around his waist, and we walked as if we were a couple.

"You haven't actually made people disappear, have you?"

Goyo stopped moving and made eye contact with me with a grin. "No," he said. Again, he brushed hair behind my ear, this time adding a soft caress along the side of my face. "I couldn't hurt anyone, Alexis. But that guy doesn't need to know that. Let him think I'm the scariest dark man on earth."

"Be careful," I said.

"I'm sorry," he said. "It's just that you have the most beautiful skin I've ever seen."

"I meant be careful about Daniel," I said. "He's not right in the head."

We walked the rest of the way to my car. After I opened my door, Goyo stood beside me and smiled at me so gently, so softly I wanted to cry. Again, he moved in, eyes on my lips. I ducked into the car, thinking of Caridad and how much I did *not* want to be anyone's other woman, how much I'd lose respect for Goyo if he turned out not to actually be a committed, loving man.

"What now?" I asked, cheery.

"I brought my surf gear. You ready?"

I had promised him that morning that I would let him teach me to surf today if he went with me to the *Times*.

"Okay," I said.

He lowered his eyelids and placed a single, soft finger on my lips, as if to quiet me. "A pretty mouth," he said.

"Goyo, please."

"Follow me," he said as he left me at my car. "To the beach."

I steered the Cadillac behind Goyo's Jeep to Malibu, and listened to his CD at top volume the entire time. His lyrics moved me, the beats excited me. This song was funny, a riff on the whole ridiculous debate between the terms Hispanic and Latino, which, Goyo pointed out, was silly. Those who hated the word Hispanic, the song said, hated it because it related to the Europeans who conquered their ancestors. But why, then, did these same people cling to Latino? "The Indians weren't speaking Latin when the Europeans got here," one line went. I laughed out loud. I'd been saying this same thing for years. His voice opened a door in my soul. The intensity of feeling I had for this man almost overwhelmed me.

I parked next to him in the beach lot. Goyo left his stereo on, blasting the weepy strings and acoustic guitar of Lydia's latest, as he unpacked his surf gear from the back of the Jeep. He still had a dream, he had told me, of recording a duet with her. Once we made him a national household name, I thought, it would be the perfect time to do the duet. He and Lydia could help bring each other into the mainstream.

I'd brought a Fendi gym bag with a wet suit and surf shoes in it, the exact ones he had advised me to buy.

"There's a woman's restroom down there." He pointed down a path to a squat cinder-block building I could smell from here.

"Do I have to?" I asked. The wind whipped the waves, and circling gulls cried out in panic at the sight of me holding a wet suit. I didn't want to drown. And, honestly, I didn't want to undress in a restroom I could smell fifty feet away.

"Come on," he said. "It'll be fun."

I fixed my gaze on the vehement waves and swallowed.

"I won't let anything happen to you," he said.

My fingers tugged at each other and chips of nail polish crumbled beneath my nervous clawing.

"I *promise*," he said.

I waddled down to the smell-o-rama, stashed myself in a stall, and did my best to change clothes balanced on one foot, careful to never set bare skin against the gritty, damp, gray floor. "Latrine" was the only appropriate word for the facility in which I found myself. "Restroom" was far too ladylike, and "bathroom" implied cleanliness at a level this place had never known. I shimmied into the wet suit with the grace of a penguin climbing a rock wall, stuffed my other clothes into my bag, and padded and chafed my way back to the light, blinking like a thing just born. I trudged back up the hill toward Goyo, feeling huge and rubbery as my thighs mashed together with a squeak. He didn't seem to notice. He grinned at me, already wearing his wet suit, which, to its credit, did not resist his flesh the way my outfit seemed to reject mine. What a body.

"How'd you get changed so fast?" I asked.

"We guys do it right here, in the road."

"That's not fair," I said. "You get t'pee standin' up, any old time and place you choose. It's not fair."

"You could change here, too," he said. "Equal opportunity for exposure."

"No!"

"You look good," he said with a crooked half-smile.

"I do *not*," I said. I lifted one foot and frowned at it. They were like big, flat rubber clown shoes, these surfing shoes. I felt like I should juggle, or tumble out of a tiny car.

Goyo looked like he felt sorry for me. "Why are you so hard on yourself?" he asked.

"I'm not. I'm honest. A girl who's thirty pounds overweight does not look good in anything, much less a skin-tight wet suit."

"*You* do," he said. "And you look good at your weight. You don't need to lose weight, Alexis."

"Oh, hush," I said.

"You look pretty great," he said. "I think so. I've always thought so. You're very pretty."

"Okay, thanks. Let's go." What I thought was: *Am I as pretty as Caridad?*

I blushed, and tried not to. Why was it that the most attractive, child-loving, talented, and intelligent man I'd ever met found me attractive and liked hanging out with me, but just happened to be in love with someone else?

Ever thoughtful, Goyo had rented a small surfboard for me, something turquoise and yellow he said was called a "Wahine" and which was supposed to be for girls only. How in the heck was I supposed to stand on something that shiny, much less in the middle of the churning, bloodthirsty ocean? I supposed I should have been grateful for his kindness, but I was still under the impression that I was about to voluntarily, politely allow myself to drown.

He showed me how to hold the board as we walked into the water, not too far out. He left his board on the shore and stood to the side of mine. He showed me how to hoist my body onto the thing, how to paddle, and as I lay prone on the board he pointed at the surfers farther out and told me what they were doing. Feeling him next to me, with his guiding hand on my arm, back, hips, it was almost too much. Even in the water, he smelled of coconuts. I wanted to kiss him more than I had wanted anything, ever—other than to be on solid ground again.

"Want to go a little deeper?" he asked. He had no idea.

"Sure," I chirped. Inside, I nurtured images of me sinking to the sea bottom covered with suckerfish and skewered with medical waste. Shudder.

"Uh-oh," he said. He stared at me.

"What?"

"There you go again," he said. "Something's wrong."

"No, I'm fine," I said.

"No, something's wrong."

At that moment, a little wave came along and I lost my grip on the surfboard. I toppled into the water before I knew what hit me. Stinging salt water flushed up my nose and down my throat. *Well, dangit all, here it comes*, I thought. I began to flail through the water, fleeing the needle-teeth of sharks and piranhas I believed would start sawing at my soft, fatty flesh any moment now. I came up for air, embarrassed and with sinuses on fire from snorting nature's saline solution. I wiped an eye and saw black smudges on my hand; the mascara. I'd forgotten about the mascara. Things really couldn't be any worse, I thought. Drowning with all the beauty and dignity of a weeping, waterlogged Tammy Faye.

Goyo seemed unshaken by my dip into the sea, the snot pouring from my nose, and the black eyes. "You look like a beautiful mermaid," he said. He reached out and messed with my hair.

"Stop it," I said. The water was shallow enough for him to stand up, but too deep for me to do so. I held onto one side of the board, with my arms and chest on it and the rest of my body below. I started panting and wished I had my inhaler. I could not afford an asthma attack out here.

"Stop *what?*" he asked. He went to the other side of the board and balanced himself like a mirror image of me, his face inches from mine, like a teasing boy. His breath smelled of mint.

"Stop saying I'm pretty. Jeez."

"Why? It's true. You're very pretty."

I wanted to cry. I looked him directly in the eyes and felt my heart explode. "Because," I said. "It hurts me every time you say it." I coughed.

"Why?" He moved his face even closer to mine. He looked surprised. "Because!" I whined. I coughed some more. I wanted to go home.

"Because why?" he asked. He smoothed my hair back. I shook myself away from his touch. A Dallas girl had no purpose floating in the ocean, much less with a Cuban rapper. I was almost ashamed of myself.

"Don't," I said. "Please."

His brows twisted in concern and his eyes softened with kindness. "What's going on?" he asked.

"Look," I said. "Maybe it's normal in Cuba to touch people all the time and tell them they're pretty even though you're in love with someone else, but I'm not used to it. It makes me uncomfortable."

He looked down at the surfboard. "No," he said. "It's not normal there. I shouldn't do it. You're right. I can't help it. I'm sorry."

"It hurts, Goyo."

Tears burned my eyes, as much from terror of the sea as from unrequited love. I couldn't look at him anymore, so I looked away, toward a seafood shack on the shore. I wanted to be there, croquettes in hand, tartar sauce in easy reach. He reached out and turned my face back toward him. I wheezed like a deflated whoopee cushion and looked away. He turned me toward him again.

"Tell me," he said.

"Are you being silly?" I asked. "Can't you *tell*?"

"Tell what?"

I stared up at the pale blue sky and felt my body sway under the water. I wasn't drowning, at least I had that. I might suffocate on my own lung tissue, but I wouldn't drown, as long as I clutched this dingy surfboard.

"Can't you te-*el* . . . that I'm in *love* with you," I wheezed. An invisible fist clenched my lungs and shook them.

His cheeks flushed deep crimson. "Really?" he asked. He smiled broadly.

"Yes, Goyo," I hacked. "Holy cow, couldn't you tell? I'm always s'nervous around you. Jeez Louise."

"You never seem nervous, Alexis. I didn't know. I'm sorry."

The tears flowed hot across my cheeks, dripping into the seawater. "Yeah, I know. You're sorry. Me, too. So please don't compliment me anymore because in my sad little twisted brain I could interpret it as you being interested in me." I hacked and coughed.

"I am," he said. "I mean, I shouldn't be. But . . ." He paused and closed his eyes tight against whatever he was feeling. When he opened them, he smiled at me and said, "I am."

"Don't be stupid," I wheezed. "We just worked everything out so your girlfriend can come be with you. You can't be interested in me!"

Goyo stared deeply into my eyes, and I felt the board start to move into deeper water.

"What are you doing?" I asked.

"I'm taking us farther out," he said.

"Don't. I have asthma. I don't want to die."

"You won't die. I have something to say," he said.

"Don't," I said.

He stopped paddling and leaned forward across the board.

"I don't know what it means," he said. "But I'm really, really attracted to you, Alexis. I shouldn't be, but I am."

And then he did it. He kissed me. Right there, in the middle of the ocean, where I couldn't turn and run away, where I had to kiss him back or be devoured by a swarm of jellyfish. Swarm? I didn't know what you called a massive grouping of jellyfish, other than terrifying.

"What are you doing?" I whined. I wanted more. It was so good.

Goyo's brow creased with confusion. "I don't know," he said.

"That makes two of us," I said.

He kissed me again.

"We shouldn't do this," I said. The cough returned.

"No," he said. "We shouldn't."

"Do you love her?" I asked.

This time, Goyo stared at the sky, and the feeling he had shut his eyes against filled them now, true and soft and yearning and sorrowful all at once. "Yes," he said. "I do. I think so."

"Then we can't do this," I said.

"You're right. And I'll stop, as soon as you kiss me again."

We kissed again. His soft, warm lips tasted like ChapStick and mint, not too wet, not dry. Delicious. I knew better. It was stupid. One thing the girls and I had always agreed on back home was that we would never, ever allow ourselves to be the "other" woman. We were worth more than that. And until this moment, I had succeeded in keeping that vow. But in the middle of this saltwater expanse, my lips did what they wanted.

"So that's it," I said when we were done. I released the surfboard and started to swim toward the shore. Actually, swimming was an overstatement. What I was doing looked more like a flailing, haphazard non-drowning.

"Where are you going?" he called. "Come back!"

"Home," I said. "No!"

"You can't," he said. "We just started. You said you'd have dinner with my parents!"

I treaded water the way they taught me in the country-club swim lessons Momma and Daddy made me take in middle school, and faced him. Part of me was tickled pink to discover the water-treading thing actually worked, out here in the ocean. But the bigger part of me was almost sure I'd never make it to shore. Goyo paddled toward me on the little surfboard, with an impish grin on his face. I wanted to grab him, take him—or, rather, I wanted him to grab me, haul me up onto that surfboard, rescue me from certain death, and then, on the safety of solid ground, take me. And I was pretty darn sure he'd do it, too, if I only asked him to. But I couldn't. Not if I was a good person who respected other women and didn't want to hurt them.

"That's the whole point," I said. "We *can't* start. You're taken. We have to *stop*." I wheezed harder. "And I have to get my inhaler. It's in the car."

"Let me help you," he said, easing the board under my arms. "And you're right. We'll stop."

Filled with the greatest confusion I'd ever felt, I turned away again, and paddled, gasping, as fast as I could toward solid ground.

OLIVIA

My mother's grubby little three-bedroom house on a hill on the border between Silver Lake and East Hollywood had not changed in the nearly twenty years since I moved out, other than to peel and crumble. The wooden floors were still faded, in need of sanding and wax, the rugs still dingy and dusty no matter how many times she ran the old canister vacuum cleaner over them, the walls in need of paint, the front yard in need of attention, the backyard a wild place with a bushy palm tree and plenty of singing birds. Nana was too busy with her writing and activism to think or worry too much about practical matters like keeping up a house, and I doubted she even noticed there was anything desperately needing work here.

Meanwhile, all around, the old shuttered houses were being snapped up by young, well-to-do couples who painted them in pastels and filled the front porches with expensive potted plants. One by one, the homes in the area were losing the bars on their windows. They called it gentrification. I could only imagine what Nana's house must be worth now. Close to half a million dollars, thereabouts. She probably had no idea.

I had long wished to have the money to help Nana fix up her home. I knew she loved it but couldn't afford to pamper it in the ways she wished. How many times had she told me about the purple picket fence she would have loved to put up in place of the old sagging and rusting chain-link? With just a little bit of improvement, the home could be worth double what it was worth now. But I doubted she would ever sell it. My mother lost everything and almost everyone when she left El

Salvador—her husband, her parents, her family, her job, her language, her customs. Through hard and often degrading labor she'd been able to create a place for herself and her children here in Los Angeles. And now that we kids had long since moved out and started lives and families of our own, her only stability and comfort came from this decaying house, which she spoke of as if it were a human being.

It was a Saturday, and I had left Jack with Samuel for the day, and, after I'd interviewed a couple of directors for a job on my movie—*my movie!*—I had gone to talk to my mother about the train wreck that was my life. How could I be having the best and worst time in my life at the same moment? How could my career blossom while my marriage tanked? That's not how it happened in the movies; in the movies, all the horrible things happen at once, and all the great things happen at once, and everyone lives happily ever after. There was no room for this kind of ambiguity in movies. Was there?

I had tried to talk to Samuel, but my feelings were too intense for me to handle. I'd asked him to allow us to coexist in the apartment and carry on with old routines for Jack's sake, with the promise that we'd talk later, in the presence of a counselor, once my rage subsided. I was not the type of person to rail and weep. I wanted to figure things out completely before talking them out. Otherwise, it seemed like a waste of energy.

Samuel said he wanted to work it out, but he said it after I told him about the movie deal and the money, and now I had no idea whether he really loved me, or if he had suddenly seen an easier path through life unfolding before him. Mostly, I was worried by my lack of emotion; everything was shut down, turned off, and I went through life on automatic. All I could see when I looked at Samuel was Lisa Benavidez and her plump little rump. Numb. It was easier to be numb.

Nana answered the door wearing a bright blue dress and perfume. She favored jeans and T-shirts most of the time, so she had primped for my arrival. I didn't know why, but this made me sad. Her wanting to look formal made the breakup of my marriage seem like a rite of passage. In America, it nearly was.

"*Hola, mi'jita,*" she said. She didn't smile the way you wanted a mother to smile at a time like this. Rather, she looked the way she had always looked, as if she were thinking about a lecture she was going to give, or a rally she was planning for striking workers. Deep in her mind, pacing through her thoughts. "Come in."

The house smelled of candle wax, onions, cooking oil, and roach spray, scents I associated with childhood, revolution, comfort, and dread. Everything was as I remembered it, even the old yellow and brown plaid Sears sofa bed with the knitted afghan on the back. I think someone gave her that sofa and she had never considered getting a new one. She'd added a few new framed Diego Rivera prints from

Pier 1, her favorite store, and a few new vases of artificial flowers, but otherwise it was the same altogether charming and rundown house. I admired her life, but I didn't want it. I wanted comfort, newness, ease.

She brought me a glass of *chicha*, a Salvadoran drink made with pineapple peel and cashews, and offered me *coyoles* with honey, which I refused. She wasn't the kind of mom who cooked often, though she was an excellent cook. That she'd made these for me also made me sad, as if she were preparing for a funeral. I still had little appetite, partly from the medication, but mostly because of Samuel.

She moved aside a pile of books and sat quietly on the sofa. I plopped into the big old black canvas papasan chair, which had collected bookish Nana dust in the button holes. I had spent hours in this chair as a child, reading.

"So," she said with a sigh that I took to mean she had something better to be doing. "What's going on?"

I told her everything I knew about Samuel's affair and she listened with the frown and total concentration of a practiced academic.

"Well," she said when I'd finished. "You're in quite a situation."

"He says he did it because of my disorder," I said, realizing only after I'd said it that I had never told Nana about the diagnosis of PTSD; telling her about it would have meant talking about what happened, and we tended not to do that for some reason.

"What disorder?" Nana looked surprised. I hadn't even told her about the nightmares or the screenplay, about how often I replayed what had happened back home in my mind. I'd hoped I could just ease it into the conversation without Nana judging me.

"Post-traumatic stress disorder," I said.

"Pssh," she hissed dismissively. "Who told you that? Samuel? He thinks he's so smart."

"No, Nana. A doctor. A very good doctor. I've got it."

Nana's mouth hardened and she looked into my eyes. "I wouldn't be surprised if you did," she said. She shook her head and sighed. "I guess I thought, I *hoped* you didn't remember it very well."

I shook my head. "I remember."

"Are you on medication?" she asked.

"Yes."

"Does it impact your libido?"

I stared open-mouthed at Nana. "What kind of a question is that?" I asked.

"Sometimes men wander if you aren't paying attention to their needs," she said.

"Are you joking?"

She frowned, judgmental. "So, how long has it been? Weeks? Months? When is the last time you slept with your husband, Olivia?"

"Nana, that's not a fair question."

"That's what I thought," she said triumphantly. "You love him, he loves you. He made a mistake. You have no sex drive. It happens when you have children. Get over it and start having sex again. You'll see, it's not that bad once you get started." She shrugged and dusted her hands together in front of her.

I gasped. "Nana! That's so sexist."

She shook her head. "It's common *sense*."

"What?"

"There are differences in sex drive for men and women. That's biological fact. We might not like to hear it, but it's true. Everyone has to make sacrifices for relationships, and sometimes those sacrifices can mean having sex with your husband because he wants to and you don't."

"That's not fair," I said instinctively.

"Who taught you life was *fair*?"

She didn't say so, but I knew Nana was talking about Tata's murder, the least fair thing that had ever happened to her.

"So are you here to ask for my advice or not?" she asked.

"I thought so but I don't know now," I said.

"Then don't question me. You need to save your marriage because there's love there. I've seen it. I know Samuel and I know that man loves you. And there's a child."

The room spun. "How do I fix it?"

"Get counseling."

"But I don't trust him, Nana. He lied to me. A lot."

She bit her lip and thought. "Then you and Jack should move in here with me for a while," she said simply.

"So I *should* divorce Samuel?" A pit opened in my gut. Who would share my joy about Jack's latest triumphs? Who would hold me in the night? Who would make me pancakes? Who would tell me jokes?

"No," said my mother. "You *separate* for a while. See what happens."

Now it was I who frowned.

"I saw Chan Villar last week," she sang suggestively, as though this news ought to mean something to me.

"So?"

"So nothing." She looked offended, though I had no idea why. "I just wanted to tell you. He was out walking with his daughter in a stroller and he asked me about you."

"What did he say?"

"He asked me how you were."

"What did you tell him?"

"I said you were fine." She looked at me with narrowed eyes. "You need a man like that, Olivia. He's a good man."

"Nana, you don't even *know* him."

"I know his *mother*. She told me about how he was with his wife when she was dying. Did you know he shaved his head when she had chemotherapy, so she didn't have to be bald alone? And he told her how pretty she was every day, even though she was sick and dying. He used to leave her notes every morning of their lives together, telling her how much he loved her."

"That's great," I said, thinking that this information did nothing to help my depression about Samuel, who would probably celebrate news of me having cancer by screwing a student.

"You should have seen him with his daughter," she went on. "I've never seen a man so loving toward a child. Not even my own sons are that loving toward their children. I haven't seen a man like Chan Villar since your father."

"Then, Nana, maybe *you* should ask him out." Her line of conversation struck me as controlling and insensitive.

She stared at me, stunned. "Why would you say something like that?"

"It's not helpful right now to hear about how great someone else's husband was, Nana. I don't really need that right now."

"Sorry," she said. "I didn't mean it like that."

I nibbled a pastry halfheartedly and looked out the window.

"How is your writing, anyway?" asked Nana.

I peered up at her, head lowered. "I've been waiting to tell you," I said with a cringe. "I sold a screenplay."

In normal families, I realized, such news would have been shared long ago, with the expectation that the parent would be happy for the child. In my family, with Nana the center of Nana's universe and mine, I was terrified to tell her I'd done anything that might overshadow her own life's work, much less something about *her*.

Nana raised her hands over her head and let out of whoop of joy. "I knew it! I knew you would! Didn't I always tell you you had talent?" She clapped.

"That woman I met at Samuel's event with Los Chimps del Norte, she was a manager for all these actors and people, and she liked it. It's crazy, because she's a Republican, and I don't usually get along with them. But I like her. She's nice."

Nana smiled hugely at me. "You see?" she said. "It's about balance, sometimes. Good things come with bad, it's all part of life." She smiled. "So, what's this movie about?"

"That's the thing." I squirmed. "It's kind of about . . . you."

"Me?" Nana put a hand to her chest and looked puzzled. "Why me?"

"Because you're the most amazing woman I know," I said. I braced for her anger.

Nana frowned at me and set her glass on the table with a snap. "You can't just write about my life without asking me, Olivia."

"I should have asked, I know."

"Why didn't you?" She crossed her arms and leaned forward. "I'm surprised."

"I was afraid you'd say no, or that you'd try to control it somehow."

Nana said nothing and sucked her lower lip. She only sucked her lip when she was angry; it made her look like a pouting baby.

"I'm sorry," I said. "But it's very flattering, Nana. It's a good movie, it shows you as a hero."

"I know how you feel about me, Olivia, that I was never there for you, that I don't think enough about your feelings. I don't appreciate you making a movie to show the world how much you hate me."

"That's *not* what I did. My *God*, Nana."

"How do I know that? It's very American to do something like that, blame your parents for everything and write a movie to get back at them."

"You can read it, if you want."

Nana shrugged. "Can I change it if I don't like it?"

"You'll like it."

"I don't know," she said. "Back home a child would never do something like this, you know that? Behind my *back*."

"I thought you'd be happy," I said.

"If that were true you wouldn't have lied about it."

"I never lied about anything," I said.

"You didn't tell me or ask me," she pouted.

"Nana, I'm a grown-up now. I don't always have to ask for your permission."

She stood up, angry. "When you're writing about my life you should," she said.

"I know, I know. I'm sorry."

I sat in silence for a minute as Nana paced and finally sat down with a sigh. "I'll look at it," she said.

"They're going to pay me a lot of money," I said. "More than Samuel makes in two years."

She stopped sucking her lower lip and grinned at me, beaming with pride. Nana was good at changing her mood in an instant.

"You better get a good accountant."

"I did. Alexis knows this Russian guy."

Her eyes took on a pleading expression. "Just don't make me look bad, Olivia. Please. I've worked too hard."

"Don't worry."

"Who do you think will play me?"

"Marcella Gauthier Bosch."

"Who's that?"

"She's a Dominican actress."

Nana looked doubtful. *"Una Dominicana?"*

"She's very good, Nana. You'll see."

"Okay," she said.

I looked out the window and felt deeply sad. "I wish I could enjoy all of this, Nana. But I can't. It's like Samuel took my soul away."

Nana glared at me, walked to a bookshelf, and took down a family portrait from when I was a child, from before the murder. "You're a survivor," she said. "Everything you told me today is nothing compared to what you've already been through. Remember that. You're a remarkable woman."

I looked at the floor in shame. We never talked about my father's death. She had tried, of course, but I'd always resisted, changed the subject, stormed out. Blamed her. Blamed her. Forever and a day I had blamed my mother for the murder of the man she loved.

"Nana?" I asked.

"Sí?" She flinched and closed her eyes with a held breath, as if she expected another outburst from me.

"Why did you spend so much time away from us? After we got here, I mean."

She looked me directly in the eye and frowned. "It's one of the biggest regrets in my life," she said. "We were running, Olivia. I was younger then than you are now. I wanted to make sure the world was safe for you." She walked over to me and touched my arm. "You were the reason I worked so hard, you and Paz and Frascuelo. But you didn't need a human rights crusader. You needed a nana. I'm sorry. I can see that now. But then, then I didn't know what was happening. I was moving so fast, Olivia, so fast you can't imagine how it felt."

I felt the pinpricks of tears forming behind my eyes.

She stared at me, unblinking. "And I know you think it was my fault, what they did to Tata. But they would have gotten him anyway, Olivia. He died to save us."

One by one, the drops fell onto my cheeks, ran down the crease next to my nose and into my mouth. Salt, and metal. Blood water.

"I know," I gulped.

My mother's lower lip trembled. In the film, Nana never cries, because I had never seen her cry since El Salvador. I put my hand on hers. "It's okay, Mom."

"You forgive me?" She knelt on the floor and began to weep, my Tata's photo in her hands; she asked him, not me.

"There is nothing to forgive," I whispered. "It's not your fault."

We embraced in silence.

Finally, Nana looked up with a small smile. "I just hope I'm a better *abuelita* than I was a mother," she said.

"You're a good *abuelita*," I said.

"If you and Jack move here, I won't work so much. I'll stay with him, as much as you need."

"I could help you fix up the house," I said.

"Oh, Olivia," she said, seeming suddenly so small and alone I could hardly bear it. "I did the best I could. I did." She looked at the walls and furniture and I realized she knew it was falling apart.

I held her again, and ran my finger over Tata's smiling face in the picture.

"Do you miss him?" I asked.

She nodded gravely. "Every day."

"Have you ever thought of dating?" I asked, thinking of Dr. Garcia from UCLA.

"Me?" my mother asked in a shocked tone, as if I'd suggested she try out for a skin flick.

"Yes, you!" I smiled. "You're beautiful. You're still young. You are a flesh-and-blood woman, Mom."

"Fifty-two is hardly *young*."

I could not believe she'd only been sixteen when she got pregnant with me. "It's *young*, Mom. And I know a great guy who's interested."

She blushed and pretended to slap my arm. "Olivia, *deja eso*."

"I'm serious. He's admired you for a long time."

She shook her head as if she weren't interested, but looked up with a girlish smile. "Is he cute?" Cute? It was such a youthful word. An eighth-grade word.

"Very."

"Is he a Republican, like this Alexis friend of yours?"

"Highly doubtful."

"Is he Latino?"

"Very."

"Is he afraid to come to this part of town, like that stupid Samuel?"

"No."

She released me and stood up, and said, "We'll see."

"So I can invite him over?"

My mother laughed out loud, and it sounded like church bells. I couldn't re-member the last time I heard her do that. Then, with the tiniest of smiles, she re-peated herself: "We'll see."

In that instant, in the warm gold of the afternoon light, she had the full, pink cheeks of a little girl. And I realized something I was ashamed to have never con-sidered before: Inside my mother, like me, *was* a little girl.

And my mother, like me, was human. And fallible.

And maybe, just maybe, so was Samuel.

Summer

It is necessary to make virtue fashionable.
—José Martí

ALEXIS

Caridad arrived in L.A. like a shiny new gift from Satan on my thirty-first birthday, and I started to wonder why God had a problem with me. It was a test. But why?

Thirty-one and single. Lordy.

I smiled for the rumpled-looking *New York Times* photographer and tried to seem happy as a baby with her hand in rhubarb pie. In truth there was no place on His great green earth I wanted to be *less* than where I was at this moment. Hell, perhaps. Or Antarctica. But this? This was hell on earth for me, and my heart was frozen as if I stood in tundra in nothing but clowny surf shoes.

In reality, I stood in a vast hallway at the airport, a few feet from Goyo, surrounded by a couple of select camera crews—we'd given exclusive coverage of the blessed event to *60 Minutes* and the *New York Times* in English, and to Jorge Ramos and Univision in Spanish. I'd been massaging the press on this for a few weeks, and they all thought it was a great story. I'd pretended, of course, that the story was pure and organic as *The Moosewood Cookbook* Olivia recently loaned me (I made one recipe and quickly went back to Carls Jr. drive-bys, thank you) even though I had plotted and schemed the whole shebang as coldly as General Antonio López de Santa Ana surrounding all them helpless cowboys at the Alamo.

I'd invited lots of dramatic, annoying Cubans, for full media sound-bite effect. Maybe *60 Minutes* would add sentimental mood music to the segment the way all the so-called unbiased liberal newsmagazines were starting to. Nothing would be better for Goyo's career than footage of a bunch of sobbing Cubans, Goyo holding his beloved (spit, spit) Caridad, while some slow, sad song piped softly through American television sets. Listening to the jabber of all these dang Cubans, I couldn't help thinking the TV people would be best off doing *something* to mask their volume. Jeez Louise but they were *loud*. They yelled everything, and their hands whipped around all over the place like a bunch of little girls doing patty-cakes. They made me nervous. You thought they were arguing with each other until you listened to their words and realized they were just shootin' the breeze.

I'd never noticed that Goyo was particularly loud, but surrounded by his people he was as much of a yeller and hand-whipper as they were. And these weren't low-on-the-totem-pole people, either. These were wealthy and powerful Cubans, who came from all over the nation and world to have their photos taken with the rising pop-superstar Goyo—already being billed as the first Cuban-born pop phenomenon since Gloria Estéfan, thanks to yours truly, the Texan media Machiavelli—and his beautiful and newly freed love, the talented and soon-to-be-famous Caridad Heredia (spit, spit). And there I was, in my navy blue suit with the white shirt and pearls, smiling like a happy camper, the sweetest li'l Breck girl in the world. *Not.*

To complete the illusion, I held a bouquet of Mylar balloons welcoming *her*. I'd arranged several large bouquets of (day-old, mildly droopy, discount—ha!) flowers on little foldout tables I'd brought in the back of Goyo's Jeep. I smiled and tried to play the part of joyous publicist while dozens of Cubans wrung their hyper hands in anticipation of the happy reunion.

Goyo, dressed in his usual jeans and tank top with a Hawaiian shirt over it, paced, shaking hands with men here and there, smiling at the benevolent expressions on the faces of the Cuban women who sniffled and dabbed in their brightly colored suits. Gosh, but these people were dramatic, weren't they? I mean, I sort of knew they were because I'd watched all that emotion with Elián González on the news like every other mystified American. But I didn't expect all this wailing and shouting.

I could tell you one thing, though: If this were a Mexican ordeal, everyone would contain their dramatic impulses a *little bit* so that at least the other people around wouldn't be scared or uncomfortable. We were thoughtful; not so, it seemed to me at that moment, the Cubans. They roared and shouted and hit their palms with the backs of their other hands. It was like our music; Mexican music was dignified, classical, orchestral, passionate—at least the kind Papi Pedro performed. Cubans sweat and shook to their music. Mexicans, if you asked me, had more class. Except Goyo.

Goyo paced the hallway like a hungry tiger. And when he didn't pace, he tapped his foot in the suede cowboy boot, his big biceps twitching. I wanted to whisk him off, drive him away from here and away from *her*. But that wouldn't happen.

He looked over at me, his eyes low and heavy with guilt. He sort of shrugged, like he didn't know what to do with the secret kisses we'd shared. *Yeah, buddy*, I thought. *Join the dang club*. I felt sorry for him, actually. But that was another problem with me; I thought about other people's feelings too much. I was capable of forgiving people for just about anything.

Goyo watched me and seemed to know what was going on inside my head. He looked at his watch and paced over to where I stood.

"Alexis," he said. "Come with me."

Goyo grabbed my hand and pulled me down the corridor toward one of those dimly lit airport bars where people like me, people who hate flying, try to drown their terror in alcohol and endless sports programming on the hanging televisions. Goyo looked around with rushed, wild eyes, paranoid, and dragged me past the hostess to a darkened corner of the pub.

"Sit down for a second," he said, helping me into a booth whose high walls created an almost roomlike privacy.

"Goyo, what are you doing? We have press here. We have to go back."

He slid into the booth next to me. "I have to tell you something," he said. Beads of sweat formed on his forehead, and his eyes squinted with worry.

"What in the world has gotten into you?"

He looked deep into my eyes and grabbed my hands in his. "Caridad is coming today," he said.

"Please tell me you didn't just figure that out."

He went on as though I had not said anything. "And I don't know why, but I have these feelings for you that won't go away."

"It's just heartburn. You gotta lay off that fried cow stuff, darlin'. Let's go."

"Alexis, stop it. I'm trying to tell you . . ."

"What?"

The tension in his shoulders exploded out of him as he sighed and slumped. He looked lost. "I don't know," he said. "I don't know."

"You drag me all the way over here to tell me you don't know something? Goyo, please. Let's go. This is silly."

"No," he said, the tension squaring his shoulders again as he sat up and leaned closer to me. "That's the whole point. I don't know what I'm doing. I don't like having mixed feelings. Until I met you, everything in my life was clear."

I looked at my watch. "Can we talk about this later? Your lady's plane should be touching down any minute and there's a roomful of crazy Cubans who want to see you out there."

He laughed, I guessed because he liked the way I referred to his people as crazy. "Fine."

Goyo started to get up, but thought better of it. He turned toward me and grabbed my face with both hands, planting a kiss right on my lips. I squirmed to get away, but he held me in place with his strong hands.

"Don't," I protested, as dishonest as I'd ever been. "Go."

"Stay," he said. And we kissed, for nearly twenty seconds we kissed, intensely.

"I'm sorry," he said. But his eyes shone. He *wasn't* sorry. He was happy as a puppy with a new chew toy, and I realized I was headed toward the same ripped-to-pieces fate.

"We should go," I said.

"I know."

"Please don't ever do that again," I said as I did my best to avoid crying.

"Why not?" he asked.

"Because I don't think my heart can take it. You've just got cold feet."

"What? My feet are fine. It's hot. I'm hot, actually, it's nerves."

"It's an American saying. It means you're just a little scared of what's about to happen. It's going to be good. You love her. You really do. Now for the love of God, don't get me stuck all up in the middle of it."

Goyo hung his head as though he were ashamed of himself. "I'm so stupid," he said. "I'm sorry. I'm so confused right now."

I smiled and stood up, walking briskly back toward the corridor. This time, it was me dragging Goyo. "Now, sugar," I said. "Let's go see Caridad, and make history."

They're here," cried the *New York Times* reporter. He pointed a pasty finger to the electronic arrival board on the wall and shoved the photographer toward the gate. The flight from Mexico City read ARRIVED instead of ON TIME and I felt the bottom drop out of my world. "Get going," the reporter said to the photographer. "Don't miss the shot." The photographer glared at the reporter like he was darn near ready to smack him one.

Papi Pedro would arrive later tonight, in his private jet. But the rest of Papi's band was here, with the beloved Caridad and her cousin Amado. Papi's guitarist had his instrument out and strummed José Alfredo Jiménez's classic ballad, "Serenata Sin Luna," singing the best he could: "*Con suelo en tu amooooorrr . . .*" Mood music! Maybe *60 Minutes* wouldn't have to overdub it themselves. Very sweet. (Spit, spit!) Smile, darlin'.

So she was here. It was over. She was here, with her false papers saying she was a member of my dad's band. I'd done this. She was here. The love of Goyo's life. And he'd kissed me, there, in the middle of the ocean, and he'd called me beautiful, and then he'd done it again, not five minutes ago. And I'd loved it. And I loved *him*.

I loved him so much I had gone through with this, getting her out, and now Goyo was promised a big piece on *60 Minutes* and a big profile in the *New York Times*, and he was promised the love of his life. That's how much I loved him. Did he recognize it? Did he see how generous I'd been with him, how I'd let him go, just like it says on those tacky inspirational posters you buy in the office stores at the mall, the ones with the photo of the white horse galloping through the misty green forest? Did he see how I'd loved him and let him go and how I stood here even now in the middle of the most exciting moment of his life, hoping he'd boomerang on back to me? I needed Marcella here, to come up with a better quote for the moment, something you couldn't buy in an airline Sky Mall shopping magazine. The whole inspirational poster thing wasn't strong enough. She'd be able to pull something out from a deep thinker or poet or something. That was the difference between me and Marcella. That and the fact that men wanted her for their beds, and they wanted me for, you know, high-fives at the sports bar.

The camera crews started to crowd around the exit from the gate corridor, jockeying for position, and I had to snap back and play publicist for a moment, reminding them to give Goyo plenty of room, saying nice things like, "I know y'all want to get your stories, but remember that this is Goyo's life, not just a photo op." Spit, spit. "Y'all are lucky to be here, because he didn't want anybody to film this." Yeah, right.

Goyo glided to where I corralled the journalists and put his arm over my shoulders, his smile bright enough to power the whole airport.

"You are such an amazing woman," he whispered, hot in my ear. "Thanks, Alexis."

He kissed my cheek too long, and too wet, and I wanted to punch him. But I didn't. I was Alexis Lopez, nice girl, so I smiled up at him and fought the urge to attach my lips to his again.

"No problem, buddy," I said. I socked him playfully on the arm and stepped back to watch. That was me, Little Miss High-Five Chick. He stared at me and mouthed, *"Lo siento, mi amor,"* in Spanish: I'm sorry, my love. Great. Could he have tried to confuse me more? I wasn't the cursing type, but *shoot*.

Caridad was skinny as a gazelle, of course. And taller than I expected. Why did I just assume everyone in Cuba would be a dwarf? That was silly of me. Anyway, she must have been about five-eight. Her skin was the color of a shiny new penny, and her hair a dark reddish brown, thick and lustrous past her shoulders down the middle of her narrow back. Her eyes were emerald green like mine, but tilted gently upward at the outer corners, with long black lashes. Goyo had told me her mother was Chinese-Cuban, and her father was mulatto, a mix of Spanish and African.

She showcased her long, shapely legs in a cheap miniskirt. How impractical, I thought. Who in her right mind would wear a miniskirt on such a long airplane flight? You'd have to sit there worrying if the world could see your coochie. Or maybe she wasn't the type who worried about people seeing her coochie. Maybe she was the type who *wanted* people to see her coochie. They existed. Look at Marcella.

I stopped myself from criticizing her any more, and realized with some shame that she had probably never taken a plane before. The poor creature probably didn't know what it was like to sit in those itty-bitty seats for hours on end. I was mean. But I was in love, with her darn boyfriend. And to look at her, I knew the same seats that felt small and tight to my enormous arse would feel large and spacious to hers. Bitch.

Goyo watched her walk toward us, and his eyes grew moist. His mouth softened into the sweetest smile. He loved her so much. I could see that. I didn't want to stand in the way; I wanted to erect an entire *army* to stand in the way.

Caridad wore a tight tank top with the American flag on it, and you could see her nips standing at attention through the stars and stripes. Oh, please, I thought, how Pam Anderson. How cheesy. She waved at Goyo and smiled, and her teeth were as white and as perfect as the rest of her. She wore large hoop earrings, and sad little scuffed white pumps that screamed "ghetto." Again, I stopped myself from being too critical. The woman just came from Cuba, I told myself. She's as poor as they come, a political exile, and there but for the grace of God go I, all that. I *understood* all of that, in my head I did, anyway. But in my heart I understood that she was gorgeous, even in those dilapidated shoes, and she was here to take Goyo away from me.

I hated her.

Traipsing along next to Caridad was her cousin Amado, a moderately handsome man six or seven shades lighter than Caridad, with remotely Chinese features as well. He lugged her bags on arms that looked too long, like the knuckles might drag the floor. He was nowhere near as good looking as Goyo, and it looked like the boy preferred to breathe through his mouth. I was poop out of luck.

Cameras flashed and popped as Caridad and Goyo finally embraced. Amado hunched to the side with his ape arms, a big, awkward yellow smile cut like a lemon wedge across his face. He waved for the cameras as if he'd been coached. He's a Gomer, I thought. A Howdy Doody. A Hallmark moment. Yay.

I had to turn away as Caridad and Goyo locked lips. I examined the arrival board, scrutinized all the city names, and tried to imagine I was there, in any city but here. I felt a hand on my arm and turned. It was Maria Teresa Rodríguez, the representative from the Cuban American National Foundation, whom I had invited to be here.

"Are you going to introduce me or not?" she huffed. Right. I had promised she would be the first speaker at the mini–press conference we were supposed to hold here, now, in the middle of the airport.

"I'm so sorry," I said. The tears dripped from my tired over-thirty eyes.

"Are you okay?" she asked.

"Oh, I'm fine." I dabbed with my tissue. "I'm just a big old sap. I cry at the littlest thing. It's so beautiful, isn't it? I just love happy reunions."

"It's *wonderful*," she said. She grabbed me by the shoulders and shook me so hard I almost screamed. "And on behalf of Cubans everywhere in search of freedom, I want to thank you for making this possible, and for bringing the world's attention to the hardships our people live with every day because of that tyrant, that son of a bitch!"

Jesus God but these people needed tranquilizers or something.

I arranged myself once more, and led her to the small podium the airport authorities had set up for us in one corner. I tapped the microphone to make sure it was on. Feedback, adjust, fine. Alexis Lopez, publicist extraordinaire, manager to the future superstars of the Americas.

"Okay, you two lovebirds," I said, as lightly and sprightly as I could. "Let's come up for air for a minute here so we can let everyone know what's going on."

Goyo and Caridad stopped kissing and looked at me. Then, the nerve, he pulled her over and introduced us. He led her gently, lovingly to the podium. I introduced the speaker from the foundation, and stepped aside so she could introduce Goyo and Caridad, or, as she called them, our modern Romeo and Juliet, but with a happy ending and symbolizing freedom from a communist dictator she despised. Cubans, in my opinion, just could not stop complaining. I mean, I hated communists, too, but I can tell you one thing—if I wasn't living under one anymore, I sure as shootin' wouldn't keep talkin' about him all the darn time. That was like letting the "son of a bitch" win, in my opinion. The best thing to do would be to just forget about it and have a great life. That would show him. But no. They wanted to whine about it for the rest of eternity.

As I pushed through the crowd to get a corner to myself, I brushed against Caridad, who smelled faintly of roses and not-so-faintly of sweat—gross. You'd think someone that pretty would wear deodorant, unless, of course, she hadn't been able to afford it, or they didn't carry it in the communist shops. She smiled and grabbed my hand.

"*Gracias,*" she said. She smacked her chewing gum as if she'd never enjoyed the stuff in her life. "Goyo told me so much about you. It's a great honor to meet you."

"I'm happy to meet you, too," I lied. She was prettier up close than I had realized. You couldn't see her pores, like a baby's skin. I hated her for that, too. But I was overjoyed, almost to the point of somersaulting, that she smelled like a barn.

Cousin It gripped my arm like a man having a heart attack. "Thank you," he said with a thick accent. He reeked of alcohol. A drunk Gomer, with massive beige teeth. Charming. He held up a hand for me to high-five him, and I simmered with rage. Even *he* wanted to be my buddy? What *was* this?

We looked up at the speaker, who was concluding her introduction: "I invite you all to join us for a welcome-home party for Caridad tonight at the Conga Room on Wilshire. It's going to be a very special night, because Goyo and Cary will play onstage together for the first time since he left Cuba about one year ago."

To my credit, I had arranged *that*, too. The concert and party at the trendiest, most glamorous Latin nightspot in Los Angeles. It would be catered by the gourmet Cuban restaurant downstairs, and a collection of A-list celebrities would be there, and Goyo and his beloved would play together, make music together. It was a brilliant publicity stunt, and a bullet through my heart.

The crowd of obnoxiously happy people clapped.

I clapped, too, and smiled until I wanted to retch.

OLIVIA

knew set designers were magicians, but I did not expect to walk into a plain, weedy warehouse in East Los Angeles and find my childhood home waiting for me under an array of lights and microphones.

Using photos of my village, two personal photos of our old home in El Salvador that my mother had managed to bring with her to the States, and interviews the set designer had done with me and my mother, the designers for *Soledad* had re-created the house I'd grown up in, with almost terrifying precision. The blankets on the bed were frayed, as ours had been, made of the same untreated wool; and even the fake foliage outside the windows was created to match the plants that grew around my old home.

"Oh, my God," said my mother, as she grabbed for my arm to steady her. She had been present for filming at other times along the way the past month or so, but she had never had this kind of reaction. I held her, and we looked at the set of the small house, walked together from room to room.

"Incredible," whispered my mother.

In a corner of the warehouse, makeup artists worked to make Marcella look like my mother. She'd dyed her hair black and cut it for the role, and when the artists had finished, her eye shape looked like my mother's, her brows were my mother's, even the angle of her cheekbones was like Nana's as a young woman. The press liked to say that Marcella was doing "plain" and "homely" for this role, but I didn't see it that way at all. She was not going glamorous, it was true, but to me, and to millions like me, my mother was the epitome of human beauty.

"The set is incredible," I said to Marcella, who had finished in makeup and joined us. "It's exactly right. You, too. You look just like her. I can't believe it."

Marcella opened her arms and held Nana. The transformation in her had been incredible. She'd been spending time with Nana, talking to her, getting to know her, and had adopted many of my mother's mannerisms. And I didn't think there was an actress in the business who could match my mother's fury and sense of injustice better with her eyes than Marcella. Watching her hug my mother now was almost like seeing the young Nana holding the old, and I got goose bumps. I watched as my mother's eyes strayed to the young actor who had been selected out of hundreds to play the role of my Tata. He was just right for the job, too; probably too right, if the sadness in my mother's eyes was an indicator. It was almost creepy to see him standing at the catering table sifting through melon chunks with a group of men dressed as death-squad soldiers, talking about baseball.

"I know this won't be easy, Soledad," said Marcella. Today was the day of the murder shoot. "I can understand if you don't want to be here."

Nana shook her head. "No," she said. "I'll stay. It's the one part I want to make sure you guys get right."

After the shoot, I drove to Samuel's in Calabasas to pick up Jack.

My estranged husband looked bad, tired and old, weak. Left to his own devices, it appeared that Samuel could not cook a meal properly, or get his clothes washed. He seemed to want to talk to me, and even tried to touch my face with his hand, but I had no interest. I felt nothing for him. It was almost a relief.

We'd been going to counseling once a week since I moved out, for four months now, and nothing had changed. Well, that wasn't entirely true. *I* had changed. I no longer believed I needed to be married, much less married to a man who did not appreciate me. I did not want to be married to Samuel anymore. We'd been civil to one another, for Jack's sake and out of habit, and I think my patience and understanding caught him off-guard because he walked around with a shocked, miserable look on his face. "Why don't you scream at me?" he asked. "Hit me! Something." When I had told Alexis of Samuel's transformation, she'd seemed impressed.

"I never thought about it," she'd said. "But I think you might have just found the best way on earth to make a man feel guilty. Do nothing in the face of his man-ness. Be nice, but not too nice. I'll remember it, assuming I ever find another man to love me enough to treat me like doo-doo."

"So I'll see you at counseling Saturday?" Samuel asked now, as I walked down the hall, away from my old apartment, toward the elevator with Jack singing softly to himself in my arms.

"No, I don't think so," I said. "I'm sorry, Samuel. I'm not going anymore."

"You can't just stop," he said.

"I can. And I have. I want a divorce."

He stared, dumbfounded. "Shouldn't we talk about this?"

"Divorce," said Jack, repeating the new word as he often did with new words, testing the weight and feel of it in his tiny mouth.

I gave Samuel a sweet smile and a wave, because nothing frustrated a jackass of a man more than having the object of his abuse and neglect treat him with the respect and dignity he himself had failed to display. "No. There's nothing to talk about anymore, other than Jack, and we'll stay in close communication on that subject, because we both love this kid so much. Don't we, baby?"

I kissed Jack on the cheek and tickled his belly. I did not want this to be traumatic for him. There was no reason his parents' divorce should not feel like the most natural, comfortable thing in the world. It wasn't divorce that hurt children, I figured, but rather all the drama and stupidity parents subjected their children to in the often messy process of parting ways. I kept my messes to myself. Jack did not need them.

I smiled at my soon-to-be-ex-husband. "Good-bye, Samuel. And good luck."

I drove Jack home—to my mother's. Jack, a creature of toddler habit, noticed instantly that we were not going back to Calabasas, and he knew where we were headed. But, as usual, he grilled me about it just to be sure.

"Where's Mommy going?" Jack demanded as I took the North Rampart exit on the 101.

Ay, mi madre, I thought. How do I explain this to him again?

"Mommy is driving to *her* mommy's house. Jack and Mommy are going to live with *Abuelita* for a little while. Doesn't that sound like fun? *Abuelita* loves you so much! She has flowers and apple juice. Jack likes apple juice."

"Where's Mommy going?" he repeated.

"We're going to live with *Abuelita*," I said. "She loves you very much. And we're going to live in her pretty blue house for a while. Doesn't that sound like fun?"

I watched his eyebrows rise in the rearview mirror. He set to work scratching lines and squiggles on the Magna Doodle, perfectly content with my explanation. I loved him so much, his adaptability, his strength of tiny character. His company.

"Where's Daddy?" he asked.

"Daddy is at Daddy's house. Mommy and Jack are going to *Abuelita's* house. Sometimes mommies and daddies live in different houses and Jack gets to go visit in two houses. Isn't that fun? There are parks and lots of good things where *Abuelita* lives. We're having an adventure!"

I pulled off the freeway and started toward the house. As we drove past the swaying palm trees and gleaming pond of Echo Park, he perked up. "Birds! Mommy, birds!" he yelped. I looked again at him in the mirror and saw that he pointed out the window toward the pond. Two beautiful swans circled in the water with the pedal boats. Families strolled the twisting paths, everywhere with strollers and children.

"Look at that!" I exclaimed. "The swans look so pretty! Swans have beautiful long necks."

"Park," he said. "Want to go there."

I knew Samuel and everyone else I knew thought of this as an undesirable neighborhood, but the sight of all of the people and families out enjoying the afternoon in the park—and speaking Spanish as if it were the most normal thing in the world—made me happy. And this was a very, very good sign.

It had been months since I'd felt anything at all.

We arrived at my mother's, and I was grateful Jack was out of the lead-paint danger age, because I was sure the house was powdered with toxic dust. It was the next thing I'd have to deal with on the long list of fix-ups to my mother's decrepit abode. Nana hadn't painted since I'd left home more than fifteen years ago. I was sure it hadn't crossed her mind. I'd have to buy smoke detectors, too, as they were part of the world of responsible home-ownership to which my nana did not belong. I'd been polite about the issues in the house before I'd made my mind up that divorce was the way I was going to go with Samuel; but now that it looked like I'd be living here for a while, with my son, I would have to start fixing things. I did not know how Nana would react to me messing with her house; but work had to be done. It seemed to me that what Nana did in this house was closer to camping than living, but I hadn't had the heart to tell her so. Now I'd have to.

"'Buelita!" Jack cried. "We're home!"

I unbuckled Jack from his car seat and set him on the sidewalk. He raced on his own across the dry yellow grass of the yard toward the porch, where my mother stood waiting for us with one hand on her hip and the other blocking the rays of the setting sun from her eyes. She wore a long, flowing dress, purple batik on black rayon, with flat hippie sandals. Her white hair flowed around her face and, as usual, she wore long, dangly earrings, the kind you could only find for sale on card tables at swap meets. Other than the color of her hair, there was nothing to indicate she was a grandmother. She could have been my twin sister. I realized I dressed a little too much like her; the more time I spent with my fashionable new friends, the more I realized I probably needed help in the wardrobe department.

"'*Buelita!*" Jack cried.

My mother squatted and held her arms open for my son. I couldn't remember her being that open to me, ever. As they embraced, my heart filled with a bittersweet joy. She would be a better grandmother than she'd been a mother.

As I approached the house, I could smell pork *pasteles* and *casamiento*, or Salvadoran rice and beans, cooking. I realized with equal shock that Nana was cooking, and I was hungry. Not ravenous, but hungry. I was starting to feel things again, including a deep, abiding sadness, laced with the excitement of my own possibilities. I'd have to get a new haircut and new clothes, and put myself out there again, single. It was so strange to think of myself as single, but exhilarating, too. I liked it. I liked it so much, in fact, that I was in no rush to change my status. I had my own money now, and my own life. I had good child care for Jack, and new friends who appreciated what I did. I didn't really think I needed a man to complement all that, not now and maybe not ever. How fun would it be to just sort of date around? Have a few male friends, maybe, that I could have sex with, even, but who wouldn't own such a large part of my heart and soul that their behavior could impact my moods? Wow. That would be amazing.

"*Que niño más lindo,*" my mother cried. She scooped Jack into her arms, rested him on one hip, and touched my arm with her free hand. "Welcome home, *mi'ja,*" she said. You hungry?"

"I am, actually," I said. I stood next to her on the porch, buried my head in her shoulder, and smelled onions and *masa*. She had smelled the same all my life.

"Atta girl," she said. "You should eat. You're getting too skinny."

"*Ay, Mami,*" I said. "I told Samuel I want a divorce today. *Que voy a hacer?*"

"You're going to come in and get on with life, that's what you're going to do," she said. "Blessings come in many forms, and this is a blessing. You'll see. Things can only get better."

"I hope so," I said.

Nana turned me around so I was facing the street, and pointed discreetly.

"Look who's here," she sang, low.

Chan Villar walked past the house, holding hands with a little dark-haired girl with high pigtails. Catching sight of me, he waved. I waved back.

"Did you tell him to come?" I hissed to my mother, horrified.

"Maybe," she said.

I felt the blood rush to my cheeks and dashed inside. Nana followed, whistling and dancing with Jack on her hip.

"Nana, how could you!" I ran to the windows and pulled the curtains closed.

"I know you," she said. "I didn't think you'd be going back to that spoiled baby, you-know-who." When Jack was around, we avoided speaking harshly of his father by name.

Nana sat down with Jack on the piano bench and started showing him how to play the old upright, which he loved even though it had never been properly tuned and still bore Paz's initials carved into the wood of the legs. I wandered through the gray light of this strange little nourishing house, wondering if I could ever get used to being back here again.

Jack's toddler bed and furniture were in Paz's old room, and my old room waited for me, scarcely changed. My speech and debate ribbons still stuck to the walls, and the closet door was still hot pink, the shade I'd painted it in the eighth grade, when I thought that color was cool. I wondered if my mother had kept it this way out of nostalgia, or sloth. Likely it was a combination of the two.

Nana found me going through one of my old high school yearbooks, sitting on my old canopy bed. "We've got plenty of space," she said. "Stay as long as you need to, Olivia. It'll be nice to have children in the house again."

S everal days later, Nana watched Jack while I went for a jog. Marcella had called as I was about to leave, to check in, she said, but I suspected it was for an ego boost because she had also bragged about how well the day's shooting went. She also said she was going to go public with some really big news to help promote the causes of justice and my movie, but would not tell me what in the world she was talking about. I was at the point where it didn't really matter anymore. Everything Marcella did Marcella thought of as big news. She was famous and getting more famous, but it was never enough for her.

"You can't jog there," she exclaimed when I tried to get off the phone.

"Why not?" I asked.

"You'll get killed, or mauled by a stray chow chow. I've seen them wandering around that area, in herds."

"You mean packs?"

"Swarms of chow chows, flying all around."

I looked at the debate ribbons and remembered what it had felt like to speak my mind, to argue—and win. There had been a time when I felt hopeful enough about my future and power to stand up to people. I was starting to feel that way again, and there was no better person to practice on than Marcella, a woman I had been afraid to confront until very recently.

"You don't know what you're talking about," I told her. It was the first time I had had the courage to challenge Marcella. And then, for the first time, I hung up on her the way she was always doing to other people.

I turned my phone off and stuffed it in the entry-table drawer. I liked Marcella, but I needed some alone time. Some time just for me. I strapped on my brand-new Asics—the first thing I bought when the movie money came in. The second thing I did was hire a contractor to build a purple picket fence for my mother's house; she didn't know yet. They'd be here next weekend. The third thing I'd done is start a college fund for Jack. He already had a semester of college taken care of, at the most expensive school in the nation. Not bad for a two-year-old. As soon as I finished with his college fund, I'd start to pay off my own college debts, loans that had all but crippled me before.

I wore green nylon shorts, a sports bra, and a Pepperdine T-shirt. I'd read that running and other forms of exercise stimulated the same hormones and brain sections as love, and that one of the best things to do for yourself during a breakup was to move your body, vigorously. I ran down the uneven sidewalks, and ran some more, until I couldn't run anymore, all the way through Silver Lake, around the reservoir, to downtown. I walked sweaty and exhausted into the Grand Central Market, took the damp, wrinkled five-dollar bill from the pocket of my running shorts, and bought myself a watermelon "agua," or iced fruit drink, from a Mexican vendor. I bought a copy of the L.A. *Times*, and sat at a table in the vast warehouse space to catch up on world events while shoppers went about their business in Spanish all around me, shuffling through the peanut shells on the floor. I didn't care what the media said about it being "dead" here; I adored downtown Los Angeles. And it was very alive, just alive in Spanish. This was the real Los Angeles as far as I was concerned, not Marcella's world. This was the Los Angeles no one knew about in the rest of the country—my Los Angeles. And it was the Los Angeles I'd write about in films for the rest of my life.

The front-page story surprised me. Daniel, Alexis's ex-boyfriend from the *Times*, had been suspended without pay for abuse of journalistic power. The paper confessed it was an embarrassing prank from an "unstable" employee and issued an apology to Alexis. I wished I had my phone on me so I could call Alexis and ask her if she'd heard from him in the wake of the news. I'd call her when I got home.

Home. The word felt just right. My heart hung in shreds somewhere in my rib cage, and every time I saw a pretty young brunette my pulse raced with jealousy and hurt. I knew I was starting a new life, one that might lead to more happiness than I'd had before, but I mourned the future I'd never have with Samuel, all those dreams I'd built as solid and reliable as mountains in my mind.

I walked home, my emotions swinging between the joy of freedom and the misery of death. I felt unhinged, which is probably why I decided to walk past Chan Villar's studio instead of taking a different street.

Chan was in the front yard, in baggy jeans and a T-shirt, kneeling down to help little Melanie take a photo of a flower with a tiny digital camera. He saw me immediately, before I had time to change my mind and run away.

"Olivia," he said, waving in that energetic way of his. "How are you?"

I walked casually. "Just out for a jog," I said, wanting Chan to be absolutely sure I hadn't come by here with hopes of seeing him. "I forgot you had a studio here. How are you?"

"Great! Can I get you some water?" he asked. "Can you come in for a few minutes?"

I wanted the water. I wanted to go inside and see what kinds of photos Chan Villar had grown up to take. But I didn't feel right about it. I no longer felt like a married woman, but I didn't yet feel single, either.

"Maybe another time," I said with a shrug as I looked at my watch. "I've got to get back to my son."

"This is Melanie," he said. Then, to the child he said, "Can you say hello, Melanie?"

"Hello Melanie," she said. Amazing how alike children were. I waved at the little girl. She had Chan's dimples, and her mother's light brown hair.

"She's beautiful," I said. And she was.

"She's smart, too," he said. It was just the sort of thing a perfect man might say about his daughter. He added, "I hear you're back in the area for a while. Maybe Melanie and Jack can get together and play one of these days?"

"Maybe," I said.

"Great!" Chan smiled broadly. "I'll call you at your mother's to set something up. Maybe we could go to the zoo or something."

"Maybe," I said. "Well, gotta run. Literally."

"Hey," he said. "I've been seeing some things in the papers about your movie, Olivia. It's really great. I just wanted to say congratulations."

I smiled. "Thanks, Chan."

"Well, see you around!"

On tired legs, I started to run.

At home, I found Jack helping my mother water her dead and dying potted plants on the back porch, enjoying the feel of the sun on his skin, and dumping more water down the front of his T-shirt and jeans than into the pots. He didn't seem to care that the plants were no longer living. There was something important to be learned from that, I realized. Sometimes it was the process, the journey, the watering, that counted. I was here. I was alive. And I had Jack. I leaned down and kissed the sun-ripened top of his head.

"Call came for you," Nana said.

"For me? Who?"

"A Dr. Garcia," she said. She looked at me suspiciously.

"Dr. Garcia? From Samuel's work? What did he want?"

"He said he wanted to check in and see how you're doing." She still frowned at me, not telling me the whole story.

"And?"

Nana coughed and dug a hole for Jack to place a seed in. "And he asked your *mother* out for coffee. Can you believe that? What an old goat."

I laughed out loud. "That's great, Mom. He's nice. You should go."

"I'll get you for this," she said, but her eyes danced with anticipation.

"Revenge," I said. "I can count on it from you."

"What on earth will I wear?" she asked. "I haven't gone on a date since your father died."

"We'll go shopping," I said.

"I can't afford . . ."

I put a finger to my mother's lips. "Shh," I said. "Yes, we can. We can afford it."

"I can't let you do that."

"I'm a grown-up," I said. "Remember? I don't need to ask your permission to shop."

MARCELLA

Carmelo the Fantasm showed up at my door wearing all black, much of it shiny, and extra-heavy eyeliner. Or was it tattooed on, permanent? He didn't ring the doorbell, or knock, and if I hadn't checked to see what the anemic scratching noise was, catlike and desperate, I'd never have known he was there, on my front porch.

He reminded me of someone from Flock of Seagulls, back in the day, a man sculpted almost entirely out of Dippity-Do. His hair had been freshly dyed, purple, and stuck up in prickly porcupine barbs, all of which went quite nicely with the pointy metal things sticking out of various parts of his body. He was willowy and feline and none of this bothered me because I was so beyond giving a shit about men anymore I couldn't be bothered to care.

"Hi." He smiled and held a single wilted red rose out for me. Not so wilted it stunk, but not fresh enough to excite a bee. Or me. One end of a delicate chain was looped through a ring in his eyebrow; the other end looped through a hoop in his lower lip. If I pulled his chain, I thought, his face might peel off. His cheek was pierced twice through with something that looked like a small railroad spike, or a large knitting needle. Grotesque.

I opened the door wide enough to let him into my house, and took the rose. "Gee, thanks, Carmelo," I said. "A dead rose, how swell."

I wondered if all the holes and metal in his head hurt. "Come in."

He stared into my eyes like a lion ready to strike, and walked right in.

"Have a seat, I'll be right out," I said, pointing to the sofas in the living room. I had to grab my purse, but that had to wait because Carmelo was off, roaming the house sort of hunched over and ghoulish, mumbling to himself.

He eventually landed like a bird of prey on one of the patio chairs in the backyard. There he perched, the scary bird man of Laurel Canyon. Not in the living room. The backyard. I followed, and found him whistling at a sparrow; it stared curiously at him and whistled back. It, for one, was unafraid of Carmelo. I stood in the doorway and watched; I'd worn a miniskirt and a lace top, with low-heeled slingbacks, and hadn't expected to spend time in the backyard.

"This is the best room in the house," he said. He stared up at the vines twisting into a blanket of green overhead. "If I lived here, I'd set up a tent. I'd never go inside. It's uncontrolled. A lot of people might look at this and say it's abandoned but that's not what we see, is it?"

"It's my favorite thing about this place." I shrugged. In the trees, my cats watched him with suspicious yellow eyes.

"It's my second-favorite thing about this place," he said.

"What's the first?"

"I'm looking at her."

He skulked at me and bared his teeth in a smile. He really was a handsome man, in spite of all the mess and metal. He could have been a classically striking guy with shorter hair and less stainless steel in his ears, brows, lips, and tongue—and God knew where else.

"Does all that . . . hurt?" I pointed to the piercings.

He stuck his tongue out and waggled the tip with its silver stud, a weird grin playing across his demented face. Lucifer, I thought. He looks like the devil. But I bet he gave good oral sex. So few men did. They tried, bless their little hearts, but they had no idea what or where they licked. Or why. That was the worst part with men; they didn't seem to believe in the fact of female orgasm as a mission in and of itself. Our O was more accessory than necessity to most males. And when you tried to correct them, point them in the right direction, they lost their erections and started to pout. It wasn't worth the effort, really. Better just to fake. That was my theory.

"No," he said, watching my eyes. "It doesn't hurt. Physical pain isn't the worst kind of pain, anyway."

"It's not?" I was still thinking about oral sex.

"Psychic and spiritual pain are the worst," he said. He jumped up and picked a pink flower from the bougainvillea train hanging overhead. He ran his thumb over its surface in a small, circular way that reminded me of a woman masturbating. "But you know that." He smiled at me as if I'd just told him a secret, which I hadn't, and said, "You know a lot more than you let on. You're a genius. *That's* what I think. But a controlled genius. And cynical as hell. That's the hard part."

"You're a little too deep for me, Carmelo," I said. "You want a drink?"

"Water," he said. "I'll get it."

He pushed past me and began stalking around the dining room. "You want me to show you where the glasses are?" I asked.

He had located the kitchen and turned in a slow circle, taking it all in. He smiled at me. "It would be an educated guess to say they're here in the kitchen, in a cabinet."

"Yeah, but which cabinet?"

He squatted down as if he were about to take a dump, ran his fingertips over the Deco tiles of the floor as if checking them for something, then stood and hopped six times in his combat boots. "That's the whole thing about getting to know someone," he said. "I like to explore people." He opened a spice cabinet, picked up a bottle or two, read the contents, and replaced them. "I want to look through your cabinets. I want to see how you organize things."

"Don't you think that's a little rude?"

He didn't answer. Rather, he took my hand and began to kiss it, ending with his tongue in the groove between my middle and ring finger, wiggling, licking. I felt the metal stud catch on my skin, hot and wet. He winked at me and strolled off into the house. "Go back outside," he said. "Your energy is better there. I'll find you."

I did as he said, but I wasn't sure why. What a weirdo. I had never met anyone quite like him. After a minute, he brought me a glass of water, with three thin slices of lime in it, just the way I liked it.

"How did you know?" I asked.

"I know things," he said. He fixed his eyes on mine, unblinking. "I pay attention. I'm not just a musician. I paint, too, so my eyes see things other people miss. I know things. Yes, I do." He still held the flower petal in his hand, darkened from so much touching.

I could scarcely remember the last time a man had made me so uncomfortable, or excited. I had no doubt he did, in fact, know things. Good things.

"You know things?" I asked.

"Uh-huh."

"Like what?"

"Like, you need something from a man."

Right. This was where the man started to whack himself off, or to tell me to show him my boobs. This was where they all thought they had the exact thing I needed—in their pants.

"I don't want to hear this," I said.

Carmelo stared at me. "I know why you're looking at me like that," he said.

"Really." I grabbed my cigarettes from the tabletop, tapped out a Capri, and lit up.

"Because you think I'm going to ask you to fuck me, like all the other assholes. And all they do is get off and move on. I know their type."

I stopped, mid-puff, and turned my eyes toward him. He smiled, pleased to have hit a home run on the first try. Then he grabbed my hand and pulled me all the way to my bedroom. He closed the shades and shut the door.

"Should I call the police now, or later?" I asked.

"I'm not like all the other assholes," he said. "I'm an asshole. I don't deny that. But not like the other assholes. A different kind of asshole altogether."

"You don't want to fuck me?" I said, glib and defensive as usual. "Yeah, right."

"No, I don't. Not now."

Part of me wanted to ask him why not. Everyone else did. That was what I'd been put here on the earth for, right? To be an object for all these other people to desire. As if reading my mind, Carmelo answered my thought.

"I don't want to because it wouldn't be a challenge."

He stood at my side, close enough for me to feel his body heat, close enough for me to smell the patchouli and nutmeg of him. He held a hand out to me, and pulled me to my feet so we were standing side by side. Then he moved us both so we stood in front of the full-length mirror on the back of my bedroom door. He wasn't much taller than me. In fact, it seemed as if we were exactly the same size.

"Go to hell," I said to his reflection.

"No, *wait*. You didn't let me finish." He moved his face close to mine, talking within my personal space, but not touching me. "It would be a challenge because you'd be *acting*. Going through the motions. Watching yourself watch yourself, the sex goddess. You'd be absent in your own flesh. That doesn't interest me, Marcella."

I turned my eyes away from him now, unable to believe he'd seen this in me. "So what interests you, Carmelo?" I shrugged and dragged on the cigarette, tried not to seem uneasy.

"You," he said. "Your relief. You coming into your own skin and being there."

"My *relief*? What are you talking about?"

"Don't move," he said.

Carmelo slid to his knees and lifted my little skirt, neatly tucking the hem into the waistband so that my lower body was exposed. I thought of trying to protest, or move away, but I didn't want to. I wanted to see what would happen. With one finger, he eased the thong out of the way.

"Very nice," he said. He breathed me in. We hadn't even kissed on the mouth yet, and here he was, sniffing me . . . there. "Move your feet farther apart," he said, as if he were giving directions to someone moving a couch. It wasn't quite sexual, the way he approached all this, or at least not the way I'd been accustomed to it. It was exhibitionist, almost auction-like, and all about me and my body. I did what he asked, and felt my center fill with heat.

"Good," he said. And then, there was the tongue, doing the little tap-dance that it had done on the webbing of my fingers, but lightly. So lightly I could barely feel it. I let out a little startled squeak and felt my knees grow soft.

"Steady," he said. I peeked down at him and he smiled up at me. He returned to his task, this time a little harder. He most certainly knew what he was doing. At the right moment, he inserted three fingers into me, and moved them at just the right speed, and a moment after that, another finger, in the other hole. Before I knew it, I had come. With a man.

For the first time. While looking at myself.

He knew precisely when I had finished, and stopped. He settled the thong back in place, lowered my skirt, wiped his mouth on his shoulder, and stood.

"You ready to go?" he asked, as if nothing had happened.

"Uh, sure," I said. The ash at the tip of my Capri was an inch long.

"I'll just wash my hands," he said with a smile.

Then, there it was. The quote, inappropriate, and I had no idea where it came from. "'*Better keep yourself clean and bright,*'" I mumbled. "'*You are the window through which you must see the world.*'"

He smiled.

"That's George Bernard Shaw."

"Genius," he said.

And then Carmelo, the creepy, telepathic, wayward Sancocho, smiled at me, and went off to find the bathroom without asking for directions.

C armelo had made reservations without asking me. This generally pissed me off because it signaled a lack of respect for the woman's opinion.

But Carmelo, unsurprisingly, chose the very restaurant I would have chosen myself: L'Orangerie on La Cienega. Considered the best French restaurant in Los Angeles by French people and others, it was close to my house, relatively speaking, and one of the only places on earth that I allowed myself to forget I was on a constant diet. It was also a French restaurant that treated vegetables with respect. It was formal, almost laughably so, and romantic in an old-fashioned way that belied what Carmelo had just done to me in my garden.

Carmelo also drove us, without asking. I might have guessed he drove a hearse. I would have been wrong, however. Carmelo drove a Toyota Prius, silver, narrow, and dull, a hybrid car with a huge forehead and a large Sierra Club sticker in the back window.

"If I could live without a car at all, I would," he explained, though I hadn't asked him anything. "Cars are disgusting. At least this burns less fuel than most. You can feel that this place is dying," he added, with a hand sweep across the dash. "It must have been amazing when no one lived here but the Chumash and the Shoshone, trading shells and acorns, rowing to Catalina Island in twenty-foot log boats. It must have been paradise on earth."

"You sound like my manager, Alexis. She hates it here, too. Though I don't think she gives a shit about the environment. She's a Republican."

"I love it here," said Carmelo. "This is the most creative city in America. There's just death all around. You can feel it."

"I never thought about it that deeply," I said.

"What a lie," he replied.

We walked out of the neon darkness of Los Angeles, into the creamy yellow light of L'Orangerie, and I let out a little gasp at the beauty of the place. Tall white candles glowed from the center of every table. A woman who looked like a wood nymph tickled the keys of a black baby-grand piano, undulating with the smears of impressionistic rhythm. As I walked across the understated black-and-white tile floor, it was like stepping back in time, to the countryside in France. Heads turned when we walked in, and a few people whispered and pointed. Mercifully, no flashbulbs went off. I marveled at the large spray of wildflowers in the enormous vase behind the bar—it must have been six feet tall.

I loved it here.

At dinner, Carmelo asked the waiter innocent, baffling questions like "How do they get oil out of the olives, anyway?" and "Why would you *want* to eat a snail, really?" He knew his wine, too. And in spite of his bodily punctures and fingernails, he was graceful with his utensils. This was a man who had been raised right, and decided to follow his own path.

"So," he said as he tasted his foie gras with fruit-compote appetizer, stopping to savor the flavor with his eyes closed. "Tell me about Marcella. What does Marcella like?"

"Why are you talking about me in the third person?" I asked.

He grinned. "Because that's what you do. Inside your head, all day long."

"I do not," I insisted. I nearly choked on a spoonful of butternut squash soup.

"I told you, I know things," he said.

The pianist stood and apologetically announced that she would be taking a short break. Carmelo put down his fork and began to sing to me, loud.

At first, I wanted to dive under the table and hide. But after the shock of having a man sing to me in public wore off, I became entranced by the song itself, by Carmelo and his gorgeous gravel pit of a voice.

It was a love song, for me. *"If you'd let them see what's inside of you, so far inside of you you've forgotten it yourself, that very little girl who liked to read and think, before she misunderstood that beauty equals silence and silence equals wealth."*

He stared into my eyes the entire time he sang, as if he were simply talking.

"What do you think?" he asked. The waiter timidly set Carmelo's venison cutlets in almond crust with cranberry sauce in front of him. A few patrons of the restaurant applauded his performance. Others shook their heads.

"I think you're the weirdest guy I've ever met," I said. The waiter shared eye contact with me, apparently agreeing, before setting down my main course, a vegetarian soufflé.

"Thanks," said Carmelo.

He gulped down a bite of food, and beamed at me as if "weird" were a high compliment he'd been waiting for all of his life.

We arrived at the party an hour after it started, which seemed about right. It was held in a Hollywood Hills mansion that belonged to a now-broke former member of the hair-metal band Bluesnake. Unable to afford the modern cube of a house, this has-been now rented it out for fashion photo shoots and parties. I wasn't sure where he went, but it might have been safe to guess he was at a Motel 6 in the Valley, waiting to come home.

The house was large and surprisingly elegant for the lair of a hair-metal musician. The entire backside of the house was a two-story wall of glass that overlooked a sloping backyard with an hourglass-shaped swimming pool and an expansive view of the city's twinkling orange lights. The floors were made of white shiny stone of some kind, and the furniture was all white or metal. Fluffy white bearskin-looking rugs stood out like fuzzy islands on the polished floors, and colorful Warhol knockoffs decorated the walls.

The usual assortment of Hollywood types talked too loudly over drinks and unrecognizable little appetizers, generally looking around as they talked to make sure someone, anyone, watched them. Hip-hop music throbbed through every surface of the house, adding insult to injury for the metal musician, I supposed. His time had come, and gone. There was probably a lesson there for me, but I didn't want to think about it at the moment.

Carmelo held my hand as we entered.

"You don't mind, do you?" he asked. "I feel like you need support, and this hand is for that, nothing else. No ownership implied, in other words."

"Thanks," I said. His hand felt good, warm and steady.

I spotted Wendy right away, leaning on the kitchen counter—which was serving as a bar—in snakeskin pants and a glittery tank top better suited to someone with toned arms. She turned her back as soon as she saw me, and marched in her tottering heels out of the living room into the backyard.

"Ignore her," said Carmelo. I had told him about Wendy, and said she would be here, but I did not tell him Wendy was the woman who just stormed out. "You don't need her. You have Alexis. And even better than that, you have Marcella."

Carmelo led me to the bar, and we ordered drinks. I had a chilled white wine, and tried to calm my nerves. He watched me sip my drink the way my cats watched birds flit in the trees. I half expected him to chatter.

"You have a drop, right there," he said, pointing to the corner of my mouth. I instinctively raised a hand to wipe it off, but he stopped me. "May I?" he asked. He moved close, so close. I could feel his breath on my cheek.

"Yes," I said.

He licked me. Not a big, sloppy lick. Just a small, delicate lick. Fast.

"You taste good," he said.

"No," I said. "*You* have good *taste*."

To my surprise, Carmelo knew more people at the party than I did, and more than a few people knew me, or knew of me. It turned out that he did quite a bit of film music, composing the scores for about two movies a year. People approached him like strays, with a mixture of respect and fear. I liked that combination. Very much.

"Oh, good," Carmelo said out of nowhere. He grabbed my hand and pulled me out into the backyard. "There's someone here I want you to meet," he said. I tripped along in the grass behind him as he barreled forward.

"Karen!" he called.

I watched as Karen Debray, the film critic, stopped in her tracks and turned to face us. In spite of her pale, mousy, pinch-faced appearance, she was the top female critic in the nation, with a lot of power. She had short overpermed hair, thick glasses, and a rayon paisley dress that seemed to collect crumbs in the creases from her large stomach. It was a great testament to her intellect that a woman who looked like this had been able to become a widely respected critic both in print—*The New Yorker, Vanity Fair*—and on television, with her own syndicated weekend-film roundup rivaling Ebert & Roeper's.

"Hey, Carmelo!" she called. "I was just thinking about you."

"I know," he said. There was no sense that he was joking.

We joined Karen and her skinny husband with the slab of Donald Trump hair on a patch of flagstone, near a sculpture of a giraffe. Introductions were made, hands shaken. Karen explained that Carmelo had written the score for one of her favorite movies last summer, a blockbuster that had starred Ben Stiller.

"I thought that was someone else," I said, the name of the composer on the tip of my tongue. "Aaron Drake. He writes a lot of movie music."

Carmelo smiled and pointed to his chest. "Nom de plume," he said, and winked. "That's obsolete French for pseudonym."

"Yeah, *merci*," I said.

He narrowed his eyes. "I'm not stupid enough to think Hollywood would hire a Puerto Rican with a Spanish name to do anything but write mambos," he said. "So I fucked them with Aaron Drake."

"Talent like you would not believe," said Karen, pointing to Carmelo.

"Talent like you would not believe," said Carmelo, pointing to her.

"We're one big mutual admiration society," joked Karen.

"You know Marcella?" Carmelo asked. "The reluctant misused star of that piece of shit known as *Bod Squad?*"

"It's a pleasure to meet you, Marcella," she said. "You're even more beautiful in person than you are on TV."

I caught my breath.

"I'm a huge fan of your work," I said, and I meant it. There were few critics I liked, or agreed with. But I believed Karen to be one of the few who knew the art of film and acting inside out, and she was *fair*. When the rest of the nation shit on Adam Sandler because he was popular, Karen Debray saw his work for what it was and reviewed it for those who might like it. She was not interested in making friends in Hollywood, and, interestingly, that made her more liked than the ass-kissers who tried to fit in. "It's really a great honor to meet you."

"I've been meaning to call you," Karen said to Carmelo, suddenly seeming to forget I was there. In spite of her girth and homely appearance, she was not in the least impressed or intimidated by me. She was, incredibly, comfortable in her baggy skin. It was rare to find anyone like that in this town. I respected it. "I got that script you sent me. I really liked it."

Carmelo squeezed my hand. "Yeah?" he asked. "What did you like about it?"

"Oh, fuck, the whole thing. It's got all the elements America's looking for right now. The Latin angle is obvious, but beyond that it's got politics that apply to what's happening today, and the love story of this mother for her children, Jesus Christ. It's beautiful. It's a parable for where we're headed in this country, that's what I think. That writer's got a future."

"What script is this?" I asked Carmelo, though I already knew.

"Carmelo sent me a script last week by a new, unknown writer he said I needed to pay attention to. He's only sent me one other thing, and it turned out to be a hit, so when Carmelo makes a suggestion, I listen." She patted him on the head as if he were her son, or her dog.

"What's it about, if you don't mind me asking?" I asked.

Carmelo stared at me as if hypnotized, smiling like a madman. "Listen good, Marcella," he said. "Pay attention now."

"It's about the life of this Salvadoran woman, Soledad Flores, based on a true story. It's like the Romero of our time. Totally beautiful. Really an incredible life," said Karen.

"You liked it, then?" Carmelo asked.

"I just don't know who they'll get to play the lead," said Karen. "Do you know?"

Carmelo beamed at me. He stood back and opened his arms to me, as if he had just made an introduction onstage at an awards show. "You're looking at her," he said. "In . . . the flesh." Something about the way he said "flesh" made me want to lie down.

Karen and her husband gaped as if they had not really, until that moment, noticed I was there.

"You?" Karen asked. She smiled so broadly I thought her cheeks might pop. Her husband choked on his drink and shot a few drops out of his nose.

"Yes," I said. I looked at Carmelo. "How? Where did you get Olivia's *script*?"

"Alexis," he said with a wink. "She's your biggest fan. She gave it to Goyo, for music, and he showed me. She's something, Alexis. I'm thinking of hiring her myself."

To Karen, I said, "I know people think of me as a tittie actress, but that's not all I want to do."

Karen, seemingly possessed, clawed for my hand. "Come here." She yanked me along the yard. "Come sit down and talk to me." She led me to a couple of lounge chairs by the pool. "Honey, go play in the champagne," she called to her husband. "Do something. Get lost. Flirt. Fuck. I don't care. Play in traffic."

Carmelo saluted me, a military salute, and wandered back into the house, singing to himself.

Then, to me, Karen said, "I'm not going to bullshit you. I loved loved *loved* the script. I think it's wonderful. And I'm really intrigued that they have you for the lead. I'd love to do the first piece about it, for *Vanity Fair*, when you finish shooting. Would you mind?" I couldn't be sure, but it almost sounded like she was . . . begging?

I didn't know what to say. "I think you should talk to my . . . Alexis—my manager, er, agent about it," I said. "But my gut tells me it'd be fine."

Karen smiled. "I know you won't believe this, but I was telling my husband just the other day that I thought you were underutilized on the show you're on. I never watch shows like that, but I checked you out. A guilty pleasure, I suppose you might say."

"Thanks, I think."

Karen patted my leg. "We'll talk more later, with your manager. I have other ideas down the road. For some other stories."

At that moment, Wendy walked by with one of the producers for the Morgan Freeman movie featuring Hispanic Stripper Number One. She nearly tripped and fell in the pool when she saw me talking to Karen. I thought of the "nice" lessons, and how I really did not like them all that much. Nice sucked.

"Wendy, darling!" I called. "Come here."

I introduced her as my former agent, and told her that Karen was interested in possibly doing a *Vanity Fair* feature about me and the new movie I was starring in.

"No," Karen corrected me. "Not possibly. I fucking want it. And I'll fight anyone to the fucking *death* to do it."

Wendy and the other producer exchanged looks.

"You're shitting me?" Wendy said. "Marcella?"

"Me," I said.

"Be careful," Wendy said to Karen. "She's a bit of a loose cannon."

Karen smiled at me.

"Loose cannon?" she said. "Doesn't faze me. Here's the deal, Wendy. In this business, and in life, it's called *balls*. And I like a chick with *balls*. I happen to be one myself."

ALEXIS

oyo stood in the little living room of the apartment he shared with his family, above the bookstore, and told me the "good" news, as if I should be happy about it. He wanted to marry Caridad, and I wanted to get out of town and away from my heart. Could you do that? Stash your heart in a storage locker at the bus station and just take off like a gosh-darn zombie? How did you live through the man you loved marrying someone else? There went my dream of Goyo standing in the bright light of the United Methodist Church in Highland Park, watching me walk down the aisle toward him. If it hadn't been overly obvious, I might have crumpled into a ball and died just then.

Goyo's eyes glowed with excitement, like he was a kid who just got picked to head the team. But there was guilt in them, too. He knew what this was doing to me, he had to. Or maybe he didn't. Maybe he realized that I was the last one on the fence, the player no one wanted, the pudgy unathletic kid everybody couldn't wait to nail with the stinky red rubber dodge ball.

"That's great, sugar," I said. I sat on the velvet sofa and crossed my hands in my lap. Caridad was out with Cousin It, helping It find a job, because her English, which she spoke about as well as I spoke Yiddish, was better than his.

"She's great to him," Goyo said. "That's what did it for me, seeing her generosity of spirit. A woman like that will make a wonderful mother. She is so family-oriented."

"Sure," I said. "She's the best." And me, I thought? What am I? Garbage? I don't love my cousins? I didn't want to, but I frowned.

"I know it's hard on you," he said tenderly.

"No, not at all," I lied. Fake smile. "I have plenty of men lined up. You didn't mean much. I always kiss my clients."

"Really?"

"No."

He hung his head and looked up at me sheepishly. "Thanks for agreeing to help me pick out the ring," he said. In his hand he gripped a selection of business cards from jewelers, the nicest ones in Los Angeles.

"Did you get her size, like I asked?"

Goyo dug in his pocket and produced a ring. A cheap ring, stained and sorry-looking, but a ring. "This is hers," he said. "I didn't want to ask her for her size because I didn't want her to suspect anything."

"That's good," I said. I reached out for the ring. It was tiny, smaller than my size. Of course. Next to Caridad, I had the hands of an auto worker.

"She's petite," I said. I didn't mean to, but I sounded sad when I said it. Goyo looked at me as if I'd told him I had a terminal disease.

"I'm so sorry, Alexis," he said. "It's hard on me, too. I mean, the things I said, about you, I meant them. I felt them. I still feel them. I have very strong feelings about you."

I'll be gosh-darned if the boy didn't look like he wanted to kiss me again. He had to be stopped.

"Shall we?" I asked cheerfully, pointing to the door. I frowned. I didn't feel like talking about it.

"Okay," he said.

We spent the afternoon looking at rings, with Goyo asking my "informed woman's opinion" on everything. He finally settled on a twelve-thousand-dollar Tiffany setting.

"She'll love it," I said, wondering where he got that kind of money. Oh, that's right, I remembered. He got it with the record deal I got for him at Wagner, and the endorsement deal I got him with Willie Esco's clothing line. He'd traded the rusty blue Jeep for a gleaming black Jeep Wrangler almost identical to his old one. He'd wanted to keep the old one, and give all his money to Caridad and her cousin, but I told him it was okay to spend a little of his cash on himself. After all, I'd spent my percentage on a down payment for an office in Sherman Oaks. Talentosa, Inc., management and publicity company of the new millennium, was up and running, just as my ova were running *out*.

"You think?" he asked as the salesman packed it in a beautiful box.

"If she doesn't, she's a fool," I said. And then, in the most generous move I'd made in years, I gave Goyo a hug—a friendly, supportive, loving buddy hug, as my heart popped open and oozed a slow death.

"You're . . . amazing," he said.

I nodded in complete and utter agreement, smiling furiously.

"Pretty much," I said. "Yeah."

The 60 *Minutes* segment on Goyo had run a couple of months before, and I was able to use the momentum of it to get Wagner Records to sign Goyo and to agree to a duet with Lydia as the first single. He was also signed on with "Aaron Drake" to do the music for *Soledad*, and Wagner wanted to produce the soundtrack.

Wagner was considering signing Lydia for an English-language pop record, too. Things were just peachy, for *them*. My clients. They were all over the place. Marcella had a *Vanity Fair* cover story coming, by Karen Debray, and Olivia was all the rage in the script-writer's universe, the hot new thing people buzzed and buzzed about like a nest of hornets. She'd appeared on the *Today* show and afterward got a call from a speaker's agency in New York that wanted to sign her to their roster, flying her around the country to talk at colleges and women's groups, for between five and ten thousand dollars an appearance. Did I mention I was a magician? But then why couldn't I make Caridad disappear like a bunny in a hat?

Goyo had a guest appearance tonight with Lydia and Juan Gabriel at the Hollywood Bowl—yet another smooth move by your smooth manager/publicist of the moment—and we had planned to go straight from ring shopping to the gig.

Lucky me.

But Goyo had forgotten to pack a new microphone he wanted to use.

Stupid him.

"Dangit," he said as he pulled his Jeep onto Rodeo Drive. *Dangit?* I'll be gosh-darned if I wasn't wearing off on the boy. At least I had infiltrated at some level, I thought. "I'm sorry, Alexis, I have to stop at home real quick to pick something up."

I looked at my watch. Stopping at Goyo's would cost us a good forty minutes. "It's cutting it close," I said. "Can you just get a new mike?"

"No." He shook his head. "I ordered this one months ago, it's the only one. I'll be fast."

He sped all the way back to Glendale. I held onto my sunglasses to keep them from blowing off in the breeze from my open window, and to hide the fact that my eyes had been leaking. Again.

We arrived at the apartment in half an hour. Goyo's parents were away for the weekend on a religious retreat in North Carolina, paid for by their generous son. Their new Buick Regal, which Caridad and her cousin had been using to get around, was parked in the driveway, indicating the luckiest girl on earth was here. They'd said they would stop by the show if they got back from job-hunting in time. Maybe, I thought with despair, if we're lucky, they'll want to join us. Peachy.

"You want to come up?" he asked. I didn't, not really. I had no desire to see her. I shook my head and crossed a bouncing leg over the other. "Oh, come on," he said. "You said yourself you had to use the bathroom."

"Fine," I said. I tried to smile, but I couldn't.

"You okay?" he asked.

"No, babe," I said, as we climbed the rickety outdoor steps to the apartment door. "I'm not. My heart is breaking. There, I said it. Let's move on."

He looked pained as he opened the front door. "There's someone out there for you," he said. "I have no doubt. He'll be lucky."

I followed Goyo into the apartment, and even though my eyes took a second to adjust to the darkness of the living room, I could have sworn I saw Miss Tiny-Fingers Caridad holding *hands* with Cousin It on the velvet sofa. I thought, for some reason, of that *Friends* episode where the siblings kiss and Phoebe tells them to "get a room." Eew, eew, get it off me. At moments like this I truly did need Marcella to kick my cultural references up a notch. Oops. Kick it up a notch. There I went again, Emeril Lagasse. Was he single? Did he need a publicist? Manager? So sexy, for a chubby guy.

"Goyo!" Caridad called out, with a surprised, scared, and simultaneously happy look on her face. She dropped her cousin's hand. She and the cousin sat so close their legs touched, and when they saw us, moved apart quickly. I am no woody expert, but I could have sworn that cousin of hers had one, poking up, up, up.

I looked at Goyo and he seemed to notice something, too, but said nothing.

"Just forgot something," he said in Spanish. "How was the job hunt?"

Cousin It frowned and shrugged, charismatic as a fallen tree branch. He scarcely talked, and when he did it sounded like machinery rumbling. I'd suspected he was mentally slow, or devious, and suddenly it was looking more like the latter.

"It was good," said Caridad as Goyo rifled through a box of musical equipment in the front closet. "I think he got a job at an electronics store." In bad English, she said, "The Good Guys." How ironic.

Goyo found the microphone and eased the door shut with a soft snap. "That's good," he said. "I'm happy for you."

He did not approach Caridad as he usually did, and didn't kiss her as he (spit, spit) usually did. Nothing. He stood, smiling.

"It's great news," cooed Caridad, still awkward.

"When do you start, *compai?*" Goyo asked Cousin It.

"*La semana que viene,*" he rumbled. Next week.

"Great. That should give the two of you just enough time to find another place to live. Sound good?" He clapped his hands together as if addressing school-children.

Caridad's eyes popped open. "What?" she gasped. "The two of us? *Me?*"

"Yep, you."

I suddenly lost the urge to pee.

"But I thought I'd live here with you?" Caridad looked confused. Her horny "cousin" rolled his eyes.

"I'm late," said Goyo. "I have a concert tonight. So that's a good thing, because I really don't want to discuss anything." He walked over to them. To Amado he said, "Do you love her?"

Amado nodded, and flinched as if he expected to be slugged.

Caridad put a "shocked" hand to her throat. Goyo fake yawned.

"He's why you stayed behind, isn't he?" Goyo asked her. "He's why we fought all the time."

"I'm sorry, Goyo," she said, her eyes filling with tears. "I loved you, I did. For a while. And I didn't want to use you like this. I hate myself for it. But . . ."

"But?" he asked. Still calm. God bless him.

Caridad squirmed. "It was our only way out. And the way the government punished me, because I'd been your woman. I just thought . . ."

"It was the least I could do?" asked Goyo.

"Something like that," said Caridad.

"When were you planning to tell me?" asked Goyo.

"Soon," said the man. "I wanted to tell you when we got here, but she didn't want to hurt you."

"How thoughtful," said Goyo.

Caridad's tears poured down her cheeks. "Goyo, I wouldn't have done it, except we're, we're—" She sobbed into her hands.

"Pregnant," said the man in Spanish. *Embarazada.* Five syllables, six, if you counted his '*ta*, the ghetto version of *está.* I was surprised he could get that many out at once. They'd throw him out of L.A. once they found out.

"Just be sure it's yours, sugar," I blurted, before I realized I'd spoken. Everyone acted as if I hadn't spoken, which I shouldn't have.

"Congratulations," said Goyo. "Do you have money?"

"No."

"Not yet," said Caridad. "But we will. We're both going to work."

"Here," said Goyo. He pulled the ring box out of his side cargo pocket. Caridad opened the box and gasped.

"Oh, Goyo, no," she said.

"It's worth twelve thousand dollars. Take it back to the store, here." He handed her the receipt. "Cash it. Get a place. Get some furniture. Eat well. Lots of folic acid. Lots of water." He bent forward and kissed her on the forehead. Cousin It stood up and sulked out of the room.

Caridad sobbed harder. "Why are you doing this?" she asked.

"Doing what?" asked Goyo.

"Being so nice! It's crazy."

"*I'm* crazy," said Goyo. "And now I'm late. See you later. Don't tell my parents anything if they call. Let me tell them."

The cousin returned, holding two suitcases with those long gorilla arms. "I'm sorry, Goyo," he said.

Goyo held his hand out to shake the man's hand. I could not believe my eyes.

Goyo turned to me and slipped the keys quietly into his pocket. He had a furious look on his face that I had only seen before when he confronted Daniel at the Times Building. I felt like I'd won the lottery. He couldn't have her! I nearly skipped out the front door. He would never have her!

But when Goyo asked me to drive the Jeep for him, and I saw the look of complete despair and terror in his eyes, my elation deflated. I loved this man, and he hurt. He hurt so much, and he'd hidden it, and he'd done the right thing.

"I'm so sorry," I said. I took the keys and settled him into the passenger seat like a sick child heading to the doctor.

"Yeah," he said, his voice a weak whisper. "Me, too."

We drove in silence for a while before Goyo began to laugh, at top volume.

"What's so funny?" I asked.

"Me," he said.

"You?"

"Yeah, me."

"How so?"

I looked at him and he smiled at me. "The way I'm feeling right now, that must be how you've felt lately, huh?"

I nodded. "Pretty much, yeah."

"So I was just thinking about that, and I tried to comfort myself with the words

I gave you earlier today, about how there's someone for you out there somewhere. I said, 'Goyo, don't worry, there's someone out there for you.' And then I realized she was driving my car. I mean, I knew that a week ago, but I ignored it. I knew it months ago. I ignored it."

"That's just rebound talking," I said. "I have no interest in being your rebound girl."

"No." He shook his head. "It's not. It's Goyo talking."

"Let's take it easy," I said.

My soul flew up the pole and flapped in the wind.

"Sure," he said. "But know this. I'm sorry. I ignored my feelings for you because I felt guilty about Cari. And now I understand this happened because God wanted me to realize what I'd ignored. That *I love you*. Because I do. I blocked it out because of her."

"We'll see," I said. "First, let's get you through this show."

I should, at that moment, have focused on figuring out how to handle this mess with the press.

But I didn't think about that. I thought about how Goyo knew that pregnant women needed to eat lots of folic acid, and wondered what it would be like to watch Goyo pushing our baby in a swing.

OLIVIA

Seeing my mother with aluminum foil rectangles all over her head was one of the nicer moments of my life. But seeing her chatting in Spanish with Marcella as their heads cooked under the hot-air helmets at the posh Lukaro salon in Beverly Hills swelled my heart to bursting. Nana had never had her hair done at a salon, in all the years of her life. She had cut it herself, or let one of the old ladies in the neighborhood do it for her, or, at best, gone to La Lupe's beauty parlor on Sunset. Now, here she was, getting ready for her close-up.

Newspapers and magazines all over the world wanted interviews. With me, with Nana, with Marcella most of all. The fact that Marcella had turned her uncle in for spying on her had pushed the *Vanity Fair* profile of her to the cover, and once you've had a controversial and moving *Vanity Fair* cover, you can all but count on the rest of the press knocking your door down.

I was getting other kinds of calls, too. People in the industry had their hands on copies of my screenplay, and a few of them had even seen advance reels of the film, which was in the very final edit. Studios wanted me to write movies for them, all of them more or less along the same lines of the movie I had already written. I did not want to do that. I had not written my mother's life for marketing purposes, or to fulfill demographic expectations. I had written Nana's life because it was an amazing life. And now that it was out of me, and I was on medication and dealing with my childhood experiences, the last thing I wanted to do was dwell on the Salvadoran revolution and death squads. It was out, and it felt good to have it out, and I was done with it.

Other producers and studios and agents were calling to ask me to adapt books into movies for them, usually books with Latina themes. I had written a gritty, moving drama, but they wanted me to write comedies, assuming, I thought, that because I was a Latina I could do the job better than someone who was a comedy writer. I had no interest in doing something that didn't come naturally to me, no matter how much money they wanted to pay me. And they wanted to pay me a lot.

Alexis encouraged me to keep my options open and wait for the success of the movie to drive the prices of my work up. But I didn't want to do that. I usually told the people who called me "No, thank you," with just two exceptions. One was a children's network that wanted me to come up with a funky drama for tweens; I'd liked the suggestion because there was nothing ethnic about it and they seemed to understand that my brain was a human brain, capable of anything. And the other was PBS; they wanted to contract with me to do a series of documentaries similar to the Ken Burns series, on immigrant and refugee communities in the United States in the past forty years. I loved this idea, and had already begun researching it. There were so many groups of people, from every continent, who had gone through what my family went through in El Salvador. I relished the idea that I might be able to tell their stories, in relation to one another. I loved most of all the idea that these stories could and would have happy endings; I was a living example of the human ability to transcend horrors, and the strength of people the world over in the face of adversity, women in particular, was something I wanted to explore.

The interest in *Soledad* had made my mother something of a celebrity at last in the city where she had for decades given voice to the voiceless. This celebrity was translating into money for workers' unions and causes that were central to life in Los Angeles but which had essentially slipped below the radar of those in the city with money. Now, Hollywood and East Hollywood were finally meeting, and discovering that we all had more in common than it might appear on the surface.

"They're like old friends," said Alexis, who sat in the chair next to mine, getting her hair trimmed. I was going for a more drastic change, short. Very short. The stylist said I had a face for long or short hair, and I'd always been afraid to cut it off. Now that I was entering the most fearless phase of my life, it only seemed right to hack it off. Just like I'd hacked Samuel out of my life. And not only was I going for short, I was going for red—burgundy, almost. I would see in a matter of minutes whether this had been a good idea; I would see in a matter of days whether my movie was, too.

"No, wait," said Alexis, pointing to Marcella and Nana. "They're like . . . twins."

As I watched Marcella, I was amazed by how well she had adopted my mother's mannerisms. She frowned like my mother, picked her fingernails like my mother. It was a little frightening. And when you spoke to Marcella these days, she even sounded like my mother, peppering her sentences with all the Salvadoran words my mother had never been able to relinquish, particularly when angry. I knew this happened with actors, and that sometime after we finished shooting the film, in a month or two, she would go back to being Marcella. But as they spoke—about my mother's life, always about my mother's life—Marcella seemed not only to mirror Soledad, but to become her.

And it was more than that. Now that I knew a little more about Marcella, I knew that she was enjoying having a mother figure she could talk to the way she'd always wanted to talk to her mother. Marcella was always over for dinner, looking through my mother's photos. And my mother was warm and loving toward Marcella, too. They held hands as they talked, and it seemed the rest of the world disappeared. Somehow, in the past year, Marcella Gauthier Bosch, the bouncing beach babe, had become the soulful, thoughtful sister I never had.

Life was strange.

As large chunks of hair fell around me, I looked over at Alexis.

"Thank you," I said.

She knew exactly what I was thanking her for, and grinned.

"You're the horse that wrote the screenplay, sugar, not me," she said. "I just led you to the water."

ALEXIS

We had finally wrapped up shooting *Soledad*, and to celebrate, I was doing nothing. Absolutely nothing, for a whole week or more. You thought the world of Hollywood and movie stars was glamorous until you were steeped in it and realized it was just flat-out exhausting. I wanted nothing in my life more difficult than prying the top off a jar of marshmallow cream for a few days.

Juanga and I were trying to read a romance novel in bed, thank you, and did not want to answer the *phone*. But the phone had this idea that it ought to be answered, and rang like there was no tomorrow. I let the answering machine pick it up three times. The annoyance on the other end had immediately called back, as if they knew I was home and didn't want to talk. Juanga yapped at the thing, and I glared. Who would call close to midnight anyway? I looked at the Caller ID box.

Marcella. Right. Marcella, queen of the acting universe, adored in highbrow publications because she had to look "homely" for parts of the movie (the male-dominated media somehow thought beautiful actresses were more serious and intelligent when they allowed themselves to be shot without makeup on), and the big-time star couldn't be bothered to check the time before bothering her friends? Jeez.

"It's late," I grouched into the phone. "You might be Miss Thang, hero to all oppressed lefties people everywhere, but it's still late. I know you've been hanging around with vampires, but we normal people still sleep at night."

"I know. But I just got an invite to play volleyball on the beach tomorrow and you're coming with me. Just wanted you to know."

"I am?"

Anytime Marcella called asking me to join her for some outdoor activity, I worried. I blamed the rollerblading incident on the beach, and others like it, where she looked great and athletic, and I fell down, scraped something, had an asthma attack, or otherwise humiliated myself.

"You are," she said.

"No, I'm not."

She gave me the rest of the details. Carmelo and Goyo versus me and Marcella. Loser buys beer. I knew this was the kind of thing hip young people such as ourselves were supposed to do in the hip young city of Los Angeles, but still. I had promised Lydia I'd go shopping with her. And when I wasn't doing that, I'd figured I would just watch movies on the Romance channel and eat ice cream with my dog. Why couldn't they just let me do that? Why were they always trying to get me to be so darn social? And worse than that, why was Marcella always pushing me to hang out with Goyo?

I sat on the edge of my bed and listened to the pitch, considered my options.

"Goyo wants to see you," she said.

"He sees me all the time," I answered. But even I was getting sick of blowing him off. It required superhuman strength, but it was part of what Momma always taught me about love—don't give in until you know he's for real. What she never taught me, though, was how you *knew* he was for real. When did that happen?

"No, you *work* with him all the time. He says he keeps asking you on dates and you blow him off. Are you *crazy*, girl?"

"He's rebounding."

"It's been *months*, Lex. He's over that bitch."

"Don't call her that."

"Why are you defending her?"

"She's human. She was in a bad spot. I might have done the same thing for freedom. You can't judge someone if you never sat in their shoes."

"You mean 'stood'? You can't sit in shoes, Alexis."

"Shut up. It's late. What do you want?"

"Just to tell you about the volleyball. Bye."

"I don't like volleyball."

Juanga, sensing my stress, yapped and growled at the phone, quivering. She was tired, too.

Marcella sighed into the phone. "You have to go. Please?"

I scratched behind Juanga's ears and tried to think of a way out. Only I didn't really want out. I really wanted to see Goyo.

"Come on, Lex."

"Fine. But don't blame me if I'm on your team and you lose, or if the big bully walks by and kicks sand in my face."

"Please," said Marcella. "I know enough not to pick you for my team."

And she hung up.

I went back to the book. *With infinite tenderness, he touched his lips to hers but almost immediately gentleness gave way to passion . . . His tongue touched her lips and she opened to him, giving everything she had and taking all he offered at the same time. His chest pressed against her breasts, his hips crushed her against the table, and even through her tears and pain she wanted him.*

Lydia could shop alone.

I turned out the lights and dreamed of Goyo.

The beach was crowded with tanned, fat-free bodies, which I wasn't crazy about because that meant more people to see me in the sports bra I had no sense wearing, particularly because I had no breasts to heave against it. Juanga wore her sports bra, too, with little jogging shoes.

We all met in front of the rollerblade rental hut. Goyo looked great in his khaki shorts and Hawaiian shirt. As always. He hugged me and looked defeated. As we embraced, I could have sworn I saw Daniel's pale ugly body swooping past on a small girl's bicycle.

"When are you going to give in?" he asked.

"Huh?" I asked. I rubbed my eyes. Did I really just see Daniel riding along the beach on a girl's bike, alongside a classic cholo-looking guy with a shaved head and long white socks? Was he really staring at us like he was crazy?

"Give in," Goyo pleaded. "Go out with me. I can't stand this anymore."

I shrugged. "I'm worth the wait," I said.

Juanga lunged toward where I'd seen Daniel disappear into a crowd of joggers and skaters, yapping.

"What's with the mutt?" asked Marcella. "Can't you ever leave her at home?"

"No," I said. "She's watching out for me. I could swear I just saw Daniel."

"Daniel?" asked Goyo. "Where?" He swung around, ready to fight.

"There," I pointed. "But he's gone."

Marcella had her hands over her ears. "Please make the dog shut up," she said. "And please quit dressing her like the Olsen twins."

"She looks very nice," said Goyo. He stooped down to pet my puppy, but kept an eye out for Daniel on the boardwalk. "Don't insult Juanga, or you'll have me to deal with."

He even defended my dog. Was there no end to his perfection?

Marcella and Carmelo, to my surprise, held hands as we walked toward the sand pit. I'd known Marcella for a long time, but I had never seen her hold hands with a man in public. She liked to seem available, and that sort of thing, well, undermined the image. I could have sworn the girl was in love with that human pincushion. What that meant, I did not know.

I tied Juanga to the little rhinestone sand stake I'd bought for just such an occasion as this, and took her pink sunshade, treats, and water bottle out of my backpack. Goyo picked me for his team, and we lost. Nine out of ten games, we lost. I dove for the ball once, hoping to at the very least illicit a raucous laughter from the gathered beachgoers, and got a mouthful of sand. Some of the grains blew into my lungs. I started to wheeze, and hated the feel of sand in my hair. Juanga panicked to see me in this state and got herself tangled up in twinkling stones.

"Want to surf?" asked Goyo. He ran from me to the dog, tending to both.

"No," I said.

"Want to go to dinner?" he asked.

I looked him over. "With you?" I asked, teasing.

"Yeah."

"Only if it's pizza, at my house, and we can watch the Romance channel and I don't have to get gussied up."

He smiled broadly and fell down in the sand. "Yes!" he cried. "She's having dinner with me! Finally."

Marcella and Carmelo stood to the side and applauded.

Juanga licked Goyo's face in much the same manner I planned to later.

And he didn't seem to mind at all.

Autumn

*When women are moved and lend help,
when women, who are by nature calm
and controlled, give encouragement
and applause, when virtuous and
knowledgeable women grace the endeavor
with their sweet love, then it is invincible.*

—José Martí

OLIVIA

pumped the comb through my now-short, now-red hair one last time, and checked the mirror above the sink in my mother's guest bathroom. I saw a new woman, more stylish than before. I'd been shopping with Alexis and Marcella, but in the end had found the endeavor boring and stupid. I liked to have good, high-quality clothes that were comfortable, but I realized I did not have any interest whatsoever in high fashion. I wanted jeans, T-shirts, and sneakers, just as I'd had before, but nicer and more expensive ones. I didn't see the point of clothes you had to iron, if you had a toddler and spent your days working with cameras, outdoors and in. I liked the hair, but not enough to keep it. I missed the days of putting my mess of hair in a ponytail and forgetting about it. This whole short thing was hard because I had to style it to avoid looking homeless, and I didn't have time for styling my hair every day. I had other things to do. My new friends saw their clothes as an extension of their souls, but I knew better. Clothes were the things that covered you and kept you warm while you got busy with the job of changing the world. And the more producers, writers, and directors I met, the more I realized I was one of them; it was rare to find behind-the-scenes people in Hollywood who worried about how they looked. We were much more interested in how other people looked, and in making the world in our films look the way it looked in our heads. Who had time for blow-outs and hairspray under those conditions? Not me.

With sleep, work, and my mother's cooking, the dark shadows had disappeared, however, and I looked healthy, youthful, and rested just in time for the premiere of our movie. Advance praise in the press was setting us up for a good run, and Columbus execs who had seen the finished product were so excited they had all but promised to distribute in a wider market than originally planned.

"*Estás lista?*" Jack asked me. He stood in the doorway wearing a tiny mariachi costume, for Halloween, complete with a fake moustache, watching me get ready. Since moving in with my mother more than half a year ago, he'd become as fluent in Spanish as English, and could tell the languages apart. If only we all had brains as supple and ready as toddlers'.

"Yes, sweetie," I said. "Mommy's just about ready. Go get *Abuelita*."

Jack scampered off to the living room, where Nana sat on the sofa next to Dr. Garcia, each sipping a cold glass of Nana's *ensalada,* a slushy Salvadoran drink of pineapple, orange, apple, and mint. I walked into the room in time to see Jack tumble into the doctor's lap, laughing. "Bad, bad, bad." The doctor, now an expert at toddler games, replied with a jolly "good, good, good." Jack smiled and announced, "Those are opposites."

The doorbell rang, and I rushed to answer it. Chan stood on the porch with a red rose in his hand. "It's lame and corny as hell," he said, regarding his flower. "But, you know. I try." At his side, little Melanie twirled in her ballerina costume, clearly proud of the way the skirt poofed and puffed when she moved.

I took the flower, trying to remember the last time Samuel had done anything remotely thoughtful for me. It had been years. "It's very nice, Chan. Thanks. Come in."

It turned out that Chan, a man I thought of as a friend and nothing more, was the same kind of person I was. He did not care about fancy clothes, and he had told me the most beautiful thing about me was my mind; he said he could see it working when he looked in my eyes. Maybe he could be more than a friend one of these days, but I was in no rush.

"Good and bad," cried Jack as we entered the living room. "Those are *opposites.*" *Like Samuel and Chan*, I caught myself thinking.

"That's right, *mi'jo*," said Nana. She set about locking the doors and windows. Dr. Garcia shook Chan's hand, then stood on the front porch, humming. It felt like a family here.

"Okay," Nana sang as she waltzed back into the room. "Everybody ready to go?"

Together, we walked all the way to Echo Park. I'd organized a Day of the Dead/Halloween festival for the neighborhood, as a fund-raiser and public awareness event for the Soledad foundation I'd started for neighborhood girls who wanted to go to college. Chan had been the first to give me money, followed by Alexis and Marcella.

Volunteers from the neighborhood had been at the park for several hours already, helping the vendors set up their tables along the walking path, and helping Alexis set up the small soundstage on the park's central island, where Goyo and Lydia would perform. Already, people had set blankets out on the grass; they'd also started to form lines at the tables for a few cell phone companies and other businesses that were handing out free pens and other graft.

"I'm going to go check on Alexis," I told Chan.

"Okay," he said. "Jack and I are going to go look at the fountain." Jack was obsessed with the fountain, which shot water two stories high in the middle of the pond.

As I walked through the gathering crowd toward the stage, I bumped into a familiar-looking middle-aged man who wore oversized jeans, an Enrique Iglesias–style knit cap, and Puma sweatshirt with a hood. He whispered madly to a younger man with a shaved head, a typical-looking gang banger. My blood ran icy through my veins, but I wasn't sure why. There was something about the way they looked around, something about the way the older man pointed and whispered, that gave me the creeps.

"Excuse me," I said.

The man cursed and mumbled and I realized as he stormed away that it was Daniel, Alexis's ex-boyfriend. What was *he* doing here? And who was that *vato* he was talking to?

I found Alexis helping Lydia with her makeup in a limo parked near the soundstage.

"Hey, girl," I said.

"Hi!" Alexis stepped out of the limo to give me a hug. Lydia waved from inside.

"Everything okay?" I asked.

"Going as planned," said Alexis. "This is gonna be a good show."

"You got everything under control with the sound equipment?"

"It's all taken care of."

"That's great." I looked around and said, "You should know, I think I just saw Daniel."

"What?" Alexis bit her lower lip and grabbed my arm. "Olivia, he's creeping me out."

"He was talking to a real sleazy-looking homie," I said.

Said Alexis, "I keep seeing him. It's like he's following me."

"I'll let the officers know," I said. We'd hired a police detail for the event. "Hey," I said. "Is Goyo here?"

"He's at one of the taco stands," Alexis said with a playful roll of the eyes. "I didn't know a Cubano could be so crazy about tacos."

"How's it going with you guys?" I asked.

"Oh, you know. Takin' it slow."

Alexis *still* had not slept with Goyo, which, she told me on the phone a few days ago, was driving the man nuts. I'd warned her about keeping a man too frustrated, but she hadn't heeded my advice yet.

"And Chan?" she asked.

"Things are good," I said. I'd slept with Chan and enjoyed it. I'd thought I had simply lost my sex drive when I was married to Samuel, but I was starting to think it was just that I didn't find Samuel all that attractive, especially not after he'd lied and cheated.

"That's great."

"Alexis!" Lydia cried from the limo. "Help! My, mascara, it, like, *smeared!*"

"Gotta go," said Alexis with rolled eyes. "Mascara emergency. I'll talk to you later."

I strolled around the perimeter of the park, to make sure all was in order, and when I spotted one of the police officers, I approached.

"Excuse me, sir?" I said, handing him a business card. Man, that felt *good*. "I'm Olivia Flores? One of the organizers of the event today?"

He smiled and nodded my way. "Officer Peter Quintanilla," he offered. "What can I do for you?"

I told him about Daniel and his *vato* friend, and gave him a description. "He might be harmless," I said. "But I thought I'd fill you in, just in case."

Officer Quintanilla thanked me and called the description in to his fellow officers via walkie-talkie. "I'll keep an eye out for them, ma'am," he said.

I thanked the officer and walked back to where Chan, Melanie, Jack, Nana, and Dr. Garcia sat on a park bench, near the center's table. Jack munched on a burrito nearly as big as he was, and gooey cheese hung in a string from his chin.

"Everything good?" Nana asked.

I said yes, and sat on the grass next to the bench. Nana took a bite of Dr. Garcia's funnel bread. He wiped a crumb from the corner of her mouth. My mother was in love. I felt safe with Chan, and I hadn't had a nightmare in almost three months.

Three hours later, Goyo took the stage. Chan, Melanie, Jack, and I wandered closer, for a better look, but Nana and Dr. Garcia said they didn't want to deal with the crowd. And it *was* crowded. Echo Park was small, so we'd closed several of the surrounding streets, but the bodies still crammed every open spot.

Goyo wore the usual jeans and tank top, with his cowboy hat and boots. Alexis stood to the side of the stage, on a small set of stairs, watching with a smile on her face. She loved him, even if she was holding out.

After three songs, Goyo invited Lydia to join him on the stage. She'd be performing her own set later, but many in the crowd today had come to see the two of them perform their duet, which was climbing the Latin pop charts across the nation. As Lydia picked her way up the steps onto the stage, the crowd roared; this was her hometown, and they loved her.

But no sooner had she begun to sing when I heard a loud popping noise behind me. I knew that sound. Then, pop, pop. Two more. Gunshots. This time, it actually was a gun I heard. It had to be.

I pushed Jack and Melanie to the ground instinctively and covered them with my body. Chan jumped on top of us, and all around people started shrieking and running. The music stopped, replaced by the high whine of a microphone feeding back. I could hear sounds of feet running on the stage, amplified through the sound system, and Alexis's voice screaming, "No!"

"This isn't happening," I said, over and over. The memories came flooding back, and I felt my heart would explode from the terror. I looked around and saw feet scrambling in every direction.

"Get up," Chan yelled. "Olivia, get up. Move!"

I felt him lift me off of Jack and Melanie, and watched as Chan threw my son over his shoulder, Melanie pressed to his chest with his free arm. It was all slow motion, just like the last time. "Let's go," cried Chan. "Move, Olivia, come on!" He shoved me through the bodies and away from the commotion.

"They got the rapper!" I heard someone shout. "They got the rapper!"

"It's the guy with the ski hat," someone else screamed.

"It was that bald guy," shrieked another. "Get him!"

I turned to look over my shoulder, and saw a group of young men from the neighborhood attack Daniel and Daniel's homeboy friend, one of them a young Salvadoran honor student named Fabian who I knew. Fabian was skinny and small, like my father, but I watched as he grabbed the pistol from Daniel's homeboy's hand. Officer Quintanilla, his gun drawn, came crashing through the crowd. He pointed his weapon at Fabian, who dropped Daniel's *vato*'s gun and raised his hands in the air. The gun went off as it hit the ground, the popping followed by a man's voice wailing in pain. I couldn't tell who had been hit, but I had to stop the officer from shooting Fabian.

"No!" I screamed. "It's not him! He's a good kid! Don't!"

The crowd started to scream that the officer had the wrong man, and to my astonishment, he listened to them, and trained the gun on Daniel, who writhed on the ground in pain. Another officer came and pointed the gun at the *vato*.

"Go," Chan screamed. "Don't stay here, Olivia, move!"

Chan pushed me until I was behind the stage. His face glowed red, and sweat ran down his face from the effort of running with two toddlers in his arms.

"Shit," he said.

"Shit," parroted Jack.

We stopped behind a van that had brought sound equipment. "Are you all right? Jack! Are you okay? Melanie? Oh, my God."

My son looked up at me with fear in his eyes, but nothing seemed wrong with him. Melanie had begun to cry.

"Shit," my son repeated, pleased to have learned another new word.

"Oh, my God," I said, holding my child. "Thank God you're okay."

"What's going on?" Jack asked.

"It's nothing, sweetie," I said. "Don't worry. Mommy's here."

Chan comforted his own child, then turned to us. "He's fine," Chan said, kissing Jack's head, then Melanie's, then mine. "Oh, God, Olivia, he's fine. They're fine. We're fine."

I looked up to find several members of Goyo's band rushing his limp body down the stairs, covered in blood. Alexis trailed them, wailing.

"What happened?" I cried.

"I don't know," shrieked Alexis. Her white sweater was covered with Goyo's blood. "Someone, call an ambulance!"

But someone already had, and I could hear the siren approaching.

Goyo's eyes were open, but they didn't focus on anything, or blink. The eyes of a corpse. His arms hung limp at his sides, and his legs looked like they'd been put on wrong. Chan covered Jack's eyes with one hand, and Melanie's with another.

"Don't look," he said.

Don't look, Nana said. And then his head exploded.

"This isn't happening," I cried, and the palm trees seemed to be closing in on me, the world seemed to be spinning.

"Not again."

ALEXIS

I sat on the small wooden chair with the plastic padded seat and watched Goyo sleep. The sun tried to break through the closed slats of the metal window blinds, but mostly there was darkness, and quiet, and the antiseptic smell of a hospital room.

He lay propped up on a white pillow, a white bandage around his head and one eye. A bullet had grazed his ear, that's where all the blood came from. And another bullet had severed the cord for a light that then fell on his head, knocking him unconscious and dealing him a nasty concussion. Beneath the cotton hospital gown, Goyo was wrapped in more bandages; the third bullet had entered the flesh just below his left shoulder, and zipped out the other side. He'd been lucky, the doctors said. Very lucky.

I picked the television remote up off of the small wooden table next to his bed, and flipped through the stations. It was six o'clock, just in time for the next round of local news. An IV bag dripped fluids and painkillers into the needle dug into the back of Goyo's right hand, held in place by clear tape. He wouldn't wake. I raised the volume to listen to the news report, but soon wished I hadn't.

Even though Daniel was in custody, under arrest for hiring a gang member to kill me and Goyo, the anchor portrayed the story as if the race of the *victim* and the ethnicity of the majority of the people at the festival were to blame. "It was another bloody chapter in Los Angeles's inner-city hip-hop war," the anchor announced, all of those the media code words I recognized for "black" and "Latino." They called Daniel the "alleged" mastermind behind the "Hispanic" shooter, even though there were dozens of eyewitnesses who saw Daniel pointing the shooter in the right direction. They showed file footage of Goyo that made him look like a criminal instead of the poetic, gentle, humorous man he was, while the photo of Daniel was clean and harmless, with him in a tie I had never seen him wear.

"I hate you," I hissed at the anchor.

I flipped to the next station, but only found more of the same. Violence in the inner city; hip-hop and rap to blame; Hispanic festival erupts in gunfire—as if all these things were related to each other somehow, as if being a minority automatically meant you'd be violent. No one bothered to mention that the mastermind behind the shooter was *white*, and *broke*, and a resident of the "Hispanic neighborhood" where the shooting took place. It's like the media was intentionally hiding the fact that Daniel was one of them, as if his downfall would be their own. No one bothered to say he was out to avenge being dumped by his well-to-do *Mexican-American* girlfriend, who lived in Newport Beach and owned her own business and drove a Cadillac.

I flipped through the stations until I came to the Home and Garden Network, the only station I watched anymore without being offended. A new show out of Miami was on, *Casas Americanas–American Homes*, hosted by a perky blonde Cuban named Sara Asis, who looked like a cuter, younger Martha Stewart. In today's episode, Sara helped a newlywed couple figure out the best design for their Kendall, Florida, family room. I stared, mesmerized, for the full half hour, impressed by the transformation of the dull, boxy space into a lush tropical wonderland of pinks and peaches. I liked this Sara's style. Miami. I'd never really thought about Miami, but it seemed like the perfect blend of Los Angeles fashion and Dallas sensibility. Might not be a bad place to raise kids, either, especially half-Cuban kids.

When the show ended, I left the television on—something called *Designing for the Sexes*—but dug my latest Linda Style romance novel out of my new Jamin Puech denim handbag. I hadn't read it yet, but when I started, I thought of Marcella's constant lectures on synchronicity. The book began with a sexy daredevil, J. D. Rivera, a navy pilot who zipped around in his jet only to have a near-crash that crushed his leg. It began in a hospital room.

So much for escape.

I shut the book and stared at Goyo. Even now, he was beautiful. I stood and walked to the side of the bed, one hand on the burgundy blanket that covered his legs, the other hand gently stroking his cheek.

"I'm so sorry," I said. "It's all my fault, for dating a loser."

To my surprise, Goyo's one exposed eyelid fluttered open. *"Hola, cariño,"* he said, his throat hoarse and dry as powder.

"Hi," I said. "How are you feeling?"

Goyo tried to shrug, but his face twisted in pain instead. "I've been better," he said. "What happened?"

I explained it to him.

"And I thought I was in love with a nice girl," he joked.

"He's in jail," I said.

"Was anyone else hurt?" he asked.

"Just Daniel," I said. I giggled.

"What?"

"Well, this kid from the neighborhood took his gun away—he saved your life, Goyo—but then the cop thought the kid shot you, so the kid drops the gun and it goes off when it hits the ground and shoots Daniel in the butt."

Goyo smiled. "Shot him in the ass?"

"Yup."

"Sounds about right," said Goyo. "So, where'd they get *me*?"

I realized Goyo didn't know where he'd been shot. He'd been in and out of consciousness and drugged up pretty good for the three hours he'd been here. I told him.

"Nothing too serious, thank God," I said. "You're gonna be just fine, sugar."

"I know a way I'd be even better," he said.

"And what's that?"

He reached for my hand with the hand with the needle taped in it. "If we lived together," he said.

"Lived together?"

"If you married me."

I stared at him and blinked tears away. "If this wasn't, you know, a deathbed proposal, I'd be really upset you didn't have a ring when you asked me."

"Who says I don't have a ring?" he asked.

"Do you?"

He smiled. "In my room, upper right-hand drawer of my dresser. Go look."

"Really?"

"I figured it was the only way I'd get you into bed," he joked.

My heart soared. "In that case," I said, "my answer is yes." I leaned over and kissed him gently on the lips. "But if that ring's no good, you can forget it."

A few minutes later, Goyo's parents returned from dinner. All three of us intended to stay all night with Goyo. I needed to get home to feed Juanga and let her out to do her business, and get some toiletries, so I offered to drive to Goyo's parents' apartment on my way, to get toothbrushes and anything else they might need. Goyo's mother wrote a list for me, handed me the keys to the apartment, and gave me a hug. As I walked out the door, I heard her say, "She's a good woman, Goyo, you finally found a good one."

Juanga was fine, but hungry. I apologized to her for not being able to take her to the hospital with me. "These human chauvinists, they don't understand," I said. "But I'll be back tomorrow."

At Goyo's parents' apartment, I packed all of the things on the list. And before I left, I checked the dresser drawer. There she was, a Harry Winston, twinkling up at me from the velvet-lined box.

"Oh, m'gosh," I gasped.

I noticed a smaller box beneath, and opened it, too. Inside was a small dog collar, diamond-studded, with an inscribed heart tag: TO JUANGA, it said, FROM YOUR NEW FATHER.

I cried all the way back to the hospital.

MARCELLA

I t was one of those clichéd moments where I had to pinch myself to realize I *was* where I *was*, doing what I was doing: In the New York studio of famed designer Narciso Rodriguez, being fitted into a delicious black-and-white dress he had made just for *me*. Specifically, he had created a long, flowing, white silk jersey skirt, form-fitting but full at the ankles, and a tunic-style transparent silk-satin top with spaghetti straps. And in my hands, I held a copy of that day's *New York Times*, with another cover story on the downfall of Uncle Hubert, grand king of the Manhattan theater world, now a "suspected" child pornographer.

"Marcella," the designer cooed, running a hand along my side as if I were a work of art. "Exquisite. Perfection." Glad someone finally noticed, without whacking off in front of me. "I should use you for some ads."

Alexis stood to the side, nodding her approval. "It's fabulous, sugar," she said. "Really great."

Alexis had been fielding calls from dozens of designers who said they wanted me to wear one of their creations to the Los Angeles premiere of *Soledad* tomorrow night, and I'd interviewed a few of them, including Alberta Ferretti, Hubert Hardy, and Carolina Herrera. I'd been most impressed with Rodriguez's portfolio, and by his sense of humor and passion for his craft. His handsome face and sexy goatee hadn't hurt, either.

"Thanks, Narciso," I said. "It's a fantastic dress."

Alexis looked at her Rolex. "Time to get going, darlin'," she said.

Several assistants helped me out of the dress and packed it into a special carrying case. I shimmied back into my jeans and T-shirt, wrapped the fat parka around my body, and gave Narciso one last hug.

"Thanks for everything, *chico*," I said.

"Good-bye, *amorcito*," said Narciso. "I love you. Knock 'em dead."

Alexis, in a hot-pink wool coat and polka-dot hat and gloves, carried the dress box down the stairs, and I carried her handbag and mine. The black hired car idled at the curb. The Russian driver had crawled into the backseat, where he watched a game show on the television.

"Hey, babe, sorry to ruin the party," Alexis said to him as she opened the door.

"Oh, sorry," the driver exclaimed, jumping up in a panic. "Let me open the door for you."

"Relax," said Alexis. "I'm from Texas. We can open our own doors."

I climbed in behind Alexis, and the nervous driver shut the door behind me.

"To the airport?" he asked as he took his seat in front.

"You got it, sweetie," said Alexis, shivering in the cold.

The American Airlines flight would land in Los Angeles with plenty of time to rest and primp before tomorrow's big event at Mann's Chinese Theater in Holly-wood.

As the lights of Manhattan whirred past, I pinched myself one more time, to make sure I was here.

"Is this really happening?" I asked Alexis.

She opened her pink suede Pucci soft tote bag and removed the latest issue of *Entertainment Weekly*, which had an alluring photo of me in jeans and a low-cut black shirt, but nonetheless looking tough and smart, on the cover and a headline across the top: MARCELLA'S *NEW* T&A: TENACITY OVER ADVERSITY.

"Look at this," she squealed. "They love you. They love the movie. They love the way you survived a perverted uncle. Everybody likes an underdog story."

"Thank God for Karen Debray," I said, thinking of how much everyone had copied her *Vanity Fair* cover story from last month.

"Even without her they'd love you," Alexis said. "Because you're amazing. Didn't I always say you were amazing?"

I tapped a cigarette out of the box and lit up, shaking my head at the stupidity of the whole situation. "Rude, I think that's the word you used."

"Well, yeah, rude and amazing. Amazingly rude. That's my Marcella."

"It's crazy," I said.

Alexis gagged on the smoke, rolled down her window, and sucked at the fresh, freezing air. "Yup," she said. "It sure is."

I t wasn't the norm to have eight and a half people accompany the star to her movie opening, but seeing as I starred in the thing, I was allowed to do whatever I wanted. And I wanted eight and a half pals along for the ride—or three couples, one toddler, and two hot girls, to be exact. Me and Carmelo; Alexis and Goyo; Olivia, Jack, and Chan; and Lydia and Sidney.

We all met at my house an hour before the two stretch limos were scheduled to arrive. In addition to the friends, my mother, father, and brother were there (Mathilde couldn't make it). To round it all out, I was also attended to by several makeup and hair artists.

"You sure you don't want to come in the limo with us?" I asked Mère as she stood in the doorway to my bedroom, watching a man named Glory brush golden shimmery blush over my cheeks with the ecstasy of a great painter.

"It's your night to shine," said Mère. It was the closest she would ever get to an apology or compliment, I realized. She smiled, and for the briefest of moments, there was nothing fake about it. I don't know what she was on, but I wanted to encourage her to take it more often.

"So you admit I can shine after all?" I asked.

"Phrase it however you like," said my mother with a sniff, before turning on her stylish heel to leave the room.

T he three couples crammed into one limo, with Lydia and Sidney gamely agreeing to take Jack in their limo, along with an arsenal of toys. "Is this like the kids' table at Thanksgiving?" asked Lydia, surprising everyone with her humor until we all realized it wasn't a joke.

"Jack's not a kid, he's a person," I said.

Olivia overheard me and called out, "Don't you mean Rhesus monkey?"

Inside our limo, Goyo, who'd healed nicely from the shooting, popped open a bottle of Krug Clos du Menil champagne, supplied by Columbus Pictures, and poured bubbly into flutes for everyone.

"To the blood in women's brains," growled Carmelo, raising his glass in the air. "To open boxes with demons inside."

"Eew," said Alexis. "Please. I can't drink to *that*."

"Do better then," Carmelo challenged her.

Said Alexis, "How about this? To a wonderful film and many more to come!"

"Here, here," said Olivia.

"Boring!" shouted Chan.

Olivia glared at him, then smiled. "Okay," she said. "How about: To a smart and beautiful actress who never takes no for an answer!"

Chan nodded once and laughed. "That's okay. But I think we're overlooking the power behind the picture again." He looked at Olivia with love in his eyes. "To the writer!"

"To the writer!" we all cheered.

"To tenacity and adversity," cried Olivia.

"Tenacity *over* adversity," corrected Goyo.

"*You* obviously don't hang out with *Marcella* much," joked Olivia.

"To the *old* T and A," I cried. "Tits and ass!"

"That's more like it," said Goyo. "Wooo!"

"Oh, *brother*," Alexis moaned, smacking her man playfully on the arm. "How about a very dignified *lack* of tits, and a whole big helping of ass?"

"Did you just curse, debutante?" I asked her.

"Maybe," she said, tipping the flute into her mouth. "I've been corrupted by a bunch of liberals."

"If you're not careful, you might join Greenpeace!" said Olivia.

"To Talentosa, Inc.!" Goyo announced.

"To Talentosa, Inc.!" everyone echoed.

We clanked our flutes together and laughed, and sipped bubbly all the way to Hollywood.

The seconds on the red carpet zipped by too fast, a flurry of flashing lights and reporters and fans screaming my name. Before I knew it, I was inside, the chaos of fame left to wave and press in from the street.

In the theater, Olivia sat on my left, Alexis on my right, which was all quite fitting, really. A few rows down, Soledad basked in the spotlight as actors, directors, producers, and reporters stood in line to shake her hand. She wore a glittering gown her daughter had bought for her, and I found myself unconsciously imitating her movements as she shook hands and smiled. Olivia watched and beamed. Alexis's parents sat in the row behind us, holding hands, and her mother could not stop crying and laughing all at once. Alexis's dad kept leaning forward to pat each of us on the shoulder and tell us how proud he was. We had invited Pedro Negrete, but he was nowhere to be seen.

"Oh, m'gosh," Alexis cooed as the lights started to go down. She reached across my lap and took one of Olivia's hands in hers.

"It's starting," Olivia breathed.

"It can't," I said, looking around at all the faces turned to look at us.

"Why not?" asked Olivia.

"The red carpet part was too fast. I want to do it again."

Olivia nodded. "Me, too!"

As we laughed nervously, the opening credits began to roll, and Alexis said, "Don't worry, ladies. Something tells me this won't be the last premiere for any of us."

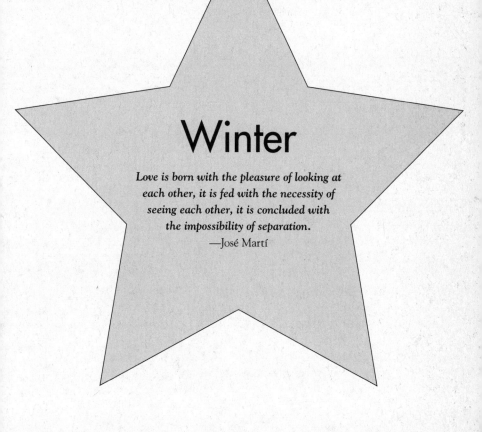

Winter

*Love is born with the pleasure of looking at
each other, it is fed with the necessity of
seeing each other, it is concluded with
the impossibility of separation.*

—José Martí

ALEXIS

When Momma first sent me the ugly yellow book with the drawing of the pregnant lady on the front, in a rocking chair and a gingham dress, I swore on all I held dear I'd never let myself look like that—or look like she looked like she felt, which was *miserable*. Pregnancy was supposed to make you glow, darlin', not fade away.

But as I passed the mirror on my dresser, en route to the bed with a plate of frozen waffles smothered in peanut butter and fake maple syrup (the faker the better for some reason), I might as well have been gaping at the washed-out model for that fabled drawing. *What to Expect When You're Expecting* had become the second-most important book in my life, after the Bible.

In my black-and-white cow-print nightgown, I climbed up onto the bed like a great big panda bear gettin' cozy in her tree. I arranged my plate on the Crate and Barrel bed tray that had taken up permanent residence there, and tried not to think about the crumbs and stains. Somehow, the books and TV shows for pregnant women never told you about the crumbs and stains, the sick feeling of your belly skin bursting like some horror-movie cocoon. I adjusted the pillows just so, trying to take the throbbing ache out of my lower back. It felt like the bones of my sacrum were cracking apart. What was this kid, a linebacker? I propped up my swollen feet on another mound of fluffy pillows and tried to remember the last time I'd seen my ankle bones. Then, I realized I'd left the remote control for the DVD player clear across the room, on the dresser. And I didn't much feel like hoisting myself up to get it. For some reason this made me cry. You'd have thought

I'd just heard someone died from the way I bawled. I couldn't possibly stand up again, could I? And waddle all the way to the dresser? It was miles away, wasn't it? I didn't want to do it. I didn't. But I knew someone who would.

"Goyyyyyo!" I called out.

Six months into our marriage, and one year removed from the release of the first movie I'd produced, my rap-star husband had learned the importance of waiting on a pregnant woman.

Goyo appeared in the doorway to the master bedroom of our new home in Silver Lake, a completely renovated Richard Neutra modernist masterpiece above the lake, near Silver Lake Boulevard and Earl Street. The three-bedroom house was not my first choice, of course. I'd wanted a suburban home with at least three thousand square feet and a huge backyard with a swimming pool. But Goyo loved Neutra, and said the house, surrounded by palm trees and succulent greenery, reminded him of "Labana," where, from what I understood, the modernist period homes were as immaculately preserved as they were in Silver Lake.

We'd endured the first three months of the pregnancy, the near-constant puking and endless sleeping, and were into the fifth month. That meant the little critter in my belly was gaining weight almost as quickly as I was, and my insatiable appetite would have made me right at home on Papi's grasslands. I knew the rest of the fetal development details by heart. She was growing a white coat of waxy stuff called vernix, to keep her skin from puckering up in all that amniotic fluid. She needed lots of iron. In the drawings in the books and on the Internet, the fetus always looks pale pink and white, but chances were good that our little girl didn't look anything like that. She'd be brown and beautiful like her momma and her daddy.

"What now?" he complained. He held music paper and an automatic pencil, which made me think he was composing. Oops, I always seemed to bother him in the middle of composing. But, honestly, did he have to give me that look? Wasn't I carrying his child? Wasn't this child more important than a little old song he could write any old time?

"Help me!"

Goyo sighed, and set the staff paper on the dresser. He rubbed his temples, and I feared for a moment he might say something unkind, like last time, when he said, "I'm sorry, Alexis, but I have a deadline and I have to get this work done." The nerve. But he didn't. Rather, he smiled, and then he laughed. At me.

"What?" I croaked.

"Cow jammies?" he asked. "Isn't that a little, I don't know, lactant?"

"That's not a word," I said. Rappers, like poets, made up words all the time.

He kept smiling. "Moo," he said.

"Shut up. You did this to me, remember that."

"What do you need?" he asked.

"The clicker?" My voice came out small and apologetic. I knew there was something not good about all the TV I was watching. But I didn't have the energy for much else. I was making a baby, after all.

"Clicker?" There were still some words in English he didn't know.

"I can't reach the remote," I whined. I was forever whining now, and Goyo didn't seem to mind. He was the calmest man ever created, patient beyond what I considered normal.

"Clicker," he repeated.

Goyo picked up the remote and joined me on the bed.

"How are you?" he asked my tummy. "And how are you?" he asked me.

"Not bad," I said. I felt terrible, but not as terrible as I had before.

He stayed to see what I was watching. When he saw, he wished he hadn't.

"Not that again, Alexis!"

I grabbed for my box of tissue and started to dab my eyes and nose. Soon, I knew, I would be full-on weeping. "It's so beautiful," I whined.

"Still. How many times can you watch that thing?"

I glared at him in mock anger. "Hey," I said. "That wedding DVD is the only thing that keeps me from ripping your guts out for doing this to me."

"I'll be in my studio," he said with a grin. "Far from the cranky preggo."

"You can't leave me," I said.

"Alexis, please. I'm sorry. I have a deadline."

Again with the deadline! And I didn't have a deadline? What nerve.

"Fine," I said, in the way I knew would make him feel guilty.

"Don't do that," he said. "I'll be back. Give me a few minutes. I'm on a roll."

"Mmm," I said. "Rolls. Can you bring back some bread?"

He grinned, then frowned and walked away.

I turned the cable to the Home and Garden Network. Somehow, with my nesting instincts on overload, no channel soothed me quite so well as this. I was learning a lot about architecture and design, too, and realized—a little late, I admit—that this house of ours was quite a catch, as was my husband, even if he was selfish and thought he had the right to work on his album instead of massaging my back at the moment.

I looked out the window of our bedroom. Trees everywhere, and hills. I was surprised to find myself quite at home here and unable to imagine living anywhere else, especially after all the time I'd spent missing Texas.

I'd even been dubious when Goyo first dragged me to see this place.

But after I'd soaked in the spectacular view the first time he dragged me to see the oddly curved Neutra, I was hooked. So what that it was perched precariously on a steep hillside in earthquake country? So what that it was right smack in the middle of the city I had once considered the first stop toward hell after purgatory? So what that I could only get a view clear to the ocean on smogless days, and those came once or twice a year? My inhaler and I were used to it now, and I was almost embarrassed to admit I actually kind of loved this city now. I didn't know if I'd ever be able to live anywhere else. And Silver Lake was an oasis in the middle of it all, a mess of winding roads, too narrow for cars to pass side by side, and steep hills carpeted with thick vegetation and flocks of birds. The astounding variation of houses, each of them a work of art really, was the yin for the yang of tract homes and McMansions I'd grown up with. My new neighborhood was unpredictable, with endlessly surprising twists and turns through miniature canyons, some ending in donut shops, some ending in thrift stores. There was nowhere else on earth quite like it.

Besides, Goyo said he felt inspired to write in our hilltop home, which was important for a man the media were calling the first Cuban-born crossover pop star since Gloria Estéfan. I hoped to God the media's knee-jerk tendency to call him a "Latin Lover" or "Latin Heartthrob" wouldn't take away from Goyo's poetic soul. I believed the listening public understood him better than the reporters. He'd sold more than a million albums already and was working hard on his second release. I was still working, of course, and I always would; but it was nice to know that if I wanted to stop working for a while and let the new, younger agents in my company handle things for a while, I could. And the bills would be paid, by my Cuban poet.

I didn't miss my hour-plus commute from Orange County, either. And it seemed I had several meetings a week in places like Santa Monica, Burbank, and Culver City. Talentosa, Inc.'s Sherman Oaks offices were no more than half an hour from my new house, and I'd gotten enough new clients—of varying backgrounds—to hire two more agents to work for me. We weren't CAA—yet. But we were formidable.

The personal bonus of living in Silver Lake, of course, was that I was super close to Olivia now; she and Chan were not married, and from what she said she never planned to be that "responsible" for a man again, but that hadn't stopped them from buying a house nearby, walking distance from her mother's *and* his mother's. It also hadn't stopped them from making a *baby*. And while I had my strong opinions on the matter of bringing a child into the world with unmarried parents, it was none of my business. Olivia told me she wasn't sure Chan was the one, but she added that as she approached forty it was silly to wait around. She wanted another baby, and she got it.

And it was nice to have her so close. It meant I had someone to share entire bags of pepperoni with, and it was plain old cute to have someone similarly afflicted to waddle around the lake with on balmy afternoons. She was finishing up writing a drama pilot for a children's network, and said she was looking forward to a few months off to absorb all that had happened to her. She had turned down almost every interested party who had come knocking on my door for her, and was planning to do a documentary series for PBS. She would never get rich off that kind of work, but she said she did not care about rich, and I believed her.

We joked that all we needed now was for Marcella to get pregnant, too, but there wasn't much chance of that anytime soon. The runaway success of *Soledad*, not just in Latino markets but across the *globe*, had made her an A-list star with no shortage of high-profile projects. (For the record, *Soledad* had made close to $70 million worldwide, so far, seven times what it cost to make.) She was in New Orleans shooting a big-budget vampire movie, and I talked to her every few days by phone. Carmelo was staying with her, and they'd rented a haunted house and had people over for séances. She told me she and Carmelo were experimenting with threesomes involving women. Very strange, and very Marcella. Her success was my success, as I was still her manager, even if I spent most days in bed eating and waiting to feel the baby move. Nesting.

Goyo finally returned to the bedroom, visibly more relaxed.

"Done," he said.

"Where's the bread?" I asked. He flinched in a way that I took to mean he'd forgotten. "Sorry," he said.

"Never mind," I said. "Big as I am, I don't need it."

"You're supposed to be big right now," he said. "Move over."

I scooted, and a sharp pain stabbed my back. "Ouch!"

He joined me on the bed, looking sorrowful and guilty. "I'm sorry," he said. "If I'd known you were going to suffer so much . . ."

"Don't even think about finishing that sentence," I said, with a protective hand over my belly. "I would suffer a hundred times worse for sweet Emily."

Goyo wrinkled his nose. "I don't think that's her name, Alexis."

"It is too."

"Her name is Gisela."

"Emily."

"Gisela."

He nuzzled my neck and kissed my cheek. I pushed him away playfully and pressed play on the remote. "Emily."

"Not the video again, please!" he said, settling into my nest of pillows with me. He wouldn't admit it, but I knew Goyo was as big a sap as I was, and he liked watching the video almost as much as I did.

"Massage, please," I said.

"Your back still hurt, baby?" he asked.

I nodded and he got his thumbs going. It was instant relief, and I knew that he would keep it up as long as I needed. He had massaged my back for three straight hours the other night, when I couldn't get comfortable and kept bursting into tears. Just about anything made me cry these days.

We'd been wed in July by Reverend Mark Craig, in the beautiful and serene Cox Chapel at Highland Park United Methodist Church on Mockingbird Lane, where I'd always dreamed of being married. Momma had helped me with near about every part of the planning, and she'd seen to it that the chapel was filled with pink and white orchids and calla lilies.

Goyo had stood at the altar waiting for me, handsome in his black tuxedo, beneath the blue and red light of the high, circular stained-glass window. His best man had been Carmelo, and as I prepared to walk down the aisle to him, you could see Goyo on the video wiping nervous perspiration from his palms and sharing a look of excitement with his best friend. But the best part had been seeing hip little Miss Marcella tucked into a line of naturally gorgeous Texan bridesmaids, my friends from high school and college. She almost didn't look unusual next to the beautiful Heathers.

I'd worn a micro-beaded tank gown by Vera Wang, with an empire bodice and a flowing skirt that draped in the back. It was simple, elegant, and flattering, and it was just right for the Texan I had been—and the Californian I had become. Both of my fathers walked me down the aisle, with Daddy on my left and Papi Pedro on my right, and while my momma sat and cried a river into her hankie, Granny Lopez did her best to stare down Grandmother Stiffler for an imagined affront in the church parking lot minutes before.

As the wedding march played on the organ, I felt the tears come. It was truly the happiest day of my life, and I remembered vividly what it felt like to walk slowly past a crowd of my family, friends, and colleagues, knowing I had launched a business with great success, knowing I had become all that I'd dreamed I could be professionally, and knowing that waiting for me at the front of the chapel was the kindest, sexiest, smartest, and most talented human being I had ever met. Knowing, too, that I would not die a childless woman.

Goyo grabbed my hand and placed a kiss on it. "My hand is killing me," he said. "Can I stop for a minute?" He placed a warm hand over my belly. His touch excited me. No one had told me pregnancy could give you such strong sexual impulses; it didn't seem right, somehow. But there was no denying it—being pregnant had made me feel very sexy, once the nausea subsided.

Goyo gave me a look. The horny-man look.

"But I'm huge," I said, dabbing the tears as the slimmer woman in the wedding dress finally reached her groom on the screen.

Goyo looked straight into my eyes and did not take the horny-man look off his face.

"I don't think so," I said. He kept staring.

"No, Goyo," I said. "It's not right." As he scooted closer, I kept my eyes on the wedding.

The couple on the screen recited the vows they had written for each other, and I mumbled along from memory. Goyo slid his body closer to mine and kissed my neck.

"Forget the wedding. Remember Canada?" he asked, as his lips moved toward my chin. Goyo had wanted our honeymoon to be something different from anything he had ever experienced in his tropical lifetime, so I had booked our honeymoon in a sweet little mountain resort in Whistler, near Vancouver. We hadn't skied, obviously, because it had been summer. But on those rare occasions when we weren't in bed together we'd biked and hiked, and Goyo and I had both been impressed by the chilly wilds and green of the mountains.

"I remember," I said, knowing from his kisses that he was talking about the indoor activities.

"Let's relive Canada," he said.

"But I'm fat," I said. "Look, I'm wearing a cow nightgown. Moo."

"You are carrying my child," he said, as if I didn't already know it. "And I can't even begin to tell you how beautiful that makes you. It makes you a goddess."

"But what if she can hear us, or feel it?" I asked.

"The baby can't tell anything." His fingers left bites of electricity across my skin, just as they had on our wedding night. "Just be with me."

As the video cut to the reception, which we'd held at the Crescent Court Hotel in Dallas, I felt myself dissolve into the comforter next to my husband, finally completely at home—with him, with myself, and, Lord forgive me, with Los Angeles.

READING GROUP GUIDE

1. Do you think the relationships forged between friends or the characters' family bonds are stronger in this book? Explain how the characters' ties to others affects their behavior.

2. Body image and looks are very important to Marcella and other characters in this book. Discuss how those perceptions change the characters' view of themselves and also whether you think the male characters in the book share those perceptions.

3. Alexis is not a typical heroine—she's Republican and Christian, among other things. Do you think those anomalies make her more or less likable as a character?

4. *Playing with Boys* begins with a satirical portrait of a typical Los Angeles party. In what other scenes did you feel Valdes-Rodriguez sharpened her satirist's pen effectively?

5. Musicians play big roles in *Playing with Boys*. Compare and contrast the styles and fans of Los Chimpances del Norte, Pedro Negrete, and Goyo. Do you think one of them is more successful than the others at being a musical ambassador for their home country?

6. Valdes-Rodriguez makes it clear how much Olivia's childhood has affected her actions and mind as an adult. Which of the other main female characters has brought her childhood into her adulthood?

7. How important is work to the self-regard of Olivia, Marcella, and Alexis? Explain why each character approaches work as she does.

8. Did you feel the city of Los Angeles was a character in this novel? How might the story have differed if it were set in New York City or Chicago?

9. What do you think happens to Caridad after the action in the book is over?

10. If you have read this author's previous novel, *The Dirty Girls Social Club*, do you think Alexis, Marcella, and Olivia are as likely to remain friends as the six characters (Lauren, Sara, Elizabeth, Usnavys, Rebecca, and Amber) in that novel? Why or why not?

For more reading group suggestions visit
www.stmartins.com/smp/rgg.html

In sunny, sultry Miami, beautiful people are a dime a dozen.
But beauty is about to take on a whole new persona—
and his name is Ricky Biscayne....

make him look good

the new novel from
alisa valdes-rodriguez

Meet Ricky Biscayne, the sexy Latin singing sensation who's turning the pop scene upside down and having quite an effect on women, especially those who circle him:

MILAN—Ricky's new publicist, smart as a whip and chubby as only a girl who still lives at home with her parents can be.

GENEVA—Milan's sister, and as lean and chic as Milan is pudgy and dowdy; her club, Club G, promises to be Miami's hottest opening ever.

JASMINKA—Ricky's gorgeous Serbian model wife, who finally might eat a little something now that she's pregnant.

IRENE—a firefighter whose high school romance with Ricky was the last love in her life, now just eking out an existence for herself and her daughter.

SOPHIA—who is beginning to suspect that she and Ricky Biscayne look a little too much alike.

JILL SANCHEZ—an omnivorous media-manic Latina singer who has crossed over into perfume, clothes, and movies.

What all these women are about to discover is that once Ricky Biscayne enters their world things will change—for better or for worse....

COMING IN